Shadow Wall

A science fiction novel by

Lucy Andrews

Published 2019 by Treeberry Press

Copyright © Lucy Andrews 2019

Lucy Andrews has asserted her right under the Copyright, Designs and Patents Act 1988 to be identified as the author of this work

ALL RIGHTS RESERVED

No part of this book may be reproduced or transmitted in any form or by any means, electronic or mechanical, including photocopying, recording, or by any information storage and retrieval system, without permission in writing from the author, except in the case of brief quotations embodied in reviews.

Publisher's Note:

This is a work of fiction. All names, characters, places, and events are the work of the author's imagination.

Any resemblance to real persons, places, or events is coincidental.

ISBN 9781916297036

Prologue

Vivid images of the burning city ran through Kalen Trinneer's mind in unrelenting intensity. He tried to push the images aside and sleep, but the horror of the day would not leave him. He saw the missiles screaming across the city of Central, throwing up columns of fire and smoke at their targets. He heard the thunder of buildings collapsing and the screaming of people. He smelled the acid smoke of destruction, tasting its bitterness, and felt it suffocating him. He was in the middle of it all, trapped underneath the Colonization Division's headquarters building with the U-Zone forces.

The wrong side. The words came unbidden into Kalen's head. He was with Unity - he had sworn allegiance to the United Colonies Time System. They had attacked the Early Colonial Time System, his people, and civil war now raged across the planet Taidor. They called the people of the Ea-Zone, Earlians, and showed them no mercy. How had it come to this? Was he responsible for any of it?

Kalen twisted about on the hard bed, trying to find a comfortable position, but sleep eluded him. He turned the events of the past year over in his mind. The year of 2235 was nearly drawing to a close. It had been a terrible year. It had started well enough; he had been employed as a chief engineer at the Division with the Ea-Zone. He pictured Halle Rison, petite and blond, all feminine curves; his supervisor and his girlfriend. She had a fair complexion and large blue eyes. How he missed her! He let out a sigh. Why did he leave her?

He hadn't wanted to leave the Ea-Zone, but he was forced to defect. Forced to choose between promoting a lie that would put workers' lives at risk or losing his liberty. He couldn't do it. The truth had to be told and he'd gone to the U-Zone with Sera Ethern, the geologist he worked with. But he missed Halle; missed her melodious voice and her laughter. He wished that he was still with her. It's too late, he thought. I'm with Sera now and have sworn loyalty to Unity. That's my reality and I have to deal with it.

Kalen rolled over onto his side, his mind still racing. His conscience prickled and he examined the sharp intrusive thoughts. He had taken part of an alien artefact to Unity, ignorant that Unity had the rest of it; and ignorant that it had the potential to be used as a weapon. They'd told him that with the artefact, they could win a war against the Ea-Zone. It gave Unity the edge. But they haven't been able to use it as a weapon yet, he reminded himself. But would they have attacked the Ea-Zone without it?

Possibly, Kalen rationalized. The U-Zone might have attacked the Ea-Zone anyway. Tension between the two zones had been high. Both zones had shared the city, taking turns to use it. When one zone used the city, the population of the other zone had been crammed into accommodation blocks on the perimeter. For that zone it would be night, their blocks closed to the sunshine in the city, a situation that was duplicated in other cities throughout the planet Taidor. Both Early and Unity had hated the system of time zoning. Like many others, Kalen had dreamed of unification. But not this way, he thought. Not this way…

Chapter One

Someone was shaking his arm. Kalen opened his eyes. A bright strip light ran across the ceiling above him and he blinked under its harsh white glare. He lay fully dressed on a narrow bed under a thin blanket. The pillow under his head smelled musty and the windowless room felt cold. He heard the distant sound of explosions and falling masonry. Taking a wide yawn, he drew in smoke that caught in his throat, and began coughing uncontrollably.

Sitting up, he tried to remember where he was. He had been dreaming of Halle Rison. He had been holding her in his arms and kissing her. The dream began to fade rapidly but he took a moment to savor it. Now she was gone, or more precisely, out of his reach. He missed her. Jealous and possessive, yes, but also fun, clever and beautiful. Was she even still alive? A terrible sense of loss washed over him. Everything had changed.

"You're needed, Sir."

Kalen turned his head. A young man, no more than a teenager, was peering at him anxiously, his hand still extended. The boy had a pimply pale face and wore a black soldier's uniform, complete with a gold triangular badge on the left breast of his jacket. The badge known as the "Divine"; the symbol of the U-Zone. The badge sported the number five on it. Kalen suddenly became acutely aware that his own Divine only boasted a lowly one. The silver vertical stripes below the shoulders of his burgundy jacket that denoted him as a chief engineer, did little to compensate for his lack of status in this society. Had the soldier noticed?

"You must come quickly, Sir. It's urgent." The soldier's eyes flickered towards Kalen's Divine.

"What time is it?" Kalen asked, sweeping the blanket aside and swinging his legs to the floor. "I was supposed to be called at seven."

"A little after six, Sir. There's an emergency and the major wants to see you."

"Okay, I'm there," Kalen muttered, bending to fasten his boots.

The teenager turned on his heel and walked swiftly to the door. Kalen followed him, brushing back his black hair with one hand while picking up his peaked hat from a table with the other, and tucking it under his arm. Outside the room, the soldier turned down a long narrow corridor. The burnished alloy floor muted their footsteps and there was little noise except for the low hum of the air supply units and the sound of distant voices. Several doors led off the passageway but the soldier ignored them, and continued to the end where another turning took them to a wide metal door.

"One moment, Sir." The soldier pressed the entry plate.

A wave of noise and heat hit Kalen as the door slid open with a gentle hiss, and they stepped into a large, stuffy, well-lit room. Several black clad army officers stood in the center, talking loudly and behind them, more soldiers sat at desks arranged haphazardly. Civilian Colonization Division personnel sat at consoles below viewscreens along one wall, that displayed external images of the city of Central, above them on the surface. Some showed views of the terraces, hewn into the sides of the crater in which Central was built, while others showed soldiers moving between damaged buildings at street level.

Kalen stood too far away from the screens to make out the detail, but he saw daylight images. Taidor's strong sun penetrated the transparent dome that protected the city from the oxygen deficient atmosphere of the planet. He considered the scene. That could only mean one thing. The air attacks had stopped and the metal safety roof covering the dome had been drawn back during the night. Was the United Colonies Time System winning the war?

He suddenly became aware of the thickness of his jacket and the damp patches under his arms. A distinctive sweaty odor from unwashed bodies permeated the room. I'm only adding to it, he thought.

One of the officers broke off from the group and came towards them. Behind him, the others stopped talking.

"Morning, Chief Trinneer," Major Reece greeted Kalen. Tall with a sharp nose, silver hair and a lined face, the Divine fixed to the breast of his black jacket proclaimed him as a twelve. "There's been an incident and we need your assistance. Come and look at this."

Major Reece ushered Kalen towards a console where an operator sat, and pointed to the screen on the wall. "See this? They've hit a monorail tower. There are people trapped in one of the cabs on the line."

Standing behind the operator, Kalen studied the screen. It showed a side view of the monorail track that snaked on high supports over the buildings of the city. Every five hundred meters, a more substantial tower provided an embarkation terminal. Comprised of a lattice of steel girders and access ladders, each tower had an elevator running up its interior and a boarding terminal at the top. The supports in the forefront of the picture appeared undamaged, but black smoke curled from one of the towers next to a tall building.

"Bring it closer," the major instructed the operator, and the scene shifted.

About halfway up the tower, a blackened tangle of warped metal girders surrounded a large gash in one of its corners. Kalen saw that it was the tower that served the civic hall.

"A laser hit?" he queried.

"Yes, it happened an hour ago. Tower Seven. The whole line's down," the major confirmed. "One of the cabs is stuck. We can't move it."

Another officer, with close cropped light hair and an open face, joined them. Kalen recognized the square jawed man, Jon Ingeston, an army captain in the Engineering Corps. In his mid-thirties like Kalen, Jon had worked with him over the previous five days, since they had been confined to the bunker below the Colonization Division's burned out headquarters building. The Divine on Jon's jacket designated him as an eight.

"The strike has probably severed cabling," Kalen said. "Although we can't see it from here, the monorail track could be sagging by a centimeter or two. There might also be damage to the guidance coils. The safety cut offs have kicked in and shut off power to the track."

"We have to get it going again," the major stated.

Kalen thought for a moment. The maglev ran from the hospital in the south to the transport terminal and military base in the north, and had several intermediate stops. Despite being the primary transportation for the army across the city, it was very exposed to hostile fire.

"Isn't it too dangerous to use the maglev anyway?"

Major Reece grunted, "Perhaps it is today but we'll have the situation under control by tomorrow. Will the tower collapse? What do you think?"

"Well…" Kalen paused. He didn't want to assist the U-Zone, but he had to play along. If they suspected he wasn't loyal, they would kill him. "It's possible. The structure has been significantly weakened. The strike is about halfway up, so the damaged section is carrying half of the weight of the tower."

"Can you repair it and get the power back on?"

Kalen carefully considered his reply, "I don't have any particular expertise when it comes to monorails. My work in the Colonization Division usually involves underground structures and mining machinery."

"But when you worked in the Ea-Zone, didn't you have to troubleshoot mining problems?" Jon Ingeston interjected. "So isn't this the same sort of thing, just another bit of machinery?"

"It's more complicated." Kalen paused to think. Appear helpful, but don't offer a solution. "The tower needs rebuilding. Any repairs we do now, may not be enough. I wouldn't chance running a cab on the track over the tower. The tower's too damaged and may give way."

"The cab was travelling north. It can't go back. There's heavy fighting in the southern section and they wouldn't make it," the major said. "It has to go over the tower."

Kalen pointed at the screen. "See where that large girder has been burnt away? That's one of the main exterior stanchions. There are four main stanchions running up the tower, one at each corner."

The major and Jon both leaned forward to see.

"Can you see how twisted the ends near the hole are? The laser shot went straight through the corner, burning a hole right through the metalwork." Kalen paused and then continued, "The lack of support leaves the girders above in danger of buckling. Part of the cabling for the elevator has also burnt away."

"We need to do something quickly," the major stated.

"You said people are trapped?"

"Show him," the Major instructed the operator.

The operator changed the shot to a different angle. Now the cab was visible, sitting stationary on the track high above a street junction, to the south of the civic hall. As the operator brought the view closer, Kalen saw movement inside the cab. He made out several soldiers and four or five people in loose tops and trousers, the typical garb of the U-

Zone. They were still too far away for him to see clearly, but sunlight glinted off their Divines.

Kalen stared at the cab. "They can't get out?"

"They can't open the doors or the roof hatch," the major informed him.

"When the line goes down the doors lock automatically," Kalen said. "A serious malfunction could also jam the roof hatch mechanism."

"We have to get them out of there. The Ea-Zone could target them at any minute."

"Even under ideal conditions, it could take two to three hours to get the line running again, and the damaged section is in a very exposed position," Kalen replied.

"We need to try. I want Captain Ingeston and you to repair the tower and get the line working," the major said. "It's our only option."

Jon stared at the screen and shook his head. "With respect, Sir, the Ea-Zone have done this deliberately to force us into the open. They'll attack as soon as we try to repair it."

"If you haven't noticed yet, captain, we're at war!" the major said angrily. "The Early Colonial Time System will stop at nothing to get the city, but they won't succeed!"

Every fiber of Kalen's being screamed against assisting Unity. The people of the Ea-Zone were trapped in the accommodation blocks that ran along the eastern side of the city. They had nowhere else to go. The blocks were accessed by the Gates that lined the perimeter of the city, and the U-Zone had closed them. The Duplicate system where the U-Zone and Ea-Zone shared the center of the city alternately, had ended when Unity activated the electric barriers in the eastern Gates, to lock the Ea-Zone out. He couldn't blame Early for fighting dirty. But his loyalty would be suspected if he didn't help.

"Are the Gates still closed?" Kalen asked.

The major cleared his throat and Kalen glanced up from the viewscreen.

"The Ea-Zone have been trying to disable the barriers and unlock them." Jon briefly met Kalen's eyes with a troubled expression, before turning back to the screen.

"It must only be a matter of time before they find a way to open them," Kalen remarked. There was something more. Something they weren't telling him.

"When that happens, we'll be ready for them," Major Reece pronounced.

Suddenly, an explosion erupted in a bright yellow flare from the roof of a building near the monorail cab.

"They're firing at it!" Kalen exclaimed. Laser fire, in the infrared. Silent and invisible until the strike. How had Early managed to hide military weapons in their living accommodation? Had they anticipated Unity's attack?

The major wheeled around and glared at Jon. "Can't we do anything about that?"

"We've set up reflectors but they're not proving very effective, Sir. The Ea-Zone are also using varying wavelengths so we can't get a lock and visibility on the beam."

"Can't we throw up a dust curtain or something?"

"It wouldn't significantly dissipate the charge. These weapons have been enhanced, Sir," Jon replied.

"Yes, but there must be something we can do. We don't even know where it's coming from!" the major snapped.

As Kalen watched, another flare erupted close to the first. The fires started to take hold and black smoke wafted upwards from the rooftop. The people in the cab ducked under its windows and the soldiers held their lasers ready, but without any tracers from the enemy fire, they had no target. The civilians shrank to the rear, farthest away from the blaze, with the soldiers in front of them. Kalen could almost smell their fear and he reached an unsettling conclusion. *Early had trapped them deliberately. The Ea-Zone was playing with them!*

"I want that tower fixed and the line back on. Captain Ingeston, get a team together. Trinneer, you are to assist Captain Ingeston and supervise the repairs," the major ordered.

"Wouldn't it be better to clear the hostiles from the area before attempting repairs?" Jon queried, frowning.

Major Reece gestured to the screen. "There's no time for that. Get your people together, get what you need and get out there. You'll only need a small team. There's no point risking more men than necessary."

"When do you want us to leave, Sir?" Jon asked.

"As soon as you can."

"Yes Sir!"

Turning to Kalen, Major Reece said, "And Trinneer, I know I can count on you to do a good job. You'll get everything you need. Just get that monorail running again."

"Yes, major," Kalen replied trying to keep his voice steady. These orders were madness. They would be in range of the Ea-Zone's lasers.

Major Reece's glance swept over both of them. "Take risks if you have to. God will be with you."

Kalen felt his innards clenching. This would be a suicide mission. Early had pummeled that section of Central since the war began five days before. Most of that area was charred ruins. To get to the damage they would have to expose themselves to enemy fire. They would be easy prey for the Ea-Zone. Beside him, he sensed Jon shaking in cold fury.

"I'll leave you both to work it out." The major turned on his heel to re-join the group of officers behind them.

Jon let out a sigh and folded his arms. "Well, it appears we're going to see a bit of action."

"I suppose that was inevitable," Kalen said with a wry smile. "I'll give you a list of what we need."

"I'll organize the transport and materials. We'll have Lee and Mik and two others from the Engineering Corps with us. Get yourself kitted out at supplies. We'll leave within the hour," Jon replied.

Kalen recognized the names and felt a measure of assurance, but this wasn't going to be easy. They would have to dodge Early's laser fire high above the city, and their chances of survival were slim. His conscience nagged at him too. He had given allegiance to Unity and played his part in the events leading up to the conflict. No amount of rationalizing his actions could take away the bitter taste of guilt he felt for the outcome. Now, he had been asked to repair the maglev that Unity would use to ferry their troops across Central.

He couldn't do it. Unity would have an advantage over Early, and he mustn't let that happen. He couldn't stand by and let Unity destroy the people of the Ea-Zone. He had to sabotage the repairs; prevent the monorail from running. And he had to find a way to do it without arousing suspicion.

Chapter Two

The air above ground gripped at Kalen's throat as they emerged from the bunker, into the shell of the Colonization Division headquarters building. The upper floors had been obliterated leaving only an open outline of ruined walls, bearing scorch marks from intense heat. He stared through his visor at the desolation around them, and clutched the stock of his laser. Army issue and bulkier than his small handheld work laser, the weapon felt unwieldy in his gloved hands. Jon had insisted that he carry it despite Kalen's protests. Together with black combat suit, body armor, helmet and small backpack containing his tool kit, he looked like a soldier.

"Keep your heads down," Jon directed Kalen and the four soldiers, from the army's Engineering Corps, who had been ordered to accompany them. "We're vulnerable to sniper fire. The trucks with the steel girders and heavy equipment are being sent direct from a nearer depot."

"Good," Kalen said. "Hopefully they'll be there when we arrive."

"Set your visors to track," John instructed. "There's a chance we might pick up visual on the lasers."

The ground around the building was strewn with twisted metal, rubble and debris. They began to pick their way carefully over it, their boots kicking up grit and powdery ash. A thick metal barrier, fifteen meters high, had been erected across the street in front of the building, but most of it had been destroyed and only one short section still stood. Kalen remembered running out of the compound on the day fighting broke out, determined to return to the Ea-Zone, and being pulled back by Unity's troops in the midst of the heavy bombardment. To the side, where the exit had been in the barrier, two soldiers crouched behind piles of twisted metal. They watched Jon and Kalen closely as they moved away from the charred doorway, and then one of them gesticulated in an attitude of warning.

"Get down and follow me," Jon ordered. He lowered his head and sprinted towards the exit, where he dipped down behind the remnants of the barrier.

Kalen went next, copying Jon's route through the detritus of battle, his strong army boots crunching the debris underfoot. Although he estimated that the laser in his hand weighed three or four three kilos at most, the body armor he wore dragged him down. Each step he took seemed to take twice the effort and he was panting by the time he reached Jon. He crouched next to Jon and hoped that the armor would be sufficient protection from weapon fire. He didn't want to die.

The other four followed them to settle behind part of the wall, constantly watching for movement around them. Kalen looked up, to inspect the dome high overhead. Despite the fighting, it didn't appear to be damaged.

Jon turned towards the group. "Okay, we've got about two kilometers to cover. We're going to head for the civic hall, and access the tower from its roof. There's a ramp across."

"The most direct route is down Main Way," Kalen said. The bitter air raked at his throat and he coughed.

"Try not to make any noise out there," Jon said. "We don't know if any Earlians have managed to get through the Gates yet. We don't want them to know we're here."

"There doesn't seem to be much fire at the moment," Kalen replied hoarsely.

"Once we've passed the barrier we're liable to attack. We'll start on Main Way, but if there's any sign of trouble, we'll take the side streets. The moving walkways aren't running, so we're going to have to do it all on foot."

Without speaking further, Jon rose and nodded to one of the soldiers at the gap in the barrier.

The soldier peered around the twisted metal. "It's clear, Sir."

Jon carefully edged through the exit and then ran towards the overhang of the nearest building. With the walkways down, this is going to be tough, Kalen thought. At least he was fit. The Colonization Division had made him adhere to a rigorous fitness program. He was thankful that Lee and the others were behind him, constantly checking for enemy fire, although he doubted that would help them against a laser strike their visors couldn't pick up.

Jon glanced back at him. "Stay close to me."

Kalen caught up with him. "I'm an engineer, not a soldier."

"If we come under attack, shoot to kill," Jon threw the words over his shoulder as he trotted down the side of the building, keeping near to the wall.

Initially, they jogged under the overhang of the building, their black uniforms merging into its deep shadow, but in places where the walls had been pulverized, they were forced to deviate around piles of rubble into the exposed sunlight. The moving walkways that ran down the center of the street were stationary, heat scars on the sidewalk evidence of the laser fire that had burnt out their junction boxes. There was no movement and an unnatural silence that Kalen was unused to. He had never seen the city like this before. There had always been crowds, and the noise of too many people. Even with only half of the population in the city, the restaurants had been full and the shops busy.

Now, they made good time, compared with a journey that he remembered taking twice as long because of the crowds, even using the moving walkways.

Jon stopped at an intersection, dipping under the lip of an awning that still hung incongruously amidst the desolation, into the shade. He waved to the others to stand back against the wall beside him, out of view of the road. Before them, the street was empty, bits of rubble and charred plastic strewn across it. Several buildings nearby had been reduced to blackened ruins cloaked in ash, after fires had raged through them, whilst stonework and paneling had collapsed on others, tearing away parts of walls. Where buildings had escaped the fires, plastic shop and café fronts dangled precariously from warped metal brackets. The smoke in the air thickened, and Kalen suppressed another urge to cough.

Jon put a finger across his mouth, "Shhh…do you hear that?"

Kalen held his breath and listened. He heard the fast beat of his own heart and then he became aware of a distant rhythmic clacking. Soldiers marching!

Jon gestured to the others with his hand to be still, while he crept forward towards the edge of the building and peered around the corner. Kalen froze, but he heard scuffling behind him. Without moving the rest of his body, Jon patted the air quickly with his left hand to signal silence. Kalen waited, swallowing to dull the tickle in his throat. His heart thumped in his chest and a spike of fear crept into his mind. Up until now it hadn't seemed real. *But now I'm in an army uniform and a target*, he thought. *The Eu-Zone have no reason to show mercy.*

The sound of marching got louder. Jon stood motionless, gripping his laser firmly. Kalen backed against the wall. The footsteps seemed to be coming directly towards them. Soon they would be in view. He pushed down his fear, but still felt a moist trickle go down his back, making his shirt stick to him. The footsteps reverberated across the empty thoroughfare.

Without warning, a dazzling flash of light erupted from the building opposite them and it burst into flames. Temporarily blinded, despite his visor, Kalen heard the roar of falling masonry and felt intense heat. Blinking open his eyes, he saw several soldiers running towards the ruins of a meeting hall on the other side of the intersection. *We are in the war zone*, he thought. He felt a strong urge to run, but Jon hadn't moved and he sensed that those behind him hadn't either. The fire took hold, sending small bits of burning plastic and debris into the air on the wings of black smoke. Kalen put his hand to his mouth to muffle a cough. Keeping his eyes on the soldiers, he waited for Jon's instructions.

Jon turned his head slightly and whispered to Kalen, "Can you see their jackets?"

Kalen pressed a button on the side of his visor to amplify his vision and studied the soldiers. "I'm not sure. They're well hidden."

"I think they're wearing Divines," Jon replied. "I'm calling base. I need to be sure."

Jon touched a control at the side of his helmet and began speaking quietly.

Kalen heard Jon say, "Yes, we'll wait."

"Base is checking," Jon said. "Even if they're ours, they have to know we're here otherwise they'll shoot on sight."

Several tense seconds passed before Jon spoke into his radio again and gave a sigh of relief. "It's okay, they're ours. They'll come to us."

Kalen watched the soldiers in the distance. They had hidden behind the ruined wall of the meeting house, and he could only see the tops of their helmets. They emerged cautiously and grouped by part of a shop front that still stood. One of the party gazed directly at the awning where Kalen and the others hid. The soldier began crossing the street, coming towards them at a jog followed by the rest of his troop. As he approached, Jon switched his weapon to his left hand and stepped out from underneath the awning.

Jon raised his right arm with the palm of his hand facing outwards and saluted the approaching soldier.

"Unity!" Jon barked.

"Unity!" The soldier saluted, and then beckoned to his men to join him. Kalen couldn't see his face beneath the visor, but his voice sounded young.

"I'm Captain Ingeston," Jon said. "These are members of the Engineering Corps."

"Base has told me who you are, Captain. I'm Lieutenant Stafford. I've been ordered to escort you to the civic hall."

"Have you seen much fire?" Jon asked.

"It went quiet until a few hours ago. The Ea-Zone have been lobbing lasers since they hit the monorail tower. We've got reflectors in place but they're getting uncomfortably close."

"What about enemy on the ground? How many have got through the Gates?"

"We saw a group of about ten men, by one of the south Gates. Unity have sealed that Gate again but of course, it won't be long before more get through."

"Which way do you recommend, lieutenant?"

"My orders are to take you through the northern side ways. We have men patrolling the periphery near the Gates to guard against any more encroachments. With your permission, Sir, I'll lead."

"Okay, proceed," Jon said.

Stafford directed his men to split and march to the front and rear of Jon's small group, and they moved off at a trot. More soldiers eased Kalen's apprehension but couldn't silence the voice in his head. Numbers wouldn't make any difference against a laser attack. Those military weapons were precise, and had a long range. From what Stafford had said, the reflectors had limited use. Their only hope was to stay out of view. If Early had wanted to destroy the monorail cab, they would have done it already. Now, they were running into an ambush. The firing would start as soon as they tried to repair the tower.

Kalen was still lost in thought when the civic hall came into view. The column came to a sudden halt a hundred meters away, in sight of the monorail supports. The majority of the buildings in this area had substantial damage and some had collapsed. Above the charred ruins, the monorail track passed overhead. Kalen took a moment to study it. He couldn't see the damage. That meant the damaged track had to be on the south side near the cab, he concluded. In full view of the Ea-Zone's weapons.

As they got nearer to the civic hall, Kalen saw black smoke rising from its roof. If they've taken out the embarkation ramp, we won't be able to reach the monorail tower that way, he thought.

They crossed the street at a run, Stafford taking the lead. Kalen thundered forward with the rest of them, holding his laser, aware of the heaviness of his backpack. Once inside the building, he took a few moments to catch his breath, thankful to be alive. His combat suit was hot and his helmet stuck to his forehead, despite the padding. He wished that he could take it off. Dim emergency lighting illuminated the hallway.

Kalen glanced around the entrance hall. He had been in it several times before but had never seen it empty like this. Power to the air supply units hadn't been restored and there was a deathly silence instead of the usual hum. He listened for other noises besides the rustling of their own movements, but there were none. This is strange, he thought. All he remembered were crowds of people, everywhere. The building had thirty floors or so above ground, and possibly as many underground levels.

"The normal elevators are down. We'll have to take the stairs to the roof," Stafford reported.

Jon turned to his unit. "The service elevators run on emergency power. Lee, take Mik with you and check that our equipment has arrived. The trucks should be in the yard at the rear. Use the service lifts to bring them to the roof. The rest of us will walk up."

"I'll go first." Stafford headed towards the stairs.

In the stairwell, Kalen smelled burning. The smoke got thicker, the higher they climbed. It scratched at Kalen's throat and he began coughing again. He lowered his visor to full head position and sucked on his helmet's integral breathing tube. Thoughts ran through his head. He had to sabotage the monorail. He would blow the track; completely destroy a section beyond repair. If he repaired the tower first, he wouldn't be suspected. He could blame an explosion on the track on something else.

Stafford opened a door at the top of the stairwell. He paused to shout back, "The roof's burning badly."

Outside, a broad path ran across the roof, to a wide ramp that sloped up gently to the embarkation terminal. Kalen recognized the low building. He remembered arriving by monorail with Sera Ethern, for their Allegiance Ceremony to the U-Zone. He pictured Sera and shuddered, pushing her image from his mind. On either side of the path, the roof had been laid out as a leisure area, with abstract shaped statues, low decorative paneling, benches and awnings. One side of the park burned ferociously. Flames licked up awnings and paneling, the floor tiles peeling up in the heat.

Stafford said, "The fire's spreading. Soon it will take the whole roof."

"The ramp is okay," Jon said. "We should be able to reach the tower that way."

Kalen squinted at the terminal. "According to the building plans, the ramp is just over thirty meters long, but this looks like a trap to me. This building is the least damaged of any in this section."

"We'll be exposed on the ramp, but it's better than climbing the tower."

"I agree, but I don't like it. I think they're waiting for us. Otherwise why leave this building standing? They've set fire to the roof so we'll be trapped on the ramp."

"If we can get to the terminal, we can repair the tower and level out the track from there," Jon said. "We're going to have to take the risk."

"I've been told to provide cover for you, in case of attack." Stafford shifted uncomfortably. "But I've been ordered to keep my people on the roof. If the fire gets worse we'll have to withdraw."

"To where?" Jon asked bluntly.

"To street level. Sorry, Sir, we don't go further than the roof."

"The fire's getting worse," Jon said. "We need to get moving."

"We'll go first." Stafford gestured to his troops and they moved off at a trot across the burning roof, fanning out towards its edge, in line of sight of the ramp.

Kalen jogged across the roof with the others, side stepping burning debris, until the ramp was immediately in front of them while Stafford and his soldiers took up position on each side, sheltering behind the low perimeter walls of the roof. After a brief nod to Stafford, Jon began running across the ramp towards the terminal and Kalen sprinted after him, swallowing down his fear. The gradual upward slope made his steps heavy, and his boots thudded loudly on the ramp surface. As he ran, he thought, *this is a trap. An ambush. They're waiting.*

Chapter Three

Suddenly part of the ramp near Kalen erupted in a fireball with a roar and blinding flash. Intense heat hit him together with burning shards that swirled around his head, and bitter choking smoke. The fire ate ferociously, spreading along the ground like a living thing. Kalen kept running, but a second later, another fireball exploded directly ahead, setting the ramp ablaze. Jon staggered backwards as Kalen drew level. They were halfway across the ramp with fires raging ahead and behind, sending up curling smoke that began to thicken in the artificial atmosphere.

With a thunderous crack, a charge like sheet lightning seared through the grey smoke ahead of them to explode on the deck, disintegrating part of the bridge.

Kalen's radio headset crackled and he heard Stafford's voice. "Move to the wall. The lasers are coming from the south. We're getting a partial visual on them."

"Acknowledged," Jon shouted tersely, darting sideways to crouch beside the ramp boundary wall.

The floor shuddered with the force of another explosion several meters behind them.

A cloud of thick smoke danced upwards from the blaze, no draught to distort its path. Bright flashes of light in rapid succession, illuminated the ramp in the smoke around them. Kalen realized that Stafford's men were firing back.

He heard Jon speaking on the radio, "Stafford, the wall's too low to protect us."

"We're targeting their lasers," Stafford replied.

"We can't move forward. The deck's alight," Jon said urgently.

"There's no way back. The fire's intense at the start of the ramp," Stafford said.

Through his combat suit Kalen felt the heat of the flames. Jon began to move forward carefully. In places the surface of the ramp had melted exposing the steel structure below, which glowed red and orange. In other places, the surface covering itself had melted into pools of a sticky black substance, still bubbling from the heat of the charge. I'll lose a foot if I step into one of those pools, Kalen thought. My boots won't protect me.

He saw Jon jump over a bubbling puddle of something dark and rubbery, and he copied him, but the smoke was getting worse. Things appeared indistinct in the murky atmosphere, and the soles of his boots had become hot. He took a step, but had to wrench his boot free from the sticky floor dissolving underneath him. Abruptly, a wall of fire ripped across the span of the ramp, shooting upwards in flaring brilliance. Tongues of flame leapt skywards, throwing out intense heat, that Kalen felt despite his body armor.

Jon stopped and took a step backwards. "We can't get through that."

Stafford didn't reply and Kalen wondered if he had withdrawn his troops. He glanced behind him at the roof. He saw only smoke and flames burning fiercely. No sign of Stafford and his men. Could they go back? Stafford had said not. The two other engineers with them, waited silently. Would their handheld lasers be powerful enough to take out the Ea-Zone's weapons? Possibly, if they had a target. He looked over the side of the ramp. Underneath there was a void and no way down.

Jon gestured towards the fire in front of them. "We're cut off."

"Aren't our uniforms environment suits? Won't they withstand the flames?" Kalen asked.

"They've got limited heat protection. There's a boost in the suit that'll provide a coolant. At these temperatures it will only give you two or three seconds at most." Jon pointed to a button on Kalen's jacket. "When you need to, press that button."

"Where are Lee and Mik with the equipment?" Kalen asked, as the flames crept nearer. The heat was searing and soon they would have nowhere left to stand.

"Last time I checked, they were coming up to the roof in the service elevator."

"Can I speak to them? I have an idea." It might work, he thought. It seemed to him their only chance. Two or three seconds might be all they needed.

"It's on a safe channel. We can all hear. Go ahead," Jon said.

Kalen tried the radio. Initially, he heard only static and then Lee replied. He told Lee what he had in mind.

"They're on the roof," Kalen confirmed, securing his laser by its straps onto his back. "They're coming over now. Get ready."

The first of the hover trucks appeared at speed out of the smoke. Lee lay straddled across its flat top, lying face down, clutching handles on its back cover. About two meters wide and three long, the truck's armored plating reflected the flickering flames on its sides, as it moved quickly a meter above the surface of the ramp. Kalen tried to estimate its speed. No more than thirty to thirty-five kilometers an hour, but enough, he decided. He had told Lee to program it to make a straight run at the terminal, through the wall of fire. As the truck approached it did not slow.

"Wait until it's nearly passed." Jon shouted at the other two engineers. "Now!"

The two engineers launched themselves at the rear of the truck, grabbing the lip of the top and scrambled up the sides, their boots only centimeters above the burning deck. One lost a handhold and half fell, her foot momentarily scraping the surface of the ramp and she pulled it up swiftly in a reflex action. They disappeared into the flames as the second hover truck appeared, with Mik lying spread-eagled across its top.

Kalen readied himself. They only had one chance at this. The truck was nearly upon them. He quickly turned on his suit coolant and then the truck was passing him. Out of the corner of his eye he saw Jon launch himself forwards, and he did the same, springing at the rear of the truck. He caught hold of the edge of the lid and then pulled himself up, swinging one of his legs over the top. Keeping his head down, he crouched as the truck hit the wall of flame. Scorching heat engulfed him, but his suit quickly quenched it, leaving only his visor burning hot. It will hold, he thought. Suddenly the truck lurched to one side, its sensors picking up a solid obstacle. Losing his grip, Kalen got thrown across the lid to dangle half over the side. A strong hand gripped his arm.

"Stay with me," Jon muttered, holding on to him. "Keep your feet up."

Kalen maneuvered his other arm until his elbow was on the back cover, and then with Jon's help, hauled himself up onto his stomach so that only his lower torso swung free. The truck suddenly reduced speed and stopped with a jerk that banged Kalen painfully against its side. The body armor bit into him and he gasped. Raising his head, he saw with a shock that they were free of the flames and at the boarding terminal. With the terminal doors closed, the trucks had stopped adjacent to its wall. Lee was already working on the keypad to open the doors.

Kalen jumped down and looked back at the ramp. The fire stretched across it, but he detected movement on the roof of the civic hall. Stafford's men. They were still there.

"Jon, we have to move quickly. That fire will spread to the terminal soon."

"Once we're inside we'll set the bots to work," Jon replied, as the doors slid open. He gestured to his team.

"Bring the trucks inside and close the doors. That might keep the fire out for a while."

The terminal was no more than a waiting room with an elevator in the center. Kalen remembered that this wasn't a public facility – it was only used by army and Government personnel. Seats and benches with small low tables lined two sides, and in the corner there was a drinks dispenser. Behind them, the walls had tinted observation windows which ran from a meter above the floor to the ceiling, giving clear views across the city. At the far end, transparent doors opened to the track.

Kalen raised his visor, swung his backpack off and began assembling his tools. "We should start with the tower and then test the track."

"Okay," Jon agreed, guiding the first of the hover trucks into the hall. It settled on the ground, emitting a low pitched buzz as its engines turned off.

The trucks took up nearly half of the space of the hall, and Jon's team hurriedly opened their lids and began unloading the bots.

"We'll need the ants," Kalen instructed. "For the girders. Spiders for the welding and cables. And let's get these doors open."

He strode to the track doors and input a code in the lock mechanism to open them. The doors slid aside. He peered out over the track in both directions. To the south, about sixty meters from his position, stood the large bulk of the cab. The track between the cab and the tower superficially appeared undamaged, but his scanner showed a small deviation in the level of the rail about fifteen meters away. He also detected damage to the guidance coils. That was all he needed, he decided. He would repair the tower beneath them, but blow the track under the guise of repairing it. The occupants of the cab could take their chance with the Ea-Zone.

He looked around for Ea-Zone soldiers but saw none. The laser strikes had stopped and everything was quiet. Too quiet. Silence always bothered him.

Kalen ducked back inside and took out one of the small wall panels adjacent to the doors, to access the power mechanism for the track. The safety had cut in and the power was off. He wouldn't restore it until he was ready to destroy the track. He tested several circuits and then shut down all of the track systems completely.

"Jon, I need to get a line of sight on the damaged section of the tower to program the bots."

"We've nearly got them all out. We're at stage two assembly," Jon replied.

Kalen went to the doors and jumped down onto the line. Aware that he was a target, he bent low and ran a few steps to the track barrier and peered over the edge, down the length of the tower. He used his scanner to take several readings and then hastily returned to the safety of the hall. He cross referenced his readings with the specifications of the tower.

"Girders 2A, 10B, 11B, 12B, and 35E, 23G and 24G are damaged, as well as cabling." Kalen studied his pad. "We're going to have to take one girder at a time. Four of the girders need complete replacement. Three of them have partial damage. Girder 2A is our main problem. It's one of the primary stanchions."

Jon glanced up from the floor where he crouched over several ant bots. "We've got eighty bots total. Enough to do the job, but girder 2A will be a heavy replacement. Now at stage three assembly."

Weighing four or five kilos each, the ant robots stood approximately twenty centimeters high, with six legs jointed in three places and flat backs. The spider bots were a similar height and weight, but had a smaller body with eight legs that were jointed in six places, and tipped by swiveling pincers that were capable of intricate repairs. The spiders also had inbuilt tools including lasers for welding. Kalen watched as Jon and the others readied each bot in turn, checking power levels and setting up the initialization sequence on each, before putting them aside.

"The ants should be able to manage that, Jon. They can carry a hundred times their weight. We can program ten of them to take each section of the main girder together. The spiders are going to have to do the welding in situ."

"We're ready to input the repair data now," Jon said.

"We're going to have to program this manually. The code plates on the damaged girders aren't working. I've got our replacement girder codes here." Kalen flicked his fingers over his pad, until the screen with the replacement girder codes was displayed. "We've got more than we need. I'm setting the sequence. Check your pad and confirm my calculations."

Kalen sent the information to Jon. "Check each damaged girder against the replacement girder code, and the specifications of each repair required."

Jon read through the sequence on his own pad. "All correct. We're good to go. We need to calibrate the bots' programming."

Kalen moved over to the bots that were lined up, their legs slack and lifeless, and began working on them.

"Lee, I'm sending you the codes for the girders and cabling we need. Get them ready," Jon ordered.

Lee checked his handheld screen and then punched numbers into the control panel of the nearest hover truck. The floor of the truck opened slowly down its center, moving outwards until it formed two shallow ramps that extended to the ground on each side. Below the floor, in the bed of the truck, the girders and cables were stacked neatly. Lee leant into the truck and activated the coding recognition plates on the girders and cables they required. Mik mirrored him with the second hover truck and then they both stood back.

"It's done," Lee confirmed.

"Are we finished here?" Jon asked Kalen.

"I think so. Let's start with girder 2A. We'll send it down in three pieces. I'll start the sequence."

"Clear!" Jon shouted.

Standing well back with the others, Kalen pressed the screen of his pad in the required sequence. He had done this many times before, but had never got tired of watching the bots come to life. The first row of ant bots immediately sprang up to their full height. Legs flexed and stiffened, pushing each of them up in a jerky motion, and then back down, bending at the joints.

A group of ten scuttled across the floor and up the ramp into the bed of the truck, using their foremost pair of legs to pick up a girder and position it on their backs. As soon as they had the girder, they scurried down the ramp, across the floor and out of the track doors to climb down the side of the tower. More and more of the ants followed them, working together to carry the girders and cabling between them. When the ants had left the trucks, the spiders came to life, springing up to run after the ants, onto the track and over the side of its barriers. Kalen and the others stood still until the bots had left.

Kalen swiped his pad to show video being transmitted by a lead ant bot. He could see upside down images of warped blackened metal struts.

"They've reached the damaged section, but we need a long view."

He went to the track doors and jumped onto the track again. Smoke from the roof had drifted across it. He ran to the edge and looked down the side of the tower. The bots were scurrying along its structure, balancing expertly on metal beams and struts. They climbed effortlessly amongst the confusion of the charred corner, the ants positioning their loads to fit into the gaps. He saw sparks flashing from the pincers of the spider bots welding the beams together.

Jon had followed him out. "The tower repairs look good. What about the track?"

"It's sustained damage. Fifteen meters south, between the tower and the cab. It deviates by nearly a centimeter from level. There's also damage to the coils in the guidance rail and barriers." Kalen hoped that Jon couldn't hear the tension in his voice. He would sort out the rail by setting a charge that would explode when the power was restored. "The bots are only capable of so much. Repairs to the coils or conductors might need to be done manually."

"That's going to be dangerous," Jon said gloomily. "We'll have to deal with it once the tower's repaired."

Kalen glanced back towards the roof of the civic hall. It blazed fiercely, throwing up thick smoke that had begun to enshroud the terminal. "We're making good time but the fire will reach the terminal soon."

"I can't see Stafford or his men. Let's get inside," Jon said, staring at the blaze.

Heat enveloped Kalen when he re-entered the boarding terminal. The temperature had risen and in places, heavy smoke obscured the view over the city. Perhaps that's why the lasers have stopped, he mused. The smoke might scatter the beams and render them ineffective. Jon joined him by one of the observation windows.

"The fires are getting worse," Jon remarked.

Kalen glanced at his pad and brought up a couple of views. "The bots are still on schedule. Main beam 2A in place. Spiders finishing the welding on it. Ants positioning secondary beams."

Jon didn't reply. He had raised his visor and stood staring out of the window, his mouth open. Kalen followed his gaze. At first he couldn't comprehend what he was seeing. Clouds of thick grey smoke surrounded the terminal. But there was something else. Black objects emerging from the smoke, getting larger. A black swarm, heading straight at them.

Chapter Four

Jon whirled around and bellowed, "Drones! Take cover."

Jon grabbed one of the benches and thrust it away from the wall, and then crouched under the window, taking hold of his laser. Kalen crouched beneath the window as well. Drones! He had seen at least thirty and they were still coming.

"We're too exposed here," Jon said.

"I'll close the track doors."

Kalen sprang up and ran towards the doors. The swarm would be upon them in seconds. Civilian drones were banned in the domed cities, but these were deadly military issue. With nearly oval shaped bodies similar in size to the ant and spider bots, their flattish fronts discharged lethal laser fire that could burn through thick walls. He reached the doors and glanced out. The track was empty but over the rim of its retaining wall, he saw the drones closing in. He quickly punched in the code. The doors slid shut with a hiss. That won't keep them out for long, he thought.

He ran back to Jon, who still crouched behind the wall, watching the drones. Lee and the others sheltered behind the trucks.

"What's the status on the bots?"

"Used fifty-five. Have twenty-five in reserve," Lee volunteered.

"Let's unload them and use the trucks as a barrier, one each end," Kalen suggested.

Jon swiveled around. "Good idea. Mik, Lee, unload the bots and move the trucks." He gestured towards the other two. "Both of you, with me. Assume defense three."

One of the engineers had raised her visor and now she lowered it again. They both gripped their lasers and ran to take up position, one on each side of the closed track doors. Touching buttons on their belts and helmets, they waited, weapons at the ready.

"You might want to do the same, Kalen," Jon said. "Enhance your visor visuals and turn on your suit reflector. It may be enough to avoid a strike."

Kalen swore to himself. He wished he'd taken time to study the specs for the army suit, but his mind had been focused on the engineering problems they faced. He quickly adjusted the settings on his helmet and suit, and held his laser in both hands.

Jon shifted his weight. "It'll take the drones a few minutes to burn through the windows."

"That might be enough time to complete the work on the tower. But we've still got the track to deal with," Kalen replied. He needed to blow the track. If he didn't, Unity would simply send another unit to repair it.

"I'm going to try and locate Stafford. I can't see him on the roof," Jon said.

With the magnified visuals Kalen studied the approaching swarm. They were about twenty meters away now and gaining rapidly. Kalen estimated about fifty of them. His knowledge of military jargon was sketchy but the orders were defense only. They must wait until the drones came nearer for a better shot. The soldiers on each side of the track doors would fire alternately if the swarm stayed together, to give continuous fire, or individually if the swarm split, which seemed more likely.

Behind him, he heard the soft hum of a truck rising, and then it swung into view and settled just behind the track doors. He heard the second truck move into place and Lee and Mik scrambling to the sides of the room.

"Wide beam," Jon ordered.

The drones were now ten meters away. They'll fire soon, thought Kalen. Are we the target or the repair bots? He had fixed his pad to the back of his wrist and he checked it.

The bots were making good time, girders in place and spiders welding.

Jon saw the movement. "How's it going?"

"Good, so far."

The drones suddenly scattered, darting all ways in rapid jerky movements. Kalen heard a loud cracking noise above his head and looked up. A glowing orange circle had appeared in the center of a window about a third of a meter in diameter. Heat emanated from it. A bright spot also appeared on a window opposite. He risked peeping out. They were surrounded. Shiny black drones hovered within meters of the tower, nearly soundless.

Up close, he could see the vents for their power units on the underside of their sleek shell-like bodies. Their rears were rounded, but the fronts were flattened out to create a mouth that displayed a miniature laser array. They darted about, taking turns to fire at the windows of the terminal. *They're firing from all sides*, he thought wildly. *We have to get out of here.*

Jon swiveled around, pointing. "Lee, guard the rear! They're opening up the building to storm it."

Kalen squatted under the wall. "How well will the suit reflectors protect us?"

"Don't rely on them. Early are using enhanced weapons." Jon paused as if listening to something. "I can't raise Stafford."

"How long before the drones get in?"

"About five minutes. I'll keep trying Stafford for backup." Jon turned back to the window, speaking quietly into his headset.

"Focus!" Kalen muttered to himself. He could taste fear in his mouth. The repairs. Once they were done, they could get out of there. He risked glancing at his pad. The bots were nearly finished. Could he send them to the track next? No human could survive on the track with the drones out there. He could send the bots to reconfigure the connections

- to create an explosion when he restored the power. The track would be totally destroyed. A small strike to assuage some of the guilt that he felt. The cab wasn't his concern. *Jon won't know I did it,* he decided. *I'll blame it on the bots.* How many spiders left? Twenty-five. Remote programming might do it.

He had a good view from the bot cameras. The ant bots had begun to climb back up the tower. A small stream of ants straddled the girder at different heights. A few spiders followed them, while a handful stayed to finish off the welding. A drone flew into view. It darted forward, jerked upwards and then a light blinked in its mouth and an ant burst into flames. The drone shot sideways, mouth lights twinkling and another ant burst into flames. Another drone appeared and hovered nearly stationary within meters of the tower. An orange heat patch appeared on the girder, shrinking quickly to a blackened scorch mark. Kalen felt a sense of relief. The drones' lasers weren't powerful enough to warp the girders.

Kalen adjusted his suit visor to enlarge the visuals further and then sprinted to the other side of the room, keeping his head down. Peering out with his enhanced view, he saw that the cab remained undamaged. The soldiers had fanned out along the windows of the cab, ready to repel an attack. The civilians huddled behind them but appeared distracted. Movement caught Kalen's eye. Tiny hands pressed against a window. A tall woman stooped to pull the child back, who waved its arms about in protest. Another woman cradled a baby, whilst a man tended to another child. For a moment, Kalen's thoughts were confused. *Children! There were children in the cab!*

"Who's in the cab? I thought it was transporting soldiers but I can see children?" Kalen asked.

"Nurses with injured children from the hospital. Seven or eight of them. Hurt in the conflict. They were being evacuated out of Central," Jon replied. "They have a guard with them."

Kalen stared at the crowded cab. What madness had led them to attempt travel on the maglev in the middle of a war? He couldn't blow the track now. If he left the cab stranded, the Ea-Zone would kill them all. He couldn't have the death of children on his conscience. The cab had to be saved. He remembered the Major's orders. He'd been insistent that the cab had to be saved. Now he knew why. But the drones will go for it once they've dealt with us, he reasoned. The cab was the bait. Now the Ea-Zone has no further use for it. He had to think quickly. They had minutes left. He returned his attention to the spiders. The spiders had finished their work and begun their ascent.

"I'm going to try and repair the track just using the bots. I need a minute to program them," Kalen told Jon.

"Okay, but if this gets worse we'll have to pull out."

How? Kalen wondered. They couldn't retreat. A wall of flame blocked the roof and they wouldn't survive on the tower access ladder, against the drones. This had always been a suicide mission.

The windows and doors of the room were now a patchwork of orange smoldering circles. Another window suddenly caved inwards with a cracking sound, about a meter away from Kalen. The interior of it melted, the material peeling back to reveal a red hot underside that glowed like a demon's eye. It gave off a pungent chemical smell that he could taste, despite using the helmet breathing tube. Kalen imagined a drone flying in and shuddered. He could feel the tension in his companions, waiting for the first drone to appear. Tense and alert they stared through the windows. He estimated they had about two minutes before the first drone got inside and hell broke loose.

Kalen scrambled towards the center of the room and huddled next to the heap of chairs they had thrown there. Taking his pad, he quickly located the first four spiders coming up the tower and began programming them. They had nearly reached the track and he counted the seconds off mentally. He saw a drone appear to their left. A bright flash and one of the spiders had gone. He programmed another spider to take its place. The first of them reached the track and it began to send readings to his pad. The track still wasn't level despite the tower repairs, but the deviation was minimal. The coils in the guidance rail and track wall, remained damaged.

"Watch out!" Jon cried, jerking backwards.

A window near Jon's head blew in with a thunderous crash, hurling a tongue of flaming splinters across the room. Chairs opposite burst into flame, throwing out scorching heat.

"They're through!" Jon yelled, springing up and firing. "Keep wide beam."

Kalen suddenly felt burning on his shoulder, despite his bulky suit. He saw a red rimmed hole, above his head, dripping bits of smoldering plastic. He brushed a piece off his shoulder, sniffing at the sharp pungent smell that invaded his lungs despite his breathing equipment. We can't keep them out for long. We've only got seconds, he thought. *Once they get in, we're finished. We have to get out. There must be a way.*

The soldiers returned fire, but the onslaught didn't lessen. Another window near Kalen imploded with a loud high-pitched sucking sound, sending shards of glass whipping past his head. He heard a scream. One of the shards had pierced Mik's suit, impaling his arm. Mik frantically yanked the shard out and tossed it aside before resuming fire.

"Try and hold them!" Jon shouted, firing through the gap in the window.

Outside, one of the drones hovered within meters, as if preparing to make a run at the gap. Suddenly it burst into flames and tumbled haphazardly downwards.

Jon chortled, "Got it!"

A sudden scream came from the front of the room. One of the soldiers writhed in agony on the floor, her suit a ball of flame. Kalen ran forward, but the heat drove him back. The woman became still as the crackling fire lashed at her. Within seconds, her body had incinerated.

Kalen ran towards the track doors and flattened himself against the side of the hover truck. Moving the cab with the children, had to be his first priority. He glanced at his pad to check the spiders' location. They had reached the damaged section of the track and started work. They weren't equipped to effect complete repairs. Four were all he needed. He monitored their actions until they were in position.

Behind him, someone shouted. He spun around. A drone had got in. It darted towards the rear of the room and a bright flash came off the truck sitting there. Kalen aimed his laser and shot at it. He clipped the drone's side and it swayed, briefly losing power. He followed it up with another shot. It burst into flames and crashed to the ground.

Kalen shouted, "I'm turning on the power to the track."

"Are the repairs done?" Jon asked, his voice staccato as he twisted about, firing at the drones.

"I've programmed the spiders to emit a magnetic field. They're overlaying the coils to create a temporary patch on the rail." He reached into the control panel on the wall and began working through the switches, to turn the track power back on.

"What?" Jon took a breath. "They'll burn out when the cab goes over them."

"It's the best I can do. We have one chance to get the cab out."

"The rail will be destroyed," Jon objected.

"Our orders are to save the cab. We can't save the track as well."

Kalen studied the control panel. There had to be a remote for the cab. Out of his peripheral vision he saw an orange hole appear in the track doors, above the parked truck. The nose of a black drone poked through it. He wheeled around, while grabbing his laser. He took a shot and sparks flared off the top of the truck, but the drone was inside. He aimed again, but the drone flew to the other side of the room, exploding in a small fireball when Lee's laser hit it.

"That was close," he muttered to himself, turning back to the control panel. "The power's back on. I've turned off the safety overrides. I'm going to try and move the cab."

Jon inclined his head. "As soon as the cab's safe, we leave."

With a limited visual of the track, he switched to a bot camera outside the doors. The cab was still stationary but the occupants were watching the drones. The civilians were bunched at the farthest end. Adults hugged crying children, comforting them. He studied the control panel. He was unfamiliar with the maglev controls and tried to recall the instructions pages he had skimmed through that morning. He inputted a code and switched to manual override. A green light began blinking. He pressed another button and waited. One, two seconds passed. Nothing. Come on, he thought. Move! The green light became solid green and the cab rose slowly by twenty centimeters, but remained stationary. How to make it move forwards?

"How are you doing?" Jon asked, his voice hoarse.

"Trying to find the forward propulsion." Kalen pressed another button. A digital display flickered to life. Flashing zeros. Speed indicator! Top speed fifty kilometers an hour, but forty-five meters to the patch. "I think I've found it."

"We can't keep them off much longer," Jon said.

Fire had begun to take hold of the terminal. Smoldering debris littered the floor and the air was hazy with smoke. Drones were visible through the holes in the roof. Mik and another soldier were attempting to fend them off while Lee covered the rear of the room. Kalen tried to focus on what he was doing. He must get the cab moving. The distant screams of children carried down the empty track.

"Moving it now," Kalen confirmed.

Kalen pressed the operating panel below the display, bringing the numbers up to five, ten and then fifteen. He kept his finger on the button to send the speed up to thirty. His eyes flicked down to the bot feed on his pad. With a sharp lurch the cab rocketed forward, skimming over the track towards the terminal. It quickly got to the damaged section. Wobbling, it stalled briefly and then picked up speed again, leaving the bots on the track burning behind it. He breathed a sigh of relief. The bots had held for the cab but the track couldn't be used again.

The drones' sensors had picked up the cab. As one, they rushed to meet it, their lasers sparking fireballs along its sides. As the cab swept past the terminal, Kalen felt the tower shudder and caught sight of white faces and terrified eyes. He pushed the speed up to forty and then fifty, to send the cab hurtling up the line, drones following.

"The sensors at track end should slow the cab automatically," Kalen said.

"Let's go before the drones come back." Jon stopped firing.

Kalen eyed the fire still raging behind them. "We can't go back over the ramp."

"Can we use the tower elevator?" Jon suggested.

"The cabling is burnt through. The bots only repaired the tower structure. We can't use it."

"Then we'll use the access ladder to climb down the tower."

"We won't make it if the drones come back. We'll be too exposed to fight them off," Kalen said.

"Do you have a better suggestion?"

Kalen ran through the options in his mind. They had the hover trucks but they couldn't use them on the track. Even if they could get over the damaged section, the guidance rails would interfere with the hover mechanism. The trucks wouldn't run.

"Can't we throw a line down the tower? Abseil or something?" Kalen asked.

"We haven't got the equipment," Jon replied. "Any other ideas?"

"No," Kalen admitted reluctantly. "We need an antigrav surround but Taidor doesn't have that technology yet."

"That's the disadvantage of living in the colonies," Jon replied sourly. "Okay. The access ladder it is."

"I'll move the truck and open the doors." Kalen pressed a sequence on his pad and reached for the door controls. The hover truck rose and glided away and the track doors slid open. "The track's live. I turned off the overrides to keep the power on. We mustn't touch the coils or guidance rail."

"There's a walkway to the access ladder," Jon replied.

"We've got about a minute before the drones return," Kalen warned.

"With me!" Jon motioned to the others, and stepped onto a narrow ledge that ran from the side of the track doors, along the outside of the terminal.

Kalen followed him on the ledge around a corner, holding onto a handrail set into the wall. A vertical ladder ran down the side of the tower and Jon began to climb quickly down it. Kalen paused and took in the view. From this angle, through the smoke, he could nearly see to the military base in the north. Slightly to the east of the military base, flashes of light caught his eye. He tried to remember what was there. The flares were in the vicinity of one of the Ea-Zone Gates. Was there fighting? Were Unity defending the base? He had no time to think about it. Swinging his feet onto the ladder, he hurriedly climbed down after Jon.

Jon's voice came urgently through his headset, "The drones are coming back. Get ready!"

Chapter Five

Kalen hesitated on the ladder. They were in an impossible situation; either climb down or fire.

"Mik, Lee, Josh, assume defense nine!" Jon shouted, without breaking step.

Immediately, in unison, the soldiers above Kalen stopped on the ladder and swung outwards, lasers in their hands.

"Kalen, follow me down. When I stop, you stop. They'll cover us, and then we cover them," Jon ordered.

Sweat broke out on Kalen's brow and his hands felt clammy. His gloves were tucked in a pocket, and his palms slid against the rough metal rungs. Behind him he sensed the presence of the drones, their lights catching his helmet visor. The rail above him suddenly flared bright, showering sparks over him. The smell of burning reached him, despite his helmet filters, and he felt sick. He heard a scream and a soldier flew past him, his boot hitting Kalen's left shoulder, the glancing blow nearly knocking him off balance. He held onto the ladder tightly.

Further up the ladder, five or six drones darted about. Their miniature laser arrays twinkled just before splashes of fire erupted on the tower trelliswork and ladder. About six meters above him, the men fended them off, targeting the drones with their lasers, drawing their fire. In the distance, a cloud of twenty or thirty drones advanced. More coming. He didn't like their odds of surviving against them.

"Ready?" Jon asked, laser in hand.

"Ready."

Kalen reached for his laser. His heartbeat pounded in his ear drums and his senses became acute. Colors appeared vivid. Jon, no more than two meters below him, holding his laser, his steps scraping on the rungs. Above, the scuffling of boots. The smell of acrid smoke tinged with plastic. Drones. Six of them. He could see every small detail of their shiny black bodies.

"Change!" Jon shouted, abruptly stopping on a rung. He began firing rapidly and hit a drone. It burst into flames and fell out of the sky.

Immediately, the remaining drones dived towards him. Kalen took aim. He clipped one. It spun and jerked about for less than a second while recalibrating its directional sensors. He swung his laser to fire at another, and then bent back to shoot a drone above. Turning to his left, he aimed at a fourth drone, but they seemed to anticipate his movements and darted about evading him. Again and again, he fired, but they continued to frustrate his attempts. He willed Jon to call time on it. He couldn't keep this up for long.

"Change!" Jon cried, and began climbing downwards again.

Kalen clambered after him, slinging the strap of his laser over his shoulder. He risked glancing down. They were still over ninety meters above the ground. The main body of drones would reach them soon. They were too few to fight them off.

A sudden humming behind his back, made him start. A bright flare burst near him and then another and another, throwing out heat that penetrated his suit. The arm of his jacket singed, turning a crisp brown. He risked glancing around. Forty or fifty drones. Within meters of them. Obsidian insectile drones and another kind. Similar in shape but with sharper snouts and dark grey shells, cutting through the others. Black drones exploding in a hail of metal parts. Yellow lights on the grey snouts twinkling like golden triangles before the strike. Comprehension struck Kalen. Unity! They had sent their fleet. Thank the planets!

"They'll cover us," Jon confirmed, his voice breathless. "Defense nine stand down. Let's go."

Jon's boots clattered on the ladder below him and Kalen quickened his steps. He looked upwards, relieved to see all of the drones engaged with each other. They were in the clear. How far to the bottom? Soon they must reach the ground. A whirring sound caused him to spin around. A black drone had followed them down. It was coming at him at an angle. Clinging to the rail with one hand, he grasped his laser with the other. Lights flickered along the drone's snout and then a blinding flash dazzled him. One of his boots slipped on the rung and for a moment he floundered.

"Got him!" a voice from above.

Kalen let out his breath and fought to regain his balance. He knocked his laser against the rail and it slipped out of his hand. Cursing, he clutched the rung to steady himself. Propelling himself downwards, Kalen saw the ground rising from below. Within moments, Jon had jumped off the ladder and was bending to retrieve something on the ground. Kalen followed him, glad to be back on a firm footing.

"Here's your gun," Jon said, handing him the laser. "Try to hold onto it."

"Point taken," Kalen replied.

Jon strode over to a bundle lying nearby. "Mik," he said, bending over the body. "He couldn't hold onto the ladder after that hit he took in the terminal."

Boots crunched on rubble as the other two joined them, standing quietly, watching Jon examine the body. "He's dead. Headquarters will arrange to retrieve him."

A sudden movement above caught Kalen's attention, and he jumped aside to avoid a chunk of burning metal that hit the ground near him. The battle above continued fiercely. He stepped closer to the wall of the tower. They were still in danger. Near him, Jon was speaking into his radio. Lee and Josh were checking their equipment. He secured his pack and did the same. At a signal from Jon, they moved off.

Jon sprinted along the side of the tower and civic hall until he reached the street, where he paused to tell the others, "We're to meet Stafford in the alley opposite."

They crossed the street and entered a dark narrow alley. For the most part it was bordered by high walls, pitted with doors and shop fronts. At intervals, pedestrian ramps led off it to elevated walkways that traversed the buildings at an upper level. Jon carried on forward ignoring the side exits, continually glancing about them, as if expecting an ambush. Kalen felt uneasy. The place was quiet. There was no sound but their own footsteps.

Jon moved quickly with economic steps, sidestepping slabs of fallen masonry that littered their path. Kalen wondered why they had to meet Stafford. They could have made their own way back to base. Why did they need an escort? Had the fighting spread from the perimeters into the city center?

A bright flash suddenly lit up the alleyway ahead of them and the walls exploded, spewing out hunks of masonry and burning plastic. With a thunderous rumble, stonework and plastic fittings fell across the passageway, throwing up clouds of ash and dust. Searing heat and the smell of burning washed over them. When the dust settled, Kalen saw that the alleyway ahead was completely blocked by rubble.

"We'll take another route," Jon said. "This area isn't safe. Follow me."

Jon turned back, to take a different pedestrian walkway up to a higher level. Bordered by transparent barriers, it provided a view over several city blocks. Lines of buildings were visible, dissected by dark scars, where lasers had demolished the structures. Smoke rose from buildings nearby, and ahead of them, laser flares exploded repeatedly.

The walkway swung around, and Kalen glimpsed the beginning of the Ea-Zone accommodation blocks. A pang of familiarity hit him. He wondered if Halle was in there. Was she in the blocks somewhere, afraid and injured? Where was she when the war started? Pointless questions. He became aware that Jon had stopped walking and came out of his reverie.

"We've come too far east," Jon remarked. "I'm going back to ground level. We'll take Main Way if we have to. We can't get through on the ramps."

Jon resumed walking, descending at the next exit to the walkway below and then down a stationary escalator to the street. Kalen heard a noise coming from somewhere ahead of them. At first it was faint, but gradually he made out the sound of voices. He strained to hear. Screaming, faint but persistent from more than one person. He couldn't catch the words but he could hear the tone of fear and desperation in the voices. Gradually, different voices became discernible, some pleading, some screaming and other voices, shouting orders.

Jon rounded a corner and then stepped back sharply. "We shouldn't be here."

Kalen moved forward, but Jon held out a restraining arm, barring his path. "Stand back! All of you. Stay out of sight."

"What's going on? I can hear people screaming?" Kalen questioned, unable to see around the corner.

"They're dealing with the prisoners," Jon replied in a flat voice.

"What do you mean? What are they doing to them?"

"They're sending them away." Jon glared, challenging Kalen to call his lie.

A piercing female scream drowned out Jon's last words, impaling Kalen with a sense of fear that he hadn't felt since he was a child suffering nightmares. Something terrible was happening. These weren't cries emitted in combat, but visceral screams of terror.

"We have to do something," Kalen insisted.

"There's nothing we can do!" Jon hissed. "Keep your voice down."

"They're getting what they deserve," Lee remarked. "They don't have the God-force. Their whole society is immoral."

"Disgusting Earlians!" Josh snarled. "Think what they would have done to those children if you hadn't moved the cab."

"Be quiet!" Jon ordered.

Kalen heard another scream, a shrill dry cry that ended abruptly. Icy horror invaded him. He wanted to do something but the others would stop him if he tried. They would quickly brand him a traitor if he tried to interfere. He didn't subscribe to the religious dogma that Unity had used as an excuse for civil war. There had always been overcrowding, but he suspected that there was another reason for the war, more sinister and pervasive.

Kalen whispered to Jon, "Can't you pull rank and stop this?"

"I have my orders. I don't have the power to intervene."

"Who are they?" Kalen asked. "I thought the Gates were locked and the Ea-Zone were inside the accommodation blocks?"

"They must have breached one of the Gates, before it was secured. The fighting is more widespread than I thought," Jon replied. "We must leave."

Jon gestured to the others to go back. "We're returning to the walkway. Let's move!"

Jon blocked Kalen's way, and he reluctantly turned around and followed the others. As he trudged back, he found himself thinking about Josh's remark. Early had intended to destroy the cab and everyone in. Had Early known that there were children in the cab? It seemed likely. A savage unreasonable act, that ran counter to any civilized society. Was the Ea-Zone now adopting the barbarity of Unity? Was there an explanation for their actions? A worm of truth began to eat at the corners of Kalen's consciousness, but he dismissed the idea. No, it couldn't be. He wouldn't allow himself to believe it. If it were so, Early and Unity faced a greater danger than each other.

Jon sensed Kalen's disquiet. "Forget them. When we get back to headquarters, I'll recommend you get leave to see your girlfriend. You must be missing her."

"Yes, thanks," Kalen muttered, a feeling of dread settling on him.

Kalen pictured Sera Ethern's pale face, with her hollow cheekbones and purple shadows underneath large brown eyes. Before they came to Unity, she had had a lithe body, but since arriving, she had become skeletal thin, all sharp angles. Her dark brown hair had thinned in recent weeks, to hang lankly to her shoulders. Kalen had thought her beautiful once, before her recent gauntness. Her thick black eyelashes had given expression to her lovely eyes. Now she had the eyes of a fanatic and a deep frown line between them. He needed to break with her, tell her they were finished, but he sensed a darkness within her, something indefinable, that held him back.

***

Halle Rison searched her bedroom for her favorite grey belt, as she got dressed for the meeting. She saw the end of it poking out from underneath a pile of clothes she had dumped on a chair, the night before. Taking two steps, she picked it up and fed it through the loops in her blue uniform trousers and then slipped on her matching jacket. After putting on her boots, she checked her appearance in the mirror. Dark circles below her eyes evidenced the horror of the last few days. She quickly brushed her blond hair and made up her face, before spraying herself with perfume.

Looking and smelling nice won't hurt, she reasoned. Russ would be there. Her heart skipped a beat when she thought about him. He was tall with broad shoulders, and strong features. A warmth coursed through her when she remembered the previous evening. She had run her fingers across his chest, tracing the outline of his hard muscles, her hands pale against his black skin. He had kissed her deeply, folding his arms about her, and she had felt his strength. She had stayed in his rooms until late, feeling safe and loved in his embrace. She glanced in the mirror again and forced her attention back to the present.

Leaving her rooms, she hurried along the interior passageways of the Ea-Zone accommodation block. She was a divisional manager of the Ea-Zone's Colonization Division and had been ordered to attend a meeting in the block canteen. The air in the passageway smelled stale with a hint of smoke, but she rejected the idea of taking a route along the external terraces. Unity had fired intermittently at the block over the previous days, and the damage to the terraces was extensive. Sections had been closed off, and many residents had been moved to safer quarters.

The corridors were empty save for a few staff from the Colonization Division, who saluted her.

At the entrance to the canteen, a grey uniformed security guard blocked Halle's path. "ID please. Access to the meeting is restricted to senior personnel."

Halle showed her Division card and the guard checked her off the list.

"Thank you," the guard said, waving her in.

The room was half full. A mixture of Division, Security and Army personnel sat in rows facing a long table on a podium at the far end. Several people milled behind the table in deep discussion, Captain Russ Thomas amongst them. She caught his eye and he winked at her. Halle smiled back at him and then made her way towards him. She reminded herself to behave formally around him; their relationship was a private matter. As she neared the podium, she recognized Sun Hider, the Ea-Zone divisional director. In late middle age, his face had grown fat and his greying hair had begun to recede.

Sun greeted her, "Miss Rison, good to see you. Let me introduce you to the others. They represent each branch of the services and like you, have been trapped in the Ea-Zone blocks and army barracks since Unity took the city."

Sun Hider began to effect introductions and eventually came to Russ. "This is Captain Thomas, Miss Rison."

"Yes, we've met," Halle said politely. Russ stood taller than her, three vertical gold stripes glittering on the right shoulder of his black jacket.

"I know Miss Rison; we've spoken before," Russ replied, his eyes twinkling.

"Good. You'll be working together," Sun Hider said, his fleshy jowls wobbling and indicated that she should sit by him at the table, facing the audience. "Major Baker will chair the meeting."

Halle noted that there was only one civilian in the group, a man of about forty-five with black wavy hair touched with grey, who represented the civilians and families. Why had a civilian been asked to attend the meeting? She hadn't been told what the meeting was about, but the people here represented all sections of the Ea-Zone. They were going to be told something important, she realized. A feeling of dread settled over her. Whatever it was, it wouldn't be good news.

Chapter Six

Halle waited and a silence gradually fell over the room and Major Baker stood up. She took off her peaked hat and surveyed the audience with serious expressive eyes. A woman in her early forties, she wore no makeup and had a pallid complexion. Her brown hair had been cut short with a fringe across her forehead. She looks tired, Halle thought, studying the lines on the major's face. Hadn't she heard a rumor that Major Baker had recently been promoted? Stepped into a dead person's boots. The five gold vertical stripes just below the right shoulder of her army jacket glinted in the harsh glare of the overhead strip lighting. Placing both hands flat on the table, Major Baker leaned forward.

"Ladies and gentlemen, the United Colonies Time System have declared war on us. I command the Army, here in Central. My colleagues, represent Security, Colonization Division and civilians. We've called this meeting to inform you of our plans."

Major Baker paused and then continued in a firm voice, "We cannot remain for more than a few more days in the accommodation blocks. The buildings have been badly damaged and the structure is failing. Food and water is running out. All our supplies came through Central. Without the use of the space port we cannot import more. We have no access to the hospital, transport terminal or military base."

Halle listened with growing alarm. If they couldn't stay in the blocks, where would they go? She listened to the low murmur coming from the audience that reached her on the podium.

"I've called for assistance, but none is coming," Major Baker announced. The buzzing of the audience grew louder. "Our situation is replicated throughout Taidor. Unity has taken all of the major cities and the building sites. The war is planet wide. We've been attempting to open the Gates into Central. We've had some success, but have been repulsed by Unity's troops. The fighting continues, but the Early Colonial Time System is losing the war."

The babble of the audience had reached a crescendo and Major Baker put up a hand for silence. Nodding to Sun Hider, she said, "Sun Hider is now going to outline our plans."

Sun Hider stood up. "All government on Taidor has broken down. We are in the midst of a civil war. The fighting extends to the building sites and mines. At present, Unity has control."

Halle tried to take in Sun Hider's summary, fear growing like a rotten fruit in the pit of her stomach. They were trapped and would have to fight to survive. Although the Ea-Zone had some military resources, the bulk of the weaponry and transportation had been seized by Unity in the coup. She pictured the city, desolate and destroyed, and remembered the busy cafés and restaurants, the music playing and people bustling about the shops. It all seemed like another life. Halle jolted at the sound of her name.

Sun Hider was still speaking, "Miss Rison will co-ordinate the Colonization Division personnel. Miss Rison, please stand so everyone can see you."

Halle pushed her chair back and stood up. "Thank you Sun, I shall be pleased to do so."

Halle stared over the audience and then sat down again, an uncomfortable feeling of embarrassment washing over her. She chided herself for putting makeup and perfume on. Next to Major Baker, it made her look trivial and foolish in the face of the threat that they all faced. She'd tried to deny the war, hiding behind her normal routine. Now she had to deal with it. She turned her attention back to Sun Hider who continued speaking, and when he had finished, the others spoke in turn.

Finally, Major Baker stood up and announced, " In twenty-four hours, we will deactivate four of the Gates that are trapping us in the accommodation blocks, simultaneously. We will get through the Gates and attack Unity and retake the city. We have a day to prepare. You all know what you have to do. Dismissed."

Twenty-four hours! That isn't enough time, thought Halle. Like everyone else in the Division, she had received basic military training, but that barely extended beyond the use of hand lasers. Now she was being asked to co-ordinate the Division personnel, in an armed attack. The scale of the task daunted her. All would be under Army command on the day.

Halle turned to speak to Russ. "I understand that I'll be reporting to you."

Russ smiled at her and then assumed a serious expression. "Yes, that's correct. You'll be liaising with me when we attack."

"That's good," she replied, meeting his eyes. He still affected her in the same way as when she'd first seen him in a corridor at Division headquarters, several weeks before. Tall with a muscular body, the confident way he carried himself, exuded power. With a commanding air, his gaze had swept over her, his brown eyes bright and intense. She had blushed and butterflies had somersaulted in her stomach. He had carried on walking but when he was very close, he had winked, and then he was gone.

"Miss Rison, we have a lot to discuss." He was studying her face now, his mouth twitching into a smile.

Remembering last night, Halle thought. They'd been too busy to discuss the meeting today. She adopted a business-like demeanor for the benefit of anyone listening. "Please call me Halle, Captain Thomas."

He gave a short laugh. "I will, Halle. It's okay to drop the Captain Thomas unless it's in front of the unit. They need to remember that I'm in charge. About tomorrow's engagement, can you tell me the number of Division personnel in the blocks?"

"About five hundred," Halle replied, acutely aware of his close proximity.

"I know the computer network is down. Can you compile a list?"

"I have a list," Halle said. "I backed up my office work so that I could access it from my quarters. I have some records that may be useful."

"Excellent. We need to go through all the staff we have available, so that we can assign them roles," Russ confirmed. "We should be a match for Unity with everyone on board. We need every man and woman who can fire a laser."

"I know." Halle frowned. "But have we got enough weapons? I was told that Unity took the military base, where the armaments are kept."

"That's correct, but the Ea-Zone started taking precautionary measures a while back, in case of an attack. We've accumulated a stock of weapons and equipment; enough to kit everyone out."

"The Division staff aren't soldiers, but we've had military training."

Russ smiled. "If this all goes to plan, Unity will find itself outnumbered tomorrow."

"I hope so," Halle replied.

"You haven't seen any action yet, have you?" Russ asked her frankly.

"Not so far." Halle repressed a shudder. "The U-Zone aren't targeting the higher floors where my quarters are."

"They're hitting the lower floors," Russ said. "They're frightened that high shots could hit the dome over

Central. We've also got orders to avoid damaging it. If we lost the air seal, the consequences would be terrible for everyone."

"It wouldn't take long for the air to run out. We can't breathe Taidor's atmosphere," Halle agreed.

"Let's hope that never happens."

"I've been told that the domes over Morten and most of the other cities are still functioning," Halle informed him. "I've been assisting in communications."

"I've heard…" Russ frowned. "Never mind. We need to deal with the plan for tomorrow. I've just been allocated one of the security offices on floor ten by Gate Six. Do you know it?"

"I can find it."

"Can you get the personnel list and meet me there in an hour?"

"Yes," Halle agreed, feeling her heart rate quicken. She would be alone with him in an hour.

"Okay. I'll see you there in an hour." Russ's eyes twinkled. He turned away from her and was soon caught up talking to another soldier.

Halle picked up her pad, nodded at Sun Hider who was in discussion with Major Baker, and made her way out of the canteen. The tension of the people around her was palpable. They were going to have to fight for their lives. She had watched the missile and laser attack over the previous days. The Ea-Zone blocks had been reduced to rubble in places and one floor had been turned into a makeshift hospital. Every hour, more parts of the blocks were hit and there were more wounded. Until now, she had been safe, but that was going to change. She tried to suppress a nasty thought but the words refused to be quashed. *I could die tomorrow.*

***

Halle found the security office easily. It was a small room just off a corridor that she was familiar with. One of the rooms near it had been converted into a temporary crèche for the children. Their squeals and laughter rang up the passageway, another reminder of their cramped living arrangements. Before the war, she had often used this route, using a nearby Gate to get into the city. It didn't seem possible that it was closed to the Ea-Zone now. The events of the last few days seemed surreal.

The door was shut when Halle reached it and she pressed the entrance panel. It slid aside to reveal a sparsely furnished office, with cabinets lining the back wall and viewscreens and consoles lining another. Russ sat at a table in the center of the room, working on a desk screen. The door slid shut behind her and he stood up and hugged her.

"You look lovely. I keep thinking about last night," he said, bending his head so that his lips brushed the side of her hair. "You smell delicious."

He kissed her, moving one hand to stroke the back of her hair, and placing the other in the small of her back, clasping her firmly to him. She wound her hands around his neck and kissed him, pressing herself against him. She felt the power of his hard muscular arms locking her within them and her legs began to go weak. He kissed her again and then stood back.

"We've got work to do." He sighed and ran one hand across her cheek, before pulling a chair out for her. "Perhaps we can find time later?"

"Work always gets in the way." Halle shrugged out of her jacket and took a seat opposite him. Underneath, she wore a tight pale yellow shirt that had magnetic fastenings at the front. Casually, she undid the top fastening to expose a pretty blue necklace that was the same color as her eyes, and a hint of her ample cleavage. She took a pad out of her bag and put it on the table. "Back to work then."

"The plan is to divide our manpower equally between four of the southern Gates. We'll launch an assault after we've deactivated them," Russ explained, his eyes flickering momentarily to her chest. "We'll create a diversion in the north, to draw Unity's troops away."

"What's the total head count per Gate?" Halle asked, switching on her pad and flicking her fingers over it to make notes.

"We think we can field about a thousand people per Gate. Mostly soldiers, security officers and Division personnel. We also have a number of civilians who will be able to fight."

"I thought that we had more soldiers in Central than that?" Halle was puzzled. She had received various reports from the Division and the numbers didn't make sense to her.

"We've already taken a number of casualties. Where it's essential that we maintain a military presence, such as the diversion in the north, we're going to substitute as many soldiers as possible with non-army personnel, so that we can use them in the assault."

"How long will it take to deactivate the Gates?" Halle asked.

"We've already done a lot of the preliminary work. We've been working on the codes and know the weak points. It will take about an hour to actually physically open them and turn the barriers off. The final push through won't happen until we have everyone in place."

"I know about the body scanners at the Gates but I'm not familiar with the barriers," Halle said, inwardly cursing the Division's climate of secrecy. "Security issues have never come under my remit."

Russ widened his eyes. "You should have been fully briefed."

"Information is guarded in the Division," Halle said crisply. "The Division doesn't interfere with security issues."

"The barriers are electronic," Russ said. "When a Gate is open, only the body scanner in the Gate's frame is activated. Behind the frame, the Gate extends for about another three meters. When a Gate is closed, the electric barrier is activated along the whole length of the Gate. The electric barrier can be set at any strength, for instance, low enough to give superficial burns or high enough to kill. You wouldn't have seen it because the Gates are hidden behind heavy metal doors when they're closed."

"Presumably if they're deactivated they won't cause a problem," Halle said. "Here's the list of Division personnel you wanted." She handed him a memory chip.

"Good, let's run through them," Russ said, pushing the chip into the bottom of his screen. "We'll divide them into four groups and I'll give you details of where they can pick up their kit. We also need to run down timing, placement once we're through the Gates, line of command and check details such as radio frequencies. There'll be a briefing for all Division personnel at eighteen hundred hours."

"Okay," Halle confirmed.

"Let me show you the Gates we're deactivating." Russ stood up and moved to the viewscreens on the wall.

Halle got up and joined him. The viewscreens showed scenes inside the accommodation block, as well as the view of the city from the terraces. Russ pressed a switch on a console and instantly the screen above it changed view, to show one of the Gates that served the south-eastern blocks. The large metal door that usually hid the Gate when it was closed, was open. Inside the Gate, flashes of electricity sizzled dangerously across it, sparking bright bursts of energy that illuminated its mouth. A panel near the metal door had been removed, and two men were working on a tangle of wiring behind it.

"That's Gate Three," Russ said.

"I wouldn't like to get caught in that." Halle stared at the bolts of electricity streaking across the Gate.

Russ leaned forward and pressed another button. Instantly the scene changed. "Now Gate Four."

"And the other Gates?"

"Gates One and Two. They're the farthest south. While Unity defends the north, we'll attack from the south."

Halle pondered his reply. "There's fighting in the south. Unity has a lot of soldiers near those Gates."

"We've begun to withdraw from the south. Pretending defeat in that area."

"But the military base is in the north? Surely it would make more sense to try and take the base?"

"Unity won't withdraw from the north. The base is heavily defended and Unity expect us to attack it. Our primary objective is to get into the city. Once we're through the Gates, we'll push north to take the base."

"Okay," Halle replied.

"I'll show you the other two Gates."

Russ shifted his position, leaning in front of Halle slightly, to press another switch. He was now so close to her that she could smell his perspiration, mixed with a faint smoky smell from his army jacket. His arm brushed hers and she savored his closeness. She wanted him to put his arms around her again. She hadn't felt this way since Kalen. How long had it been since Kalen left? She tried to remember and then told herself to forget Kalen. She'd heard that he'd been at headquarters when it was hit by the Ea-Zone. No one had survived. He was gone and there was nothing that she could do about it. She had Russ now.

"I'm sorry. I didn't mean to crush you." Russ moved away from her.

She put a delicate hand on his lower arm. "It's all right. You're not crushing me."

She smiled at him, blue eyes ingenuous. He held her gaze for a moment and then resumed studying the viewscreens. "You're distracting me. We have work to do."

"I thought we were nearly finished."

"We are. I've just got a couple more bits of the city to show you." Russ brought up views of the streets near the Gates. "We'll discuss where we're putting people after the briefing, but it's important that you're familiar with the layout of the area on the other side of the Gates."

"I know the area. I've often walked through there," Halle said.

"Okay, we're done here." Russ shut the screen off. "Anything you're unclear about?"

Halle faced him and took a deep breath that made her breasts strain against the thin material of her top and asked, "How bad is it really going to be? I've seen what the lasers can do."

"We have almost equal numbers to Unity, so with good planning we should win," Russ said.

"Good. We have to take Central back," Halle said.

"We'll field a strong force if we all work together."

"You have the experience. This is all new to me." She gazed at him, the overhead lights creating bright ripples in her blond hair.

He put his arms around her and said gently, "Don't worry, you'll be fine. But things will be different after tomorrow."

If we survive, Halle thought. *If we survive the lasers and missiles. And the drones.* Their chances were slim. She tried to shut out the images of death from her mind.

"I'll do my best. We mustn't let them win." Halle raised her chin and gave Russ a long look. She had to act brave even if she didn't feel like it. It wasn't as if any of them had any choice. What she really felt was anger: anger at Unity and their terrible destruction. She dropped her eyes for a fraction of a second before lifting them again, to regard him with a determined expression.

"We will win," Russ said emphatically. He bent his head and kissed her.

She returned his kiss and felt his hot breath as he nuzzled her neck.

He gently nibbled her ear and then whispered, "This can't wait until tomorrow."

"No it can't," Halle murmured, as he unfastened the clasps of her top and slipped a hand inside.

Chapter Seven

Kalen stared into the face of the madman sitting at the desk. He had been ordered to report to Javed Durton at the Colonization Division's makeshift offices in the U-Zone accommodation blocks. He had last seen Javed when the headquarters building had been hit at the start of the war. Javed had refused to leave the burning building, and Kalen had run out into the maelstrom of the battle, only to be pulled back by Unity's troops. Now he wondered how much of their last conversation Javed remembered.

"Thank you for coming straight here, Chief Trinneer. I was told that you survived the initial attack unharmed. The God-force protected you," Javed said.

"Yes Sir," Kalen replied automatically, assessing the U-Zone divisional director.

"Major Reece has told me that you've done some good work."

Kalen studied the short, bald headed man, behind the desk. He almost looked sane. Except for his eyes. Unnaturally bright and dark, they fixed on him unblinking.

"Thank you Sir."

"The fighting has been intense but we hold all key areas of Central." Javed touched his Divine. The gold triangular badge on his jacket had number thirteen inscribed on it. "Once we subdue the Ea-Zone completely, we'll be able to start rebuilding the city."

"I understand that most of the Ea-Zone are still in the accommodation blocks, Sir?" Kalen ventured.

"Yes, they are, but not for much longer. Once we take the blocks we can use them to house our own people," Javed replied.

Kalen waited for him to continue, his eyes drawn to the triangular plaque on the wall behind Javed, inscribed with the word "Unity" in gold lettering. The heat in the room was stifling and Kalen sweated under his jacket. He wished that he could take his hat off, but protocol forbade it.

"The air supply units aren't working properly," Javed said mildly. "But that isn't why I wanted to see you."

Kalen said nothing and Javed regarded him steadily, as if deciding what to say next. "Aren't you going to ask where we're putting them?"

"I'm sorry, Sir. I don't understand?" Kalen feigned ignorance. He balled his hands into fists to stop them shaking. He had to be careful. Javed was a powerful man.

"The Ea-Zone population."

"They aren't my concern," Kalen said emphatically, looking Javed straight in the eye. Would Javed buy that? It wasn't enough. "They have no morals. They're child killers. We're all well rid of them, whatever Unity decides to do."

"I'm glad to hear you say that, Trinneer. Their corruption taints this planet. They have no God-force. After our last conversation, I was concerned that you might be sympathetic towards Early."

"No Sir," Kalen said. What could he say to convince him? "They don't have the God-force. We shouldn't have to share the planet with them."

Javed smiled. "At last, you're seeing things how they are."

"I understand it now." Kalen clenched his hands behind his back.

"We're going to send them to the mines to work. They can supplement the machines. It will accelerate the whole building program," Javed informed him.

"I see."

"What was it you said to me about the Uveid rocks, the last time we met?" Javed asked suddenly.

He remembers, thought Kalen, but how much? "I told you that the Uveid deposits have an energy field," he replied cautiously, recalling their last conversation. He had called Javed infected; infected by the energy field exuded by the Uveid rocks. The strange pyramid shaped crystalline rocks that had been found on Taidor, seemed to affect most people who came into contact with them. He had told Javed that his actions weren't dictated by God, but caused by exposure to the Uveid. Such was Javed's fanaticism, Kalen doubted whether he had even heard him.

Javed's eyes glassed over for a fraction of a second and then flickered back to Kalen. "That's right. We were discussing the weapon that we've developed from the alien artefact you brought to us. It utilizes the Uveid energy."

Kalen clenched his hands tighter. The trident. An alien device found in the mine at Three-Craters, a city that was still being constructed, level by level, deep underground. He had found a small piece of metal tubing on the forty-seventh level and taken it to Unity, not realizing its significance. Fitted together with parts that Unity had found, it formed a trident. The trident was small enough to hold, but when used in the vicinity of the Uveid rock deposits, capable of harnessing their powerful energy. From what he had seen, it had the potential to wreak terrible destruction, much worse than the lasers. "Has it been deployed?"

"So far we've only been able to use it in limited conditions, underground, but it's being modified for use above ground. We're nearly ready to test it."

Kalen went cold. Use of the trident at ground level would be devastating. It could destroy entire cities. He opened his mouth to reply and then thought better of it.

"Once we have it working properly, we should be able to end this war quickly," Javed said.

"Where are you going to test it?"

"You'll be informed in due course," Javed replied. "Right now I want you to assist Paul Neill in finalizing the modifications to the trident. There are still one or two technical aspects that need to be dealt with."

Kalen stared at Javed. "Isn't Paul Neill at Three-Craters? That's a full day's journey."

"No, he's in Morten. You're to meet him there and then go on to Three-Craters. You can catch an overnight transport tomorrow."

"Isn't there a lot of fighting in Morten?"

Javed grimaced. "There's still a lot of resistance, but Unity has taken most of the city."

"The God-force is with us," Kalen replied, thinking quickly. Perhaps this was his chance to escape. Morten was Taidor's second city. Once he reached it, he could try and get to Early's forces. But where did Unity intend to use the trident? He had to find out first. Wherever it was used, it would cause horrific devastation. And now Javed expected him to help Paul Neill. Perhaps he could stop Unity using it. Destroy it? Or try to reason with Paul? No, Paul was one of Unity's top physicists. He wouldn't listen. He would have to destroy it.

"Your work with us is appreciated, Trinneer," Javed said. "I have something for you." He placed a gold Divine on the table. "This is for you. Put it on."

Kalen picked it up. It had a number two on it. "Thank you Sir."

"Normally there would be a formal ceremony to celebrate your elevation," Javed said seriously. "But we are at war, so you'll have to do without that. However, you are now at stage two and that has been recorded officially. Congratulations."

"Thank you, I'm honored." Kalen nearly choked on the words, but managed to keep a passive expression on his face. He was still a lowly two, ranked under nearly everyone else.

"That's all. I know Sera Ethern is waiting for you. She has something to tell you."

***

The U-Zone accommodation blocks seemed very much the same to Kalen, as they did before the fighting. Laser and missile launchers had been placed on the terraces, but the substance of the blocks was the same. He walked through the corridors, towards Sera Ethern's quarters, with a feeling of trepidation. He had agreed to collect her for the evening meal but he was not looking forward to it. She had changed since he had brought her to Unity. The sweet intelligent geologist he had fallen in love with, had become a cruel humorless zealot. He found her door and pressed the entry plate.

The door slid aside. Sera stood in the doorway, dressed in a long sleeveless turquoise gown. The neckline of the bodice had been cut into a deep "V" and the gown had been shaped to accentuate her waist. The sides of the gown were split up to the top of the knee, providing Kalen with a glimpse of her slim calves. She wore matching shoes, with a small heel. On her breast, a Divine shimmered denoting her a six. She regarded him with large brown eyes, thick black lashes fluttering under his scrutiny. He stared at her in surprise. Her face had filled out and the frown line between her eyebrows had gone. Her glossy hair fell luxuriously to her shoulders.

"Sera, you look well." He tried to inject warmth into his voice.

She gave him a shy smile. "I am. How about you? I've been worried about you."

"I'm fine. Just tired." He was suspicious. Something had brought about the change in her. The gown was unusually colorful. Even her eyes had lost that dangerous glitter. "Have you stayed in the blocks during the fighting?"

"Yes, I've been working from here," she replied.

"Shall we walk to the canteen? You can tell me about it on the way," he suggested.

"Why don't you come in?" Sera asked.

Kalen tried to keep the surprise off his face. This was new. Unity had very strict rules about such things. They weren't married and he would be committing an offence if he entered her quarters.

"You know I'm not allowed to come in."

"There are exceptions." Sera blushed. "In any case, I wanted to celebrate your elevation."

"I'm still only a two, Sera," Kalen said warily, making no move to go in. "But I see you're now a six. Congratulations."

"Thank you, I've been working hard. I heard you risked your life in the fighting. I'm very proud of you," Sera beamed. "But there's another reason I asked you to come in. I've got something else to tell you and no one will mind if we celebrate that together, in private."

Kalen heard footsteps at the end of the corridor. An elderly woman, dressed in a long blue tunic was walking towards them. She squinted at them curiously as she went by.

"Well, are you coming in?" Sera asked, turning away from the door and disappearing inside her room.

All of Kalen's senses warned him not to trust her. A true citizen of Unity, she embraced the U-Zone's strict regime wholeheartedly. Conformity in the U-Zone was mandatory. No exceptions were allowed, and Kalen had no doubt that Sera would denounce anyone she thought was breaking the rules. The consequences of non-compliance were severe, especially now they were at war. If she suspected he sympathized with the Ea-Zone, she would give him up without hesitation.

"Are you testing me?" he asked her. "Are you trying to see if I'll break the rules?"

"Don't be silly," she called from the depths of her dimly lit room. "Come in. Once I've given you my news, you'll understand."

Kalen reluctantly entered the room. She had turned the overhead lights off, and the wall lights gave a gentle glow that softened her features and cast her shadow across the room. A blue sofa had been pushed against one wall and a table and two chairs along another. The table had been laid out for supper and a dish with a lid had been placed in the center.

"Come over here."

She led him to a sofa and sat down. He cautiously sat beside her, trying to keep a few centimeters between them.

"We have to discuss our Commitment Ceremony," she said. "You told me that you'd think about it and give me an answer."

"Sera..." Kalen hesitated. An unequivocal negative response would evoke her wrath. Her revenge would be terrible. He was under suspicion already and vulnerable to accusations of treason. He had to keep her on side, if possible. "We discussed this. I thought we agreed to wait before we took the final decision?"

"Oh Kalen, I don't need more time. I know I want to marry you. I want to be your wife. I thought that's what you wanted as well. Otherwise, why did you bring me to Unity?"

She has a point, thought Kalen. He should have left her in the Ea-Zone when he decided to defect. But they were both in danger and he had thought that he loved her then. Now he did not. And he did not want to marry her. He tried to think of something to say. "You know you mean the world to me..."

She suddenly reached for his hand. "I've got something to tell you. I know you'll be pleased. I'm pregnant!" Sera announced with glowing eyes. "We can't wait now. We have to go through the Commitment Ceremony as soon as possible. Especially now that there's a war. I've told the Division and we can get married tomorrow."

"The Division know?" Kalen stared at her aghast. "Aren't they going to sanction us?"

"Don't worry!" Sera said brightly. "I've explained that our indiscretion took place in the Ea-Zone; that the moral climate of the place caused it. The Division supports our marriage."

Kalen squeezed her hand and attempted to smile. "That's wonderful."

"You are pleased aren't you?" Sera searched his face. Doubt began to cloud her eyes and she started to frown.

"Of course," Kalen said in a softer tone. Drawing her to him, he put his arm around her so that her head was against his shoulder. "It's wonderful news. I'm just a bit surprised, that's all."

He found it difficult to think. An overwhelming feeling of entrapment rose up with the acid in his stomach. He had to say something. She was gazing at him expectantly.

Taking one of her hands in his, he asked, "When did you find out?"

"Only a couple of days ago."

"When is it due?"

"It's a boy and he's due in August," Sera said contentedly.

He tried to think of an appropriate response. "I've always wanted a son."

The words sounded strange. He was going to have a son. This was a new idea that he would have to get used to. He had no doubt that he was the father. He didn't think she'd been with anyone else.

"I would have been happy with either," Sera said.

He would have to go through with the ceremony. There was no way out, not now. He would have to take care of her and their son. He couldn't leave her. In any case, Unity would insist that he married her and if he demurred, they would arrest him for immorality.

"I don't know if we can have the ceremony tomorrow. I have to go to Morten to work with Paul Neill."

"The Division has already arranged the ceremony for tomorrow morning."

"Good," Kalen forced the word out. "But I have to leave for Morten tomorrow evening."

"Didn't Javed tell you? I'm coming with you. I've been asked to survey the underground levels in Morten for the Uveid rock. After all, I'm the geologist who discovered the Uveid originally. So we won't be apart."

"That's great," he replied. The net is closing, he thought. It was going to be difficult to destroy the trident with Sera there. She would watch him the whole time. Javed Durton had given her this assignment so that she could watch him.

She interlinked her fingers in his and gazed at him. "I thought we could have supper here tonight. I've prepared a stivey casserole."

Kalen groaned inwardly. He could almost taste the bitter flavor of the yellow watery stew with purple lumps in it and felt nauseous.

"And you can stay over if you want to…we have permission," Sera continued.

Pushing the image of the stew out of his mind, he thought about his situation. There was no escape. He had to make the best of it. He brushed a stray lock of hair away from Sera's cheek and looked into her face. Her dark eyes questioned his. He could see no hint of the cruel fanatic in their black depths. Had he imagined her earlier irrationality or was her pregnancy disguising it? Had she shaken off the influence of the Uveid? She had handled the Uveid stones frequently and he was convinced that she had been infected.

However, tonight she seemed sane and looked beautiful. Either way, he must hide his true feelings. Perhaps he could learn to care for her again. He placed a hand on her waist and drew her to him. She came willingly into his arms and turned her face to his. He gazed into her lovely brown eyes and kissed her.

Chapter Eight

The Gates had been deactivated and Halle had been amongst the throng of Ea-Zone troops streaming under the metal archways into the city. Following orders, she had massed her people in the main body of the assault, whilst the vanguard forged ahead taking out the enemy positions. Focusing on Russ's voice through her helmet radio, she had detached her emotions, and acted mechanically, returning laser fire and directing Division personnel.

She was vaguely aware that the buildings around her were gradually disintegrating, as explosions and laser fire ripped through them. Columns of fire sprang up around her sending masonry crashing down. Taking cover behind a wall, she viewed the bodies strewn across the ground dispassionately. Suddenly, a tongue of white flame flared from an awning near her, followed by billowing acrid black smoke.

"Are you all right?" Russ's voice in her headset.

It took a moment for his question to penetrate her woolly senses. "Yes, I'm still here."

"Wait where you are. I can see you. I'm coming over to you."

She scanned the ruins. She saw him on the other side of the street, in the shelter of a damaged escalator. The twisted metal steps, warped by heat, were charred black and smoking and part of the metalwork dangled above him. She watched as he ran towards her, willing him to make it safely. He was one of the few left. Nearly all of the others were gone. Hundreds of people. Incinerated by lasers that continued to sweep the area. Only a handful of their soldiers still fought, using hand lasers, crouched behind low walls. The larger armaments and drones had already been destroyed.

Russ reached her. "We've lost. I can't make contact with Major Baker. She's either been killed or captured. I'm now the ranking officer. I've given orders to withdraw to the blocks."

Halle couldn't see Russ's face beneath his visor, but his voice sounded crisp and matter of fact. Wasn't he affected by all this?

"Some of them are still fighting," she said.

"I know. I've told them to pull out if they can. We have to move back. This way." Russ took a step towards the remains of a café. "I've ordered them to follow us."

Halle went with Russ numbly, the laser a dead weight in her hands. Her short stride made it difficult for her to keep up with him. Exhaustion dogged every step. *I will survive*, she repeated over and over to herself silently, but another voice in her head told her to be realistic. Their forces had been destroyed and they were surrounded. A blink of light caught her eye. She swiveled towards it, raising her gun. Sunlight glinting on a badge. She didn't hesitate. The black clad figure let out a blood freezing scream and burst into crackling flames.

"Got him," she said. A feeling of steely determination began to creep over her. She would kill them all if she had to.

"Now they know where we are." Russ quickened his pace.

A blast shook the ground, tearing through the walls of a building ten meters away, throwing up slabs of masonry. Halle ducked and when she raised her head again, she saw that there was only rubble left where the building had stood. A loud screeching sound suddenly drowned out everything else and a missile screamed overhead, its tail blazing comet bright. Its glare dazzled her but she followed its trajectory with a morbid fascination. As it veered downwards, time seemed to slow.

"Please no!" she muttered under her breath.

Beside her, Russ had stopped moving. He grabbed her arm and pulled her down into the rubble. The thunderous sound of an explosion rolled over them, followed by the screech of another missile closely following the first, to find its mark in the accommodation blocks.

"They've hit the blocks. We can't go back," Russ shouted. "We need to regroup."

Halle surveyed the blocks. Badly damaged, the buildings were under heavy bombardment. Anger coursed through her. They had destroyed her home. They would pay. It took a moment to absorb Russ's words. They weren't going back.

"And then what? There aren't many of us left."

"We'll have to use guerrilla tactics. We're surrounded. Still with me?"

"All the way," Halle said angrily. She stared at the smoking accommodation blocks, rage seething inside her. "I have no intention of dying in this disgusting place."

Russ glanced back at her, as he led her down an alley. "I've told the others to meet us at the shopping complex."

A blast several meters in front of them, rocked the ground. Halle felt the vibrations under her boots and flinched.

"This way," Russ shouted urgently, veering into another alley. "The others are up ahead."

At the end of the alley, Russ paused, shrinking back against a half ruined wall that bordered a wide street. "They should be near the shops across the road."

Halle stared at the shopping parade on the other side of the street with a feeling of disbelief. The complex had taken heavy damage. In places, walls had been reduced to rubble or left with gaping holes, while elevators and walkways to the higher floors had been ruined. Halle cursed Unity again for the destruction. It would take months to rebuild their beautiful city. Before the war, there had been rumors that Early and Unity could not agree on major policies, but she had never thought it would come to this. She wished that she had taken more notice. Perhaps if she had, she could have stopped Kalen leaving.

Russ assessed their surroundings. "We have to make a run for the shops on the other side. There'll be snipers waiting for us to cross over. When I say go, run for your life. Ready?"

"I'm ready," Halle confirmed.

"Now!"

They took off together, and in less than a second, flashes of scorching heat exploded around them. Russ kept going, ignoring the bombardment but Halle began to drop back.

"Keep running!" Russ screamed through her headset.

A laser flare reared up in Halle's path, lashing her with silvery yellow fire. She blinked away the white dots playing in front of her eyes and swerved to avoid the heat spot. Gathering speed again, she ran onwards, focusing on Russ. Another blast took out part of a shop ahead of them, and Russ altered course towards a stone archway. Blast after blast shook the parade and dust and debris showered down on them.

The stone archway led to an inner courtyard and more shops. Several soldiers stood in the shelter of a doorway set back a little from the wall. Halle counted seven people, two women and five men, all dressed in army uniforms of black jacket and trousers. Halle thought that she recognized one of the soldiers, and then realized it was the man who had been introduced as the civilian representative. She tried to recall his name, Seth Wayland. She didn't recognize anyone else. She ran after Russ into the recess, out of range of the snipers.

"Sir," one of the soldiers called out. "We're waiting for orders."

"Is that all of you?" Russ asked, surveying the group.

"Yes Sir, no one else is coming."

"Glad to see you made it," Russ said to Seth.

"This is Nadia," Seth replied, indicating a tall woman with auburn hair standing next to him. "We're the only ones from the civilian unit to get out."

Russ stared at Seth for a moment before replying. "All of the units have taken heavy losses."

"I know," Seth said. "Nadia and I are lucky to be alive."

Russ spoke to the group. "Anyone from the Colonization Division or Security?"

"I'm from Security," a lanky, pale young man stepped forward. "My name's Milan."

"The rest of us are regular Army," one of the others chipped in.

Halle blanched. "No one from the Division?"

"I'm sorry, Halle," Russ said.

"Okay everyone," Russ spoke to the group. "Unity's troops know we're here. We're going to have to fight our way out. If we can break through, I propose trying to join the diversionary force near the northern Gates."

"How are we going to get across the city?" Seth asked. "We'll never make it. We'll be picked off before we even get halfway."

"Our first priority is to get out of this area," Russ replied. "We'll deal with our route after that."

"You take the lead. I'll follow your orders," Seth said.

"Okay then, let's go." Russ stepped out from the shelter of the doorway and a flash of white gold light streaked across the pavement in front of him. He stepped back quickly. "They've got us pinned down. We'll have to find another way out."

"There might be a rear door to this shop," Seth indicated the doorway behind them.

"We came through that way," the first soldier informed him. "Unity also has the rear door covered. We're surrounded."

Halle thought hard about the layout of the city. "I know a way out. You've forgotten that I work for the Division. The Division built this city."

"How?" Russ asked doubtfully.

"We can get out of this building below street level," Halle explained. "I know a direct route to the transport terminal. The terminal is near the north Gate."

"Below street level?" Russ asked simply.

"We can use the supply lines that run underneath the city. The cars carry food and general cargo. We should be able to use the cars or we can walk through the tunnels."

"Do you know their layout?" Russ questioned her.

"They connect the transport terminal and port to several depots inside the city."

"You think we can get through the tunnels?" Russ looked skeptical.

"Yes, I'm sure of it. The maintenance crews go down there," Halle replied.

"How do we access them?"

"There's a supply depot underneath the shopping complex. All of the shops are connected to it at basement level. There should be a service elevator at the rear of this shop." Halle indicated the partially open door behind them.

"When we came through, we had to force the door open. All of the electrics are out so the elevator won't be working," one of the soldiers volunteered.

"Over there." Halle pointed into the blackness of the shop interior. "There'll be stairs down, at the rear. There are about ten levels before the basement."

"Okay, let's try it. We've got nothing to lose. Listen up, everyone. Unity may have followed you into the building, so watch out for them inside," Russ said. "You go first Halle, but stay vigilant."

Halle entered the shop, switching on her helmet light. In the darkness, she found the familiar surroundings spooky. She walked past the counters and racks of clothes, trying to remember the way from previous visits. Russ and the others followed her in silence. She headed towards the stairs at the rear of the shop, and found them, after making one false turn. The doors to the stairwell were closed.

"Let me." Russ came up behind her and wrenched the doors open with the help of another soldier.

They made their way down quickly, the lights from their helmets throwing bobbing shadows on the walls. At the bottom, a wide corridor led to another room. The outline of rows of trolleys became visible, and further on, they came to storerooms containing stacked rectangular boxes. The air supply units were off, and although the air was still breathable, Halle began to perspire under her heavy military suit.

After passing through the storerooms, they entered an open area. In the darkness, Halle made out three low bullet shaped cars no more than a meter and a half high and a meter wide. The curved lids on the top of the cars were open and they stood on a single rail that ended in a low buffer. The rail disappeared under a metal door set into the far wall. A series of large metal clamps secured the door on each side, while a parallel track ran up the wall vertically above it. Plastic boxes of different colors and sizes had been stacked into tall piles near the depot walls, and to one side of the bullet cars. More boxes lay strewn across the floor, left where they had toppled or been thrown down.

"This must be the depot," Halle said. "People left in a hurry."

"They were taken by surprise," Seth remarked. "The U-Zone didn't even warn their own people about the attack. What craziness is that?"

"Unity have been doing a lot of crazy things," Russ replied. "It's almost as if they're suffering from mass insanity."

"Yes, mass insanity, but there's no point discussing this now," Halle said. "I see the cars, but where's the tunnel?"

"Behind that door." Russ indicated the metal door set into the wall. "It'll slide up to let the cars into the tunnel. We need to find the controls for it."

"There'll be a control room somewhere," Seth said.

Russ took a torch from his belt and shone it around the depot, moving it systematically along the walls. The mouth of a corridor and several exits became visible, and then the beam hit the transparent surface of windows.

"That way," Russ said, heading to a door next to the windows.

Halle went after him, into a room containing a console with flickering lights, underneath a length of windows adjacent to the depot. Seth followed them in, while the others waited in the central area.

"These controls must be on a different circuit from the store," Russ said, inspecting the console.

"Let me see." Seth joined him. "I'm an electrical engineer. I should be able to figure out how it works."

Seth sat down and began pressing buttons on the console. Suddenly, overhead lights lit up the depot, gleaming off the stainless steel surfaces of the tunnel door and bullet cars. A whooshing sound flooded the depot as the air supply units came back on, and the temperature began to cool.

"That's better," Russ muttered.

Seth frowned. "The tunnel has an airlock and is depressurized."

"We overlooked that," Russ said. "We can't go through there."

"What?" Halle asked. "Can't we use the tunnel?"

"No, it works on a vacuum system," Seth explained.

"We can't go back up," Halle objected. "Isn't there a way we can use the tunnel?"

"To send a car off, the outer door is sealed, and a vacuum is created before an inner door is opened. The cars are propelled through a vacuum in the tunnel," Seth told her.

"So we can't use it?" Halle asked again.

"We can't get through a vacuum," Russ said. "We'd die pretty quickly. The pressure differential would have some nasty effects. I've heard reports of blood boiling and bodies exploding but I think we'd probably die from heart and lung failure before that."

"We might be able to pressurize the tunnel," Seth suggested.

"Is that possible?" Russ asked.

Seth studied the console. "It might be. There could be a system to pressurize the tunnel for maintenance work. Just a minute, I'll bring up the schematics."

Seth flicked switches on the console and a screen on it came to life. He switched through several pages before stopping at a complicated diagram.

"Okay. There are vents along the tunnel walls that can be opened to pressurize them. We don't need to pressurize all of them, just the tunnels that we'll be using. There's a system to shut off other intersecting tunnels."

Russ stared at the diagram. "If you can pressurize the tunnels, we can walk through."

"Someone might use the system while we're in the tunnels," Halle interjected.

"No one's going to use it while the fighting is going on," Russ replied.

"I don't like it," said Halle, tapping her fingers on the edge of the console in agitation. "I wouldn't have suggested this route if I'd known about the vacuum. I think we should forget this and go up top."

"Provided we pressurize the tunnel, it should be perfectly safe," Seth confirmed. "There are also escape hatches along the tunnels, presumably for maintenance safety."

"The transport terminal is about five or six kilometers away," Halle informed him.

"We can walk that quickly," Russ said. "Seth, can you see that tunnel on the diagram?"

"Got it. It's straight except for one intersection."

"Where do the vents lead to?" Russ asked.

"Let me try another page."

The view changed and Seth studied it. "From what I can tell, the vents serving this tunnel exit somewhere outside the city. That means the tunnel must be pressurized with Taidor's natural atmosphere."

"Taidor's air is too thin for us to breathe. I think we should abandon this idea," Halle objected.

"There should be breathing equipment around here somewhere. Normal atmospheric pressure won't be a problem," Russ replied.

"I still don't like it," Halle said. "We'll be in the tunnel for too long."

"There isn't another way," Russ said. "We can't ride in the cars. They won't work without the vacuum."

"How long will it take to pressurize the tunnel?" Russ asked Seth. "Unity may be on their way down here. We need to get moving."

"It isn't a long process. Once the vents are opened, the alien atmosphere will be sucked in. There should be filters on the vents. Possibly twenty minutes. There are pressure monitors here." Seth pointed to the console.

"Okay, start the pressurization. I'll ask the others to look for oxygen equipment for the tunnels," Russ said, switching on his radio.

"The tunnels are pressurizing." Seth pressed a button on the panel.

Russ's radio crackled and Halle heard him say, "Okay, we're coming, Aris."

"Have they found the equipment room?" Seth asked.

"Yes, Aris thinks he's found it."

The equipment room was through a door on the far side of the depot. Halle and Russ went to it, leaving Seth working at the console. Inside the equipment room, one of the soldiers, Aris, had begun pulling out masks, breathing tubes and oxygen canisters from the lockers. He was slightly built and of medium height. Halle guessed that he was in his late twenties and she glimpsed dark hair under his helmet. He caught her glance when she came into the room and gave her a wide smile. She found herself smiling back.

Halle inspected the canisters. "If we take two each, that should give us enough time to get under the city."

"We'll have to use the masks but we'll also take the breathing tubes as backup," Russ said, taking the equipment to pass to the others. "We'll need to use our radios in the tunnel."

Halle took a set, and moved out to join the others around the mouth of the tunnel. She put her mask on, clipping in the radio attachment from her helmet, and secured an oxygen canister to the front of her jacket. She wished that she had spent more time in the mines instead of working in her office. If she had, she would have been more familiar with the equipment.

"The tunnel is pressurized. I'm opening the outer door now," Seth said over the radio.

The clamps on either side of the tunnel door sprang open with a discordant clanking sound. The door slid up slowly on its tracks, uncovering an obsidian blackness behind it. Halle checked her mask was securely over her mouth and nose, and switched on her oxygen. She wished that she hadn't suggested using the tunnels. The dark space looked ominous. Her heart began to thump and she felt anxious. She saw nothing to be afraid of, but she was still filled with a sense of imminent danger.

Chapter Nine

Squeezing in front of the bullet cars, Halle entered the tunnel after Russ, with a feeling of trepidation. Heat hit her and she began to take quick shallow breaths before reminding herself to breathe normally. Inside, the central rail for the cars protruded a few centimeters from the ground. It had been deactivated, but all the same, she tried not to step on it. The tunnel was circular, like a tube, just under two meters in diameter. The curved walls were made of smooth grey steel and the depot lights penetrated about ten or eleven meters inside. The frame serving the inner door was visible a few meters from the entrance, and rubber type seals ringed both the inner and outer door frames. The airlock itself was unremarkable, save for a control panel on the wall, near the outer door.

Russ walked cautiously forward towards the inner doorway, ducking under the low curvature of the roof. Halle went next, walking to one side of the central rail. The others followed them, their footsteps sounding hollow in the eerie noiselessness of the tunnel. At the inner doorway, Russ paused and looked back. Halle also glanced back to see Seth studying the control panel for the airlock, near the outer door, his face mask slung over one arm. Apparently satisfied, he put on his oxygen mask.

Seth looked towards the others. "I'll shut the outer door, in case Unity come down here."

"Good idea. Unity might try and follow us," Russ agreed.

"I'll catch you up in a minute."

"Okay." Russ stepped through the inner doorway, into the main body of the tunnel. He walked for several meters until the tunnel lost the light fed from its entrance, when he paused again. "Switch your helmet lights on. Seth, are you coming?"

"Yes, just shutting the door now," Seth confirmed, his body silhouetted in the light from the tunnel's mouth.

A low whirring sound travelled up the passage and the light began to dim until darkness cloaked everything outside the beams of their flashlights. The outer door slid shut with a clank that reverberated inside the tunnel. Halle could hear Seth moving around somewhere near the tunnel entrance.

"We're waiting, Seth," Russ said.

"Just a moment," Seth's disembodied voice reached them.

Halle strained to see his helmet light and thought she could pick it out; a tiny faint pinprick, some way behind. She felt a tremor underneath her boots and glanced down. Her helmet light created a golden puddle which stretched into her feet. A strong vibration tickled the souls of her boots, and she looked at the others to see if they had noticed. In the glare of their lights she couldn't see their faces, but she saw Russ swivel around in an attitude of concern.

"What's going on Seth? The rail's vibrating."

"I think I caught the wrong switch. It's okay, I've switched it off."

"Good. Come on!"

Halle heard a gentle thud followed by a hissing sound that snaked around them. She squinted at the place where she had last seen Seth's light, but could see nothing. It was as if a black veil had been drawn across the tunnel.

"Where are you, Seth?" Russ demanded urgently.

"I'm stuck inside the airlock," Seth shouted. "The inner door's come down. I can't get out! The airlock's depressurizing!"

Russ swung on his heel, and sprinted back to the inner door in a few steps. "Is there a way to open it?"

"I'm trying, but I can't get the door up," Seth shouted.

"Then open both doors again," Russ yelled.

"I've already tried that but nothing's happening."

Russ took a flashlight from his belt and frantically shone it over the surface of the inner door and walls. "I can't see any controls in the tunnel."

"I'll try again," Seth screamed.

"Have you tried it? The door isn't moving."

"The airlock's still depressurizing!" Seth's voice rose in fear.

"It must be an automatic sequence," Russ shouted.

"You have to get him out of there!" Nadia cried, rushing up beside Russ and running her hands over the door. "Can't we pull the door up?"

Russ flashed his torch beam across the door again. "There's no levers to open it manually. It's solid."

"Get me out!" Seth shrieked.

Russ spoke to Seth in measured tones, "You must remain calm. Try all of the controls. There must be an off switch."

"The pressure's dropping quickly," Seth gasped.

"Stay with it, Seth," Russ urged. "Keep trying the controls."

"I can't…" Seth screamed and then screamed again.

Seth's screams, amplified over the radio, scorched Halle's eardrums and her legs began to shake. She stood back, giving room to Nadia, who began hammering on the door. In under a minute, Seth's screams reached a crescendo and then he gasped once as if unable to breathe, and suddenly became silent.

"No, no, no!" Nadia shrieked, pressing herself to the door, her face contorted with grief.

"Come on," Russ said gently, taking her arm to move her away from the door. "He's gone. He's another casualty of war."

Halle walked back towards Aris and the others, who waited quietly. She felt unsteady and faint and disbelieving. It seemed impossible that Seth was gone, so suddenly and quickly. Russ was still with Nadia at the door. Halle could hear him comforting Nadia, the words too quiet to be audible. He had put his arm around the tall woman who stood with her face in her hands. Gradually, she regained her composure, and Russ led her back towards the group.

Russ took the lead, bending under the low tunnel roof, the beam from his helmet light piercing the blackness. The flashlights of the others behind him, threw shafts of light forward, creating patterns on the walls through which their shadows moved. Intermittently, Halle caught sight of the silhouette of Russ's broad shoulders, and then his shape would blink out, eaten by the darkness. Side-stepping the single central rail, Halle followed him, their footsteps loud on the metal floor. Every now and again, the sound of a cough would bounce off the curved tunnel walls.

Halle could see very little in front of her, except for Russ and the outline of the tunnel. The sound of Seth's high pitched screams still rang in her ears and the feeling of terror it had invokcd in her was visceral in nature. She fervently wished that they were above ground. The tunnel was hot and it seemed to close in on her. She found herself gulping air and her heart started to race. With sticky palms, she adjusted her face mask and tried to slow her breathing.

They passed steel hatches set into the walls at regular intervals, about half a meter above the floor. They were big enough for a man to crawl into and had handles to open manually. The escape hatches, Halle thought. Every ten meters or so, there was a row of eight or nine rectangular vents near the base of the wall, no more than a few centimeters high. Each vent had a flap fixed to a track above it. In front of the vents, dust, tiny rocks, and other debris lay on the floor.

"I can't see any filters on those vents," Halle said. Her gut told her that something wasn't right. Why would a bullet car run through dirt?

"They must be on the outside. Try not to talk. We need to conserve our oxygen," Russ replied, without breaking his pace.

They walked for several more minutes, their group making the only sounds. The atmosphere seemed dry to Halle. Like the surface of the planet. The landscape had flatlands broken by ranges of sharp tipped mountains. Taidor's sun burned for eighteen hours a day, and much of the terrain was inhospitable desert and barren plains. She tried to remember the last time she had gone outside the domed cities, which were constantly lit by a combination of natural and artificial light. She hadn't had much cause and such outings were rare.

In front of her, Russ stopped suddenly. Catching him up, Halle saw that the tunnel branched to their right. A steel barrier closed off another opening to their left. This has to be the intersection, she thought. We're halfway to the transport terminal. She estimated that they had no more than three kilometers to go. After pausing, Russ began walking again, heading north.

The northern tunnel was the same as the first tunnel. Halle wondered how they would find the northern task force. Were they still fighting up top? She could smell nothing in the tunnel, except smoke clinging to their own uniforms. It had a greater pungency in the closed environment. She thought she heard a sound and strained to listen. Nothing. She had been mistaken. She heard something again. She held her breath and listened. This time the sound was audible. Something making scraping noises nearby.

At first, the scraping was hardly discernible, but then the sound became louder. Halle listened more carefully. There was something scratching the tunnel floor. A high pitched tinny sound. Perhaps from more than one location.

The sound didn't have the rhythm associated with someone walking.

"Russ, can you hear that scraping noise?" Halle called out.

"It's probably from above."

"No, there's definitely something down here. It's getting louder."

"We're nearly out, so don't worry about it," Russ replied dismissively.

"No, listen. Something is moving down here. Near us," Halle insisted.

Russ stopped walking and turned around. "Okay, what is it?"

"Listen."

Russ stood still and listened. The sound had increased in volume. A scraping accompanied by a low soft hum.

"You're right. I can hear a rattle. Behind the walls," Russ said.

"I don't know what it is." Halle stared at him.

Russ's face creased into a frown. "I'm not sure, but it sounds mechanical. Nothing can live down here. I think we should keep moving."

Russ began walking again and Halle preparing to follow, glanced back. The rest of their group had become strung out, and the last of them were outside the beam of her flashlight. Halle hurried on, but the noise bothered her. Barely audible at first, it was now distinct and had changed into a chittering sound, getting closer. Something was down there with them. Something moving about. She shone her torch over the walls and floor, but the beam only lit up the small mounds of dirt, under the vents.

Halle skipped over the central rail to walk on the other side. Her boot connected with something small and hard. She gave a short scream and kicked out.

"There's something here!" she shouted. "It just touched my foot."

The beam of her torch caught a glint of metal, that disappeared quickly into the darkness. Ahead of her, Russ had paused and was shining his flashlight at a row of vents in the wall. Halle glimpsed small, grey, shiny creatures scurrying around a heap of shingle. Low and oval shaped with snouts, they were sucking in the debris, making crunching sounds. They skimmed just above the floor, darting about, in and out of the torchlight.

"They're dust-grubbers," Russ said. "Designed to clear up the mess from the vents."

"Bots?"

"Yes, they take the dirt in. Keep the tunnel clean. They've come from the vents."

"Are they dangerous?"

"Depends on their design. We need to keep going." Russ resumed walking.

Halle followed, trying to avoid stepping on the bots. Whenever she walked past a row of vents, there seemed to be more of them. She crossed the central rail again, but the dust-grubbers were on each side. The bots ignored her, busily clearing the debris on the tunnel floor. She pointed her flashlight ahead and watched Russ walk through a clutch, kicking them out of the way. He had quickened his pace and she strove to keep up.

"We need to hurry," Russ urged.

"The bots are ignoring us."

"For now."

Halle heard a yell behind her.

"It bit me! I can't get it off!

Halle looked back to see Aris, several meters behind her, kicking out at a dust-grubber that had attached itself to his ankle. He frantically shook his leg to try and dislodge it. Handling his laser, he swung the butt of the gun at the bot, sending it flying with a piece of his trousers still in its snout.

Another dust-grubber had hold of his other foot, and he bashed at it with the butt end of his gun. A circle of bots surrounded him and he stamped and kicked out at them, before forcing his way clear. No sooner was he clear, than a scream came out of the darkness behind him.

"Help me, help me."

Aris turned around and shone his flashlight back along the tunnel. Halle saw the female soldier standing in a pool of grey bots, scuttling around her feet. The mass of bots obscured her boots and ankles, and were climbing up the woman's legs. The woman swatted at them, but the bots were gaining on her. Some of the others were pulling the bots off her, but for every one they removed, another took its place. Aris ran to them, and joined in, but the bots surged up her, even higher.

The woman screamed, "Get them off me! They're biting!"

"What the…they're going for her." Russ started back towards them and Halle ran after him.

At first the bots ignored the others, but after a few seconds, they sensed their presence. Turning on them, they skimmed quickly over feet and ankles, delivering razor sharp bites, that sent the soldiers springing backwards. A bot jumped on Halle's ankle, delivering a vicious nip that sent her stumbling to one side. Russ and Aris persisted, clubbing the bots with their gun butts. The woman began to succumb. While the vanguard bit her legs, others shot up her torso, gnawing at her uniform. She screamed shrilly when they reached her neck, and tried to burrow under the front of her jacket. More bots piled onto her, until her face was no longer visible, and her screams became incoherent.

"Aris, Russ, get back," a soldier shouted, aiming his laser at the bots around the woman's feet.

"You'll hit her, Jed, " Russ bellowed at him.

A bright flare erupted, and when it subsided, charred black metal casings littered the ground. The woman fell backwards, hitting the central rail. Lying sprawled across the rail, she began to moan, her legs bloodied and burnt. She attempted to push herself up, but more dust-grubbers rushed at her, streaming over her torso. The outline of the woman's body swam with grey movement, and her moans gave way to raw screaming.

Aris and Jed, stepped back awkwardly. As the mass of bots around the woman grew larger, they retreated out of range and then Russ tried again. He waded into the dust-grubbers around the woman, crushing them with his boots. Bending down, he used both hands to pull several bots off her, flinging them to one side. They quickly retaliated. When he lifted the next one, another jumped onto his hand, shot up his arm and bit his neck.

Russ dropped the dust-grubber he was holding and used both hands to wrench the other bot from his neck. Drawing his laser, he fired around the pool, leaving burnt shells, but more machines poured out of the vents in the tunnel walls. They skimmed over the woman and up Russ's legs. He kicked and stamped at them but was forced back. The woman's screams echoed through the tunnel.

"The bots are constantly reprogramming themselves," Russ exclaimed. "The more we destroy, the more are coming to clear the debris."

One of the men had made no attempt to help. Halle recognized the pale young man with the skinny frame, Milan. She thought him strangely placid. He stood beside her, stooping slightly to avoid the curved roof. He was from Security, not regular Army, but still his lack of action seemed strange. He had stood watching the activity dispassionately, his body throwing a short black shadow across the steel walls.

"After they finish with her, they'll turn on us," Milan said bluntly.

In the torchlight, Halle saw that the woman no longer moved. Her screams had faded and now she was quiet. A number of dust-grubbers roamed over her body, chewing up material and flesh, while others had begun to ingest the remains of their fellow bots. Although Milan's words sounded cruel, Halle thought his warning valid. The attempts to save the woman had been abandoned, and now they were in danger of being attacked themselves.

"We should go, before the bots attack someone else," Halle urged.

"Halle's right. We need to hurry." Russ turned away and began to jog back up the tunnel, deftly stepping over puddles of dust-grubbers milling in front of the vents, cleaning the floor.

Gradually, the number of bots in the tunnel decreased as they cleared away the debris. The dust-grubbers glided back into the vents and Halle felt relieved.

"We haven't got much time," Russ called over his shoulder.

"What are you talking about?" Halle asked. "The bots are leaving."

"That's what I'm worried about."

All the dust-grubbers had disappeared and Halle used her flashlight to illuminate the central rail to avoid tripping over it, but movement in the walls caught her eye. Unexpectedly, the flaps above the vents dropped down with a gentle whoosh, sealing the tunnel. She heard a hissing sound and felt the whisper of a breeze at the top of her neck, just below her jawline where her mask did not reach. Her only frame of reference was the breeze from the air supply units, and she wondered at this, as the tunnel had no air supply.

"The tunnel's depressurizing," Russ shouted, still jogging ahead of her.

"It's restoring the vacuum?" Halle asked, alarmed.

"It's a sequence. The bots clean the tunnel before use."

Terror coursed through Halle. "How long have we got?"

"A few minutes at best."

Chapter Ten

Russ shouted to the others, "The tunnel's depressurizing. Keep up with me."

Halle heard the others behind her break into a run, while in front of her, Russ lengthened his stride. She willed her legs to run faster. She didn't want to die like Seth. "We need to get to an escape hatch."

"There should be a hatch soon," Russ called out. "Keep up, Halle."

"The last one was quite a way back," Halle panted.

"We're probably nearly on it." Russ slowed slightly, shining the beam of his torch along the walls of the tunnel.

Halle stumbled, recovering herself in time to avoid falling. "I can't see one."

"We'll find it," Russ urged.

Halle ran forward, keeping as near to center as possible, so that her helmet didn't hit the roof. She remembered Seth's screams and fear lanced through her like an electric shock, propelling her forward. She could no longer feel her legs, and as she ran, her heart thumped in her chest and she began to lose her breath. She had to get to a hatch, to safety. Nothing else mattered. She had to keep running. She felt a stitch forming to the lower right of her belly with a sharp stabbing pain. She ignored it, focusing on Russ running slightly ahead of her.

After three or four minutes, Russ slowed down. In the patchy light of their torches she saw that he had stopped in front of a grey steel hatch, set into the tunnel wall. She caught up with him and fought to catch her breath, taking in large gulps of air. She remembered vaguely that this was her second canister.

"Make your oxygen last," Russ snapped at her. "We're not out of this yet."

Halle didn't reply. She discarded his remark; the hatch was more important. Russ grabbed the heavy lever on the face of it and pulled it down. He wrenched the door open and shone the beam of his torch inside, lighting up a small cylindrical space.

"We have a problem," Russ said.

"Isn't it big enough?" Halle asked.

"Not for all of us."

"We can try for the end of the tunnel," Halle suggested.

"It's too far. There's still over a kilometer to go." Russ took hold of Halle's arm. "Get in."

"We need to be fair about this. Draw lots or something," Halle objected.

"Don't argue, Halle. We don't have time. I can run to the next hatch faster than you." Before Halle could object further, he pushed her inside. "Stay inside, whatever happens out here."

Halle scrambled into the cavity and curled against the side. Shining her torch around, she picked out the grill of a speak station on the wall. With its switches dark, it appeared dead. To the rear, another hatch sealed the cubicle. There were no levers or control panel in view, just the cool bare metal of the surface of the tube. It reminded her of a coffin; the sides were only centimeters from her face. She felt as if she couldn't breathe and her heart raced. Russ's voice outside, interrupted her thoughts.

"It's too small for all of us to get in. It'll take four people at the most. Nadia, Aris, Milan, get in. Nik and Jed, you're with me."

"Why them?" a voice demanded.

"Three of us have to run to the next one," Russ replied.

Halle peered out. She found it difficult to distinguish the others' faces in the darkness. The beams from their flashlights danced about as they moved and argued. At one point the light caught the white of Jed's eyes, flickering between the speakers. The light switched again, and she caught sight of the pale emotionless face of Milan, watching with cool eyes. Nadia stood near Jed, her mouth slightly open and eyes wide. A young soldier with an olive complexion and stocky build was arguing with Russ, his eyes full of rage.

Jed touched the young soldier's shoulder. "Come on Nik, time's running out."

"We might not make it to the next hatch," Nik insisted.

"I'm going. See you up above." Jed disappeared from view and Halle heard his heavy boots pounding along the tunnel.

"There isn't enough room for all of us," Russ snapped. "We've got time to get to the next hatch if we hurry."

"The air pressure's dropping. We won't make it," Nik argued. "We need a better way to decide."

"I've already decided," Russ replied firmly.

"We should leave the weakest. The rest of us have a better chance that way."

"Enough arguing. Nadia, Milan, get inside," Russ ordered.

"Why them?" Nik shouted. "They're the weakest. Not Army."

Milan screwed his eyes up and drew back his lips in a snarl. "I'm not weak."

"You're not one of us," Nik yelled at him.

"I'm Security and I'll match you any day," Milan hissed back.

Nik glared at Milan, and reached beneath his jacket, drawing out his laser. Milan's hand moved in a blur and a burst of flame exploded in the place where Nik had stood. Nadia let out a short scream and Halle tried to blink away dazzling spots that seared her vision. When the flare died,

Nik was gone, leaving only a burning carcass, from which threads of smoke rose in the thin atmosphere. Opposite him, Milan stood staring at the body. He held a hand laser and his face was contorted with anger.

Russ swiveled towards Milan. "Stand down!"

"He was going to kill me," Milan snarled, still holding the laser.

"He's right. He would have killed us both. He was insane," Nadia exclaimed, her voice tremoring with fear.

"Put your gun away!" Russ bellowed.

Milan glared at him, making no move to comply. Russ lunged forward and knocked the laser out of Milan's hand. He grasped the front of Milan's jacket and shoved him violently against the wall.

"What are you doing? Stop this. Now!" Russ shouted.

Halle shut her eyes and pushed herself backwards, further into the safety tube. Putting her hands over her face, she took a moment to process what she had seen. The falling air pressure had not begun to bite but it would soon. The urgency of their situation did not inform the violence she had just witnessed. How had Milan become a killer so quickly? Outside, the argument continued and Halle opened her eyes.

"It was self-defense." Milan pushed back at Russ.

"When you're with me you take my orders! Understood?" Russ shoved Milan against the wall again, and Milan's helmet cracked against the steel.

"Understood," Milan muttered resentfully, and Russ let go of his jacket and stepped back.

Aris still stood in the tunnel, watching the exchange. "I'm going to catch Jed up. See you all later." He turned on his heel and began running, his footsteps echoing from the darkness.

"Aris?" Russ called after him, but Aris had already left the pocket of light cast by their flashlights. "I hope he makes it. We're running out of time. We have to get inside."

Halle shuffled to the end of the tube, pulled her knees up and sat with her arms around them. Russ bent down and crawled in, nodding to her as he crouched beside her. The others clambered in after him, squeezing into the small space. Milan knelt near the hatch door and gripped the lever with both hands, pulling it shut against the rubber surround.

"Pull the lever down. It has to be airtight," Russ instructed, as Milan locked the hatch into position with a click.

"You all right?" Russ asked Halle, putting his hand over one of hers.

"Yes, I'm okay." Halle smiled at him.

"Now what?" Milan asked.

"I think we're safe for the moment. This cubicle should be designed to stay pressurized, while the people inside wait to be rescued," Russ said.

"There's only one problem," Milan said. "I can't see a way out."

A chill went through Halle. *This could be our tomb*, she thought. She chided herself for being weak and dismissed the idea. She stared at the intercom set into the wall.

"There's a speak station but I don't think it works."

Russ studied the unit. "It's dead all right. We can't use the com."

Milan shone his flashlight on the rear door. "Without the com, how are we going to get out? I can't see a lever on the rear hatch."

"I need to get a better look at it," Russ said. "Milan, Nadia, can you move back as far as possible? Halle, can you get to my other side so that I can reach the rear hatch?"

Halle began to squirm her way in front of Russ, but he took hold of her waist with both hands and lifted her over his legs. She squeezed in beside him and hugged her legs. She wished fervently that they were above ground, somewhere quiet and safe, and that this terrible nightmare had ended. She scrambled into a kneeling position and watched Russ run the beam of his flashlight over the rear hatch.

"There's an elastomer seal around the rear hatch, in case the tunnel hatch hasn't closed properly." Russ indicated the thick rubber seal around the rear hatch. "It must only open from the outside. Halle, have you any idea where this comes out?"

"I think the emergency hatches come out near the depots."

"This hatch doesn't need to be as secure as the tunnel exit, as it's only a secondary hatch. The lock system may not be as secure," Russ said.

"How does that help us?" Milan asked. "It's pretty solid."

"The seal's on the inside, attached to the cubicle, so that the door sits on top, outside. My guess is that the door is smaller than the gap."

"Can we push the door out?" Milan queried.

"It's worth a try. Halle, can you give me some room?"

Russ swiveled around and leaned backwards and used his feet to kick at the door. The hatch didn't move. He changed position, and tried using his shoulder instead. Finally, he placed both hands against it and pushed hard, before giving up.

"It's solid. It won't budge. We might have better luck if we destroy the seal. Get back."

Using his hand laser, Russ burnt away the seal around the rear hatch. The rubber flamed as he carefully traced his laser around it, filling the cubicle with fumes that created a haze. Halle was thankful for her face mask and oxygen canister. The flames quickly subsided as each portion burnt away, until a charred ring surrounded the metal panel. Russ paused for a moment to inspect his handiwork and then arced the gun around the rubber seal for a second time.

"That should do it. I'll see if I can kick it out."

Russ kicked at the hatch. The panel slowly detached from the rubber, leaving a black sticky band in a comb around its edges. He grunted and kicked it several times more until he had widened the gap around it. Finally, he put his shoulder against it and the hatch came away. Kicking it flat, Russ shone his torch into the darkness beyond. Halle shifted position and tried to see over his shoulder.

"Can you see anything?" Halle asked.

"We're in some kind of equipment room. There's welding equipment. I'm going through." Russ put on his gloves and crawled through the gap. "Watch the rubber, it's still hot."

Halle went after him into a large room, lined with racks along one wall, lockers along another and on one side, larger pieces of machinery. There was no light in the room and the darkness hung like a blanket around her. Russ moved towards the center, his helmet light casting a beam in front of him, while he used a torch in one hand to sweep a shaft of light across the room. She heard the crunch of Milan and Nadia's boots behind her and wondered at the silence otherwise surrounding them.

"There's no lights or air supply units working," Halle remarked. "The power's down."

Russ flipped the front of his mask up and inhaled deeply. "There's still enough oxygen in here. The power must have been shut off recently."

Halle raised her mask and took a breath. "We're in a maintenance room. We must be in one of the main depots."

"Any idea where?" Russ asked her. "Can you remember where the depots are?"

"We should be near the transport terminal."

"So we're in the north of the city? Our diversionary force was fighting up here."

"I can't hear any fighting," Nadia said.

"We're at least ten levels underground," Russ replied. "We have to get up top."

"What about Jed and Aris?" Halle asked.

"They should have found a hatch further down. They could be a block away," Russ answered.

Russ made his way to a closed door on the other side of the room. Nothing happened when he pressed the exit panel.

"The power's off. I'll burn out the locking unit." Russ fired his laser at the door controls, and then wrenched the door open.

Halle followed him into a pitch black corridor, with the others behind her. Their lights picked out doorways, elevators and further on, a stairwell. Russ took the stairs and Halle went next, with Milan climbing after her. She saw Milan's black shadow dancing along the walls and shuddered. She didn't trust him. Their boots clattered loudly on the hard steps and then eventually the blackness began to turn grey, and she saw daylight ahead through an open door.

She stepped outside gratefully, blinking in the sunlight and breathed in deeply. Smoky air filled her lungs and she spasmed into coughing. Suddenly, rough hands gripped both of her upper arms, and forcefully threw her to the ground. Her helmet made a loud crack when she hit the pavement and the vibration jolted her head and neck. She fell face down, and the flashlight in her belt jammed against her stomach, shooting a knifing pain through her. Hands wrenched her arms backwards and Halle felt handcuffs tighten around her wrists.

"We've been waiting for you," a deep malevolent voice said loudly. "Ea-Zone scum. So stupid, burning stuff and setting off the alarms."

Halle could see a black boot near her face, and when it moved, she saw Russ's prostrate body about a meter away from her. She tried to raise her head and a hand pushed her down.

"Stay down," an angry voice shouted.

She tried to focus, breathing heavily. The corner of her helmet bit into her cheeks and her stomach hurt where her flashlight dug in. She saw the boot move again and kick Russ in the side. He let out a gasp on impact. Her legs and knees felt bruised where she had hit the ground and she began to shake. She tried to ignore the pain, as a sense of frustration enveloped her. They had come all of this way for nothing. Unity had them now. What would they do to her? Fear tried to creep into a corner of her mind, and she pushed the feeling away. Being afraid wouldn't save her now. She needed to keep her wits about her. She focused on the voices above her.

Another voice, "Take them to holding. Put them with the others."

Hands yanked Halle to her feet and a voice hissed in her ear, "There's no escape now so don't even think about it!"

Chapter Eleven

Kalen boarded the transport with Sera, in good time for its departure to Morten at twenty hundred hours. They wore their Divines, as required, his sporting the number two, and Sera proudly displaying her number six. The transport had been commandeered by the U-Zone army, and would travel overnight at high speed through tunnels below Taidor's surface. He led Sera through the corridors, until he found their compartments.

"It's a shame we can't sleep together," Sera remarked, at the door to her narrow cabin.

"They've only got single compartments on the transport," Kalen replied. He was thankful for that. He didn't know how he felt about her and needed time to think. Her recent sweetness and affection had begun to win him over, but he still held a suspicion that the fanatic lurked underneath.

"It seems wrong now that we're married," she said.

Kalen remembered that morning with discomfort. The Commitment Ceremony had gone ahead as planned. He had stood beside Sera and made a vow to commit the rest of his life to her. The Administrator who had taken the ceremony, had asked him three times to affirm his resolution to commit to her. By the third time, he had been tempted to say that he wouldn't, but had told himself not to be stupid. He had felt more than a tug of uncertainty inside, but swallowed his misgivings, because ultimately, there wasn't any other option. Images of a little boy came to mind and whatever he felt about Sera, he couldn't desert his son. Now, he was committed to her for a very long time.

"But we can eat together?" Sera reached for his hand, her big brown eyes imploring him to agree. "You're not going to hide away and work, are you?"

"Of course not." He held her hand and squeezed it. He met her eyes, deep soft pools, and briefly wondered whether he could have imagined her previous fanaticism. "We can have supper together. Let's go and find the canteen."

They walked through the transport until they found a small dining area at the end of one of the cars. It was full of soldiers and they squeezed through the crush until they found seats. Kalen left Sera at the table and went to collect the food. He inspected the selection and involuntarily twisted his mouth in disgust. Why didn't Unity have the same food as Early? Nothing appealed to him. He collected two meals and made his way back to Sera.

When he put the plates on the table, Sera smiled. "This looks nutritious. The food in Unity is very healthy, don't you think?"

"I suppose so," Kalen mumbled trying not to frown. The grey hard protein cubes on his plate had an odd fishy smell and tasted even worse. Served with stringy orange vegetables, they killed Kalen's appetite and he had to force them down. He remembered the tasty vegetable steaks that he used to eat in Early and fervently wished he was back in an Ea-Zone canteen.

"After supper, we must go and pray for success in the war," Sera said brightly.

"Of course." Kalen continued stirring the food on his plate with his fork, stealing himself to take another mouthful. He would pray for better food, he thought.

"You're playing with your food. Just eat it," Sera exclaimed in exasperation. "I've been watching you. You've hardly eaten anything."

"I would have preferred something different."

"We're at war, so we're lucky to get a good meal at all," Sera said.

"I know." Kalen speared a cube on his fork with the orange vegetables and took a large mouthful. He chewed and swallowed and speared another cube.

"It isn't bad, is it?" Sera asked anxiously.

"No, not bad at all," he assured her. He wondered what he was going to do. He couldn't leave her now and return to the Ea-Zone. But he still had to destroy the trident. He had to convince Sera that he was happy in Unity. If she suspected that he sympathized with the Ea-Zone, she would denounce him. His Divine was only a two; he was considered virtually worthless in the eyes of the citizens of Unity. He smiled at her and reached over the table to take her hand. "You're right. The food is very good here."

***

The transport arrived in Morten at breakfast time the next day. Kalen and Sera disembarked with a group of soldiers and showed their identity cards several times before they reached the terminal's exit. At the checkpoints, the soldiers took note of Kalen's chief engineer's uniform and saluted, palm forward, but became uncertain when they saw the number on his Divine. He ignored their confusion, being careful not to acknowledge it, and returned their salutes. At the exit, they were joined by an armed escort and quickly ushered into the ruined streets beyond.

"The dome has held, thank the planets," Kalen said, staring at the transparent dome overhead.

"I can't tell the difference between the natural and artificial light anymore," Sera replied.

"There's eighteen hours of natural daylight, the rest is artificial."

"I know, but I don't understand why the city is still being lit up continuously? Unity doesn't have to take turns sharing the city with Early anymore, so why do we need the artificial sunlight?"

"The dome's filters haven't been adjusted yet," Kalen said. "I suppose there's still some benefit to having twenty-four hours of daylight in the city center."

"I suppose so," Sera conceded.

"Morten isn't how I remember it," Kalen said, surveying the surrounding streets.

He saw that Taidor's second city had suffered more destruction than Central. Hardly a building remained standing. Rows of ruins marred the center, and the acrid smell of burning lingered in the air. Kalen heard the crack and rumble of explosions some way off. *It's under siege*, he thought. *Early are holding their own here.*

"The Division's offices have been destroyed, so they've set up headquarters in the accommodation blocks," Kalen informed Sera, as they approached the U-Zone Gates leading to the blocks. An unwelcome feeling of trepidation had begun to sting him. He glanced at Sera walking beside him, her dark shadow mirroring her steps. "It feels strange to be here."

Sera gave him a beatific smile. "We'll be staying in married quarters. This is the beginning of our life together!"

"Yes, it is," he agreed, disarmed by her smile. Could she really have changed? Perhaps pregnancy had changed her. A large part of him wanted to believe that she had changed. If she had, perhaps he could rekindle his feelings for her.

***

Halle's handcuffs chaffed at her wrists, where she had been straining against them. Hours had passed and she estimated that she had sat through the night, and now it must be morning. They had been taken to a long warehouse, in an area of the city near the most northern of the Ea-Zone Gates. Inside the warehouse, prisoners sat on rows of low benches, with their arms handcuffed behind their backs and one ankle cuffed to a bench leg. Halle had recognized several faces from the previous day's fighting. There were people dressed as civilians, too. She had been searched roughly, her helmet pulled off and stripped of equipment, before being pushed down onto a bench next to Russ.

When they'd arrived, Halle had estimated that there might be over a hundred prisoners in the building, guarded by at least thirty security guards and as many soldiers. Over the following hours, more prisoners had been brought in and rows of others taken out with their hands still cuffed behind them. Most were subdued and quiet as they were herded out, but occasionally a scuffle had broken out, to be quelled quickly by the guards' gun butts.

Now, she was hungry and thirsty. Cramp had set into her cuffed leg and she tried to wriggle it, but the restraint made that difficult. She had fallen asleep sometime during the night and her neck and back ached from the lack of support. Her hands felt numb from being cuffed behind her back and she wriggled her fingers, trying to get some feeling back into them. She looked at Russ. He was already awake, watching the guards under lowered eyelids.

Near her, Nadia whispered, "I wonder where they're taking those people?"

"Nowhere good. I can guarantee it," Russ replied bitterly.

"We need a plan," Halle said angrily.

"If I had a gun, I would give them a good fight," Milan snarled, from the other side of Russ.

One of the guards turned and glared at Milan. "Shut up."

"We have to wait until they take us outside. We might get a chance then," Russ answered, after the guard had wandered away.

"Maybe we can take a gun off them," Milan suggested, eying the lasers held by the soldiers.

Russ slumped his shoulders. "Act as if you've given up. It'll be easier to surprise them."

Russ fell silent and Halle thought about ways to escape. She studied the U-Zone soldiers. Like the Ea-Zone forces, a number of them were female, as were the security guards. They wore black army uniforms, similar to that of Early, except for the triangular badges on the left breasts of their jackets with numbers on them. Most were designated as fives, but those in charge, seemed to be sevens or eights. Those with the higher numbers must be the officers, thought Halle. They carried both utilitarian handheld lasers of the type used for work in the Division, in addition to longer military issue lasers.

"Look at the guards' weapons," she whispered. "And the way they're unlocking the cuffs."

She watched a row of prisoners being uncuffed from a bench. The soldiers touched the lock on the cuffs with one end of a small cylindrical device, the size of a lipstick. She guessed it worked magnetically. She saw a soldier return the cylinder to a small pouch on his belt. There was something else on the belt and she tried to make out the shape. A knife concealed in its handle. She studied the other soldiers. They carried them too. Next to the knife on the belt, she saw a thin metal rod, about twenty centimeters long. Possibly a stun stick. Unity's military were carrying more weapons than Early, she mused.

A curious thought struck her. Kalen had joined these people. How could he have done that? Their last argument had been about the Uveid rock. He had insisted that it made building at Three-Craters unsafe. As his manager at the Division, she had pleaded with him to change his mind and say that construction could go ahead. He had refused. It meant stopping the building program. The Division had put pressure on him to conform but instead he had defected to the U-Zone. He had left her, taking that woman with him. Losing him felt like a physical ache, somewhere deep inside. She pushed the thought aside. *He was dead now.*

She heard footsteps coming towards them. Looking up, she saw five or six soldiers approaching. While two of them began to free Russ, another one bent to uncuff her ankle.

"Get up!" The soldier ordered.

Two soldiers took hold of her arms and hauled her up, pushing her into a line behind Russ. She heard scraping, as the soldiers forced Milan and Nadia into line behind her. There were others in front of Russ, that she didn't recognize. Several soldiers surrounded them, overseen by an eight, to whom they deferred.

"Move," the officer ordered.

Halle was herded with the others outside and marched through the ruins of a street. Soldiers on each side guarded them. She saw no way to escape. Her legs and knees felt stiff and bruised and she stumbled from time to time. She concentrated on keeping her footing over the rubble and debris that littered the ground. Russ trudged slowly in line ahead of her, head bowed and dragging his feet. *I don't need to act*, Halle thought. *I feel bruised and sore.* She recognized the street, it led to an Ea-Zone Gate, some way ahead.

A number of other prisoners were brought into the street, from a road on their right. A few were in army uniform, but a large number were dressed as civilians. A long line of prisoners stretched in front of them, and Halle's group were steered to the end of it. The Gate was further up the street, and although Halle couldn't see it, she could make out the sign above it, that proclaimed in bright red lettering, "Early Colonial Time System."

"Get behind the others," the officer ordered.

Over the next few minutes, the line shuffled forward slowly. Halle began to hear shouting and crying, as they got nearer to the Gate. Intermittently, she heard faint screams that seemed to be coming from the head of the line.

"Keep moving," the officer ordered. "We're sending you back."

Hope surged through Halle for a brief moment, but when the Ea-Zone's accommodation blocks came into view, her hope turned into despair. A missile had torn through several floors leaving a large gash where there had been terraces and apartments. Barriers had been destroyed, so that parts of the terraces gave way to a precipice, and in places, the structure hung down precariously. Windows were blackened and several columns of smoke trickled upwards.

Eventually she caught sight of the Gate itself. The tall metal framed archway that led into the accommodation blocks was open. Security guards stood on each side of it, managing the controls. The prisoners approaching the Gate struggled and shouted. A handful nearest to it were screaming. One by one, the captives were uncuffed and pushed into the Gate. The fear of those ahead seized Halle. Her heartbeat quickened and she began to hyperventilate. She wriggled her wrists, twisting them in the cuffs. A hand in her back thrust her forward.

"Move on!"

Ahead of them, a young woman dressed in green trousers and top, was dragged to the Gate. Her short bright purple hair, contrasted starkly to the black uniforms of the soldiers around her. She screamed and struggled as they uncuffed her. One of the soldiers signaled to the guards at the controls, and then they pushed her into the Gate. Light briefly flickered from its mouth, and then they dragged another person forward.

Halle sniffed the air. There was an unpleasant smell and she tried to identify it. Today, she had smelled something similar in the fighting. Now she was close enough to see inside the Gate. It was three meters long and led into one of the Ea-Zone block corridors. She had walked through it many times before, aware of the body scanner, but had never seen the electric barrier functioning. She opened her mouth in shock. In a storm of electricity, searing bolts zapped across its length with ferocious force. A hellish maelstrom of electric charge streaked across its sides and ceiling, sizzling loudly.

The soldiers pushed a man into the Gate. Instantly, the burning bolts hit him with a cracking sound. He writhed and twitched as his clothes incinerated and his skin peeled back, quickly becoming a charred corpse.

Halle flinched and screamed. Terror gripped her throat and her mouth went dry. The smell of burning flesh suffocated her. Her heart pounded and she squirmed away, but a soldier got hold of her arm and held her, roughly pulling her forward. She screamed again and struggled against the vice-like grip. She estimated that there were about six more people in the line before Russ and herself. She became transfixed on the sparking bolts that flared across the Gate, striking haphazardly. Against an ominous hum, the power surges cracked and sizzled, swiftly burning up the people thrown into it.

Russ stiffened and whispered, "Wait until the handcuffs come off."

A soldier began uncuffing Russ, while two others held his arms. Another soldier gripped Halle's other arm and she felt her cuffs being taken off. Behind her, she heard soldiers uncuffing Milan and Nadia. Ahead, Russ struggled as he was dragged forwards towards the archway.

"No!" Halle screamed. "No! No!"

Chapter Twelve

A backhand across Halle's cheek sent her reeling and she began to fall but the soldiers yanked her up, their hands iron hard on her upper arms. Her eyes smarted with the blow and she blinked away tears. Russ was in front of the Gate now, within a meter of its mouth. She saw the soldiers loosen their hold on his arms, as another prepared to shove him forward. Suddenly, he twisted about, using his foot to trip up the soldier at his side. Ducking, he head-butted the soldier behind him.

Halle felt the hold on her arms slacken, her guards distracted by the struggle. She wrenched her arms free and grabbed at the belt of the soldier on her right. Her hand closed on his knife. She tried to take it but the soldier gripped her wrist, and began to prize her hand away. The top of her hand brushed the stun stick. There has to be a switch on it, she thought. Desperately, she felt for it and her fingers found a button. She pushed the button hard. A trembling vibration shot up her arm.

"My leg!" the soldier yelled, letting go of her. He fell to the ground writhing and clutching one of his legs.

An arm about her throat choked her, pulling her backwards. She kicked out and her boot connected. She heard a grunt and forced her elbow back and jabbed it against the man. He loosened his grip and she threw herself downwards, but he caught hold of her by the waist. A bright flare dazzled her and his hands fell away. She heard shouting and the sound of heavy boots running towards her. Another burst of flame nearby left bright spots dancing before her eyes. She staggered and someone pulled her up by the arm.

Milan thrust a gun at her. "Use this!"

Halle grasped the gun and glanced about her. Nadia was struggling with a guard, kicking out at him as he held her wrists. Halle pointed her gun at him. A bright flare exploded in the guard's chest and he fell backwards. He released his grip on Nadia, who stumbled, momentarily stunned, before regaining her footing. Spasmodic laser fire erupted near them and Halle looked around wildly to see where it was coming from. Both Russ and Milan held guns, but the fire came from the other side of the street.

"It's Jed and Aris. Over there!" Russ pointed towards the ruins of a low brick wall. He grasped Halle's arm and propelled her forward. "Run!"

Halle ran towards the other side of the street, following Milan who took the lead. The lanky young man seemed unafraid and loped forwards, ignoring the laser flares exploding around him. Halle heard soldiers running after them, but Aris and Jed cut them down. Suddenly, a soldier ran at Milan from the side. He slowed his pace and fired at him. The soldier fell in a twitching heap, his legs a charred mess of blood and flesh. Milan sniggered. Two more soldiers came at Halle from the other side. Halle ignored their angry shouts and saw them fall back, in the face of Jed and Aris' fire.

"Keep going; we're nearly there," Russ yelled from behind her.

The ruined wall lay ahead and Milan jumped over it. Halle scrambled over the brickwork after him and crouched down. She prayed that the soldiers would give up, but the hard thump of boots on the road increased. Several soldiers were running towards them, while others had taken up position to give covering fire. The ruins around her began to light up with rapid bursts of laser fire. Jed and Aris continued to return fire at them, their guns letting out a soft whooshing sound.

"We're outnumbered but we may be able to hold them off," Russ shouted.

Milan swung his laser up and fired, aiming low. One of the soldier's legs burst into flames and the man fell screaming. Milan laughed.

"It would be better if you shoot to kill," Russ told him. "You're just condemning them to a painful death."

"Those crazies deserve everything they get."

In the street, the group of soldiers began to retreat, carrying their maimed colleague. Two of their number walked backwards, continuing to fire towards the wall. Milan got them within his sights, and fired. One of the soldiers burst into flames instantly. The other fired again before lowering his laser and running after his comrades. Behind them, the line of handcuffed prisoners were still being fed into the Gate. Milan raised his laser to fire again.

Russ put a hand on the barrel of Milan's laser gun. "No need. They've given up."

Milan lowered his gun. "We should leave before they change their minds."

"What about the people in the line? Our people?" Halle asked, staring at the line of captives before the Gate. "We can't just leave them here."

"I count at least thirty guards," Russ replied. "There are only six of us."

"The odds are against us," Milan added.

"Can't we pick off the guards?" Nadia asked.

"We could do it, if we're careful, " Jed said. "If we spread out and shoot at different targets. They would have problems coming after all of us at once."

"We'd never succeed," Milan argued. "We'd just be condemning ourselves to die like them."

"It might be worth a try," Russ conceded.

"There's too many of them. We should go now," Milan insisted.

Halle heard shouting and she raised her head to see over the wall. Another detachment of thirty or more soldiers had entered the street. Heavily armed, they took up positions in front of the Gate and along the line of prisoners. Halle felt crushing disappointment. They would never win a fight against them all.

"They've called in reinforcements. That seals it. We're definitely outnumbered," Russ echoed her thoughts. "If we try anything, they'll pin us down and we won't have a chance. We need to withdraw."

"Withdraw where?" Aris asked.

"Out of the city. Our forces have been decimated here."

"How are we going to get out?" Nadia's voice was high with tension. "Even if we could get out, where would we go?"

"She's right." Jed frowned. "There's only the transports and shuttles and Unity have control of those."

Russ hoisted the strap of his laser over his shoulder and began to stand up. "We'll find a way to leave. The fighting in Central is over for now."

***

Paul Neill was waiting for Kalen at his office, working on his computer pad. Save for the pad, his desk was bare, except for a triangular plaque on a stand, bearing the word "Unity". Kalen thought that the middle aged physicist looked older than when he had last seen him, only a few weeks before. Dark grooves ran from his nose to the sides of his mouth, and his sallow face had thinned, accentuating his high forehead topped by prematurely grey hair. He was dressed in a blue jacket and trousers, the standard uniform of the Colonization Division.

Paul's face creased into a smile, yet when he stood to greet him, his eyes burned with a ferocity that Kalen hadn't seen before. Paul raised his hand, palm forward, in a salute. "Unity! It's good to see you again."

Kalen copied his salute. "Unity!"

"Please sit down." Paul gestured to the chair in front of his desk and sat down himself. He fixed Kalen with an intense gaze. "A lot has happened since you left Three-Craters. It's very exciting. We're on the verge of a real breakthrough with the trident."

Kalen settled into the chair, resting his elbows on its arms. "I understand that it's already been used as a weapon?"

"Only to a limited degree at Three-Craters." An expression of triumph passed across Paul's face and he leaned forward, as if about to impart a secret. "It was magnificent. We used it on the sixtieth level underground in the main crater. We restricted its use to a small area."

"Why there?" Kalen frowned. "Three-Craters is still under construction?"

"Some of Early's construction crew got down to level sixty when the war started. They barricaded themselves in and we couldn't shift them. There are large deposits of Uveid rocks on that level, giving out an enormous energy field. We used the trident to direct the energy and collapse the area."

"Collapse the area?" Kalen stared at Paul, trying to keep the revulsion off his face. For the first time, he noticed the number twelve on Paul's Divine. A reward for good work?

"Yes, we collapsed part of level sixty, sealing the workers in. We created a huge rock-fall that brought down a whole wall, completely cutting off the area."

"What about Early's crew?" Kalen kept his expression neutral. He had been in a rock-fall before, deep underground. He remembered the terror of burial beneath the rubble, the dust choking. He had survived but others had died. A terrible death. He noticed something glinting beneath Paul's open jacket; something that hung around his neck.

"Most of them wouldn't have survived the rock-fall. Those that did, were trapped. They wouldn't have lasted for more than a day or two, without oxygen. We're not planning to return to that section and clear the rock-fall, until we've finished the rest of the building down to the eightieth level." Paul gave Kalen a sharp look, his eyes black.

"How many people?" Kalen shuffled, uncomfortable under Paul's gaze.

"Why do you want to know?" Paul demanded, sitting back in his chair. "They're only Earlians. Surely you don't have any sympathy for them?"

Kalen stared at him steadily, mustering all of his self-control to stop himself from balling his hands into fists. "I wanted to know what to expect when we have to re-build that section."

"There were about one hundred and fifty workers. It wasn't my decision, of course." Paul smiled, leaning forward again. A flash of light caught on the object underneath his jacket, throwing out blue sparks. "Still, it was an excellent opportunity to test the trident and I wasn't disappointed."

"I'm glad the trident worked." Kalen tried to sound convincing. He could no longer think of Paul as an ally. He had changed and become a fanatic. He had handled the Uveid stones, like Sera.

"I've something to show you." Paul beamed and rose from his chair. He took a box from the shelf behind him and put it on the desk. As he stooped, the front of his jacket gaped open and a glittering piece of quartz on a chain, dangled down.

"What is that?" Kalen asked. "The crystal around your neck?"

"I wondered if you'd notice." Paul sat down and took off the pendant, and proffered it to Kalen in the palm of his hand. The tiny sky-blue stone had been cut into a pointed shape and threw off blue patterns when it caught the light. It was fixed onto the chain by a delicate claw that held the top of it, so that the pendant hung down like a tiny triangular dagger. "It's a piece of Uveid. It looks like crystal, doesn't it? It's what I would call a live piece. It can hold a small amount of energy for a few days. After that, it's possible to recharge it by placing it near one of the large seams of Uveid rock."

Kalen took the necklace and turned the stone in his hand, studying it carefully. Blue needles of light reflected off its facets. When he closed his fingers around it, the stone's color began to fade and when he uncurled his fingers again, the stone returned to its vibrant shade of blue. A strange prickling sensation extended up his arm, becoming a warmth that began to spread through his body. Was he imagining it, or could he feel its energy? He put the crystalline stone back on the desk quickly, and took his hands away.

"You felt it, didn't you?" Paul asked him eagerly, putting the pendant on again.

"I think so," Kalen replied warily. "Why are you wearing it around your neck? I'm not sure that the stones are safe."

"Nonsense, they're not going to explode or anything." Paul laughed at him.

"The energy they give off may influence our thinking," Kalen ventured. He was on risky ground, but he had to try. Surely, Paul, who was an intelligent man, would appreciate the risks.

"I heard that you said something similar to Javed," Paul said. "Miners have reported hallucinations near the big deposits of Uveid, but that's all. These tiny pieces aren't big enough to do any harm."

"Don't you remember when we experimented with the trident before? We saw shapes in the energy field."

"So? I told you at the time, that it was just our brain's interpretation of something in the energy." Paul appeared bemused.

Kalen gripped the arms of his chair. "I think the shapes might be a form of alien life that could affect us."

"I don't think so." Paul began to smile, his eyes flashing. "The trident is of alien origin, but it's from a dead civilization that's probably been extinct for hundreds of years. The U-Zone has made a thorough investigation, and we've found no alien life. As for the shapes in the energy field, they're not alive."

"Isn't the possibility worth considering?" Kalen asked.

"The nearest we've come to discovering anything alive on any of the planets that we've colonized, has been a form of bacteria. I think at best, the trident was designed as a communication device. The shapes we saw have something to do with that."

"The alien life could be something akin to bacteria," Kalen countered. "Something that could infect us."

"Nonsense!" Paul replied. "I'm a physicist, so I think you'll agree that I'm better qualified to make an assessment than you are. The energy is just invigorating, that's all. You don't feel any different now, do you?"

"No, of course not. I'm sure you're right," Kalen dissembled, recalling the first time that he'd come into contact with the Uveid in the rock-fall at Area Nine. He had shaken off the hallucinations and developed an immunity, but only to a degree. He tried to remember the other times that he'd touched the Uveid, but his mind went blank. A shadow image of a dark wall intruded into his mind, in the place where his memories should have been. "I'm just being cautious."

"Let's discuss the trident." Paul opened the box and brought out a shiny metal trident with three cylindrical prongs, about fifteen centimeters high. He held it up for Kalen to see. It was shaped like a "V" with a center prong. The outer prongs had horizontal lines indented along their outside edges, while the center prong had similar markings up both of its sides.

Kalen stared at the trident in surprise. "That can't be the trident? It looks new?"

"You're right. The original trident is safely back at Three-Craters. This is a duplicate. Here, take it." Paul handed it to Kalen. "The original is made of an alien metal that we can't replicate. The metallurgists have made this one out of a mixed alloy with similar qualities."

"Does it work?" Kalen ran his fingers down the indentations on the side of the tubes, trying to disguise his shaking hands. If Unity had found a way to duplicate the trident, destroying the original would be pointless.

"Not yet, but I'm working on it. My first priority is to make the original trident mobile, so that we can use it above ground. So far, we've only been able to use the trident at the big Uveid seams, where there's a strong energy field." Paul paused and clutched at the blue pendant he wore, before continuing. "I'm working on a way to charge the trident with smaller pieces of Uveid stone."

"That's outside my field of expertise, but I'm sure you'll succeed eventually," Kalen said levelly. So, they hadn't duplicated the trident yet. He had to get to the original and destroy it before they did.

"If I can find a way to use the alien trident with small pieces of Uveid, I'm sure that I'll find a way to activate the duplicate. After that, we'll start mass production. I've worked out different sequences to control the device. Let me demonstrate." Paul reached for the trident and Kalen handed it back. Paul held it in both hands. He pressed down on the center prong and ran his fingers over the horizontal indentations on both outer edges of the other two prongs. "I've done tests in controlled conditions. The power and range are governed by pressing the markings in different sequences. This sequence would direct an energy beam that can destroy an area in the region of five square kilometers."

"That would be impressive to see." Kalen kept his face impassive.

Paul put the trident in its box, and placed the box on the shelf behind him, before turning back to Kalen. "Exactly.

We have to keep the original safe. It's a formidable weapon and once we find a way to use it above ground, we can defeat the Ea-Zone quickly and end the war."

Kalen linked his hands together in his lap. "So how can I help?"

"We're going to mine the Uveid. Remove blocks of it and position it in or near the major cities, so that it's in situ and ready to use with the trident-weapon. The current mining machinery we have is insufficient for this task. We want you to design and build a drill to excavate the Uveid."

Kalen stared at Paul, momentarily speechless. "That's a big undertaking. The Uveid rock is brittle. It can't withstand pressure. Trying to mine it could create rock-falls. In addition, the energy field makes machinery play up."

"Sera will report on the stability of the Uveid rock. She's mapping the Uveid deposits in Morten, but the initial mining will be done at Three-Craters. You can start on your preliminary designs here, and then both of you will come to Three-Craters," Paul said. "We'll meet again tomorrow and go over the outline for the machine."

"I'll start straight away and have something to show you tomorrow," Kalen said, standing up. Paul remained seated, watching him. *He suspects me*, Kalen thought. *I need to say something convincing.* "I'm sure we'll succeed. We'll rid Taidor of all the Earlians."

"Yes, we'll cleanse the planet." Paul's mouth twitched into a smile but his eyes glinted darkly.

"Unity!" Kalen saluted, before turning on his heel and leaving the room.

Chapter Thirteen

Halle picked her way through the ruins of a building, keeping her head low, listening for the sound of Unity's troops.

Russ gestured to the others to follow him. "Our diversionary force was positioned just south of the transport terminal, near Sol Square. Let's check for survivors. It isn't far."

"We lost heavily. There won't be many left," Halle remarked.

"I'm not counting on it." Russ continued walking without breaking pace.

"Then what? We'll never get on a transport," Jed said. "The terminal will be heavily guarded."

"So will the shuttle port," Milan added.

"There might be a way," Russ replied. "We're near the square but I can't hear any fighting."

Russ led them down a narrow passageway. Stopping halfway, he said, "Keep quiet. This leads to the square. Unity might still have troops there."

Russ edged forward again, until he reached the mouth of the passageway. Halle came up and stood at his shoulder. She put her hand to her mouth and gasped in horror. A field of bodies littered the square, spread haphazardly over the ground. Nothing moved and the vestiges of acrid smoke curled up into the air. Black clad soldiers lay where they had fallen, most with burn wounds, that in many cases had charred large sections of their bodies. Some had been cut down near the exits and Halle found herself staring at a dead soldier lying no more than two meters in front of them. His abdomen had been burned away but the gold badge on his jacket shone in the sunlight. She noticed another body next to his: no badge, but gold vertical stripes just below the right shoulder of the jacket.

"There's both Unity and Early dead here," Halle whispered to Russ. "Some of them have the badges on their jackets."

"I know," Russ glanced around at her. "The majority are ours, though."

Halle felt Milan brush her arm lightly, as he stepped forward. "No one alive."

"No," answered Russ thoughtfully. He tilted his head back and surveyed the tops of the surrounding buildings. "I can't see any of Unity's troops but it's still very exposed. We need to check the bodies. Keep to the edges of the square."

"It's hard to tell which are ours and which are theirs," Nadia said.

"The basic black uniforms are the same. They always were under the duplicate system before the war, when jobs were shared. Only the equipment and insignia differ," Russ said. "Take their helmets and packs. We need to collect their identity cards, weapons and those badges they wear, so that we can pass ourselves off as U-Zone."

"That won't work," Halle said. "They'll know our identities as soon as they scan our wrist chips."

"We'll have to take that chance," Russ replied. "The systems have all been disrupted because of the war. I doubt that they'll have operating scanners at the shuttle port."

Cautiously, Russ stepped into the square, knelt by the nearest body and searched it. He took the soldier's identity card, badge from the jacket and weapons. As an afterthought, he removed the soldiers backpack and rifled through it. Returning to the shelter of the passageway, he checked his haul.

"This one is male and a number five. You have his stuff, Aris. We need their packs and equipment; anything we can use. Take the stripes off your own jacket and fix the badge on the left side. We have to find badges and identity cards for all of us. At least one of us needs to be a seven or eight so that they can pass as an officer."

Swallowing back her distaste, Halle tentatively entered the square with the others. She scanned the buildings around the square, looking for signs of Unity's troops, but saw no one. Satisfied, she began searching the nearest body. Near her, Nadia rifled through a female soldier's jacket.

"This one's about the same age as me, called Kira Tull. She's a five," Nadia said.

"We still need an officer. We've got enough but no one higher than a six. That isn't going to work. Keep searching," Russ replied.

"I've think I've found one." Jed bent down at a body and fingered the badge. "It's a number eight. A blond female. Just a minute let me check her I.D. Yes, she's a Captain Essy Ronnard."

"Good work, Jed." Russ turned to Halle. "That one's for you. You'll have to pass yourself off as our captain."

Halle took the badge and identity card from Jed, quashing a feeling of disquiet at handling the dead woman's things. She also took a dead soldier's pack and equipment. Fixing the badge to her jacket with its magnetic clasp, she stared at the name on the card before putting it away. She was Essy now; she must remember that.

"Okay, I'm now in command," Halle said.

***

The shuttle port was busy when they arrived. The wide entrance was closed by a high mesh barrier, leaving narrow gaps at the sides serving as an exit and entrance, each guarded by two soldiers. Halle saw lines of troops entering and exiting through the respective gaps. The guards weren't scanning wrist chips. She composed herself and marched forward. She heard the others fall into step behind her, two by two, as previously agreed. This is going to be tricky, she thought.

She addressed the guards, "Captain Ronnard reporting as ordered. I have five with me."

They stared at her for a moment, and then in unison both raised their right hands, palms forward. "Unity."

Halle copied them, cursing herself for forgetting the salute. "Unity."

The guards put their hands down and one of them said, "I.D please."

Halle produced the stolen identity card and proffered it to him. She held her breath. Her hands were shaking and she tried to steady them. Would the guards check the card against their records?

The guard glanced at it and then returned it to her, and stepped aside. "You're clear to pass Captain Ronnard."

"Thank you." Halle tilted her head slightly in acknowledgement and walked through the entrance, the others following. The guards made no move to stop them.

She entered the terminal building, which had a large hall bounded by a wall of windows overlooking the concourse. Outside, a line of docking platforms stretched across it, in front of fuel stations and passenger depots. Halle counted five large shuttles sitting on the platforms. They had sleek grey rounded bodies and small windows, and were each capable of holding a dozen passengers as well as two pilots. Behind the shuttles, two larger interplanetary craft stood unattended, and further down the airfield, a number of much smaller shuttles were parked. The smaller craft looked like shiny grey or black beetles, with rounded bodies. Two of the passenger shuttles had ramps attached and were being boarded by soldiers.

"This is the civilian area. The military airfield is behind it," Russ whispered to Halle. "We need to find a shuttle ready to leave."

Halle shook her head. "That's going to be hard to pull off."

"Stay with me on this. I know what I'm doing. The army has requisitioned the use of all transport. I suggest we check out the passenger shuttles."

"We need a destination," Jed remarked.

"That will depend on how much flying time the shuttle can do. We need to try and join an active Ea-Zone force," Russ replied. "There are Ea-Zone troops stationed at mountain bases."

Milan glowered. "I'm looking forward to killing a few more of those crazies."

Halle strode towards a bank of elevators and called one. "Okay, but we still have to get onto a docking platform and get clearance to leave. Who's going to pilot it?"

"I've had training on the bigger craft, civilian and military," Russ said.

"I know how to pilot a small shuttle," Nadia added. "But nothing military."

Halle had her misgivings. They needed to find a fueled craft and persuade the military authorities to let them leave. They had to give a destination. She clicked her tongue in irritation just as the elevator doors opened. Stepping inside, they stayed together, grouped at one end of the car that could take over fifteen people. Four other soldiers also entered the car and Halle avoided eye contact with them. The elevator doors closed and she gripped the handrail in the wall to steady herself, as the elevator dropped several floors.

The doors opened onto a wide underground walkway bustling with port and military personnel. Further walkways led off the main one, the exits signed to different parts of the shuttle port.

"The passenger shuttles are usually fueled on landing, ready for the next trip. I think we should try one of those first," Russ suggested.

"What about the military craft?" Jed asked.

"I think that might be more difficult. It will be easier to bluff our way onto one of the civilian shuttles. We'll say we've been ordered to requisition it."

"Here's the entrance to the first docking platform." Halle stopped by a corner and pointed down a short corridor which had doors at the end. At that moment, the doors slid open and a soldier emerged. Halle glanced at his badge. An officer: a number eight. She raised her arm in the Unity salute. "Unity!"

"Unity!" Eight replied. "Are you lost?"

"We've been ordered to report to Morten. I was told our shuttle was here?"

"This shuttle's full," Eight replied. "You must have the wrong bay. Try the next one."

"Thank you." Halle began to turn away and then turned back. She raised her arm in a salute. "Unity!"

"Unity!" Eight returned her salute.

Halle led the others away quickly. The next bay wasn't difficult to find. She pressed the entry plate at the doors and they opened onto an empty room, with cages for baggage on one side and consoles on another. The tread of their boots echoed on the chrome floor as they walked across it, towards the door at the far end. Suddenly, a man dressed in the overalls of a mechanic, appeared from a side door. He stared in surprise at Halle and the others, and then stopped and saluted. "Unity!"

The man stood nervously eying Halle. She stretched her arm out, palm forward. "Unity! Is our shuttle fueled and ready to leave? This is the right bay isn't it?"

"The shuttle's fueled, but I haven't been told that anyone was taking it out today." The mechanic fidgeted with a radio in his hand. He wore a badge with the number four on it.

"My assignment is urgent. That's probably why the orders haven't reached you yet," Halle replied smoothly. "We need to board now."

The mechanic frowned. "If you're piloting it yourself, I can open the doors and put the ramp up so you can board."

"Thank you. Unity!" Halle saluted again, and continued towards the far door.

They entered a bright waiting room at ground level, surrounded by transparent windows, giving good views across the shuttle port. Outside, a twelve seater commercial shuttle sat on its docking platform, its door situated about two meters above ground level. The craft's doors were closed and there was no ramp. Russ tried the waiting room exit doors but they were locked and Halle wrung her sticky hands impatiently.

"He'll put the ramp up soon," Russ said, watching the shuttle. He turned to Nadia. "Can you fly this with me?"

"I can try. I know the principles but I haven't flown anything this big," Nadia said.

"The basics are the same. You can co-pilot the plane as soon as we're up."

"Okay," Nadia replied.

Russ turned to Halle. "You'll have to sit with me until we're out of the dome."

The control panel at the side of the waiting room doors began to blink, and in front of it, a ramp emerged from a portal at the edge of the platform. It stretched slowly upwards towards the door of the shuttle, and attached itself with a metallic clank. The shuttle door and the waiting room doors slid open together.

"This is where we get on," Russ said.

"I'll go first in case someone's watching us." Halle walked briskly up the ramp and stepped inside the shuttle.

***

Leaving the port, Halle sat with Russ at the controls, as if she was a pilot. She had taken her helmet off and had it stowed beside her. The others sat in the passenger seats, behind the flight deck. Russ studied the console in front of them, before switching the engine on. He checked readings and flicked switches while Halle waited tensely.

"There's enough in the fuel cells to fly this shuttle for fourteen hours. Morten is about six hours away and we'll tell them that's our destination. I know the location of an Ea-Zone base in the mountains, near Three-Craters. We can go there," Russ informed Halle. "I've plotted a course and inputted the co-ordinates into the navigation program. The radio's on the channel for port control. You know what to say?"

"Yes, I pretend to be the pilot," Halle said. She took a deep breath and prepared to speak with confidence. If she spoke with authority, port control should believe her.

"Now." Russ switched the radio to transmit.

"This is Captain Essy Ronnard onboard shuttle three eight one, at bay two, bound for Morten. Permission to leave requested," Halle said crisply.

"Captain Ronnard, we don't have a manifest for your flight," the controller replied.

"I have urgent orders to report to Morten. I'm carrying a total of six. Please confirm clearance."

After a short delay, the controller replied, "Clearance approved. Please prepare for platform ascent."

"Acknowledged." He can't be bothered to check, Halle thought. She waited for several seconds and then the shuttle began to rise on the platform, towards the roof of the dome. The platform paused and then part of the dome slid aside and the shuttle ascended into the first of two airlocks. Giant clamps gripped the shuttle. The platform retracted and the airlock closed beneath the shuttle. Another platform edged into position under the shuttle, the clamps were released, and the shuttle settled onto the second platform with a jolt. The procedure was repeated again, before the craft finally sat underneath the roof of the dome itself.

"This is port control," the radio squeaked into life. "Final ascent is confirmed. God speed your journey. Port control out."

"Acknowledged. Three eight one out." Halle switched the channel off. She sighed with relief. They were nearly clear.

A square portion of the roof of the dome slid open, revealing a patch of blue sky. The brilliant sunlight flooded the flight deck despite the tinted windows. The platform rose to draw level with the roof, so that on each side of the craft, the transparent dome curved away glistening in the sunlight. Above, Taidor's bright sun burned fiercely and below, the ruined buildings of the city of Central appeared small. A flat barren plain surrounded the city, stretching out to distant sharp peaked mountains. With no vegetation, the desert was spotted by rubble and boulders.

Russ surveyed the bare sandy plain. "We're lucky we've got a fine day. There can be dust storms out here."

"And on very rare occasions, meteor storms," Halle added.

Russ took the controls and eased the shuttle up, clearing the roof of the dome, which slid shut behind them. Checking their direction, he grinned at Halle. "We've done it."

"I'll be glad when we get to the base."

"Unity doesn't know the location of Early's mountain bases. There are twelve bases. We're going to Base Four," Russ said. "It's within range so we should be able to reach it."

"I'll go and sit with the others and let Nadia take the controls." Halle unbuckled her seat belt, picked up her helmet, and stood up. She beckoned to Nadia. "The co-pilot's seat is all yours."

Halle found a seat in the main cabin and settled into it. Taking the shuttle had been easy. Too easy, she reflected. A nasty sense of foreboding began to creep over her. She looked around her at the others and stared out of the window. Everything seemed normal, but the nagging anxiety wouldn't leave her. It was the same feeling that she'd had going into the vacuum tunnel. She pushed that particular nightmare to the back of her mind and closed her eyes.

Chapter Fourteen

The dust storm blew up suddenly when they were nine hours out of Central. The first indication was the horizon blurring and a darkening of the sun. Halle stared hard through the windows. The light was fading outside. By her calculations there was another hour before nightfall. Why was the light going? In front of her, Russ and Nadia were talking quietly. She glanced around to see if the others had noticed. Jed and Aris were asleep but Milan, who was nearest to her, met her gaze.

"The light's going," Halle said.

Milan twisted his mouth, eyes dark. "It's probably a dust storm. We have all the luck, don't we?"

A jagged shard of fear bit into Halle's guts. The passenger shuttles didn't usually fly in dust storms. Why hadn't the control center warned them? She chided herself for blaming them. They were at war and the dust storms were unpredictable. She hadn't given them their real destination. Outside, the mountain range they were heading towards had become nothing more than a faint outline.

The shuttle began to vibrate and suddenly jolted violently. She put her seatbelt on and looked outside again. The mountains were no longer visible, as if a thick fog had descended. She heard the wind blowing up outside and everything started rattling. The shuttle's engines changed to a high pitched whine and began laboring, the roar of the wind almost drowning their sound out. The craft shook and all at once, tipped to one side, before levelling out.

Russ's voice came over the cabin intercom, "We're going to try and outrun the storm. Keep your seatbelts on."

The howling wind worsened and nothing was visible outside the window except a thick greyish smog. Halle wondered about Russ and Nadia flying the craft blind. She hoped the onboard computer kept them on course. She began to feel nauseous. How much longer? The craft suddenly tipped to one side again and as it righted, it bucked throwing Halle back against her seat. She gripped the arm rests and braced herself as the craft pitched downwards, slamming her against her seatbelt, before jerking to the other side. The sky was now black and Halle was unable to work out which way was up, in the pitching craft. *They're losing control,* she thought. *We have to land.*

With no warning, the shuttle dropped straight down. Halle felt her stomach flip and gripped the sides of her seat tighter. The engines kicked in, and they began to climb, the craft shaking fiercely in the turbulence. The shuttle jerked to one side again, pummeled by the raging storm. Halle held her breath and it righted and continued to climb, but the shaking increased. Suddenly the craft lurched sideways, as if thrown by a sudden gust of wind and then tipped downwards in a steep dive, engines howling. Halle glanced at the window but only saw her own terrified reflection.

The seat belt bit into her. She looked at Milan who was nearest. He sat rigidly, staring straight ahead. She heard a roar in her ears. The pressure of the belt against her chest made it difficult to breathe. She fought to take a breath. The craft's velocity increased and it shook ferociously. The vibrations jarred Halle's body and her seat belt tightened further. A terrible cracking sound filled the cabin and a split appeared in the plastic lining of the bulkhead. Russ shouted something that she couldn't hear. She interlaced her fingers behind her head and bent down, head touching knees. Screwing up her eyes, she waited for the impact, curled between the seats.

***

Halle became aware of intense pain at the back of her head. Her skull felt almost numb where something had hit her. She didn't move or open her eyes, taking a moment to assess her injuries. Her legs felt fine but her arms felt sore. A stabbing pain in her neck sent spasms of agony to her shoulders and upper back. A deep pain in both of her ears made her feel dizzy. She gingerly probed the back of her head, and her fingers felt a bump. Someone near her was groaning, and outside the storm still raged. *The shuttle hasn't broken up,* she thought. *I can still breathe.*

She opened her eyes and carefully straightened up. The interior bulkhead had cracked and swords of jagged plastic had splintered off. Aris sat behind the bulkhead, immobile and head limp, with a piece protruding from his chest. On the other side, Jed sprawled across the arm of his seat, only held in place by his belt, half of his head a red mass of blood. Above Jed, a storage compartment had sprung open. A heavy metal box rested on the floor, blood smeared across its sharp edges. To Halle's left, Milan slumped unconscious in his seat, groaning. Outside, everything was black.

Coughing up front caught Halle's attention. She saw Russ's head dip and he coughed again. A rustle of movement and he was standing up, holding onto the back of the pilot's seat to steady himself. He came towards her, blood trickling down his face from a gash on his forehead. Stopping, he reached up to touch it and brought his hand down to study his fingers. Wiping his hand on his trousers, he surveyed the cabin. A grimace passed across his face and then his eyes met hers and lit up.

"Thank the planets you're still alive." Russ started towards her. "Are you trapped? Can you get up?"

"I don't know. I've had a knock on the head." Halle undid her seat belt. "I must have hit it on the seat frame."

"Let me see." Russ stooped over and studied the back of her head. "Stay still."

She felt him gently part her hair. "There's a nasty bump. If you need to take something, there'll be a medical kit onboard."

Milan groaned again and Russ spoke to him next, "Milan, can you hear me?"

Milan's eyes remained closed and he didn't respond. Russ carefully raised Milan up into a sitting position. Milan's head flopped sideways at an unnatural angle. Russ eased his head back again.

"I can't see anything but he might have hurt his neck. Milan, can you hear me?"

Milan didn't stir and Halle stood up slowly, holding onto the back of her seat for support. She felt dizzy and unsteady.

"Careful." Russ gripped her arm. "You've got concussion. Take it easy."

"What about Nadia?"

"She hit the console when we came down. Cracked her skull. I'm sorry, she's dead."

Nausea and dizziness swept over Halle and her legs buckled. She would have fallen if Russ hadn't held her. She felt his arms around her and let him guide her back into her seat.

He knelt in the aisle at the side of her seat and took her hands in his. "Give yourself a little time before trying to stand up again."

"I'll be fine." She saw concern in his eyes. "I just couldn't keep my balance."

"It will pass. We can't go anywhere in this storm, anyhow."

"What happened?" she asked weakly.

"Sand and dust got into the engines. Wrecked them and we came down," Russ said wearily, surveying the cabin. "What a mess."

"Will we be able to fly it again?"

"No, there's too much damage. But the shuttle's body has held. There's no sign of an air leak."

Milan's eyes blinked open. He slowly turned his head towards Halle. With dilated pupils his eyes were black.

He stared at Halle with naked hatred; a piercing stare that made her recoil. For a second, she read his hate and anger, evil twisted emotions. She shrank back into her seat paralyzed by his venom. Suddenly, the glittering black stare faded to be replaced by soft brown tortured eyes. He grimaced, his mouth contorting in pain.

"I touched the Uveid stones," Milan gasped, his voice so low that Halle could barely make out the words. "I saw the shapes. They don't want us here."

"Who don't want us here? Do you mean Unity?" Russ squatted near Milan's seat.

"They hate us." Milan's eyelids flickered and then the light died from his eyes.

Russ felt for a pulse and then stood up, shaking his head at Halle. "He's gone. It's only you and me now. I didn't understand what he said. We know Unity hate us."

Halle tried to remember what she had heard about the Uveid rocks. "The Uveid stones are shaped like tiny blue pyramids and they give off some kind of energy. The Division got reports that they can cause hallucinations. Some people have reported seeing shapes in the energy."

"I wonder if it's true?" Russ mused. "I've heard rumors that people have been affected by the energy. Makes them do strange things. Anyway that's not going to help us now. How are you feeling?"

"A bit better." Halle stood up again and tentatively took her hands away from the seat back. "I think I'm okay to walk around now without falling over."

Russ bent to see out of the windows. "It's dark at the moment but the storm's dying off."

"Do you know where we are?" Halle asked.

"According to the onboard computer, we were about sixty kilometers away from Base Four when we came down. It should be due west of us. We're going to have to walk. Do you think you're up to it? It'll be a two or three day walk."

"I'll be fine," Halle said briskly. "The U-Zone will have discovered that we stole the shuttle. They'll be searching for us."

"We should rest and then leave at first light. It's too dark at the moment for Unity's patrols to see the wreck from the air," Russ said. "It's going to get very hot during the day and cold at night. We'll need oxygen as well as food and water."

"There should be emergency equipment stored at the back," Halle replied.

"Let's get our packs ready now, and then get some sleep." Russ unlocked one of the storage cubicles at the rear of the shuttle. He took out several oxygen canisters and gave them to Halle. "Check that you've got breathing tubes and a mask."

Halle took the canisters and put them in her backpack. She checked through its contents and opened up a pack one of the others had used. "Okay, there's two packs here. Hand me the rest of the oxygen canisters and water."

Halle searched the compartments for food and added rations to the packs. Fixing a military issue laser and stun stick to her pack, she asked, "Have we got a compass?"

"There should be one on the flight deck." Russ stopped searching a locker. "Here, I'll get it."

Russ squeezed past Halle. He doesn't want me to go up there, she thought. He doesn't want me to see Nadia.

Russ came back and checked through one of the packs. "I've got the compass and we've got radios in the helmets. Anything else you can think of?"

"No, I think we've got everything we need," Halle replied.

"Let's get some sleep then. We've got a few hours." Russ drew Halle into his arms and kissed her lightly on the forehead. "It'll be all right. We'll make it to the base. Get some rest and we'll start out in the morning."

***

Strong vibrations woke Kalen from a deep sleep. The building was shaking. He glanced at Sera lying beside him, but she slept on peacefully, apparently undisturbed by the sound of explosions and whine of missiles outside. War raged in Morten and their accommodation block had taken heavy damage. Their quarters were scantily furnished and Kalen vaguely questioned whether the building would still be standing in a few days. He closed his eyes and tried to sleep, but his mouth was dry. He got up and quietly padded across the room.

"Where are you going?" Sera's voice rang out.

He stopped and turned. "I'm getting some water. Go back to sleep."

"Come back to bed."

Kalen heard the air of command in her voice. He wondered if he was imagining it. Imagining that she watched him the whole time and only feigned sleep to wait and see what he would do. He collected a tumbler of water and returned to lie at her side. "The fighting's getting worse. It's very near now."

"We've got God on our side," Sera replied, snuggling up to him. She stretched an arm across his stomach and fell back asleep.

Kalen lay awake in bed. Beside him, Sera slept soundly. As he listened to her regular breathing, he reviewed his plans. They were leaving for Three-Craters soon with Paul. Once he got there, he had to find a way to destroy the trident before Unity could duplicate it. He didn't want to design the mining machine; he would design it with faults to delay its use, for as long as possible. He would delay everything, until he could destroy the trident.

Since handling the Uveid pendant in Paul Neill's office, the image of the shadow wall had hovered in Kalen's mind. He hadn't been able to shake it off. Something to do with the Uveid, he thought. He felt himself drifting and began to dream. He saw the shadow wall and a crack appeared in it, to reveal a golden light. The crack got wider until it was a window in the wall, and the glow from it pulled him towards it. He felt a primeval terror, and had an overwhelming urge to throw himself through the window, to escape from the terror. He wanted to fall into that golden light, but a tiny voice intruded into the dream. *Death awaits me in the light. If I enter the light, I will lose myself.* In his dream, he walked away from the window, but his terror increased with each step he took.

Raw fear gripped Kalen in a frozen embrace and from somewhere outside of the dream, his mind told him that it wasn't real. He woke up, the nightmare still vivid. Jumbled thoughts rushed at him. Death was preferable to the terror; it would be a release. The window had felt like a magnet, drawing him into it. He opened his eyes, careful not to make any sudden movement that would wake Sera. He searched his mind. The shadow wall was still there, like a dark cloud. He had been touched by the power of the Uveid. It's energy was still with him.

***

Halle felt a light touch on her shoulder. She opened her eyes and stretched her legs. Her neck ached and she put up a hand to massage the back of it. Sleeping in the shuttle seat had not been comfortable. The remnants of her dream still lingered. Something dark and horrible. She pushed the feeling away and looked at Russ. He stood in the center aisle bending over to see out of a window. Outside, the sun had already risen, to illuminate a flat sandy plain and everything seemed quiet.

"It's time to go. It's morning. The wind has died down," Russ said, straightening up. "We should leave before Unity spots the shuttle."

Halle began to rise and then hesitated, swallowing hard. She felt like vomiting. The bodies of Milan, Aris and

Jed, were still in their seats. Rigor mortis had set in and they sat stiffly, frozen at the point of death. The grisly scene struck her as if a burning torch had been plunged into her stomach. How could she have slept with their bodies so near?

Summoning all her reserves, she said, "I'm ready but I don't like leaving Nadia and the others like this."

"There's nothing we can do for them now. Someone will find them, eventually."

"Okay," she replied, moving into the aisle, to stand facing him. He was right but it still didn't feel like the right thing to do.

Russ gently placed his hands on her upper arms and said, "I promise you we'll come out of this alive. The base isn't too far. We can make it."

"I know, I trust you." She gave him a weak smile.

Russ hugged her and kissed her lightly on her forehead. "Let's get our things together and get out of here."

Halle reached for her helmet, fastening the oxygen canister and breathing mask in place. She hoisted a pack onto her back. Her eyes met Russ's eyes. "I've hardly been outside the domed cities before."

"Don't worry. I've been outside several times." Russ moved towards the shuttle door. "Here goes."

Russ pressed the exit plate and the door slid aside slowly with a creaking noise, to reveal a blazing tableau of sand and rock.

The heat hit Halle as soon as the door opened. She paused at the exit and lowered her visor against the glare that left sparks dancing before her eyes. A harsh alien landscape lay before them, as far as she could see. Heaped sand lay against the sides of the shuttle and Russ stepped into a mound of it, under the exit hatch, leaving deep footprints. Halle glanced back over her shoulder at the bodies of the others and felt a terrible sadness. How had it come to this? It seemed barbaric to leave them sitting in the seats they had died in, but there was no choice. They had to leave and the sooner the better.

Halle walked with Russ across the sandy plain towards a ridge of mountains, her legs aching. In places the sand had banked following the wind storm and it sucked at her feet, making them feel impossibly heavy. Her breathing mask felt sticky against her face and her top was damp with perspiration. Russ stopped and took out a compass. Grateful for the brief respite, Halle waited while he checked their direction, before he resumed walking again.

After two hours walking in the hot sun, Halle began to get thirsty and her legs ached. They no longer obeyed her commands briskly, and she dragged her feet along the ground. She wanted a rest and a drink, but Russ carried on walking, setting a pace that she found difficult to match. The water she carried had to last until they reached the base and she dismissed the idea of having a drink. Glancing upwards, she looked for signs of Unity, but the sky was clear.

"We have to keep going, Halle." Russ turned his head slightly, his voice crisp over her helmet radio. "You're falling behind and we have a lot of ground to cover."

"I know, I'm trying." Halle quickened her pace to catch up. "I can't walk as fast as you."

"Unused to it, more likely." Russ chuckled. "This'll toughen you up."

"Thank you for being so considerate," Halle replied with an edge in her voice.

"We've only gone a few kilometers." Russ stopped walking and smiled at her.

"How many times have you walked about on the surface of this wretched planet?" she demanded.

"Several times, actually. The army trains out here. It'll be easier once we get to those mountains and a bit of shade."

"I know it will," she said.

"We're an easy target in the open. If a shuttle goes over, we'll be seen. We can slow down once we get into the mountains." Russ began hiking again.

She followed him, willing her legs to keep going. The pack on her back seemed to be getting heavier. "How far is it to the mountains?"

"It's another five or six kilometers," Russ called over his shoulder. "Not far."

Not far for you, Halle thought irritably. At least when they got there, she could get out of the sun. She trudged on silently, remembering the others they had left behind. She pictured Milan dying in his seat. There was something strange about the venom in his eyes before he died. Something…she searched for the word: alien. Yes, alien. Why hadn't she seen it before? He had talked about touching the Uveid stones. Had they affected him? She had heard rumors at the Division, that the stones changed people. Could that be why Unity had turned on the Ea-Zone?

The air cooled and she realized that they were in the shadow of a mountain. Ahead of her, Russ strolled on, saying, "We better not stop yet. We're still very visible. Just a bit further."

Chapter Fifteen

Kalen sat in the office that had been allocated to him in Morten, and waited for Javed Durton's call. At the appointed time, Javed's face appeared on the desk screen.

"Unity!" Javid declared.

"Unity!" Kalen replied automatically, meeting Javed's black eyes. Something glistened around Javed's neck. With a shock, Kalen recognized a Uveid pendant, similar to the one that Paul wore.

"Paul's told me that you've started working on the Uveid mining machine. When will you finish the design?"

"I need another week or so. There are some technical aspects that I need to smooth out." Would Javed buy that? A feeling of terror and a mental image of the shadow wall hit Kalen. The window in the wall glowed golden, and he had moved away from it.

Javed screwed his face up. "A week? We need the machine before then. You leave for Three-Craters tomorrow – you can work on the shuttle. I want it ready in three days. We need to start mining the Uveid as soon as possible."

"Yes, Sir." Kalen stared impassively at Javed. In his mind, the shadow wall seemed nearer and his feeling of terror eased. The window was open and the golden light beckoned him to the other side.

"Send the design to Jon Ingeston as well as Paul Neill when you're finished. Jon will be joining you at Three-Craters."

"Will Sera Ethern and Paul Neill be traveling with me to Three-Craters?" Kalen asked.

"Yes, you'll travel together on one of the military shuttles." Javed's eyes flickered to Kalen's Divine as if assessing him. "You need to prove yourself to Unity to advance up the stages. You can't stay a two. Now is the time to show your loyalty. Unity rewards hard work. Do you understand?"

"Yes, Sir. I'll do my best." Dare he risk asking Javed about the war? "How is the conflict going in Central?"

Javed's eyes lit up. "Unity has got control now. We've destroyed the Ea-Zone's blocks and we nearly have all of the city."

"What about the Ea-Zone population?"

An expression of satisfaction passed across Javed's face. "We're holding most of them, but a few escaped. We're going to use them as the labor force in our new mines."

"You're holding them in Central?" Kalen asked, wondering how Unity had taken the Ea-Zone blocks.

"Not all of them. We've shipped some of them out on the transports to our construction sites."

Kalen thought back to the transport terminals in Central and Morten. He hadn't seen prisoners at either terminal. "The ones that escaped, where have they gone? There's very little on the planet's surface."

"The Ea-Zone have mountain bases. They've probably gone there. We think they're planning a large air offensive," Javed said. "We've got the trident-weapon so they'll never succeed. As soon as. we've duplicated it, the war will be over."

"Yes, we have God on our side," Kalen replied solemnly. Better to act the patriot, he thought.

"You need one of these." Javed fingered the pendant around his neck. "It'll help you think clearly."

"I've seen Paul Neill's pendant."

"Good. Get on with that design and then join Jon Ingeston at Three-Craters. We're on a tight schedule."

"Yes, Sir."

"Unity!"

"Unity!" Kalen responded, and the screen went blank. Kalen sat for a moment reviewing their conversation. He could finish the machine design easily within the next day or two, but if Early were massing forces in the mountains, he needed to give them as much time as possible. If he could destroy the trident, what then? He couldn't desert Sera and try and join Early. He would have to remain with Unity. Perhaps he could make contact with Early's forces and help them.

***

Halle and Russ walked all day without seeing any sign of Unity's shuttles. For Halle, the hours seemed interminable, the landscape endlessly the same. They walked in the shadow of a mountain that towered over them, rising almost vertically in places. Ravines dissected sheer cliffs that rose raggedly up to a sharp peak. Nearer to the ground, dark gullies scored the mountain's steep slopes and around the base, the black holes of caves were visible. Halle shuddered at the idea of sleeping in one.

She sweated in her jacket and trousers, her helmet heavy against her skull. They had stopped several times to rest, but she didn't get the sense that they had covered much distance. Eventually the light began to dim and the temperature started to drop. She wondered how much daylight they had left. They were walking towards a gap in the mountain range, still visible in the light from the setting sun, but soon to be lost in the darkness.

Russ paused, and then pointed to the pass. "There's a building over there."

"I can't see anything," Halle said.

"It's over there, in front of the pass. Turn the view on your visor up."

Halle switched her visor to long range vision and made out a low building. "It looks like a factory."

"It could be. There are a number of them on the surface. We might be able to get inside to sleep."

"It might be guarded," Halle replied, scrutinizing the building for signs of people. "It could have been taken over by the U-Zone."

"I think we should chance it. The alternative is sleeping out in the open."

"I don't fancy that. It doesn't look far." Halle stared at the building.

"Maybe a couple of kilometers. It's difficult to tell distance out here," Russ replied. "I think we should investigate."

"We need to be careful," Halle said. "I can't see any movement but the U-Zone could be manning it."

"They won't have spotted us yet. If we keep close to the mountains, they won't see us."

"They might have seen us already. They could be waiting for us."

Russ laughed shortly. "In that case, even if we sleep outside, they'll come for us."

"I see your point," Halle conceded. "Okay we'll have to take the chance."

Russ began walking again, hugging the side of the mountain, so that they were hidden in its shadow. Halle hurried after him, fear gnawing at her innards. The enhanced visuals of her visor gave her a clear view of the building. At any moment she expected U-Zone troops to come streaming out of its doors. Her legs felt like jelly but she forced herself to go forward. If the U-Zone had taken this building, there would be nothing to save them. She cursed Unity. She wouldn't let them beat her. Whilst she had breath in her body, she wouldn't let them win.

***

The building was a long low structure that nestled at the base of the mountain at the mouth of the pass. Solar panels lined its sides and roof, bathed in the last light of the day from Taidor's setting sun. As they walked towards it, Halle realized that it was further away than she had first thought. The light was failing fast and the sun had turned into a burning orange ball as it lingered just above the horizon. With a jolt, Halle realized that she had never seen Taidor's night sky; she had always lived in the cities under artificial lighting.

"How much further do you think it is?" Halle asked.

Russ glanced over his shoulder. "Not far now. Probably another twenty minutes."

"We're losing the light and it's getting cold."

"The temperature is going to dip right down," Russ replied.

"We need to arm ourselves and be ready in case it's manned by the U-Zone," Halle remarked.

"It'll be dark soon. We'll get a little nearer and then go in after dark."

"I still can't see any movement," Halle replied.

"We may be lucky and it may not be manned."

"I hope you're right." Halle adjusted her face mask and tried to calculate how much oxygen she had used.

Russ glanced at her. "Even the unmanned factories usually have a breathable atmosphere to facilitate visits by the maintenance crews. We might not need oxygen inside."

The sun began to disappear below the horizon, and color drained from the desert. The toe of one of Halle's steel tipped boots snagged on a rock and she stumbled. She caught herself from falling and cursed silently. They couldn't walk far without any light. The factory remained dark, with no sign of people. Above the horizon, three pale orbs had risen in the night sky and a sprinkling of stars had begun to emerge.

Halle stared at the moons. "I've never seen the moons before. I can't remember their names."

"They're called Esus, Hesus, and Aisus, but don't ask me which one is which," Russ replied. "We're nearly at the factory."

The building was now no more than a silhouette against the gloaming. They approached it cautiously, and Halle saw no windows or lights, but heard a persistent hum coming from it. Although low, the building was much larger than Halle expected. She looked for a doorway, and eventually saw a door set back in a recess in the wall.

"There's a door over there." Halle indicated the far end of the wall.

"No sign of anyone yet. Let's check it out." Russ moved forward quietly.

The black night enveloped them so that Halle could see nothing except the walls of the building. Metal paving, several meters wide around the walls, made it easier for Halle to keep her footing in the darkness, but when they walked across it, their footsteps tapped on its surface. *That's bound to alert anyone inside*, Halle thought. Save for the low hum from inside the building, she couldn't hear any other noise.

"I don't think there's anyone here. Do you think it's okay to turn our torches on?"

"Yes. If there was anyone here, they would have confronted us by now." Russ switched his helmet light on and took a torch out of his belt, to shine a wide beam in front of them.

Halle did the same and their lights illuminated the door in the recess of the wall. It was made of grey metal and a keypad was fixed onto the wall beside it. Halle directed the beam of her flashlight at the keypad, lighting it up.

Russ studied it for several seconds. "I don't know the code to unlock it."

"Can't we just use our lasers and burn it out?" Halle asked.

"If we do that, we risk setting off an alarm somewhere." Russ swung his pack off his back and opened it.

"You're right." Halle remembered the guards waiting for them at street level in Central. She wouldn't make that mistake again.

"Shine your torch over here, will you?" Russ crouched down and began rifling through the contents. "I'm going to open the keypad up. If I can disable the lock, we can lever the door open manually."

Halle used her torch to give Russ light. "I hope we can get inside. Anything would be better than staying out here all night."

"We'd definitely be better off inside." Russ straightened up, holding a small tool. He loosened the cover and carefully worked on the mechanism underneath. "I've switched the lock off. It shouldn't trigger any alarms. Now we can force the doors."

"Can I help?" Halle asked, holding her flashlight steady to illuminate the door.

"It's okay, I've got it." Russ inserted his fingers around the edge of the door and pulled. There was a loud sucking sound which abruptly stopped when the door broke away from its seal and slid open. Behind it, a short corridor led to another door. Russ picked up his bag and went inside. "It's an airlock. I'll have to close the outer door, before we can open the next door."

Halle followed him in. "Thank the planets. There'll be oxygen inside."

Russ pressed buttons on a wall panel to close the outer door and increase the oxygen in the airlock. "The inner door will unlock as soon as the oxygen level is normal."

"What do you think the factory makes? Why would it be all the way out here?" Halle asked.

"We'll know in a minute. How's the oxygen doing?"

Halle lit up the display with her flashlight. "It's back to normal."

Russ glanced at the gauge. "The door will open now, but keep close to me. We don't know what's in there. It could be dangerous."

They entered the factory through the inner door. Lights near them suddenly flickered on, illuminating one end of a large hall, holding rows of huge circular metal containers. The containers stood proud of the floor by over a meter, and on the side of each container there were controls and pressure gauges. Each tank had a lid and a rectangular metal grill in the floor near its base. A steady hum came through the grills from below. As they moved about, the lights came on overhead and died behind them, so that Halle could not see the end of the hall where the rows of tanks disappeared into the darkness.

"The temperature seems a bit better in here," Halle said.

Halle disconnected her oxygen canister and took off her mask. She sniffed the air. It smelled slightly of chemicals that she couldn't identify. Taking a deep breath she yawned, suddenly feeling the fatigue she had spent the last few hours ignoring.

Russ also took his mask off. "There's not much to see up here. I think it's a fuel plant. All the production and storage will be below. There'll be elevators down somewhere."

"It's in the middle of nowhere. There aren't any settlements near here," Halle said.

"There's underground water on Taidor. They'll be using an underground reservoir near here to produce the fuel, which will then be pumped to a refueling station nearby." Russ began walking towards one of the walls.

"I don't think we should go any further into the plant," Halle said. "I would prefer to stay in this part."

"Agreed." Russ selected a sheltered space behind one of the tanks and sat down with his back against the wall. "Here will do. Let's have something to eat."

Halle joined him, sitting with her legs outstretched, and helmet off. The floor was made of a metal alloy and cool to the touch, but was spotlessly clean. Halle's feet felt hot and sore, so she bent her knees and took off her boots, arranging them neatly to one side of her. She had a swig from her water bottle and took a meal bar out of her bag and began chewing on it. The lights near the door had died, leaving most of the hall in darkness. Russ shone the beam of his flashlight towards the door, as if checking they were alone.

"We should be okay in here. The door is shut and the lights aren't visible from outside. We're well hidden behind this tank," Russ said.

"It's only six hours before it gets light again." Halle twisted to reach into her bag and drew out a blanket. "At the beginning of today, I never expected to end up in somewhere like this with you."

"I'm sorry it's turned out this way, but at least we're safe. We should reach Base Four either tomorrow night or the next day."

"I hope so," she replied, flipping open the top catch of her jacket. "I need a proper wash and to get out of these clothes."

"Really?" Russ chortled. He dipped his head and kissed her. "We should make the most of being here."

Halle giggled. "Any opportunity?"

"That's right," he whispered, putting his arms around her and kissing her again.

Halle curled into his powerful arms and snuggled against him. She returned his kisses, the stubble on his cheeks brushing the delicate skin of her face. He slid one of his hands under her jacket, caressing her, so that she tingled. His touch sent waves of pleasure through her and she moaned softly. His jacket was open and she used a petite hand to explore the firm musculature of his chest and his softer belly. He lifted her away from the wall, so that they could lie on the floor. His breathing become ragged as he gently kissed her lips and then moved his mouth downwards, the heat of his body over hers deliciously warm in the cold of the night.

Chapter Sixteen

A rasping sound woke Halle from a deep sleep. At first she wasn't sure that she had heard it. For a few seconds she wondered whether she had been dreaming. Her head rested against Russ's chest, and it rose and fell, in line with his regular breathing. He was still asleep and she didn't want to wake him, but she could see nothing in the darkness. If she moved the lights would flicker on, so she stayed still, listening.

She checked the time and it was morning. How could she have slept so soundly through the night? It seemed as if it had only been minutes ago that she had closed her eyes. Outside there would be daylight. Another day of blistering heat and kilometers to walk. Inside the factory, she felt cocooned. A temporary safe haven from the deprivations of the war. She listened to the hum of the machinery for a minute or two before she heard the rasping sound again. This time she was sure. The noise came from outside the building, near the door. Something was trying to get in.

Halle lay with Russ behind one of the tanks, out of sight of the door. She lifted her head from his chest and he began to stir. She moved her arm and the lights flickered on overhead. The sound of heavy breathing and scraping came again, from outside. *There's more than one of them*, she thought. *They're waiting for us. They know we're inside.*

Russ opened his eyes and smiled. "Hey! Are you awake already?"

"I can hear something outside."

Russ was instantly alert. "What sort of sound?"

"A sort of rasping, grating sound. And breathing. It's coming from near the door."

Russ sat up. "There shouldn't be anything out there."

"It woke me," she replied, pushing herself into a sitting position.

"You should have woken me up straight away." Russ was on his feet now, collecting his things together and putting them in his bag. He took a swig of water and then handled his laser. "We need to be careful. Unity might have found us. They could have followed our footsteps and be waiting outside."

"They would have come in." Halle put her boots on and fastened her jacket.

"Not necessarily." Russ peered around the tank towards the door. "They might not want to risk a firefight inside the building. It would cause too much damage. If the fuel caught fire, the whole building could blow."

Halle's throat constricted and her heart began to race. She took out the military issue laser that she had taken off the dead soldier in Central, and checked that it was set to ready. Taking a final gulp of water from her bottle, she stowed it in her bag. Her insides felt as if they had clenched up and frozen. Slinging her pack onto her back, she put her helmet and oxygen mask on.

Russ turned back to her. "I can't see anything in here."

Suddenly, another scraping sound came from the doorway, as if something hard had been raked across it. It was followed by a high pitched piercing shriek, that jarred Halle's teeth.

"What is it? Why would U-Zone soldiers make that noise?" she exclaimed.

"I don't know." Russ adjusted the straps of his backpack. "Are you ready to leave?"

"I'm ready, but aren't we safer in here?"

"Not if they know we're here. We need to find another way out." Russ held her arm and guided her behind the next tank.

"Let's try the other end of the hall. There might be another door there," she suggested.

They crept stealthily behind the row of tanks, towards the rear of the hall. The overhead lights following their progress. Whichever part of the factory they were in, the lights would give them away, Halle mused. They passed numerous containers, their footsteps soft on the gleaming metal floor. She imagined the soldiers waiting for them, in crisp black uniforms. There would be no need to take them prisoner. They would probably kill them immediately and leave their bodies in the desert to rot. At least she and Russ were armed. She would make sure she took a few of them down with her.

The back wall came into view and Halle scanned it for a door, shining the beam of her flashlight where the light was dim. "I think there's a door over there."

"Yes, it's a door," Russ agreed, as they cautiously made their way over to it.

"Let's hope that Unity is guarding the other door and don't know about this one."

Russ pressed the exit controls and the door opened. "It's another airlock."

They entered the airlock and the lights flickered on. Russ closed the inner door behind them and checked the air gauge on the wall. "They won't see the lights outside. The oxygen level is normal in here so we can open the outer door. Put your mask on."

Halle fastened her oxygen mask in place and secured her backpack. She checked that the hand laser attached to her belt was within easy reach and held her military laser firmly. She nodded to Russ and he pressed the exit panel to open the outer door. It slid aside quietly, exposing blue sky and an expanse of sandy desert, shimmering in a heat haze. He took a tentative step forward and surveyed the area.

"It's clear. Come on!"

They jogged briskly away from the factory, westwards towards the mountain pass. Their footfall was soft across the sand that sucked at Halle's ankles. Ahead, a ridge of sand dunes had formed, and as they climbed, Halle found herself staggering when her feet sank into it. Russ gripped her elbow and propelled her forward until they reached the top, where he looked back.

"I can't see anything following us."

"They'll be able to see our footprints," Halle said.

"Not if there's a sandstorm. We must keep going. They could come back at any time." Russ slid down the other side of the dune, pulling her behind him.

"Perhaps it wasn't soldiers?" Halle suggested.

"I don't know what else it could be." Russ began jogging.

"I can't keep up this pace for long," Halle panted. "My backpack's too heavy."

The sand began to disappear and Russ slowed a little. "The earth isn't so sandy here. It's quite firm so we should make better time. I want to get off the plain."

They entered the pass and were now in the shade of the mountains. The landscape changed and Halle found the cooler air refreshing. Large boulders lay strewn across the dry ground which was hard and rocky underfoot. Halle's heart raced and she found herself gulping at the air fed through her mask. Her lungs began to feel as if they would burst and a stitch had developed low on her left side, that stabbed at her with increasing frequency. She panted, trying to draw the breath into her lungs but her legs had begun to drag. Suddenly her legs buckled and she put a hand out to a large boulder to stop herself falling. Bending over, she fought to regain her breath. Russ stopped running and came back to her. He took hold of her arm to steady her.

"Sorry. I'll be all right in a moment. I just need to catch my breath," she gasped.

"Here, sit down. We'll take a break." Russ helped her to sit on the boulder. "Have some water."

He handed her a water bottle and she moved her mask aside to take a mouthful. The cold water slipped down her throat, soothing it. Gradually, her labored breathing subsided.

She handed the water bottle back to him. "Thank you."

"We're making good time," he said encouragingly. "The going will get easier."

"I hope so." She closed her eyes, luxuriating in the brief respite, listening to the silence of the mountains. A strange snuffling sound interrupted her thoughts. She opened her eyes. "What's that?"

"What's what?" Russ asked.

"That sound, like something sniffing," Halle replied.

"What?" Russ scrutinized their surroundings. "Are you sure?"

Halle heard the sound again. This time it was louder. "Did you hear it?"

"Yes, but I don't know where it's coming from." Russ put the water bottle away. "We better go."

Halle got up and they began to jog again, away from the sound. Halle's legs felt weak as she pounded over the rocky terrain. Beside her, Russ seemed to be searching for something.

"Up here." Russ took her arm and pulled her up a slope. "If we get up high, we can see what it is."

She scrambled up the scree after him, towards an outcrop of rocks that overlooked the pass. Kicking up rubble that trickled down the slope, they ploughed upwards until they reached the rocks. Hiding behind them, Halle had a good view of the pass. The factory was still visible, a distant tiny building on the vast plain. Their footsteps showed their route across the sand, from factory to the mouth of the pass.

In the other direction, she saw that the pass led into a valley bordered by mountains.

Russ pointed to the valley. "That's where we're heading. Base Four is at the other end of the valley. It's still another thirty or forty kilometers away."

"I wish we were there now," Halle muttered, staring at the ground below them. She saw sudden movement, somewhere in the rocks. Several tawny brown things were moving about, for the most part hidden in the shadows. "There's something down there."

"You're right." Russ raised his laser.

"There can't be animals here," Halle whispered.

"There shouldn't be. The air's too thin."

"Then what are they?" Halle asked.

"I'm not sure, but I doubt they're friendly." Russ watched the creatures approaching.

Halle counted about ten light brown creatures milling around the floor of the pass. High thin ears protruded from the tops of their heads, quivering as they spun this way and that, nudging sand and rubble with their long thin snouts. Their tails whipped around excitedly while they roamed about. With a shock, she realized that they were moving over the route Russ and her had taken. Now the creatures were at the bottom of the stony rise.

"They've followed us," she hissed at Russ. "They're sniffing us out!"

"Some kind of dogs?" Russ pondered.

"How? Dogs can't live out here."

"They've got six legs," Russ said. "They must have been bred for the planet surface."

"Perhaps they guard the factory?" Halle suggested.

"They must have been genetically modified. There's two joints on each leg and they've got flat paws. Look at how they're using their front paws to grip! They're designed to climb and run, especially over sand. I hope we've got far enough away."

"I don't think so," Halle said, watching one of the dogs climb towards them.

Four slits positioned at the front and side of the dog's head blinked constantly over piercing yellow eyes and the black nose at the tip of its snout twitched erratically. When the creature got within ten meters of their position, it's jaws opened along the length of its snout to expose a double row of sharp yellow teeth. The skin covering its body was mottled and smooth. It reminded Halle of pictures she had seen of snakeskin. It stood still and howled. The pack behind it began to shriek; a terrible high pitched sound, before descending into barking.

"They're vicious," Russ muttered beside her.

"We'll have to take them out with the lasers," Halle said. "They haven't got any shielding."

"That would have made them too heavy." Russ shifted his position to the other side of the rocks. "I'll take this side and you take the other."

Halle poked the barrel of her laser out from behind the rocks and sighted the first of the creatures. "Okay."

"Wait until more of them are within range. Once we fire, the others will come on fast. Switch your laser to wide spread." Russ pulled back a catch on his weapon.

"Can't we distract them or something?" Halle braced herself.

"Unlikely," Russ said.

The first dog raised its head and sniffed the air. Snapping its jaws, it suddenly sprang forward. Russ swung his laser high and fired. The dog disintegrated into a sizzling mess, its body hitting the ground with a plop. The pack rushed at them, snarling and barking. They bounded effortlessly up the bank, bunching their rear legs to leap forward.

The lead dog came at Halle, snarling. Baring yellow fangs, it flew over the rocks. Halle flung herself backwards and fired upwards. A blinding flash exploded its body.

Before she had time to think, another dog hurled itself at her. Eyes fixed on her, it snarled, spewing saliva. She screamed and fired. It burst into flames, screeching. Burning pieces of its hide floated onto her oxygen mask. More dogs followed. She fired, sweeping the laser in an arc. The air around her was hot. Beside her, Russ moved about firing, cutting off barking and snarling abruptly. A choked off cry ended the attack and everything went quiet.

Halle, laser poised, waited. Nothing happened and she steeled herself to peer around the rocks. Burning carcasses smoked in the sunlight. She glanced around at Russ. He had stood up and was staring out at the slope below them. She flexed her shaking legs and searched the landscape. She couldn't see any more animals and sighed with relief.

"Can you see anything?" Russ called to her.

"Nothing. I think we got them all." She leaned against the rock.

"We don't have time to relax. We better move fast." Russ stowed his laser and began to climb down.

"They've all gone," Halle replied, securing her laser to her pack.

"There could be more of them. We don't know where they came from." Russ turned back to her. "There could be more on the way, as we speak."

"We have a good view up here. We would see them."

"I bet those dogs have an enhanced sense of smell. They can probably smell over huge distances. That's how they found us." Russ continued down the scarp.

Halle scrambled down, trying to avoid the patches of scree that sent her slithering towards the bottom. She pictured the dogs and shivered. Nasty creatures that could tear someone to bits. A horrible thought flashed across her mind. If mutant dogs had been created, what else? Something bigger and more vicious? She listened for animal sounds. She heard their own boots scrunching on the shingle, but there were no other sounds. Everything seemed peaceful, for now.

***

Halle couldn't forget the dogs as she hiked down the valley with Russ. The ground had become sandy again, slowing them down. Every so often, she glanced behind them, to check that they weren't being followed. She listened for animal noises and searched for paw prints in the sandy ground. Beside her, Russ seemed less concerned with the animals than with keeping to the rim of the valley, in the shadow of the mountains.

"I wish we could take a direct route," Halle said, as Russ deviated again from the straight, to follow the base of a mountain.

Russ scanned the sky. "We need to watch out for Unity. They might fly over this valley."

Halle's feet felt hot and sore in her army boots, and her pace slackened.

"We've got another twenty kilometers to cover. We can take a short break if you want." Russ gestured towards the shade of an overhang. "We can sit under that."

"That's better." Halle sat down and took the weight off her feet. "I'm looking forward to a hot meal."

"Don't hope for too much." Russ adjusted his mask to drink from his water bottle. "The base will be on a war footing. There'll be rationing."

"There's something over there." Halle pointed towards a circle of tall flat-sided stones that protruded from the sandy ground, about a hundred meters ahead of them.

"They look like ruins," Russ remarked.

"The storm must have blown the sand away." Halle squinted into the sunlight. A distant howl cut through her and she let out an involuntary gasp. "The dogs! They've followed us!"

"Come on." Russ jumped to his feet and pulled her up after him. "We can't stay here."

They ran across the sandy plain, Russ searching about them. "We need to find a good place to fight them."

The mountainside near them was mostly sheer vertical cliffs and Halle saw nowhere viable to climb. The sand became thicker making it hard going. The noises became louder and now she heard fierce growling. The dogs were nearly upon them. They had to find somewhere to stop and make a stand. The ruins loomed large in front of them. Within seconds, they reached the first of the stones, and they darted behind it. Swinging her laser up to take aim, Halle peeked around the stone.

She estimated that there were at least thirty creatures in the pack; a mass of reptilian flesh hurtling noisily towards them, with bared teeth. Their beady yellow eyes darted about, searching the ruins, above the rows of sharp teeth. They came on, barking and snarling, excited by the prospect of a kill, running in a vicious mass. Halle levelled her laser, ready to fire, waiting for them to come within range.

Suddenly, the creatures abruptly stopped running, almost as one. Whimpering mixed with snarls, they shied away, their tails flicking downwards, heads low.

"That's odd," Halle muttered, without taking her eyes off the dogs. "They're backing off."

"Something's stopping them," Russ whispered, looking puzzled.

"They don't like the ruins." Halle watched the dogs slink away, cowering from some unseen force.

"If we try to leave they'll come at us again." Russ stared after the creatures.

"Perhaps if we wait long enough, they'll lose interest." Halle lowered her weapon. The creatures had retreated but still lingered twenty meters or so away.

Russ adjusted his face mask and checked his air canister. "We should be near the base now. I'm going to try and raise them on the radio."

Halle listened to Russ speaking into his radio. "Base Four, this is Captain Russell Thomas formerly stationed at Central. Please respond."

Russ tilted his head. "I'm only getting static. There may be too much rock to get a connection."

"Try again," Halle urged.

Russ tried his radio again, shaking his head. "I can't get a signal."

Halle stared at the creatures waiting for them. They wouldn't survive another attack – there were too many of them. They couldn't stay in the ruins indefinitely either. They only had a few hours oxygen left. Her water was running out as well. Overhead, Taidor's sun was high, and it's harsh rays beat down mercilessly. She moved back further into the shade of the stone and saw that it had strange swirling markings on its side. She traced them with her finger, fascinated.

She heard Russ move behind her, and turned to him. As she turned she glimpsed something moving deep in the ruins. She craned her neck to get a better look, but it was gone. Suddenly, a deep howl ricocheted through the stones and the howl was taken up by more of the creatures until it was a cacophony. She peered around the stone at the creatures. They had begun to creep forward, preparing to attack.

Halle watched the dogs creeping forward, with bent legs and low slung bodies. They approached tentatively, with hind quarters bunched and teeth bared, snarling ferociously. About ten meters from the ruins, the pack paused. One of the dogs in the lead, raised its snout and sniffed the air, before letting out a high pitched shriek. The rest of the pack took up the call, screaming their cry across the ruins. The sound went through Halle like a blade. There was no mistaking the pack's intention.

"They're coming for us," she yelled to Russ. "We need to get further into the ruins."

"Go!" Russ replied. "I'll cover our rear. I'll come after you."

Halle scrambled through the ruins, heading towards a narrow alley, where parts of the original walls still stood. The ground was paved, but the stones were uneven. In places sand partially covered the surface, and she slipped. She put her hand on the wall to stop from falling. A shock, like electricity, struck her hand and ran up her arm. She snatched her hand away and gasped in surprise. Swirling patterns on the wall jumped out at her. For an instant, the center of the swirling pattern opened into a dark hole and she was falling down it. She swayed and suddenly Russ was there, gripping her arm.

"Don't fall." Russ held her firmly and pulled her upright. "You all right?"

"I think so…I got a shock from the wall," she said, dazed.

"The dogs have retreated. I'll try the radio again."

Russ spoke into his headset. Halle waited, hoping desperately that he would get through to the base. The dogs weren't going to stay back for long.

Chapter Seventeen

The shuttle flight to Three-Craters was full. Kalen boarded the flight with Paul Neill and Sera. The remaining nine seats were taken up by Colonization Division personnel. Kalen sat near the front with Sera beside him and Paul Neill on the other side. After leaving Central, they flew over desert and sandy plains, burning bright in the glare of Taidor's sun. Mountain ranges came into view and at times the shuttle flew through mountain passes, the peaks rising sharply on each side of it. Kalen saw no structures or vegetation out of the windows. He saw nothing of the Ea-Zone's military. All he could see was a dead desolate landscape until they approached Three-Craters.

The massive transparent dome covering the main crater stretched to the horizon, glittering in the sunshine. Beneath the dome, the sides of the main crater dropped two thousand meters to its floor, which stretched some forty kilometers in diameter. As the small craft flew around the western perimeter of the main crater, Kalen studied the new city below the dome. Construction had progressed since the last time he'd been here.

The terraces lining the crater's cliffs were visible and below them, built on the floor of the crater, row upon row of empty buildings were in various stages of construction. Elevated walkways, narrow passageways, parades of restaurants and shops, and open spaces, all constructed to appeal to the city dweller. A half-completed monorail track snaked through the buildings, high above the ground. As the shuttle swung north-east, Kalen saw the result of the recent conflict in the eastern section of the city. Tendrils of black smoke rose up from ruined and charred structures, and in places, there were dark gaps in the rows of buildings.

"Has there been much fighting here?" Kalen asked Paul Neill.

"We managed to squash the resistance of the Ea-Zone construction workers but the Ea-Zone sent troops. Most of the fighting was on the south-eastern side of Crater One but we quickly got that under control," Paul replied.

"What about Craters Two and Three?" Kalen recalled his briefing notes. The domes had been completed over the two smaller craters to the north and they had air, but building inside them was still at an early stage.

"A good portion of Early's forces retreated to Crater Two when the U-Zone began to get the upper hand. The final stages of the battle were fought out in Crater Two but that's over now." Paul Neill leaned in his seat to peer out of a hatch near him. "Ah… I see the shuttle port. Quite a feat of engineering."

"So there are prisoners here?" Kalen asked. Paul was trying to change the subject. He needed to know what had happened to the Ea-Zone military and workers.

Paul shifted his gaze to Kalen and his eyes appeared to darken. "Most of Early's forces were killed along with a good number of the workers. The survivors are being held in Crater Three and doing the building work there."

"How many prisoners are there?"

"I don't have that information but Javed might know. Some of the accommodation had been completed in Crater Three, so we're keeping them there, using the Gates to lock them in when they're not working."

"See how large the shuttle port is!" Sera interjected, staring out of the window. "It's grown since we were here."

Kalen looked out to the city below. The port had been built on the north-east perimeter of the main crater so that it could serve Craters Two and Three to the north. Built for interplanetary traffic, port control jutted out from the side of the main crater, over the airfield on the crater floor. A system of airlocks had been built into the dome above it. Before

Kalen could see the detail, the shuttle suddenly veered around and began a steep descent. He felt a shudder when the pilot switched from manual to port control, and the port's sensors took hold of the shuttle to pull it in on a set course.

Within minutes, the shuttle landed on a docking platform, on the roof of the dome. The pilot cut the engines and Kalen marveled at the sparkling roof, that surrounded the shuttle on all sides, like a vast silver sea. His view was quickly lost as the platform descended slowly through the system of airlocks, into the port, until it finally rested in a bay where maintenance crews waited for it.

"Good, we're here," Paul announced getting out of his seat. "Your colleague, Captain Ingeston should be here already."

The shuttle doors slid open and Kalen and Sera followed Paul out onto a ramp that led to the ground. At the base of the ramp, a young soldier in a black uniform and peaked hat, stood waiting. Twinkling flashes of blue light lit up his neck and jawline above the top of his jacket, and his figure cast a short shadow across the ground. When Paul approached, the soldier raised his right arm, palm forward, in a salute.

"Unity! Welcome to Three-Craters, Sir." The soldier lowered his arm. "I'm Captain Rajari. I'm to show you to your quarters."

"Unity!" Paul Neill returned the salute. "Thank you Captain."

The officer escorted them through the security checks and then led them away from the docking bay and the rest of the passengers, to a doorway numbered "D9", pausing to explain, "This route is reserved for senior personnel of nine or above." His eyes flickered to Kalen's Divine and he added quickly, "And their guests."

The door slid aside and they stepped into a wide, spotless corridor, with a floor constructed of a polished alloy, that deadened their footsteps. The walls were painted peach and ceiling lights gave out diffuse illumination. The air smelled fresh and clean, the supply units humming gently, providing a soothing ambiance. Speak stations were positioned every ten meters along the wall. The corridor eventually branched into two, each route guarded by the metal archway of a Gate.

"We've opened all the Gates, now that we're not using them," Captain Rajari informed them. "Except for the areas where we're keeping the Ea-Zone prisoners."

"That's good news, Captain," Paul remarked. "The birth of our new city will be with a unified population."

Captain Rajari took the right hand fork and carried on walking. "The city and the western accommodation blocks aren't habitable yet. Until the building is finished, the administration center – the central hub, is still located just south of the port and you'll be accommodated on the east side of the crater."

"According to my briefing notes, we're still mining on the south-east rim. We've got down to level sixty-three in that section," Kalen said. "I hope that it's easily accessible from my quarters."

"Yes it is, Sir." The officer stopped before a bank of elevators opposite a small lounge area. He motioned to Kalen and Sera. "Please will you wait in the lounge while I show Mr. Neill to his quarters. His accommodation is on level seven. I will return shortly. Mr. Neill, this way, Sir."

Captain Rajari left with Paul and Sera and Kalen went into the lounge. The walls were an appealing shade of light blue, and several comfy seats were grouped in a social arrangement. They settled into seats to wait.

"They must be housing Paul in one of the larger guest suites. They're usually reserved for high ranking Government personnel," Kalen said.

"I hope we've got good accommodation as well." Sera replied, gazing around the lounge.

"I'm sure we have." Kalen saw that Sera was staring vacantly at the walls.

After several minutes, Captain Rajari appeared at the door. "Apologies for the wait. I'll take you to your accommodation now."

The officer led them along corridors and then ushered them into an elevator. Pressing the keypad near the door, he indicated the handrails around its sides. "Please secure yourselves. The elevators in this block drop quickly."

Kalen glanced at Sera. She hadn't grasped the rail and appeared distracted.

"Sera, hold on. Get hold of the handrail."

Sera's head jerked up at his voice, her movement throwing a squat black shadow against the side of the car. He caught a glimpse of glazed eyes before they became aware.

Grasping the handrail Sera said, "I'm sorry, I was far away. It seems like a long time since we were here. I was thinking about how everything had changed."

"You must be careful, Sera." Kalen smiled at her. "Hold on to the rail."

The doors slid shut and the car dropped suddenly, falling thirty floors, pulling up sharply to a stop. The doors opened onto another corridor with the number twenty-eight written on its pale yellow walls. This corridor was brightly lit and Kalen realized that they had left the executive area. He felt a slight tremor from the floor and heard the base throbbing of the drills, still mining out the levels below. Their heart-beat pounding resonated along the corridor.

They followed Captain Rajari to their quarters and he left them at the door. Inside, Kalen could still hear the drumming of the drills. Sera wandered around their quarters, inspecting everything. The suite had a separate bedroom and living area, but no cooking facilities. We'll have to eat in one of the block canteens, Kalen thought. He pictured the food and his mouth filled with saliva that he had an urge to spit out. He grimaced and swallowed.

"What's the matter?" Sera had stopped pacing, and was staring at him. "Don't you like the rooms?"

"Oh nothing, don't worry. The accommodation is fine. It was just a passing thought about the war." He gave her a warm smile, hoping that his eyes weren't betraying him.

"Yes, it's hard to forgive the Ea-Zone isn't it?" Sera's eyes grew dark and the frown line between her eyes deepened. "They've killed a lot of our people. We should never have been expected to share the planet with them. They have no morals and no God."

"It'll be over soon." Kalen put his arms around her. Something sharp pressed against his chest and he stepped back. A glittering blue stone on a chain sparkled beneath her jacket. "What's this?"

"It's lovely isn't it." Sera took off the pendant and proffered it to Kalen in her palm. "Javed gave it to me as a leaving present before we set off."

Kalen picked up the stone. Immediately shards of energy prickled up his arm and he flinched. An image of the shadow wall blinked into his mind and the golden glow from the window beckoned him. If only he could jump through it into the light. If he had a pendant he could do that. He gripped the pendant hard. He wanted it more than anything he had ever wanted before, but something was wrong. Death lay on the other side of the window. He mustn't give in. In his mind, he stepped away from the window and raw fear swept over him. His hand began to shake and he dropped the pendant back into Sera's palm.

"It's very pretty but it's got a kick to it."

Sera laughed, and put it around her neck. "That's just the Uveid energy. You get used to it quickly. I'll get you one and you'll love it."

Sera began to take her jacket off and Kalen grasped her arms, stopping her. "I want you to listen to me. I'm worried about you wearing that thing. I don't think you should wear it. You don't know what it's doing to the baby."

"You're worrying too much," Sera said lightly, her eyes dancing. "A lot of people are getting these. It's harmless. I would know if it was bad for the baby."

Sera shrugged away from him and went into the bedroom. Kalen sat for a moment, thinking. This wasn't the Sera that he had met all those months ago, here, at Three-Craters. That girl hadn't been cruel or a fanatic. This was a different Sera. A Sera who was beautiful and confident. An affectionate Sera. A Sera influenced by the Uveid energy. The mother of his child.

***

Kalen left Sera in their quarters for a meeting with Jon Ingeston in the central hub. The booming of the drills followed him until he took an elevator and stepped out at the sixth level. Stopping at a small canteen on the way, he ordered a quick breakfast of coffee and biscuits. He bit into the first one and nearly gagged. It had a spongy texture and a sour taste. Why couldn't anyone in the U-Zone cook? Shaking his head, he abandoned the biscuits and swigged his coffee down. Perhaps lunch would be better.

He passed a number of Division personnel in the corridors, most wearing Uveid pendants that matched their uniforms, but none made eye contact with him. Dread sliced through him. Were they all infected by the Uveid? How much was the Uveid influencing their behavior? He had seen no construction workers, but that wasn't strange. They would be massing in the main mess hall for breakfast, before taking the large elevators down to the mines on the southeast rim. He had read that they were due to start work on the sixty-fourth level soon. There was still a long way to go before Three-Craters was complete, he reflected.

Jon was already waiting for him in his office and gave him the formal salute when he entered. "Unity!"

"Unity!" Kalen responded, his eyes flicking to Jon's neckline to see if he was wearing a pendant. Nothing.

"Take a seat." Jon gestured to a chair in front of his desk. "I've been here for a couple of days sorting out a problem with one of the primary drills on sixty-three. I've managed to avoid being in another battle. No more monorail repairs! Mind you, I hear that the fighting in Morten is fierce. I'm glad that I wasn't posted there."

Kalen drew a chair back and sat down. "There's still a lot of fighting in Morten, but Unity seems to be prevailing."

Jon remained standing and looked thoughtful. "That's what I heard but I think that Morten might fall. The word is that Early is gaining ground there."

"Do you have any news about Cherer or any of the other settlements?" Kalen asked.

Jon began to pace. "There's a rumor that Early is winning. We've taken back control of some of the smaller settlements and construction sites. Although Unity has Central and Three-Craters, they don't hold the rest of the planet."

Kalen was surprised. Early winning! "Is that true?"

"It's only a rumor at the moment, but I think there's some veracity in it." Jon stopped pacing and faced Kalen. "We have to be prepared. I don't like this conflict but if Early win, I don't think they're going to treat us leniently."

"You know that I came from Early, don't you?" Kalen paused, weighing up how much he should say. "Unity's view of them seems very harsh to me at times."

"Loyalty and belief is everything in this society, Kalen." Jon's jaw tightened and he gripped the back of his own chair. "Whatever your personal feelings, you should keep them to yourself."

"I understand," Kalen replied. What did he expect? That Jon would suddenly change sides and agree with him.

He cursed himself for being so stupid. He should have kept his mouth shut.

"Let's go over your design for the Uveid drill. There are one or two modifications I need to discuss with you," Jon said. "Overall your design is good, but I'm concerned about the geology of the areas where the mining will take place."

"I've got concerns about that as well. We usually cut through granite, but according to Sera and the other geologists' reports, the Uveid rock is brittle and will crack under pressure," Kalen replied.

"We've got a meeting set up later today with Paul Neill and Sera to visit the Uveid fields."

"Are those on level sixty of the main crater?" Kalen saw an image of bodies lying trapped in rubble.

"No, there was a huge rock-fall on that level. We've found a large Uveid field at Crater Two."

So Jon didn't know about the atrocity on level sixty. Perhaps this was the time to tell him. "I was told that the trident-weapon was used on level sixty to quell fighting by the Ea-Zone crews. Apparently the rock-fall trapped and killed about one hundred and fifty of them."

Jon went quiet for a moment and then said, "I wasn't told that. Do you mean the bodies are still down there?"

"Paul Neill told me that they trapped the workers. Their bodies are still there. I wouldn't want to be on the detail having to uncover that section." Kalen searched Jon's face. He thought he saw doubt and concern in his eyes.

"That's a problem for another day," Jon sighed. "Let's just deal with our immediate task."

"How far down is the Uveid at Crater Two?" Kalen asked.

"It's on level fifty-one. There's a huge underground cave with Uveid lining the whole length of one side. It was only discovered recently. The plan is to build a factory in Crater Two and mine Uveid." Jon swiped his fingers across his desk screen and pivoted it around so that Kalen could see it. The screen exhibited Kalen's design for the Uveid drill.

Kalen ignored the screen. "Have you been to Three-Craters before?"

"Why are you asking?"

"I'm just curious. This is a huge site. I was here before the war, but it wasn't so developed then. I just wondered whether you were ever stationed here?"

"I was posted here temporarily, before the war. I know the site quite well." Jon pointed at the desk screen. "About your design, I think that the lateral edge needs modification to allow for the brittleness of the rock. What do you think?"

Kalen considered Jon's suggested modification. Things were falling into place, slowly, piece by piece. Jon had been here before and knew the site well. Who better to keep a check on him? But Jon didn't have a pendant and he had never heard him utter religious fanaticism or seen him be deliberately cruel. Was he immune to the influence of the Uveid? Were some people immune and others vulnerable? Kalen could feel the draw of his own shadow wall. He felt it hovering on the edge of his consciousness trying to suck him in continuously, but he knew about the Uveid; he had been exposed before and had become aware. Perhaps that was the key to immunity, awareness of the alien influence.

Chapter Eighteen

Crater Two was just over a kilometer to the north of the main crater. A maze of underground corridors and walkways on different levels ran between the two craters. With no access at ground level, Kalen and Jon took an underground moving walkway from the shuttle port. Kalen had digested his briefing notes about the development of Crater Two during the previous evening. As yet, there was no sign of the small transport systems that would eventually run between the two craters above and below ground. Nor had the bulk of the building work been completed.

They arrived at an open concourse, boarded on one side by buildings and terraces that lined the crater wall, and on the other by a construction site. The sound of drilling and shouting traveled to them from the site, where men and large machines worked. The air had grit in it and Kalen found himself squinting his eyes in the dust. Above them, the transparent dome arced over the crater, sunlight poring through it.

"The lifts to the lower levels are this way," Jon said, guiding him towards the mouth of a wide corridor, ringed by the metal archway of an open Gate.

"There's grit in the air," Kalen remarked. "The air filters need adjusting."

"The fighting interrupted everything. They only resumed work two days ago, but it shouldn't be too bad below," Jon replied. "Level fifty-one was opened up several weeks ago, but they're not mining any deeper in that section until the extent of the Uveid seam is known."

"That's probably wise, given that the Uveid is unstable."

They passed under the archway of the Gate, and Kalen saw a bank of elevators ahead. A tall locker had been fixed to the wall, near the elevators, and Kalen walked towards it.

"It's okay, we won't need breathing gear below," Jon said. "Oxygen has already been installed through these levels."

"That makes things a bit easier." Kalen opened the locker door. "But I think we should still take hard hats and oxygen down with us, as a precaution."

"Okay, but we shouldn't need them. We've got radios already." Jon took the hat, oxygen canisters and rubber tubes Kalen passed to him. "I suppose it's better to be prepared."

"Have you been to level fifty-one before?" Kalen asked. Had Jon already been exposed to the Uveid rocks? Would he be affected by their energy field?

"No I haven't. I'm not usually involved in mining work." Jon put the oxygen and breathing tubes in his pack and put on his hard hat.

"Have you seen any of the other Uveid seams?" Kalen started for the elevator. "I mean, have you been exposed to the energy field before?"

"I've only seen those small pieces that people are wearing around their necks." Jon pressed the elevator controls and wide doors opened. "It feels like an electrical charge when you touch it."

"And you haven't got one?" Kalen continued, gripping the handrail inside the empty car. Would Jon change when he came into contact with the Uveid? Was he about to lose his colleague?

The doors closed and Jon selected the fifty-first level. "Those necklaces are being produced on site with the permission of the Site Commander. I can't see the point of wearing them, but they are becoming popular. I think they're a fad."

"A lot of people think the energy is invigorating. Apparently the charge in those small stones doesn't last long." Kalen wondered how much Jon knew about the pendants.

"When the charge dies, they're simply swapping the stones for another that's been recharged. I think they're producing the necklaces in an area near the shuttle port," Jon replied.

Kalen noted that the elevator car could hold at least thirty people. He imagined it bustling with workers, once mining the Uveid started. "I'm sure that you're aware of this, but when the miners encountered the Uveid seams before, a number of them suffered hallucinations because of the energy field."

"I've read that, but I don't think I'll be affected."

"I hope you're right." Kalen removed his hand from the rail when the car stopped. We'll see, he thought. Nearly everyone was affected by the Uveid, in one way or other. It was only a matter of degree. There was no reason to think that Jon would be immune. "Here we are."

The doors slid open at level fifty-one to reveal an empty vast natural cavern. Kalen estimated that it was over two hundred meters long and at least half that in width, its walls rising up twenty meters to the roof above. Lighting had been installed in the roof and around the sides, and rows of steel lighting columns ran along the floor, so that the whole area had dim illumination. Vertical fissures ran up the striated walls, patterning the dusty floor with long shadows in the artificial light.

"I can't see Sera or Paul," Kalen said. "They must already be at the far end by the Uveid seam, otherwise we would have passed them."

"I've only been in a mine a couple of times. I've never seen anything like this before." Jon stared around them.

"This is all granite. We usually have to drill out the floors to create the levels. We use the granite for the surface buildings. It's not unusual to come across a natural void like this cave, and when we do, the plans are changed to incorporate it." Kalen began walking. "The size of this is unusual though. We only occasionally come across caves this big."

"And there's Uveid here as well," Jon added, still staring around them.

"At Crater One we didn't find the Uveid until the forty-seventh level, although the machinery began playing up below level thirty. Mobile drills ran out of control for no reason or lost power suddenly. That sort of thing."

Jon turned towards him. "So you think there could be problems with mining down here?"

"Quite possibly; we know the problems are caused by the energy field. We'll have to find a way to compensate for that."

Kalen slowed his pace. Ahead of them, was a wall of dazzling blue stone. The cavern lights struck the crystalline rocks to throw out glittering blue patterns, as if the end of the cave was lit up by blazing blue fire. Nearer, Kalen saw that the Uveid seams were comprised of pools of tiny, pyramid shaped, blue crystalline stones. In places, the pools ran into each other, creating the impression of a wide deposit, and in other places there were gaps between the seams. The color of the stones varied between light blue and a deep indigo.

The sound of low voices echoed across the cavern, together with tapping and scratching sounds. Sera and Paul stood directly in front of the wall, silhouetted against the brilliance of the Uveid array.

"Be aware of the energy field. We'll be within its influence in a few meters," Kalen told Jon.

"I didn't expect it to be this beautiful," Jon remarked.

"You'll see when we're close up that there are grooves in the rock around some of the Uveid stones. When we first tested the trident-weapon, the grooves opened up and we collapsed the whole wall."

Paul and Sera swiveled towards them, as one. There's something unnatural about their movements, Kalen thought. He felt the terrifying presence of the shadow wall and forced the image out of his mind. He had been exposed to the energy field before and could resist the hallucinations, but the wall disturbed him. Beside him, Jon stared at the Uveid rocks, his face taking on a bluish tinge from the reflected light. His eyes were unfocussed and Kalen lightly touched his arm. "Sera and Paul are here, come on."

Jon started at the touch and turned his head. "Sorry, I was just lost there for a moment. This is amazing."

"Can you feel the energy field? If you think you're beginning to hallucinate, say something and leave immediately. I've seen a lot of miners get sick from the energy," Kalen advised him, as Paul and Sera approached them.

"No, I'm okay. My skin's prickling, that's all." Jon stopped walking and saluted Paul Neill. "Unity."

Kalen copied him. "Unity!"

Paul returned their salutes, his eyes bright. "The Uveid is stunning, isn't it?"

"Yes, Sir," Jon said automatically.

"It's impressive," Kalen agreed.

"Captain Ingeston, I don't believe that you've met Miss Ethern?" Paul stood to one side and ushered Sera forward.

"I'm pleased to meet you Miss Ethern," Jon said formally. "I've heard that you've done some excellent work with the Uveid stones."

Sera dipped her head modestly in acknowledgement. "Thank you Captain."

Paul turned towards the Uveid seams. "We've already started extracting small pieces of the Uveid stones, using hand tools. The drill machine you've designed has to be capable of extracting cubes of at least a third of a meter, to use with the trident-weapon. I think that sort of size will give optimum mobility while retaining enough of a charge to power the trident. Sera is going to explain where the best seams are."

"First of all, I want to show you the Uveid itself." Sera walked right up to the wall and shone a flashlight on a patch of Uveid. "You'll see that these seams are more dense than the ones we've come across before. There are no gaps between the little blue pyramids in the seam. There are no grooves running between them."

Kalen leant forward to examine the patch that Sera had lit up. She's right, he thought. These were solid patches of the stone, albeit of a spiky nature.

"Now look over here." Sera shone her torch to illuminate the edge of the deposit. "You'll see that the individual stones thin towards the edge of the seam. There are small grooves running between them in those areas."

"What's the significance of that?" Jon asked, peering at the rock face.

Sera shifted slightly and illuminated another patch of the wall. "Here you can see two large seams of Uveid. There's a gap between them, but there are grooves that run between the two seams. These grooves are much wider and deeper."

"So that makes these areas more unstable?" Kalen asked.

"That's correct," Sera confirmed. "Now I want you to see what's under the top surface of the deposits. The tiny pyramids only occur on the exposed face of the rock."

Sera walked towards the scraping sounds that were coming from a corner of the cavern. Six or seven miners, in light colored jackets and trousers, were busy chipping away at the face of the wall with hand tools, collecting small crystalline pieces of the stone in buckets. The beams from their powerful helmet lights bounced across the Uveid wall, lighting up thousands of the small crystalline protrusions, so that they blazed in varying shades of blue. The miners were focused on their task and ignored Sera and the others as they came up. All of the workers wore pendants around their necks, sparking in the beams from their lights.

Sera stopped near the workers. "These are for the pendants and experimentation. But see what happens when a piece of Uveid is chipped off."

Kalen watched the nearest miner use a hammer and chisel to extract one of the tiny blue stones. Where the stone had been removed, instead of granite underneath, he saw that there was a smooth blue crystalline surface. "How deep do the seams go?"

"According to my scanner, the seam at this point is over fifteen meters deep." Sera shone her flashlight towards the ceiling. "And about the same height."

"It's a huge seam. Do you think the drill you've designed will work on this?" Paul Neill asked Kalen.

"I've designed it as a mobile drill that can be ridden by one operator. It has four laser heads that are arranged in an adjustable square, to cut cubes up to a meter in diameter. Each of the laser heads is designed to adjust to a ninety degree angle, so that the inner side of the cube can be cut out cleanly," Kalen said. "I can't see any problems except for drilling near the deeper grooves. That could cause a rockfall. The mining captain will have to be briefed fully on the location of the deposits and the depth of the seams."

"It should be possible to have several drills running at the same time," Jon added.

"Good," Paul said. "Anything else you need to tell us, Sera?"

"No. I think that's all. I've got to map out the seams properly." Sera switched off her flashlight.

Kalen saw Jon sway slightly. "Are you all right?"

Jon briefly shaded his eyes with his hand. "I'm fine. I think it's just the wall."

Kalen scrutinized Jon's face, but he looked normal. He glanced at Paul and Sera. They stood staring at the wall while the miners near them continued to chisel away at the stones. He coughed to try and attract their attention.

"Is there anything else for us to see here?"

Paul turned around. "No, that's all for now."

"What about the tests on the original trident?" Kalen asked. He wondered where it was kept. Paul had an office in the central hub near the shuttle port. Perhaps it was kept there.

"I'm setting up those tests at the moment. We'll do the tests in Crater Three. I'll be in touch shortly about that," Paul replied. "You can leave now with Captain Ingeston. I want to talk to Sera for a while."

Kalen saluted and walked back to the lifts with Jon. He would get his chance to destroy the trident soon. But what then? If they traced the sabotage back to him, he was a dead man. He would deal with the situation when he got to it, he decided. Beside him, Jon was quiet.

"Are you feeling okay? Did you feel the energy field?"

"I felt it but I'm fine. I don't think we need any more modifications to the drill, now that I've seen level fifty-one. I'm going to recommend that the drill goes into production." Jon strode towards the bank of elevators.

"Aren't prisoners being used to do the building in Crater Three?" Kalen pressed the control panel to open the lift doors. "That's what Paul Neill told me."

"I don't know anything about that. I haven't been to Crater Three yet." Jon got into the car and selected the ground level.

"The last time I was there, the dome wasn't finished," Kalen remarked. "It must be substantially developed now, if there's a work force living there."

Jon frowned. "How many prisoners are they holding?"

"I don't know. Paul Neill said they were being held in the new blocks, and were doing the construction work. I'm surprised that Paul intends to test the trident there." Was he going to test it near the prisoners? Use it on them?

"Access to Crater Three is heavily restricted. I've heard rumors..." Jon glanced towards Kalen, his brow furrowed. "I won't add to them. We'll get our orders soon."

Chapter Nineteen

Crater Three was the smallest of the three craters, but still a substantial size. The dome over it had been installed and the air and light balanced. After going through checkpoints, Kalen came out of an underground corridor, into the crater. Like Crater Two, he found himself standing in an open area bordered on one side by a terraced cliff face, and on the other by a construction site. A wide moving walkway ran around the perimeter of the crater, with five tracks moving at different speeds, running in each direction. A gap ran down the middle of the walkway.

Kalen had agreed to meet Paul and Jon at the east perimeter of Crater Three. He stepped onto the outer track of the walkway, that crawled in an anticlockwise direction. Taking another step onto the next track increased his speed. The walkway quickly approached the construction area, but just before it, Kalen's view was cut off by a high wall.

"Of all the …" he muttered angrily to himself.

After a minute or two, the walkway emerged from behind the wall, to pass an undeveloped area. Kalen checked the time. He had half an hour before he was due at the meeting. He decided to go back to see the building work. He hopped over the tracks onto the middle gap, and then stepped onto the track going back. As it approached the wall, he stepped off and found an underpass that led to the construction site.

A tall building was being erected near the entrance to the underpass. A steel skeleton several stories high, was surrounded by three huge cranes moving girders and building materials. The floors were in place, but the outside walls were missing. Men and women were working on the building, some balancing precariously on the steel girders. They wore light covered overalls with "EA" written in large letters on their backs. Grey uniformed security guards roamed about the floors amongst them. At ground level, guards ringed the structure, each carrying lasers, their Divines shining brightly in the sunshine.

Behind the massive steel skeleton, more buildings were being erected. A row of huge structures rising upwards, each full of workers toiling under the eyes of their guards. *There must be hundreds of prisoners*, Kalen thought. *Don't they outnumber the guards? Why don't they escape?* A shout caught Kalen's attention. He glanced at the nearest building, where the sound came from.

"No!" a voice screamed.

A burst of light flared, high up the skeleton and a body plunged down, bouncing twice off the metal girders before it landed in a crumpled heap in the rubble. Kalen watched two security guards drag the body away by its feet. Something shiny attracted his attention. Restraints had been attached to the worker's ankles. *That's why they can't escape*, he thought. *They can't run.* He recalled the sort of restraints the military used. They were virtually unbreakable.

Rage hit Kalen like a fist in his gut. Unity were treating his people as slaves without any regard for their safety. He had to do something. He had to free them. His first impulse was to run at the guards and shout, but that would be suicide. He turned away, fury coursing through him and sprinted back to the moving walkway. Jumping on the anticlockwise track, he felt as if he would explode with anger. He took a few deep breaths to calm himself. He couldn't let Paul or Jon see how he felt.

He had been told to get off at "fifteen" and he counted the numbered posts. The walkway ran alongside half completed buildings as well as empty plots, but as it travelled eastwards, the building became sparse until there was desolate empty ground. No preparatory work had been done here, and the ground was raw sand and rubble. Near the east perimeter a solitary structure rose out of the flat landscape. Several floors high, it had walls and a roof, but appeared unoccupied. Nearby, Paul and Jon were waiting for him - with Sera. Kalen stepped off the walkway to join them.

Kalen saluted the group. "I didn't expect to see you here, Sera?"

"Paul asked me to come at the last minute," she replied, smiling brightly at him. She looks beautiful, he thought. Almost unnaturally beautiful. He squashed the niggling doubt worming into his mind. Weren't pregnant women supposed to glow with health?

"That's right," Paul added. "I thought it might be useful for Sera to see the test first-hand, so that she can report on how it affects the geology of the crater."

"As long as it's safe. I don't want Sera put in danger," Kalen replied. "Where are we testing the weapon?"

"I've had a team set up everything for the test over there." Paul gestured towards the crater's edge, a hundred meters away, where the cliffs rose vertically towards the roof of the dome.

A group of soldiers stood in the distance. As they got nearer, Kalen saw that the soldiers were guarding the trident-weapon, that lay on a bench behind them. Near the bench was a large cube of blue Uveid rock.

"We excavated it this morning using a prototype of your drill," Jon informed Kalen.

Paul picked up the weapon from the bench. "We're going to use the rock as the power source. If that works, we'll be able to use the trident above ground."

"We're going to test it on that building." Jon pointed to the large solitary building Kalen had seen.

A horrible thought crossed Kalen's mind. "Are you using the prisoners? Is there anyone in it?"

Paul laughed. "Of course not! They're more useful working on the construction site."

"I see," Kalen replied. Sera was looking at him curiously. He'd better say something else. "It wouldn't make sense to use good workers."

"Everyone get ready. Here goes." Paul held the trident in both hands and pressed the center prong. A high pitched noise came from the device followed by a clicking sound. Paul ran his fingers along the edges of the trident's prongs, and his eyes became unfocused.

He's seeing the shapes, Kalen thought. *They're in the energy field.* Could the shapes be a message or could they even be alien beings existing in an incorporeal form? He glanced at Sera. Her eyes had also become unfocused and she had tilted her face up, as if seeing or listening to something. He looked around at the soldiers. Their eyes had glazed over and they all stood with faces tilted upwards. Beside him, Jon stood silently. He wondered whether he was affected as well.

"Jon, have you seen the weapon working before?" Kalen turned towards him.

"Not yet, but I'm very interested to see what it can do."

The clicking from the weapon became louder and a base rumble began to reverberate around them. It echoed off the cliffs, seeming to bounce off their vertical face and the dome. Kalen turned around to survey the sheer walls of the crater behind them.

"Perhaps we should be standing further away from the cliffs?" Kalen suggested.

"Paul assured me that the weapon was directional," Jon replied. "But I take your point. Something's happening now."

The rumble became thunderous and tore through Kalen, filling his ears, so that he couldn't hear anything but the growling of rock and stone being torn away, and the groaning of the ground. Suddenly, an image of the shadow wall thrust itself into his consciousness, so that all he could think or feel was paralyzing terror, and the invitation of the golden window that would end it. In his mind's eye, spherical shapes floated on his side of the shadow wall and surrounded him, as if they wanted to push him through the window to the glowing world beyond the wall. *I'm hallucinating*, he thought. *I can't give in.*

The test building began to waver as if in a heat haze and the ground began to vibrate. Tremors tickled the soles of Kalen's boots and became stronger with each passing second. The distant crater walls, appeared to be tilting inwards and several black fissures streaked up them. The building in front of them began to shake violently and began to topple, stonework and metal tumbling from its roof. Around it, cracks had appeared in the earth, tearing it away in uneven chunks. The building swayed and then crumbled in a cloud of dust.

"It's tearing the ground apart!" Jon exclaimed, alarmed. "Why isn't it stopping?"

"It's causing an earthquake," Kalen shouted. "Paul, shut it off!"

Paul stood as if frozen with eyes glazed, gripping the weapon, his fingers playing along the outer edges of the prongs. Kalen looked behind them again. The nearest cliffs were holding. Paul was right about the weapon being directional, the devastation was all in front of them.

"Paul, you've underestimated the power, turn it off!" Kalen shouted.

"He hasn't heard." Jon took hold of one of Paul's arms and shook him, but he didn't respond. "Sir, you must turn the weapon off now!"

The ground around the building tore itself up. Huge chunks of rock sprang up, cracking the fabric of the surface, erupting from below. The disturbance widened into an area of sandy ground to the south of the structure. Sand and dust shot into the air, forming clouds that kicked and jumped about the surface. But there was something more. Kalen spotted large chunks of stone emerging, rearing up from the sand. Huge rectangular stones shooting up vertically through the sand, as if propelled from beneath, weathered to a dull grey. Patterns emerged amongst them, forming walls and doorways, streets and alleys.

"What is it?" Jon yelled beside him.

"They're ruins exposed by the quake," Kalen exclaimed, as the ground continued to crack and seethe, parting along jagged lines that ran outward from the initial destruction point. "Soon there'll be nothing left for us to stand on either."

"Stop!" Jon shouted at Paul. "Sir, you must stop. The weapon works, but stop now. We're destroying the crater."

A muscle in Paul's face twitched and he blinked. He widened his eyes at the ruins. Moving his hand, he pressed the center prong of the trident, and the clicking sounds stopped. The weapon went dead and he lowered it. In the crater, the rumbling died away and the earthquake settled. The ruins remained, standing proud amongst the sand and unlevel ground. Sera clutched the pendant around her neck and stared at the ruins. Kalen saw that the soldiers were also staring, and that some were holding their pendants.

Jon stood at Paul's shoulder. "Sir, it's thrown up ruins. Something was here before us."

"I can see them." Paul continued to stare straight ahead.

"We should call up an archaeology team. This is an important discovery. Do you want me to organize it?" Jon asked.

"I want to see the ruins," Paul replied, handing the trident-weapon to one of the soldiers. "Make sure this gets back to the locker on level five."

"It might not be safe to walk over there. We don't know how firm the ground is," Kalen said.

"He's right. It would be best to let the archaeologists go in first," Jon added.

"I want to see it as well." Sera stepped forward. "I can tell if the ground isn't safe."

"Sera, I don't think you should do this." Kalen touched her arm. "Let someone else check it out first. Those ruins could be dangerous. You don't know what's in there."

Sera ignored Kalen and began to walk towards the ruins with Paul. Kalen and Jon followed after them. The ground underfoot was uneven. In places, chasms had appeared that they had to jump over, and in other places, the fissures were so wide, they had to take detours. Paul and Sera walked ahead purposefully until they were several meters in front of Kalen. He couldn't hear any of their conversation and he glanced across at Jon who frowned as he watched his footing. At least he's still behaving normally, he thought.

"That weapon could destroy a whole city. If Paul hadn't turned it off, it would have brought the side of the crater down. We're lucky that the dome is still in place. And now they want to explore ruins, without checking they're safe," Kalen remarked.

"We could find more weapons," Jon replied. "I expect that's why Paul wants to get into the ruins first."

"Have you noticed how many people are wearing those blue pendants?" Kalen asked. "Everywhere, people seem to be wearing them."

"I did notice," Jon said.

"You still haven't got one?" Kalen enquired cautiously.

"No, and I don't intend to either. There's something strange going on. I've noticed that people get an odd expression on their face. Whenever I've mentioned it, they say that they're enjoying the energy charge."

"And you believe them?" Kalen pressed.

"I think there's more to it than that."

"Do you think it's affecting them? It is an alien energy." Kalen kept his voice low.

"It's possible," Jon conceded, sidestepping a large rock in his path.

They had come to a deep fissure and stopped at the edge. Kalen estimated that it was just over a meter wide.

"Jump it?"

"No, it would be better to go around." Jon began walking along the side of it. "I can't see how deep it is."

Kalen followed him over a narrow point in the fissure. "I saw the Ea-Zone prisoners today, working near the entrance to Crater Three. There must be seven or eight hundred of them."

"I came into the crater with Paul. He took the walkway straight up here, so I didn't see them."

Sand sucked at Kalen's feet and he stumbled before regaining his footing. "They're being held in the blocks on the west side. One of them fell from the top of a building. Both of his ankles had been cuffed."

"That's probably why he lost his balance. Stupid to cuff people if they've got to work high up," Jon replied.

They were nearing the ruins and Kalen had lost sight of Paul and Sera. He studied the shells of the ancient buildings, that in places stood a floor high. Strange markings had been carved into some of the walls and flat paving stones lay between the structures. A thin gritty layer of sand covered much of the stonework, and pools of sand had banked in corners. Kalen gazed around with interest. A settlement of some kind, he decided. Built by aliens who must have been a similar size to humans, but were probably a different shape. The sound of Paul's voice came from deep within the ruins.

"Let's find them." Jon started off towards the sound.

Kalen followed him along a narrow passageway, catching his boots on the edges of the paving stones. "I wonder how old the ruins are?"

"They could have been buried for centuries," Jon replied.

"Whoever built this must have created the trident. I wonder what happened to them?"

Jon shrugged. "We'll never know."

"Having ruins here will play havoc with the building program," Kalen said.

"I'm glad I work for the Army and not for the Colonization Division."

They rounded a corner and came into an open space in the middle of the ruins. There were three or four exits from the square, leading to other passageways, and the walls of the buildings were marked with circular patterns. At one end, a rectangular stone plinth stood between columns under an architrave. The columns had been set wide enough to leave room on each side of the plinth to walk by it. Paul and Sera stood in front of the plinth, staring up at the stone cross-beam, that had been carved with swirling patterns.

Neither Paul or Sera acknowledged their presence, their shadows merging with those of the columns. They stood silently staring upwards. Kalen remembered the cave on level fifty-one. They had stood staring at the Uveid wall in the same way. There had to be a connection. This was all wrong. Jon had to suspect it as well. He glanced towards him, but Jon was staring at something else. Kalen tried to see what had caught Jon's attention on the other side of the square. In the mouth of a passageway, for an instant, he caught sight of a translucent shape. Something akin to human size, but its form undulated fluidly, before it suddenly disappeared.

"Did you see that?" Jon muttered, still staring across the square.

"Yes, I'm not sure what it was," Kalen replied. "It could be an hallucination."

Jon raised his eyebrows. "Both of us?"

"Did you see something?" Paul was staring at them with glassy eyes. Sera had also turned towards them, her eyes blank.

"There was a shadow but it was probably just a trick of the light," Jon replied.

"Isn't this fascinating? There are patterns in the stone." The corners of Sera's mouth curled up into a smile that didn't reach her eyes.

"Do you think they have a meaning?" Jon asked politely.

"They might represent water." Sera drifted away from the plinth to stare at the patterns on a wall.

Paul touched the pendant he wore. "I haven't found any artefacts."

"I can organize a team to search the ruins thoroughly," Jon replied. "Are you feeling all right, Sir? You seem a little distracted?"

Paul blinked several times and then he smiled. "I'm fine. The test was successful. The trident is ready to use above ground. We already have a target in mind."

"Is the trident going to be duplicated first?" Jon asked.

"No, we need to use it now." Paul stroked the pendant he wore.

Kalen had been listening to the exchange. Now, he couldn't stay silent. "What is the target?"

"Morten." Paul's eyes glazed over and a wide smile spread across his face. "Early have gained too much ground. We'll use the trident to defeat them."

"Use it in a city?" Jon blurted out.

"Yes. We have no choice. It we don't, they'll have a stronghold."

"But the dome…" Kalen began. "If you destroy the dome, it will take years to rebuild."

"It has to be done," Paul said in a flat voice.

"Of course. Unity must succeed," Kalen said quickly, clenching his fists. First, it had been Javed and now it was Paul. Unity would destroy the planet. He had to destroy the trident before it was too late.

"I agree," Jon parroted the sentiment. "Early must be defeated whatever the cost."

Paul turned away from them, to stand by Sera in front of the wall. They seemed transfixed by the swirling lines that wound in circles over its surface.

Jon stared at Paul's back. "Sir, do you have any further orders? Are we finished here?"

Paul half turned. "Thank you Captain Ingeston. You may leave."

"Do you need me for anything else?" Kalen asked. So the trident was on level five. Perhaps he could find a way to get to it.

"No, that's okay. Go back with Captain Ingeston," Paul replied. "I'll come back later with Sera."

Kalen saluted and left with Jon. They were both quiet as they picked their way across the jagged landscape to the walkway.

"I've been told that Javed Durton is arriving at Three-Craters tomorrow," Jon said.

"Are you sure? I thought he was based in Central?"

"Yes, I was told officially." Jon jumped onto the moving walkway. "They must be going to co-ordinate the attack on Morten from here."

"You're probably right." Horror swept over Kalen. Unity would use the weapon from the air to attack Morten. He had to destroy the trident before it was too late. Somehow he had to do that today, now, while Paul was still at Crater Three. He tried to remember if he had seen the locked safe facility on level five where the trident was being kept. A metal safe inside a secure room. With tools he might be able to break in. As soon as they got back, he would make an excuse to Jon and go search for it.

Chapter Twenty

When Kalen got back to the main crater, he excused himself from Jon and took the elevator to level five in the central hub. He had been allocated an office in that section, albeit on a different level, and was ready with an excuse if challenged. The doors of the elevator opened onto a beige corridor with the number five prominently displayed on the wall. He glanced to left and right but the corridor was empty.

He walked down the corridor briskly, passing numbered offices and a small lounge. Eventually, he came to the wide doorway of a private meeting room. He recognized the room. He had been here before, when he worked for the Ea-Zone prior to the war. He punched the entry panel to open the door. The room was empty except for a table and chairs, but there was another door at the far end. He slipped inside, closing the door behind him and made his way to the other door.

The interior door led into a small room that contained a metal safe built into the wall. Kalen studied the locking mechanism on the front of the safe. It required a ten digit code. He couldn't disassemble it with his tools, and trial and error wouldn't work. He needed the code itself to break in. Who would know the code? Would it be recorded somewhere?

The answer came to Kalen in a flash. Paul had forgotten that Kalen had worked here before, for the Ea-Zone. He wouldn't have known that Kalen had been the most senior engineer on site. As chief engineer, he'd had access to secure information. He wondered if his original access codes still worked. Cancelling his access may have been overlooked by the administration here.

Kalen took out his handheld screen and searched the pages, until he found site administration. Using his original

Ea-Zone codes, he accessed the daily coding page for Three-Craters. Scrolling through the lines of codes, he eventually found an entry for locked storage, level five. He quickly entered the numbered sequence into the safe's digital display. A green light came on and the safe made a satisfying clicking sound.

Inside, the trident nestled in its box. Kalen took out the trident and put the box back in the safe, closing it quickly. He could be under surveillance or accessing the safe might have sent a message elsewhere. He twisted the trident about in his hands, feeling the metal. He needed to dispose of it carefully, somewhere where the pieces couldn't be found. He tucked it under his jacket and prepared to leave the room.

Jon stood at the inner doorway staring at him. "What are you doing?"

He eyed Jon. Would he set off the alarm? "Paul asked me to bring the trident to him."

Jon looked skeptical. "I don't believe you."

"He's working on a duplicate and needs it."

"Don't take me for a fool," Jon replied, scathingly.

"I can't let them use the trident. Morten will be completely destroyed."

"That sounds more honest. What are you planning to do with it?"

"Destroy it. Break it up into little pieces so that no one can use it." Kalen waited for Jon's reaction, keeping his face impassive. He had been caught in the act. If he couldn't persuade Jon to cover for him, he would have to kill him, and they both knew it.

Jon regarded him intently. "If the trident is missing they'll know it's you."

"I could deny it."

"You're not that stupid."

He's right, Kalen thought, the cold reality settling in his stomach. They'll know it's me. "I'll have to leave."

"What about Sera? You can't take her with you. You've got a life here. Are you really prepared to throw it all away?"

"Sera will be safe here until after the war. I can come back for her then."

"What you're proposing to do is treason," Jon said.

"Then turn me in," Kalen challenged him. He sensed an uncertainty in Jon, an indecision in his response. "Or join me."

Jon stared at him silently, as if weighing up his options.

"How did you find me?" Kalen could feel the trident digging into his side where he had hidden it.

"I was ordered to follow you. If you leave with the trident, I'll get the blame."

"Can't you see that Unity are crazy?" Kalen blurted out. "They're infected by those blue stones they wear around their necks. They've stopped thinking rationally."

"I agree, but there's nowhere to go."

"You don't seem affected by the alien energy," Kalen said.

"No. I can feel its presence but I seem to have an immunity."

"Some people are immune to it," Kalen replied. "I have to get out and warn the Ea-Zone."

"Warn them of what?" Jon said sharply. "Early know they're at war. If you take the trident to them, they'll use it against Unity. I can't let you do that."

"I promise I'll destroy the trident. I won't give it to the Ea-Zone. Just let me leave." Kalen took a step towards him. "I don't want to fight you."

"I'll be blamed. They'll execute me."

"Unity are holding hundreds of prisoners in Crater Three! Treating them like slaves!" Kalen exclaimed. "I have to tell the Ea-Zone about the prisoners."

"This is a war. I've watched my men become fanatics over the weeks and I've seen the atrocities. I've wondered about the blue stones, myself. They seem to change the way people think," Jon said fervently. "All that's true, but the Ea-Zone have committed atrocities as well. Why would the Ea-Zone welcome you back? Don't they regard you as a traitor for defecting to Unity?"

"What's the alternative, Jon? Stay here and watch the U-Zone rip the planet apart? Come with me. I'm sure they'll treat both of us leniently when they hear what we tell them."

"What about Sera? You're really going to leave her when she's pregnant?"

"She's infected along with the rest of them. She's loyal to Unity. Come with me." Kalen paused for a moment. "We'd have a better chance if there are two of us."

Jon didn't reply at first. He clenched his hands into fists and then relaxed them again. Taking a deep breath, he said, "Okay, you've convinced me. I don't want to betray Unity but you're right. Those blue stones are affecting people. Making them act weird. I have no ties here."

"You'll come with me?"

"Yes, but on condition that you destroy the trident, so neither side can use it. If you don't go through with it, I will kill you."

"I'll destroy it," Kalen confirmed.

Jon glanced back over his shoulder.

"Is someone coming?"

"Paul will be here soon," Jon replied.

"We'd better get out of here."

Jon turned to the door. "And find a way to leave Three-Craters."

***

Under Jon's authority they commandeered a small four seater shuttle at the port, under the pretext of surveying the area near Three-Craters. No one stopped them and Jon took the controls. Sitting beside him, Kalen considered their position. If they left now, they should get away before the theft of the weapon was discovered. He checked the fuel gauge. The shuttle only had a limited range.

"We need to join Early's forces," Kalen said, as they cleared the dome. "We don't have enough fuel to reach Morten."

"There's a refueling depot in the mountains." Jon adjusted their course so that they were heading south-east.

"Isn't it manned?" Kalen asked. The chances are we'll fly straight into Unity's troops, he thought. We'll have left Three-Craters for nothing.

"No, not usually," Jon replied. "Have you got a better suggestion?"

"Okay, let's head for the fuel depot. After that we can fly to Morten."

Kalen took out the trident and studied it. He tried to bend the outer prongs but the metal was too strong. Abruptly, a powerful image of the shadow wall thrust itself into his mind. Icy fear struck him. The golden window in the wall sucked at his consciousness imploring him to throw himself through it. Below his irrational fear, the voice of reason told him that to give in was death. He jerked his head up and stared fixedly out of the windscreen, focusing on the distant mountains, to shake away the intrusive image.

"Are you all right?" Jon asked him.

"The trident's affecting me," Kalen answered, turning his attention to the weapon again. "If I can break it into pieces, I could scatter them in the desert."

"There should be tools in that locker." Jon pointed to a compartment under the control console. "You might find something in there to smash it with."

Kalen opened the compartment and selected a small hammer. Laying the trident across the arm of his seat, he pummeled the prongs with the hammer, ignoring the growing feeling of terror that threatened to overwhelm him.

I mustn't give in to it, he thought. *I must ignore it, otherwise I'll become one of them.*

A crack appeared at the base of the center prong and he used pliers to snap it off. The tubular bits of alien metal began to get warm in his hands. He ignored the heat and turned his attention to the outer prongs. They were harder to destroy, but eventually he snapped the weapon into five or six pieces. The pieces were now hot and had a faint blue glow. He realized with a shock, that his fingers were paralyzed around the metal.

Jon gave him a sideways glance. "Get rid of it. I've opened the disposal chute for you. Put it in the chute and chuck it out!"

Kalen looked down at his hands. With an effort of will, he slowly reached for the chute underneath the console. Raw fear assaulted him and his heart raced, its beats accelerating until he thought his chest would burst. His head felt as if it was about to explode, with a growling thunder and pressure building in his ears. His hands felt as if they were a dead weight, and he fought to move them. One by one, he fed the pieces of trident into the chute, and watched the wind whipping the small bits of metal away as they fell towards the desert below.

"Good," Jon said, when the last piece had gone. "I hope that's the end of it."

The pressure in Kalen's ears subsided and normal feeling began to return to his hands. "It may not be. Paul was working on the duplicate trident. He told me that he thought he could get it working."

"Won't he need the original to do that?" Jon asked.

"I don't know," Kalen answered, flexing his fingers.

"The fueling stop is up ahead," Jon said. "You can't see it yet. It's hidden just on the other side of the pass."

Kalen surveyed the terrain around them. They were flying parallel to a range of mountains, over flat desert. To their left, a line of sharp rocky crags rose up jaggedly, overshadowing the empty landscape. Ahead, the range broke to form a pass, and Jon veered the shuttle into it, passing close by the vertical cliffs and jagged rocks that guarded the valley beyond. Once through the pass, Kalen saw a small metal building with a landing platform beside it.

Jon dropped the shuttle expertly onto the landing platform. "We'll need to get out to refuel."

Kalen handed Jon an oxygen mask and put on his own, connecting it to a canister at his belt. Jon did the same and they climbed out. The refueling equipment had been designed for easy use, and Kalen opened the shuttle hatch to access the fuel cells. Jon walked to the platform's control board and switched on the station's refueling mechanism. Suddenly, Kalen heard the crunch of heavy footsteps near him. He turned around. At least twelve black clad soldiers surrounded them, pointing guns. With lowered helmet visors, he couldn't see their faces.

The soldiers hustled them into the small building where an officer waited. He made a hand signal to his men, and two soldiers gripped Kalen's arms while another searched him. They found his hand laser and took it away together with the rest of his equipment. Jon struggled while they searched him as well. Their arms were stretched behind their backs and handcuffed. The soldiers said nothing and Kalen wasn't sure who they were. Had Unity been waiting for them at the refueling station? It was entirely possible. The theft of the trident-weapon must have been discovered by now.

"Who are you?" Kalen asked.

The soldiers ignored Kalen's question. He studied the design of their helmets and uniforms for a clue. The visors were full face masks with internal breathing equipment, designed to be worn in Taidor's thin atmosphere. Apart from the laser guns, their black jackets hid any other tools or weapons. They carried no backpacks. They haven't come far, he decided, as they forced him to kneel near the wall. Jon was shoved down after him. A soldier came to stand guard over them, while the others left the building.

The depot itself consisted of no more than a single room with a control console and two large hatches in the floor. Kalen assumed that the hatches led to the tanks and refueling equipment underneath the platform. There were no windows and the room had no oxygen. A clanking sound came from outside. Kalen realized that they were refueling the shuttle. He listened to the shuttle doors closing and then heard its engines start up. A few seconds later, he heard it ascend, the sound becoming faint as it flew away.

"Why are you keeping us here?" Kalen asked the guard again.

The guard didn't reply and Kalen whispered to Jon, "They have to be from the U-Zone. They must have tracked us here."

"They're checking our identities."

The guard was near them and Kalen kept silent. His thoughts were spinning. It wasn't going to take the soldiers long to find out who they were and what they'd done. Jon might be spared, but he would be denounced as a traitor and executed. They'd always suspected that his sympathies remained with the Ea-Zone. It could all be over very soon.

The heat of the day beat relentlessly on the low metal roof of the depot. The minutes began to stretch into hours and the room became hot. Kalen felt sweat trickle inside his shirt and cramp beginning in one of his legs. He shifted his position slightly and wriggled his hands about. He wondered what the soldiers were waiting for – they seemed to be in no hurry. Beside him, Jon pulled at his cuffs uncomfortably, grimacing at the perspiration pooling in his oxygen mask. The guard leaned against the wall watching them, casually twisting his gun about in his hands.

"How long are you going to keep us here?" Jon asked, but the guard didn't respond.

Suddenly, Kalen heard a low hum outside and heavy footsteps on the platform. Four soldiers came into the depot. Two of them took hold of Kalen's arms and pulled him outside, where a hover truck waited. Large enough to hold eight people, including a driver, the back was open with a flat interior. The soldiers pushed Kalen and Jon into it and climbed in behind them. Squatting against its side, Kalen watched the landscape slipping by as the truck skimmed over the sand towards the end of the valley.

"Where are you taking us?" Kalen asked.

"You'll find out soon," a female voice replied.

Kalen studied the guard. With helmet and full visor, and a bulky jacket, he couldn't tell who was behind the uniform. Being female gave no guarantee of leniency he reminded himself. He wondered if they would have a trial. He doubted it. Probably a few words to tell them why they were going to be executed, to make sure they understood.

The truck skimmed towards a tall jagged mountain, dissected by a large crevice that cut into its base. The driver steered the truck into it, so that they were moving between vertical rock walls. The crevice snaked into the mountain to end at the mouth of a large cave, a black hole in the shadows. The hover truck entered the cave and icy cold hit Kalen. He shivered in his damp shirt and blinked, his eyes adjusting to the darkness. Abruptly, the truck lights came on, illuminating the variegated sides of the cave. Deep inside the cave, the truck slowed to a stop in front of a smooth metal barrier. After a brief pause, the barrier began to rise, flooding the cave with bright light from the passageway behind it.

Chapter Twenty-One

Halle luxuriated in the comfort of her bed, savoring the welcome sense of security. Russ had made contact with Base Four and they had rescued them before the dogs came. Since arriving at the base, she had felt safe for the first time since the war began. She had been taken to the base with Russ, and treated to basic, but welcome, facilities. Built deep within a mountain, the base had a hidden shuttle port and three thousand troops were stationed here. Now plans were afoot to strike back at Unity, and regain cities lost during the first round of the conflict.

After taking a shower and dressing, she walked to the mess hall where Russ was waiting for her. One of three canteens, the hall was about half full with soldiers, eating and talking. The subdued rumble of chatter was broken occasionally by someone laughing and the cooking smells of fried tofu wafted across them. She glanced over the sea of black uniforms trying to spot Russ. She saw him on the other side of the hall, sitting with an older man with grey hair who she recognized as the base commander, and a female officer about her own age. They stood up when she approached.

Russ gestured to the two officers. "Halle, you've met Commander Callard, but I don't think you've met Lieutenant Abbott. We served together about two years ago."

"Commander, Lieutenant." Halle dipped her head.

"Please take a seat." Commander Callard gestured to an empty chair.

"Thank you." Halle sat down and crossed her legs. Commander Callard's brow was lined and he had hollows beneath his eyes.

The commander put his hands flat on the table. "When we first found you, we thought that you might be from Unity. We've discovered the badges they wear are called Divines and the numbers on them denote rank."

"We thought as much," Russ said, nodding. "We tried to steal the identities of the most senior soldiers."

"We've also had information that the U-Zone adhere to a set of beliefs known as the "Tenets of Cinall". Some of them have become quite fanatical. Their society has become highly moralistic."

"That doesn't surprise me." Halle clasped her hands in her lap.

"They tend to regard us as immoral and inferior," the commander explained. "It's become apparent that they have no regard for human life, or rather I should say, the lives of anyone who doesn't adhere to their beliefs."

"They were murdering people in Central. They set the Gates to kill and were pushing people into them," Russ informed him.

"That accords with our intelligence." Lieutenant Abbott's eyes were tinged with sadness. "They haven't been taking prisoners in Central."

"Well there's something more." Commander Callard leaned forward. "Their behavior is being influenced by a blue rock that was found on this planet. It's an alien mineral, called Uveid. It gives off energy that affects people."

"I know about the Uveid," Halle said. "The miners got hallucinations. My chief engineer didn't want to build on it."

"Well, it's worse than hallucinations. Most people who come into contact with it are affected. Their personalities change as if they've been taken over by something."

Russ folded his arms. "Perhaps they have."

Commander Callard gave Russ a hard look. "That's how we're treating it. The energy affects them and they change. They stop caring about human life."

"Does everyone change?" Halle asked.

"No, a few people are immune," the commander replied.

Russ shuffled in his seat and frowned. "One of our group said something very strange before he died. His behavior was odd."

"There's something else as well. The ruins we found you in, are alien. This planet was occupied before humans came here."

"But they must be extinct?" Halle speculated.

"There's nothing alien living on Taidor," Commander Callard continued. "The six legged creatures you ran into are genetic mutations, created by us."

"Nothing in corporeal form, but the Uveid energy changes people," Lieutenant Abbott said. "The rocks have affected people in the Ea-Zone as well as the U-Zone, so we're taking counter measures."

"So how can we guard against it?" Russ asked.

"We've designed a special alloy lining for our helmets that protects the brain," Lieutenant Abbott confirmed. "They shield our troops from the effect of the alien energy."

"The troops wear the helmets anytime they're near the Uveid deposits," Commander Callard added.

"We've got a problem with people who've already been affected. They don't seem to recover and we can't trust them." Lieutenant Abbott wrung her hands.

"The miners' hallucinations were only temporary," Halle mused. "They recovered."

"They mustn't have been exposed to the same degree, or perhaps the energy is getting stronger." Lieutenant Abbott shrugged. "All we can do is try to avoid getting infected in the first place."

"I'll leave you to your breakfast." Commander Callard stood up, pushing his chair back. "I'm liaising with the other bases about a joint offensive on a major target. I'll brief you both about this in the next day or two."

***

Kalen sat on the bunk and stared around at the stark windowless cell. He had been separated from Jon and bundled into the room, which had a bunk and small shelf fixed to the wall. The cell was cold and had a hard shiny green floor and white walls. Harsh bright strip lighting ran across the ceiling and security cameras were inset high in the corners. His helmet and mask had been taken away and he had been uncuffed. He rubbed the sore red rings around his wrists where the cuffs had cut in. My own fault for struggling, he thought.

He wondered what would happen next. Surely they'd traced his identity by now. Were they arranging a trial for Jon and him? Perhaps Unity were organizing a show trial. They would take them both back to Three-Craters or Central and make an example of them. Execute them so that everyone knew what happened to traitors - like him.

The cell door slid open and a grim faced soldier entered carrying a water bottle and plate of food, which he put down on the shelf. He didn't make eye contact with Kalen and left briskly, the door sliding shut behind him. Kalen got up and inspected the food. It was some kind of vegetable casserole with bread, and smelled good. He noticed the spoon beside the water bottle and smiled. At last, something decent to eat.

After eating the food and drinking half of the water, Kalen lay down on the bunk. It had been a long day, and he was tired. If they were going to put him on trial, there was nothing he could do about it at this moment. He dozed off and began to dream of Halle. He was holding her, the light shimmering on her blond hair. She tilted her chin back and laughed. The melodic cadence of her voice and large blue eyes made him forget about everything else. She had her arms around his neck and he was kissing her.

The sound of boots in the hallway brought him awake with a start. How he missed her. He should never have let her go.

The cell door opened and a soldier put his head in. "Come with us."

Kalen shrugged off his drowsiness and got up stiffly. Outside the door, the corridor smelled of cleaning fluid. More green floors with white walls, and strip lighting across the ceiling. Three guards waited for him, their lasers holstered at their belts. They stood aside as he came out and then two moved to his sides, while the third took the lead. He was marched through a complex of interlinking passageways, until they reached a wide door. The lead soldier paused briefly to press a control panel, and the door slid aside. Inside, an officer sat behind a desk, and Kalen was pushed to stand in front of him. One of his guards stood behind him, while the others waited outside.

"I'm Commander Callard, in charge of this base. You are in the Ea-Zone. Who are you, Number Two?"

Kalen was taken aback. If this was the Ea-Zone, they would have recognized his name. They'd scanned the identity chip in his wrist. Were they trying to trick him? Was he still in Unity? Were they trying to make him believe that he was in the Ea-Zone to see what secrets he would give up? He stared at the commander. He wasn't wearing a Divine. Now that he thought about it, none of the soldiers had worn them. There were no signs of Unity here. The food was better too.

"Well?" the commander demanded. "Say something! Your badge designates you as menial, but you're wearing a chief engineer's uniform. Who are you? What were you doing at the fueling depot?"

Kalen stood squarely and clenched his hands behind his back. "My name is Kalen Trinneer." Surely they knew that he'd originally defected from the Ea-Zone to Unity?

Would they call him a traitor? Or listen to what he had to say?

"Untrue!" the commander snapped. "The real Kalen Trinneer is dead. Try again."

"I am Kalen Trinneer. I worked in the Ea-Zone before I went to Unity," Kalen replied steadily, meeting the commander's eyes. "I was trying to escape from Unity and get back to the Ea-Zone."

"Hmph…Even if I was to believe that, you were found with an U-Zone officer?" The commander glared at him, rapping his fingers across the desk top.

"We were trying to get to the Ea-Zone to warn you." Was there anything that he could say that would prove who he was? Even if he did, why should Early believe him? He had defected to Unity and they must believe his allegiance lay with the U-Zone.

"Where did you come from? Warn us about what?" Commander Callard raised his voice.

"We're from Three-Craters. They're holding hundreds of prisoners there. They're planning a large attack on Morten," Kalen replied. He stood at attention keeping his chin up. He had to be believed. This was their only chance. If Morten fell, Unity would take the lesser cities one by one. "You have to stop them!"

The commander's lips thinned. "I don't believe a word you're saying. The real Kalen Trinneer wouldn't come back to Early. This is a trap. Officer, remove him."

Kalen felt a hand on his arm and he resisted the tug for a moment. "I'm telling the truth. You have to believe me."

Commander Callard stared at him, his mouth twisting as if he had tasted something unpleasant.

***

Halle had been asked to assist with the work of the base, and she made her way along the corridors to her office. She found Base Four claustrophobic after living in Central. She was used to the openness of the domed cities and constant sunshine, whether natural or artificial. The base was built inside the mountain, although extending to many levels. The corridors stretched interminably, the levels painted different colors. Everywhere, the lights were harsh and the furnishings utilitarian.

She had been allocated a desk in one of the offices near central command. She shared the office with five other people, all army, and they were busy at their stations. She found her own desk and switched on her viewscreen. Her first job was to assess the adequacy of the armaments stored at the station. This is going to be tedious, she thought. She had lists of personnel and weapons held at the base. She envied Russ his role at central command in the main control room, at the heart of the action. Scrolling through the pages of equipment, she thought about her life before the war. How different everything was then. She wished she could go back, to just one of those carefree days.

Suddenly the page she was reading blinked out, and Sun Hider's face appeared on her screen. "Good morning, Miss Rison"

"Good morning, Sir." Halle sat up straight. What did he want? Where was he?

As if reading her mind, Sun replied, "I'm still in Central, Halle. I should have warned you I was about to call. I'm glad to see that you're safe."

"Thank you, Sir." Halle composed herself. "I didn't realize that the Ea-Zone still held parts of Central?"

"We've managed to hold the southern section of the city, but our forces are greatly diminished. If we're not relieved soon, we're going to have to pull out entirely." Sun's jowls wobbled.

"I'm sorry to hear that, Sir. What can I do for you?" Halle asked.

"I've had a very strange call from Commander Callard, asking me to verify the identity of a man who was captured yesterday about thirty kilometers from Base Four." Sun glanced down at a pad on his desk, just within Halle's view. "Two men were found at the depot refueling a small shuttle. They were both from the U-Zone and one was dressed as an army captain and the other as a chief engineer. They claim to have come from Three-Craters."

"I heard that two men had been detained," Halle replied. "But no details."

Sun continued, "The commander called them a "two" and an "eight." He said that they had some wild story about prisoners at Three-Craters and a plan to attack Morten."

Halle waited for Sun to go on. What did this have to do with her? She knew nothing about Unity.

"I've been asked to verify the identity of one of the men. The engineer said he was Kalen Trinneer and that's the name on his micro-chip, but the information on those chips can be falsified. The man looks like Chief Trinneer, but Unity could have also altered his appearance. It's easily done. We had reports that the real Kalen Trinneer is dead. Are you all right? You've gone very pale," Sun asked with concern.

Shock spiked through Halle and she felt the blood drain from her face. She gripped the edge of her desk as nausea swept over her. Kalen alive? An image of him flashed into her mind; his even features and the way the corners of his mouth crinkled up when he gave her a wide smile, displaying his perfect white teeth. Impossible. It couldn't be him.

"It can't be him, he's dead."

"I know and I'm sorry to have to bring this to you, but you knew him well and you're there, at the base. I want you to see this man, so that we can put an end to this nonsense." Sun leaned forward and said earnestly, "Don't distress yourself too much over this. Just see him for a couple of minutes to confirm that it's not him. I'm sure he's an imposter."

"Thank you, Sir." Halle felt herself trembling. It couldn't be Kalen. No one could have survived the strike on the headquarters building.

"Commander Callard will arrange for you to be taken to see him. He's waiting for your call. If you speak to the man, you should be able to tell if he's Chief Trinneer straightaway."

"Of course, Sir," Halle said. "I'll report back once I've seen him."

"Good." Sun Hider gave her a faint smile. "I'll look forward to hearing from you soon."

Sun Hider's face blinked out and Halle found herself staring at the list of armaments again. She uncrossed her legs; she had been holding them rigid. She trembled. Take a minute, she thought. The man couldn't be Kalen. That would be impossible. He was dead and Unity knew that. This was a trick to put a spy inside the base. She called Commander Callard.

His face appeared on her screen. "Miss Rison, you've spoken with Sun Hider?"

"Yes, he's told me that you're holding someone who says they're Chief Trinneer?" she answered steadily, trying to stop her voice from rising.

"That's correct, Miss Rison. We've detained two men. Neither of them are showing symptoms of the alien infection. One of them says he's Chief Trinneer. I'd like you to speak to him. I understand you knew the real Chief Trinneer well. I'll send someone to take you down to him. Can you go now?" Commander Callard asked. Halle could hear the noise of other voices behind him.

"Yes, of course," Halle replied. "It can't be Kalen Trinneer, Commander. He died when headquarters in Central was hit."

"We have to be sure. Please call me as soon as you've seen him." Commander Callard turned his face slightly, as someone came up behind him.

"Yes, I will." Halle waited for Commander Callard to turn back to her.

"Thank you, Miss Rison." The commander broke the connection, and Halle switched her screen off. She didn't feel like working on the long lists again today.

Within minutes, a young soldier entered the room and came to her desk. He was dressed as a private in a smart black uniform but had no hat. Clean shaven with short blond hair, he was clear eyed. *He hasn't seen any action yet*, thought Halle. In the midst of the war, there could be very few soldiers who hadn't been in combat. How long had the army been stationed at Base Four? With a shock Halle realized that Early must have been preparing for war, to have troops stationed at the base, ready for the conflict.

"This way, Ma'am," the soldier gestured her to follow him. "We keep the prisoners on the lower levels. We have to take the elevator."

Chapter Twenty-Two

Kalen had been taken back to his cell and left there. He hadn't passed anyone in the corridors or seen Jon. Once his cell door had closed, there had been silence. Would they check his identity again or simply keep him locked up? Jon would corroborate his story but why should they believe him either? These people didn't seem to be possessed like the U-Zone people. They weren't wearing Uveid stones around their necks. But that was no guarantee that the madness hadn't reached here.

He heard a whirring sound and part of the back of his door changed into a black rectangular screen. He realized that the door had a double layer. They could open it fully or slide one layer back to see through. Someone was out there watching him. They could already see him through the cameras, so perhaps they were coming in. He stood up from his bunk, straightened his jacket, and faced the door. The door slid aside with a hiss. A young soldier blocked the exit, holding a laser.

The soldier pointed the laser at him. "Sit down!"

Kalen took a step back and perched on the edge of the bed. Sitting put him at a disadvantage. It made him appear weak and forced him to look up at whoever came in. The soldier came into the cell and stood to one side of the door. A small woman stood in the doorway behind the soldier, dressed in a sky blue jacket and trousers, the uniform of the Colonization Division. She had light blond hair, cut neatly at a level with her chin. She had pursed her lips giving her an expression of distaste. Her large blue eyes were the same color as her uniform and they opened wide when he met her gaze.

"Halle?" Kalen jumped up.

The soldier darted forward and shoved him back with the butt of his laser. "Sit down!"

"You can't be…" Halle stared at him. "The real Kalen Trinneer is dead. You're a fake."

"Halle, who told you that?" Kalen felt the shock hit his mouth and his throat constricted. Halle, alive and well, but her face betrayed her suffering in the war. Fine lines had appeared at the corners of her eyes, and between her eyebrows. Her lips were flaking and she wore no make-up. "It's me."

Halle's eyes bore into him. She opened her mouth as if to say something, and closed it again. He saw her hands trembling, and then she clutched them together in front of her. She stood frozen, staring at him. Memories of their time together came flooding back. Halle laughing and giggling at his jokes. Halle passionately kissing him. Holding her, warm and soft in his arms. The familiar ache whenever he smelled her perfume. He wished that he had never left her. What had he ever seen in Sera? But it was too late now.

Kalen extended his hands, palms up, in supplication. "It is me, Halle. I went to the U-Zone because my life was in danger. The Ea-Zone wanted to silence me when I exposed the problems with the building program."

The color drained from her face and she said stiffly, "The real Kalen was killed at the beginning of the war. You can't be him."

"I didn't want to leave you," Kalen tried again. *She must know it's me*, he thought. *What else can I say?* "I wasn't leaving you. I had to go; I had no choice. I've thought about you ever since. I was at Division headquarters when the war started. I tried to get back to you, but couldn't."

"Headquarters was burnt down during the first skirmish," Halle said resolutely. "Everyone in it was killed. There was nothing left of it."

"The command center was set up in the underground levels." If he could remember something that only Halle knew, she might believe him. "Before I left, you visited Sera Ethern in the hospital. You were jealous of her."

Halle flinched and put her hands up to her mouth. "How do you know that?"

"Sera told me. I went to see her. You tried to warn her off me." Kalen watched the uncertainty in Halle's face.

"It is you, isn't it?" Halle swayed slightly.

"Ma'am, we should leave now." The soldier hustled Halle out of the door and it slid shut behind them.

***

Halle Rison stood shaking in the corridor, thoughts crowding her mind. *It couldn't be Kalen, but it was.* A frisson of recognition had struck her as soon as she'd seen him. He had looked the same, although a little tired. He had sounded the same. When he'd met her eyes, she'd known it was him, although at first she couldn't believe it. Had he changed? What had happened to Sera Ethern? She had left the Ea-Zone with him. A pang of jealousy hit Halle. Sera Ethern had taken Kalen from her. *Kalen loved me, not Sera,* she told herself. She'd always viewed Sera as a temporary fling, and then when she'd heard that Kalen was dead, she had discounted her entirely. Was Sera Ethern still alive?

"Ma'am, I'll take you back to your office now," the young soldier said.

Halle dabbed an unbidden tear from the corner of her eye. "Yes, I must report to Commander Callard immediately."

"This way," the soldier ushered her towards the elevators.

The soldier led Halle back through the corridor. An image of Kalen standing in the cell, filled her mind. She tried to push the picture aside and focus on something else. She looked around at the corridor. The lower level seemed sterile and unfriendly. It was meant to be that way, she decided. She wondered how many prisoners Early was keeping down here. There was no way to tell. No sound permeated the passageways from behind the thick metal doors. The white walls reflected the harsh lighting, unbroken by any kind of decoration. She followed the soldier mutely back to her office and then called Commander Callard.

The commander's face filled her desk screen. "Halle, how did it go?"

His familiarity warmed her. "It's him, it's Kalen Trinneer."

"Are you sure?" The commander looked surprised.

"Yes, it is him. I recognized his voice. He said something about Sera Ethern only he would know." Halle's voice wavered and she began to tremble.

"I wonder what he's doing here? He's got some explaining to do. Defection to Unity and then coming back?" the commander replied.

Halle swallowed hard and said briskly, "He left the Ea-Zone because of problems with the Division. I can vouch for that. I don't know why he's come back."

"Well, we'll debrief him and get all the facts. Perhaps he can give us some useful information about Unity's plans. I may need you to substantiate what he tells us. That's all for now." Commander Callard terminated the call.

Halle sat staring at the blank screen. Kalen was back, but she had Russ now. Kalen had betrayed her when he'd left with Sera. She couldn't trust him and their relationship was over. It was in the past and had to stay there. Russ was steady and perhaps he loved her. She could never feel the same way about Russ, as she had for Kalen. But Kalen had made her jealous and insecure, and in the end she had been right. He'd cheated on her with Sera.

***

A few days later, Halle sat in one of the small lounges of the base, waiting for Russ. It was empty and she'd found a comfortable chair to sit in while she waited for him. Over the previous days she had had trouble putting Kalen out of her mind. She had learned that he was still imprisoned with the other man, on the lower level. Knowing that he was so close, if unseen, tortured her. She couldn't stop thinking about him. The memories of their time together before the war, kept flooding back.

Russ appeared at the door holding two cups of coffee. He handed a cup to Halle and sat down. "Are you all right? You've been very quiet lately."

"I'm fine." Halle attempted a weak smile. She'd avoiding speaking to him about Kalen.

"The commander told me that you know the engineer from the U-Zone?" Russ was watching her closely.

"Yes, they asked me to verify his identity." She studied her coffee cup. How much did Russ know? Did he know that Kalen had been her lover?

"Something about him defecting originally from Early?" Russ pressed. "It sounded like a strange story."

"He left a few months ago and went to the U-Zone," Halle said neutrally.

"Was he a friend?"

Halle found herself avoiding Russ's gaze, afraid that her eyes would betray her. "I was his manager and he reported to me."

"Why did he leave?"

"He was under pressure from the Division to falsify a report that affected the building program. I thought he was dead."

"He told the commander that he's married and his wife's pregnant. A geologist, I think. He says that she's at Three-Craters and he's worried about her."

Russ's words hit Halle like a hammer. She went cold and gulped down a mouthful of her coffee. Searing jealousy knifed through her. She stared at Russ. Did he know? She couldn't read his expression.

"Did he say why he's come back?" Halle asked.

"He's got information about Three-Craters," Russ continued. "Apparently they're holding prisoners there."

"I hope it's useful," Halle replied, trying to keep her voice steady.

"It may be. The base is on standby for a big offensive. How well did you know the engineer?" Russ drained the last of his coffee and put his cup down.

Halle felt her face redden. Anger suddenly coursed through her. She was stupid to feel anything for Kalen. Stupid, stupid, stupid! She'd thought him dead, when all of this time he'd been carrying on with Sera. He'd probably never even thought about her since the day he'd left.

"I worked quite closely with Chief Trinneer, but he was often away on assignment."

"I mean, do you think he's trustworthy?"

"Yes, I do," Halle said immediately. In his professional life, if not his personal life, she thought. "I think the Ea-Zone can rely on what he says."

"Good. The commander has to be sure before he orders an attack," Russ answered.

"An attack? On where?" Halle put her coffee cup down.

"If there are prisoners at Three-Craters, we have to get them out," Russ took hold of her hands. "Only Chief Trinneer and the other man, Captain Ingeston, know where they're being held."

"He's being sent back?" Halle asked. Kalen had only just come back into her life and now he was leaving again. Something wrenched inside her and she began to feel sick.

"If the commander decides to send him back, he won't be alone. He'll be sent in first with a small task force, to sabotage key installations. The prisoners will be released during the main offensive, after that."

He's not telling me everything, thought Halle. Something about Russ's expression, the way he avoided her eyes, made Halle wary.

"You're going with Chief Trinneer, aren't you? That's why you're telling me this?" Halle's heart missed a beat. She didn't want to lose him as well.

"Probably," Russ said, gazing at her frankly. "I haven't got final orders yet."

"If there's going to be an attack on Three-Craters, I want to take part," Halle blurted out. "I don't want to be left here."

"You're not a soldier."

Halle folded her arms. "I've had combat training. I've been to Three-Caters so I know the site."

"I'll see what the commander says."

"I'll ask him myself," Halle replied defiantly. "I can be of more use taking part in the assault than staying here, sorting out the filing."

Russ laughed and stood up, pulling her out of her seat. Putting his arms around her, he gently stroked her hair. "You like being in the center of the action, don't you?"

"Don't patronize me!" Halle snapped at him.

"Of course not." He laughed again, and when she opened her mouth to reply, he planted a kiss on it that silenced her.

***

Kalen and Jon sat in front of a curved table in the briefing room, answering questions from Commander Callard and Lieutenant Abbott. Kalen had been questioned by the commander on several occasions over the past few days. Most of the questions had been about the prisoners held at Three-Craters, but he had also questioned Kalen about Sera; her role, her attitudes. He had challenged Kalen to convince him that he would have left her voluntarily. Kalen felt pangs of remorse and guilt whenever he thought about Sera. He had tried to explain that she was safe, that he'd believed that it was his duty to return to the Ea-Zone with the information he had.

Kalen imagined that Jon had gone through a similar grilling. Today's interview was the first time that he had seen him since their detention. He wondered if Jon had convinced the commander of his sincerity. The fact that he had made the decision to leave Three-Craters with Kalen, must weigh in his favor, he mused. This session was focused on the trident-weapon and Kalen waited patiently with Jon, while the commander consulted his pad, resting on the table in front of him. At last, the commander raised his head and stared at them with hard eyes.

"I want to speak to you about the weapon that Unity has developed. We heard that it was used at Three-Craters with a large loss of life."

"I believe that's correct, Sir," Kalen said. "The weapon is an alien artefact that uses the Uveid energy to cause rock-falls or earthquakes."

"And you say you destroyed it?" The commander asked sharply.

"I've destroyed the original, but Unity was attempting to duplicate it," Kalen replied.

"This artefact. You say that it is a weapon?" Lieutenant Abbott tapped her fingers on the table.

"It might not have been created as a weapon originally," Kalen replied. "It only works with the energy from the Uveid rock."

"So who made it?" Lieutenant Abbott asked.

Kalen glanced at Jon and replied, "There are ruins in Crater Three. There were aliens on Taidor before us. It's likely they made it."

"We've also found ruins a few kilometers from here," Commander Callard added. "No sign of life, though."

"The weapon is useless without the Uveid stones. Unity plan to mine the Uveid in Crater Two," Kalen continued.

"And you say that people seem possessed after coming into contact with the Uveid stones?" Commander Callard stared at him intently.

"I think there's something in the energy," Kalen replied. He suspected that they were testing him; that they already knew that the Uveid infected people.

"Alien?" Lieutenant Abbott fixed him with a piercing stare.

"Yes."

"Isn't that far-fetched?" the commander asked.

"Not really. I've seen shapes in the energy." Kalen's gaze swept across them all. "People have started wearing the stones around their necks. They want to mine the rock and use the weapon."

"If there are aliens in the energy they would be incorporeal. They couldn't have built the ruins or the trident," Lieutenant Abbott said reasonably.

"I think there's a connection," Kalen said. "I just don't know what it is yet."

"It might not be important," Commander Callard opined. "What is important is taking Three-Craters and releasing the prisoners."

Chapter Twenty-Three

Halle had arranged to go with Russ to the main mess hall for supper. She led the way and the sound of animated chatter hit her as she entered the hall, together with the smell of cooking. The place was busy and there were lines at the food counters. Halle surveyed the room and thought she recognized the back of someone's head. He was sitting at a table near a wall and there was something familiar about his thick black hair and the shape of his ears. She peered through the sea of faces trying to make out the man's features. She felt Russ gently touch her elbow, to guide her towards the center of the room.

She saw that he was heading towards Commander Callard who was eating at a table. A man who Halle hadn't seen before, sat with him. She judged the other man to be in his late forties, with hair cropped so short, he was nearly bald. He wore a formal black uniform with five gold vertical stripes just below the right shoulder of his jacket, denoting him as an officer. He appeared to be in deep discussion with the commander.

Russ approached the commander. "Good evening, Sir," Russ said.

"Good evening Captain Thomas, Miss Rison," the commander said politely. "I'd like to introduce you to Major Terry."

"Good Evening, Major," Russ replied.

"Pleased to meet you," Halle said, standing beside Russ.

"Why don't you join us?" The commander gestured to empty chairs at the table. "The Major has come from Morten to lead our next offensive."

"Thank you, Sir," Halle said, taking the seat he indicated.

"I'll get us some food and be back in a minute," Russ said, before turning towards the food counter.

"Does he always play waiter?" Commander Callard laughed.

"We take it in turns." Halle smiled. "He knows what I like."

"I expect you've heard that we're going to launch an attack on a major target." Commander Callard impaled a vegetable on his plate with his fork. "We've had key personnel come in from other units and it will involve two other bases. We'll be coordinating the attack from here."

"I want to have an active role," Halle said. "I know that I'm Colonization Division, but I took part in the assault in Central."

"I heard that you said something along those lines to Captain Thomas. There may be a place for you in one of the units. I'll tell you about it at our briefing meeting tomorrow morning." The commander popped the vegetable into his mouth.

Major Terry put his knife and fork down and addressed Halle, "I understand you know Chief Trinneer who came from the U-Zone?"

"That's right." Halle felt her face go warm. "I worked with him in the Division."

"I don't want to pry, Miss Rison, but according to Sun Hider you were more than work colleagues with this man." Major Terry studied her keenly. "Would your history get in the way, if you had to work with him?"

"Our relationship was over before he defected to the U-Zone," Halle replied, feeling her face redden more. "I can work with him, if I have to."

Commander Callard seemed to sense her discomfort. "Good. Well, that's cleared up. I'm sure Miss Rison won't let her personal feelings get in the way."

"We still can't be sure that Chief Trinneer is loyal to the Ea-Zone." Major Terry picked up his knife and fork again. "If he turned out to be a traitor, how would you feel?"

"I would have no hesitation in turning him in," Halle said emphatically.

"It's possible that he's been infected by the Uveid. This could be a masquerade for our benefit." Major Terry ate a mouthful of food.

"From what I understand, that applies to anyone. Their side as well as our own," Halle said. "We're all at risk of this alien infection."

Major Terry chewed on his food and Commander Callard frowned. Halle saw Russ making his way towards them, deftly carrying two plates of fried vegetables with soya burgers. The food smelled delicious and her mouth watered. She waited while Russ put a plate in front of her, and smiled at him when he sat down.

"Thank you. You always know what to get me."

"You're welcome." Russ returned her smile.

Halle saw someone moving across the room out of the corner of her eye. She had a mouthful of food on her fork but stopped eating, while she turned her head to look. The man was white and above average height. He moved with a confident gait and was dressed in the dark burgundy uniform of a chief engineer. He carried a peaked hat in one hand, casually swinging his arms as he walked. He was followed by another man of similar age and height, dressed in an army uniform. As if aware of her interest, the first man glanced towards her. She couldn't mistake Kalen's even features and strong jaw. Her heart leapt into her throat. She turned away quickly, refusing to make eye contact.

Russ had followed her gaze and had seen Kalen, and now he stared at him with narrowed eyes. Halle bowed her head and pretended interest in her food. She felt Russ's gaze on her and wondered what he knew. What had Commander Callard told him? The truth, she supposed, but she had to hide her feelings. She told herself to forget Kalen. Their relationship was finished and he had a wife. She tried to push the image of him out of her head. She had Russ now, and he was worth ten of Kalen.

***

At the meeting the next morning, Commander Callard's suggestion took Halle by surprise. "You want me to be in the advance team?"

"That's right." Commander Callard's eyes twinkled. "I know you're keen to play an active role."

"I am," Halle assured him. "It's just that I didn't think you'd want to rely on me for this."

"Of course I won't force you to go, if you don't think you can manage it," Commander Callard said. "It's just you expressed a wish to do something more than administration."

"Yes, but…" Halle tried to think how best she could put it. "I do want to take an active part. I'm just not sure that I'm the best person to do this. You seem to have more confidence than I have, in my own abilities."

"You can fire a laser, you're quick and intelligent, and you're resourceful. And equally importantly, you know Chief Trinneer better than any of us. We intend to send both Captain Ingeston and him in. You have a good knowledge of Three-Craters. You'll know very quickly if Trinneer has been infected or is misleading us."

"I do know Three-Craters well," Halle agreed. "My job involved overseeing a lot of the building program, so I know the place. But I don't know Captain Ingeston."

"Ingeston has given us information about the strength and deployment of Unity's forces, that we have verified independently. He seems to have genuinely switched sides."

"I've got some reservations about my abilities in hand to hand fighting."

"You shouldn't need to be involved in any personal combat. The whole point about the advance team is secretiveness. We send a small team in to sabotage their major defenses, before the main attack on Three-Craters," Commander Callard assured her. "With your senior rank in the Division, and knowledge of Three-Craters, you would be an asset."

"Don't Unity have a lot of troops based at Three-Craters?" Halle asked.

"They have some, but most of the regiment are stationed at a fourth crater about three kilometers south of Three-Craters. We have to launch our assault on Three-Craters before Unity has a chance to mobilize them." Major Callard paused for breath. "Once the main attack is underway, you'll join the ground forces, who'll also be liberating the prisoners in Crater Three."

"Who else will be on the advance team?" Halle asked. Everything Major Callard had said was true. She couldn't tell him that she wanted to avoid Kalen, although she suspected that he'd already guessed.

"We're sending in Trinneer and Ingeston because they're both engineers and have recent knowledge of the installations at Three-Craters. They'll be under the command of Captain Thomas. There'll be two other soldiers from our Engineering Corps and yourself. A total of six people. Any more, and the task force will be too large."

"How do we get into Three-Craters?"

"We've given this careful consideration. Once you're inside, it should be easy to blend in. Only Trinneer and Ingeston are liable to be recognized by a few individuals. We propose to send the team in posing as U-Zone troops. We'll alter your wrist chips to give you real U-Zone identities and use one of their shuttles we've captured."

"I'm flattered by your confidence in me," Halle replied, thinking hard. She wanted to be with Russ. Better to be with him, than left at Base Four worrying about what was going on and hearing everything second-hand.

"Your role will be to watch Trinneer and his colleague, to ensure that the information they've given us about the location of the installations at Three-Craters is accurate. You know the site well and you'll be able to tell if they're lying to us. This is the perfect role for you," the commander said encouragingly. "There's also something else we need you to do. Captain Thomas will give you all the details."

Halle made up her mind and smiled brightly. "I'll be pleased to do it, Commander."

"Good. I won't pretend that it won't be dangerous, but you're equal to the task. There's a team briefing this afternoon."

***

Kalen had grown used to the army uniform, and now he had the full complement of equipment and weapons, together with the special helmets that the Ea-Zone used to ward off the alien infection. He hoisted the pack onto his back easily, and fastened the straps. Beside him, Jon mirrored his actions and they nodded to each other. They would work with the Ea-Zone to sabotage Three-Craters' defenses and put a stop to the madness that had overtaken Unity. Two other soldiers from the Engineering Corps had been assigned to their team – a woman called Rena and a man called Piers. They stood slightly apart from Kalen and Jon, completing final checks on their own equipment.

The door slid open and Captain Russ Thomas strode into the room. Kalen watched him cautiously. He had an air of authority and scrutinized the assembled group with hard eyes. Kalen had seen him in the mess hall with Halle. There was some connection there, he decided. He'd watched them at the team briefing and there seemed to be a familiarity between them. He had spoken to Russ during that meeting and had sensed a degree of antipathy. At the time, he'd thought that it was because he had come from Unity. Now, he wasn't so sure.

Halle appeared at the door of the room. She was kitted out in army uniform, complete with pack, and carrying her helmet. The pack was large for her small frame, but she moved easily as if she was used to its weight. Her blond hair shone in the light and provided a stark contrast to her black uniform. Without makeup, her pale skin emphasized the blue of her eyes. She walked to Russ's side and he bent to whisper something in her ear. She gave a low laugh and smiled at him.

Kalen felt his stomach churn and anger began to seep through him. He watched Russ return her smile and saw Halle's hand briefly touch his arm. So that was it. Halle was sleeping with Captain Thomas. *She's replaced me already*, Kalen thought furiously. He wondered if the others had noticed. Would it affect their mission? Possibly, if Russ wasn't objective because of her. He stared at Russ. He was a professional soldier. No, he would carry on regardless of Halle.

"All ready?" Russ asked the group.

"Yes, Sir," Rena replied in a strong voice, and the others murmured their assent.

Kalen glanced at his companions, assessing them. Rena was only a bit shorter than him, with honey brown hair that she had tied back. She had an air of detached professionalism. Piers was a short man, in his mid-twenties, with a stocky build and determined expression. They were both engineers. He could work with them. His gaze rested on Russ. He couldn't hide his distrust of Jon and him. Kalen had seen it in his eyes and his curt remarks. He would be careful around him.

"We all know the plan." Russ surveyed the group. "You've checked all your equipment? Has anyone any questions or requests before we leave? Now is the time."

Russ's gaze lingered on Kalen and Jon. "You both have all you need? Any questions?"

"Is Miss Rison coming?" Kalen asked, thin lipped. Halle had been in the briefing meeting but it hadn't been clear what her role would be, or even that she would be accompanying them.

"Yes, she is. Do you have a problem with that?"

"She's not an engineer. What is her role going to be?" Kalen asked bluntly.

Russ glared at him. "She knows the layout of Three-Craters. She can assist in guiding us around the site."

"I understand." Kalen decided against objecting further. It wouldn't achieve anything.

Standing beside Russ, Halle glowered at him, white faced and lips compressed. Kalen tore his eyes away from her and focused on Russ.

"Is that all? Any more questions?" Russ asked again. "Okay, we're ready to leave. Remember, I give the orders."

***

They took a small military shuttle designed to carry troops, to Three-Craters. Russ and Rena piloted the craft, while Kalen sat with the others in the rear seats. They all wore Divines on the left breasts of their jackets and carried Unity identity cards for casual inspection. With the fabricated information on their wrists chips, they should all pass for U-Zone army. Kalen had been amused to discover that he had been promoted to a seven while Jon kept his rank of eight. Both had been given new identities.

"If we're recognized they'll arrest us for being traitors," Jon said from the next seat, as if reading his thoughts.

"We'll have to keep away from anyone who might know us," Kalen replied. "It shouldn't be too difficult if we're careful in the central hub."

"What about Sera?" Jon asked. "She must be worried about you."

"I can't risk seeing her until the main attack is underway." Kalen remembered Sera fixated by the patterns on the walls of the ruins, with the blue stone around her neck. "I think she's been infected by the Uveid energy. If she sees me, she'll turn me in. She's very loyal to Unity."

"If this goes to plan, the civilians at Three-Craters shouldn't be hurt. She should be all right," Jon said.

"As soon as it's feasible, I'll look for her and make sure she's safe. I hope that she'll recover, once I can get her away from the Uveid energy. I'm concerned about the effect on the baby."

Kalen looked out of the window at the barren landscape below. It was a clear day and the sky was blue. They had left the mountains behind and would be at Three-Craters soon. It was strange to think that Sera and his baby were there and he wouldn't be able to go straight to them. Someone near him gave a short cough and Kalen looked over the seats in the direction of the noise. He could see the side of Halle's face, and she was staring straight ahead. She's been listening, he thought. He wondered how much she had heard over the hum of the shuttle's engines. She had refused to look at him when they boarded the shuttle, and had pointedly turned her head away when he had walked past her to get to his seat.

"There's the dome of the main crater." Jon broke into his reverie.

The transparent dome spanned the horizon for forty kilometers, its surface glinting in the sunlight. The sight never failed to impress Kalen.

"It's a marvel of engineering," Kalen said.

"We have to save the domed cities," Jon remarked. "We have to stop Unity destroying the domes. If they come down, we'll have nothing left."

"The plans for this offensive should leave the dome intact."

The shuttle approached the lock system and then jiggled as the dome's sensors caught hold to pull it down automatically. Kalen heard Russ's voice from the flight deck speaking to port control at Three-Craters. He couldn't catch the words, but Russ's tone sounded normal. The tractor beam pulled the shuttle in on a vertical descent until it came to rest on the first platform with a gentle bump. The glittering dome spread out around them in all directions. With a clanking sound, the platform grips took hold of the craft and they began to descend through the lock system into the port.

The shuttle's engines went dead, and in the quiet, Kalen sat back contemplating their initial task. Beside him, Jon had taken out a pad and was sweeping his hand over it, skimming through pages of schematics.

"Is it all there?" Kalen asked.

"Yes, I don't think we've missed anything. We have to disable Unity's defenses and find a way to get the Ea-Zone army inside the dome when we launch the attack."

"There'll be over nine thousand troops coming in," Kalen said.

"We have to shut off the defense systems in such a way, that the damage isn't discovered immediately." Jon studied a diagram on his pad.

"The damage has got to be virtually undetectable, so that when Unity realize something is wrong, they have trouble finding the fault," Kalen said.

"Let's start with the most important installations and work our way down the list."

"We've got three hours to sabotage their equipment," Kalen reminded him.

"I hope that's enough time," Jon said.

"It's got to be. Any longer and Unity will notice the alterations we've done to the systems." Kalen began counting on his fingers. "The first task is to set up an override so we can divert the control of the main dome's airlocks, from the port to our air fleet. That'll let our air fleet open all of the airlocks at once, to bring the shuttles in."

"Agreed. There are ten locks for planetary traffic and two for interplanetary ships in the dome of Crater One – the main dome. The other domes don't have aerial access, except for one airlock that's being built at the north side of Crater Three."

"We have to set up the relay to our aerial force, ready to trigger the override," Kalen added. "We also need to disable the main dome's safety roof."

"Correct. We'll have to get onto the roof of the dome to do that," Jon confirmed.

"Next, we have to reconnoiter the drone and laser defense systems and if possible, sabotage them. That's a difficult one. Security will be tight and we mustn't do anything that will warn Unity of the impending attack. We also need to destroy the drones' in-flight charging systems." Kalen tapped his left index finger against the fingers of his other hand. "After that, we need to find a way to open the ground entrances to all three domes. The ground forces will be disembarked from the primary shuttles about two kilometers from Three-Craters, where they won't be seen."

Jon referred to his pad again. "I had an idea about that - let me check. It should be possible to set up an override for the domes' ground entrances at the same time as Crater One's port locks."

"That might work," Kalen said thoughtfully. "The domes' ground and air access might be controlled together at the program inception."

"There's no long range missile launchers at Three-Craters. They would be redundant given the power of the new lasers they have," Jon said.

"We'll be down soon. Better get ready. Remember, we wear our helmets anywhere near the Uveid fields." Kalen lowered his voice. "It's a good thing we've both got some immunity to the energy. I just hope that the others aren't affected."

"It's going to get difficult if they are." Jon put his pad away and closed his pack.

The platform came to rest with a creaking sound in front of a building. Outside, two of the maintenance crew were standing, watching. One of them put a radio to his mouth and spoke into it, before walking away with his colleague to the edge of the platform. A hatch opened in the platform and a ramp extended out of it, upwards towards the shuttle's door. Lights on the shuttle's interior door panel turned green.

Russ came out from the flight deck. "From now on, we are a small Engineering Corps, loyal to Unity. You take your orders from me. You do as I say with no arguments. We follow the U-Zone protocol. Remember your assigned identities at all times."

Kalen said nothing and the others remained silent. He wondered if he'd be recognized? Would anyone recognize Jon?

Russ went to the shuttle's door, and then hesitated before pressing the exit plate to open it. "And don't do anything to call attention to yourselves."

Chapter Twenty-Four

The shuttle's door slid aside and Russ stepped onto the ramp. The others followed him out, ignoring maintenance personnel who tended to the craft. They passed through a security check without being challenged and entered a long corridor. Walking in silence, Kalen averted his face from security cameras along the walls and ceiling. They might be looking for me, he thought.

Russ guided them to a passageway leading out of the shuttle port. "We have to find the servers controlling the domes' access programs."

"According to the plans, the servers and mainframes are housed underground in the computer room on level twenty, in the central hub of the main crater," Kalen replied.

"Okay," Russ said, checking their route against signage at the corridor junction. "So our first task is to re-program the servers to override port control."

"We can deal with the ground entrances from there as well," Jon said.

"We need to set up the relay system on the roof of the main crater's dome, so that our aerial assault team can transmit the override signal to the servers," Kalen informed Russ. "We can do that at the same time as disabling the main crater's safety roof and drone charging station."

"We'll have to split up," Russ replied.

"I know how to get to the computer rooms," Halle spoke up. "I'm also familiar with the programs."

"Halle, Rena and Jon, you go to the computer room and re-program the servers. After that, begin reconnaissance of the drone and laser defenses," Russ ordered. "I'll go up top with Kalen and Piers and we'll meet you at ground level later. Jon, keep your head down, in case you're recognized."

Kalen glimpsed a figure walking towards them in a black uniform. The gold of a Divine winked in the overhead lights. He wondered if the others had seen the person.

"There's someone coming," Kalen warned.

Russ immediately faced Jon, and gave him a palm forward salute. "Unity! Dismissed!"

"Yes, Sir!" Jon saluted and walked away, followed by Halle and Rena.

"With me," Russ addressed Kalen and Piers, before taking the other corridor, in the opposite direction from the approaching figure.

Kalen strode behind Russ with misgivings. Russ didn't trust him, that much was clear. He'd separated him from Halle. Deliberately. Perhaps that was for the best - Halle had made her antipathy obvious. Still, he hadn't known that Halle had computer knowledge. He'd always thought of her as an office administrator. Perhaps it was time to reassess his opinion of her abilities. Their task was complex and the invasion depended upon their success. The first thing to do was to get up to the main dome and jam Crater One's safety roof.

"Only Crater One has a metal safety roof for meteor storms at present," Kalen said. "When not in use, it's kept open. We need to disable it, so that Unity can't close it when the invasion begins."

"According to the plans that I saw, we can access it from the maintenance ladders on the north side," Russ replied.

They emerged from the passageway into sunshine, streaming through the glittering dome that spanned the sky above them. The city streets of Crater One had begun to take shape and new buildings surrounded them. Some appeared occupied, while others remained empty husks. Construction workers dressed in beige overalls busied themselves fitting doors and windows, while others still worked on the moving walkways and escalators. Only a few people dressed as civilians wandered about the streets, and Kalen guessed these were off duty Division personnel. All wore Divines on their jackets and blue stones around their necks. The people they passed ignored them.

Above them, the port control jutted out from the sheer cliff that bordered the north-east side of the main crater. The transparent roof of the dome arced down behind it.

"That way." Kalen drew level with Russ and pointed discreetly towards an area on the other side of the port, where the cliffs had been only partially terraced. "We can reach the safety roof controls from the utility center."

"Are you sure?" Russ asked. "I thought we gained access from east of the port?"

"No, the central hub is to the east, housing the Division's administrative offices. The dome's utility center is on the north-west side of Crater One. It serves Craters Two and Three as well," Kalen replied.

"We have to find a way in," Russ said, altering his direction.

"We can get up to the utility center from ground level and take a lift to its roof. After that we have to use the maintenance ladders," Kalen confirmed.

"Aren't we going to be noticeable?" Piers questioned. "What if we're stopped?"

"We're conducting an inspection," Russ said confidently, as they boarded an escalator leading to the utility center. At the top, a wide terrace ended in a bank of elevators. Russ took out his identity card and scanned it, and the elevator doors slid open. "We'll take it to the roof."

The elevator ascended slowly through the levels. Kalen counted the seconds in silence. He had inspected the operation of the safety roof before, on his first visit to Three-Craters. He had met Sera on a roof like this, in Central, just after she had discovered the Uveid. Where was she now? How would she react when she saw him again? Suddenly, the elevator doors opened and bright light flooded the car. Leaving the elevator, Kalen squinted against the glare.

The flat roof stretched out before them, interspersed by large round water tanks. Something moved behind the tanks - black shadows flickering in the blazing light. The hard crunch of boots on the metal roof reached them. A voice issuing orders. Kalen's blood froze; the place was guarded. He cursed under his breath. Beside him, Russ had also heard the sound, and he gestured to Piers and Kalen to stand back. Several grey clad figures came from behind a water tank. A patrol of security guards. All wore Divines, blue pendants and peaked hats. They were led by a female supervisor, an eight, who carried a laser.

Russ stopped with Kalen and Piers standing behind him. Putting his hand up, he gave a salute. "Unity!"

The female guard saluted in return, her eyes dipping to Russ's Divine which stated that he was a nine. "Unity! What is your purpose here?"

"We're from the Engineering Corps and we're doing routine inspections of the roof mechanisms," Russ replied smoothly.

"I haven't received any instructions that engineering was due today. Access is restricted. Please supply me with your identity and authorization code, so that I can check." She reached for her radio, eyes dark in a pale face.

Russ handed her his identity card and she studied it. "Authorization code?"

"Ten zero eight two five nine," Russ said.

Kalen recognized the generic engineering inspection code. Would that be enough? He became aware that the guards were staring at the neckline of their jackets.

"You don't wear the Uveid stones?" the supervisor asked.

"It was deemed inadvisable while carrying out inspections at height. The strings could get in the way."

"I have to check your authorization."

The supervisor began speaking into her radio. She stared at Russ suspiciously as she listened to the reply. The guards in her party also carried lasers, and they began to fan out around them.

After several seconds, the supervisor switched off her radio. "There's no inspection due today. You must come with us to sort it out."

Russ straightened his back. "You are mistaken. This is urgent and important. I must insist you let us proceed."

"Not without the proper authorization." The supervisor gestured with her laser towards the exit. The other guards circled them, fingering their lasers.

Russ stood his ground. "My orders come direct from Major Reece. Check with him."

The supervisor regarded him for a moment before repeating, "Major Reece?"

Suddenly, a laser shot exploded at Russ's feet and two guards leapt at him.

"Get them!" The supervisor's face dissolved into a mask of hatred.

A blow across Kalen's shoulders sent him to the ground. He hit the side of his head with a crack and pain seared through his cheek. Twisting, he drew his laser from his belt and fired upwards. A guard kicked the gun out of his hand, and another aimed a kick at his side. Gripping his arms, they hauled Kalen to his feet. They ripped off his pack and cuffed his wrists behind his back. He glared at them, face smarting. Beside him, Russ struggled with two more guards until they also cuffed him.

The supervisor drew her lips back and bared her teeth. "Major Reece is dead. You're Earlians!"

***

Halle went with Jon and Rena into the main administrative center for Three-Craters. Civilian personnel from the Colonization Division worked here, in the central hub, as well as army personnel, and the corridors were busy. Jon, as the eight, assumed the lead role, while Rena and her, as sevens, acted as subordinates. Halle felt irritated to be playing subordinate to a man. It won't be for long, she reminded herself.

"Unity!" Jon saluted a passing army captain, while ignoring the civilian personnel in the corridors.

Halle avoided eye contact with anyone else, but surreptitiously studied the people they passed. Nearly all wore blue stones around their necks and walked silently without chatting to each other. There was something unnatural about their dark eyes and faces devoid of emotion. Halle found the quietness strange. The only sounds were soft footsteps and the hum of the air supply units. How could Kalen have lived in this environment? Had he walked about here with eyes downcast and silent?

She had been aware of Kalen's closeness on the shuttle. It had torn at her that he was with someone else. It hadn't seemed real – it had seemed all wrong. Kalen had ignored her. He didn't care for her anymore. She had had to pretend that it didn't matter. But it did, and she couldn't get him out of her mind. She had tried to avoid him and avoid thinking about him, but it wasn't working. *I'm jealous*, Halle chided herself. *I must let him go.*

Walking swiftly, they made their way down to the computer room on level twenty, without incident. The door was locked.

"I have the codes - I took them before I left here," Jon said, opening the door easily. Banks of computers and consoles lined the walls, under large viewscreens that were turned off. Jon took his pack from his shoulder and began to rummage in it. "We need to open servers twelve and fifteen."

"They're over here." Rena knelt down before the housing underneath one of the consoles.

"The programming for the airlocks is routed through server twelve," Jon said. "And the ground entrances through server fifteen."

Halle crouched behind Rena. "If we can insert the override Unity won't notice anything is wrong, until it's activated at the time of invasion."

"I'll get server twelve, if you two can get server fifteen." Jon took out a small tool from his pack and opened up a panel.

"Security seems light?" Rena questioned.

"That's right," Halle said. "Any problems with the programming are usually picked up quickly. They haven't anticipated the possibility of an aerial override. This is a civilian facility anyway, so there isn't the same level of security as an army base."

Halle stood up and watched Jon and Rena begin work. Russ had made an excuse for her presence to the team, but her real job was something different.

"I have a task to perform," Halle told Rena and Jon. "I'll be back in an hour to see how you're doing."

Jon looked up from his work. "Where are you going?"

"Back up to the Division's offices, I've worked here before. I'll see you shortly. Any problems, radio me on the agreed frequency."

Halle left them working and made her way to the nearest restrooms. Locking herself in a cubicle, she took blue trousers and a jacket from her pack and changed into them. She stashed her army uniform into her bag. Slipping a string with a blue stone around her neck, she came out of the cubicle. She needed one final touch and felt for the Divine in the jacket pocket. Kalen had reported that the Division managers were normally a nine. She fixed the new badge on the breast of her jacket and went to the mirror.

Halle practiced a vacant expression a couple of times, and then set her face and left the bathroom. She walked back to the elevators that led up to the Division's offices, keeping her eyes fixed in a glazed expression. She wasn't stopped and eventually reached the management suite. She'd been told that Javed Durton, her counterpart in the U-Zone, was at Three-Craters. She'd never met him, so he wouldn't recognize her. He could be anywhere on site at this moment, she thought. With luck, he wouldn't be in his office.

Halle approached the Division manager's office cautiously. In the Ea-Zone, before the war when jobs were shared, this had been her office, albeit at different times to Javed. She paused in front of the door, before pressing the entry plate. The office was locked but Jon had supplied the door code. She quickly entered it and went inside. The office had been occupied recently - a hat still rested on the desk, and the desk screen was on. A strange triangular plaque rested on the table with the word "Unity" written on it.

Halle sat down at the desk and began scrolling through the pages on the screen. The U-Zone's plans didn't interest her. The Ea-Zone would attack before Unity had time to implement them. What she wanted was the overall site controls. Halle heard the door swish open and a cough. A short bald man stood in the entrance. He took in Halle at a glance and glared at her.

"Who are you?" Javed Durton demanded.

***

The security guards dragged Kalen and Russ towards the roof elevators. Kalen had guards on each side and his vision was restricted. He wondered where Piers was. Had he got away? Or was he behind them? Ahead of him, Russ struggled. He's trying to slow the guards down, he thought. Inside the building, it's going to be more difficult to escape. We've got to do something now, before it's too late.

Kalen worked the fingers of one hand up the sleeve of the other arm of his jacket. They had prepared for the possibility of capture. The U-Zone cuffs all had the same magnetic lock system. Kalen's fingers curled around the lipstick sized key he had hidden in his sleeve. He manipulated the small cylinder to the cuffs and felt them unlock. He resisted the guards' pull on his arms, making them force him forward. In front, he saw Russ surreptitiously reaching inside his own sleeve for a key.

A blinding light dazzled Kalen unexpectedly, and fire ripped through the supervisor's torso. She uttered a short scream and collapsed, limbs twitching. Flames flared, burning her up.

"Now!" Russ shouted, swinging violently to one side, both wrists free, to fall on a guard.

Another flash, this time to Kalen's right, and he felt one of the guards loosen his grip on his arm. Kalen launched himself at the other guard to his left, shouldering him sideways and punched him in the face. He caught the guard off balance and he staggered backwards. Kalen aimed another blow at his face and wrenched the guard's laser out of his hands. Using the stock, he struck the guard across his head, sending him reeling to the ground. Another flare blinded him and he smelled burning flesh. Acrid black smoke wafted upwards and his eyes watered. He saw figures in the haze - Russ grappling with a guard and another body on the ground.

"I'll get him," Piers shouted, emerging from behind a water tank, holding a laser.

"No!" Kalen yelled. "He's too close to Russ."

Piers lowered his laser and came forward, watching. Russ and the guard continued struggling. Russ punched the guard's neck and used his other hand to force the guard's arm backwards. The guard dropped the laser and it hit the ground with a clatter. Russ head-butted him in the face and then punched him in the stomach. When the guard doubled over, Russ kneed him hard, catching his jaw. The guard's head snapped up with a crack and he collapsed to the ground. Russ touched the body with the toe of his boot.

Russ glanced at the others. "He's dead."

"Quickly, let's get our lasers and equipment." Kalen began to retrieve his things from the bodies.

"What are we going to do about them?" Piers asked. "Do you think they'll be missed?"

"Possibly," Russ replied, bending down to pick up a laser. "Piers, clear up as much as you can and drag the bodies behind one of the water tanks. I'll go with Kalen to start the work. Join us when you're finished."

Chapter Twenty-Five

The bald headed man stared at Halle, his eyes black. A blue stone glittered on a string at his throat. Halle stood up immediately from the desk.

"Sorry Sir. I was coming to see you and found you gone."

The man eyed her warily and took two steps forward. "What are you doing at my screen?"

"I was looking for the day's work details," Halle replied guilelessly. "I've been sent from Central to assist."

The man's eyes dipped to her Divine and he let out a suppressed breath. "What's your name?"

"Lindy Shrover, Sir." A real person who had died in the conflict but had never been a divisional manager.

"And what are you supposed to assist me with?" Javed asked suspiciously.

Halle assessed her chances of physically tackling the man. Although short, he was still taller than her. She needed unimpeded access to his desk screen to carry out her instructions, and he was in the way.

"The mining of the Uveid, Sir."

"I think we've got that well in hand." Javed still looked wary.

"I understood you needed extra support to ensure that the rest of the building program is kept on track. I was told that there would be a vacant office on this floor for me to work out of." Would he believe her? How could she get him out of her way?

Javed stared at her and then his eyes became glassy and his expression went blank. *It's as if he's listening to something,* Halle thought. She carefully slid her hand beneath her jacket.

"Sir?" Halle ventured again. "An office for me to work out of?"

Javed's eyes flickered and he focused on her with a malevolent stare. "You're not who you say you are. I'm calling Security."

With a flick of her wrist, Halle aimed her hand laser at Javed and fired. He reacted with inhuman rapidity and lunged at her. The shot missed and he struck out at her arm, as he crashed into her. The wall near the door flared red hot. The gun flew out of her hand, and she tumbled backwards under the impact. As she fell, she twisted about and grabbed the edge of the desk to save herself. Javed roared and hit out at her. A glancing blow caught her side but she scrambled out of his grip. Grabbing a chair, she hurled it at him. He deflected it with an arm and came at her again, eyes blazing.

Halle snapped the stun stick off her belt, and stuck it between his eyes. Javed froze and screamed. He put both hands up to his face, and then crumpled to the floor, hitting his head on the side of the desk as he went down. A large gash appeared on his forehead and blood began to dribble over his face.

Halle bent down and checked that Javed was unconscious. She searched his pockets and found his Divine, a number thirteen, and a small laser gun. She took both, together with his identity card. How had he got to be a thirteen? She considered killing him, but discounted the idea. Whatever he had done, he was unarmed and powerless now. She cast about the office for something to tie him up with. There was nothing she could use.

With distaste, she reached under his jacket to slip off the belt around his trousers. She took off her own belt and used both belts to tie his wrists and ankles. After ripping off a piece of his shirt and stuffing it in his mouth, she dragged him by his ankles to a large locker set into the wall, and stuffed him inside. Halle closed the locker door with relief. The locker opened from the outside, so even if he came to, he would have trouble getting out. Righting the desk and chair, she resumed her work.

Javed had access to more than usual, for a manager, she mused. She found the video feeds for the site easily and reprogrammed them, so that the feeds to the offices in the central hub would go dead at the appointed time, leaving only the feed to the computer room on level twenty. When Early attacked, the central hub would be effectively blind. She wished she could have shut them off for the whole site, but the port and any army systems would still be functional.

Next, Halle went to the programming for the Gates. Since the beginning of the war they had been left open, their original use of separating the two zones being redundant. She reprogrammed them, to ensure that the U-Zone could not close them in the usual way. Halle studied the rest of the site facilities that Javed had access to and set about finishing her task. She tampered with the controls for the mines: half of the mine elevators, large drills, lighting and air, would fail fifteen minutes before the attack. Enough time for Unity to send crews to try and find the faults which would distract them.

"What next?" Halle muttered to herself as she stared at the screen. The Army had requisitioned a number of buildings near the central hub to run their operations. She had no access to their controls, they fell outside the province of a Division manager. She needed something that would create a big enough diversion to draw the site commander's resources. She couldn't sabotage anything to do with the construction above ground, but scrolling through the pages, something caught her eye.

"The light filters!" she exclaimed. "I can alter them!"

This would be delicate, she decided. The attack was due to happen soon, when Taidor's sun was high in the sky. If she shut off the domes' filters, the harsh sunlight would shine straight through the domes. Anyone above ground, without eye protection, would be very uncomfortable. The

Ea-Zone army would be wearing their helmets and visors and wouldn't be affected, but everyone else without eye protection, would suffer.

"There we go," she said to herself, as she adjusted the light filters for the domes, so that each dome's filters would begin to fail ten minutes before the allotted time. It would cause chaos, but not sufficient time to trace the fault to Javed's work station or warn Unity of the attack.

***

After changing back into her army uniform, Halle returned to Rena and Jon. They were still working on the servers.

"How are you doing?" Halle asked.

"We're nearly finished." Jon knelt in front of one of the open panels, checking circuits. "We've put the overrides in both servers and installed the transmitters. I'm setting the frequencies now."

"Any word from Russ?" Halle asked.

"Not yet," Jon replied, lifting a panel and positioning it back in place. "But we're keeping radio use to a minimum, so that's not surprising. We can go up top and find them."

Beside Jon, Rena had also finished and Halle bent down to give her a hand with a panel. "I'd feel more comfortable if we'd heard from them."

"Maybe, but they're probably busy," Jon said, checking the panel's fixings. "That's back in place. Nobody will know we were here."

Halle stood up and looked around the room. It appeared untouched. In the corner, one of the screens had been turned on. It showed a long view of the inside of the main crater. "Did you turn this on?"

Jon began putting his tools away. "Yes, to check that we'd covered all of the entrances. I wanted to show you Crater Three."

"Unity can't trace this viewscreen can they?" Halle asked in alarm.

"No, don't worry." Jon went over to the screen. He pressed buttons on the console beneath it and the view changed. "There's a small military port in Crater Three."

Halle peered at the screen. "I thought that it was still being built?"

"It seems to be operational now," Jon replied. "The controls for it aren't routed through here, so we haven't been able to set up any overrides to open it."

"That's a shame." Halle shook her head. "I suppose we can't stop anything leaving or coming through there."

"Not easily, although it's so small, traffic through it will be limited anyway," Jon said thoughtfully. "There's something else you should see."

The view changed again, and Halle found herself staring at the construction site in Crater Three. Numerous people were working on several tall buildings, with grey clad guards watching them. Peering at the detail, Halle saw the letters "EA" on the back of the workers' overalls. Although she had been told about the prisoners, she still felt shocked to see them working like this.

"The construction is underway there," Jon shifted uncomfortably. "I want you to know that I have never been a part of this."

"So you say." Halle eyed him cynically. How far could she really trust someone from Unity? He must have known how the Ea-Zone prisoners were being treated. He had done nothing to help them and from what she understood, only left Three-Craters when Kalen persuaded him to escape.

"Now, have a look at the rest of Crater Three." Jon changed the scene.

Halle stared at the screen. At first she couldn't understand what she was seeing. As comprehension dawned, a feeling of disbelief swept over her. This was impossible.

***

The transparent dome of Crater One, began fifty meters above the roof of the utility center, extending upwards from the rim of the crater. To reach it, Russ and Kalen walked through the maze of water tanks and equipment on the roof, until they reached one of the vacuum elevators that had been installed around the crater's circumference. Similar to a vertical cylinder, the elevators had been designed to shoot up or down at high speed, connecting the crater's rim to the buildings or ground below.

The dome itself had been set back from the steep cliffs of the crater, so that Kalen and the others stepped out of the elevator onto a wide walkway, bounded on one side by the cliff edge of the crater, and on the other by the gently sloping wall of the dome. The ground entrances built into the dome, opened out onto the walkway, that completely encircled the city. In time, buildings would appear, but for the present, this section of the walkway was largely an empty space.

"The machinery for most of the roof mechanisms is installed further up, inside the dome itself." Kalen pointed to a labyrinth of metal steps, ladders and mesh walkways, that snaked upwards. "We have to climb up to it, but no one should notice us from below. We're too far away and we won't be directly over the city."

Kalen paused at the foot of the steps and tried the straps of his pack and equipment, making sure that they were fastened properly. "If anyone does notice us up here, they'll assume it's for routine maintenance."

"You go first," Russ replied. "You know this section."

"Okay." Kalen began to climb.

The flight of narrow metal steps zig-zagged upwards to the first walkway, high above the main crater. The mesh treads underneath Kalen's boots clanged shrilly with each step. Through the treads, he could see the buildings of Crater

One below, appearing tiny from his viewpoint. The dome, above and behind him, was now near enough for him to make out the many panes that it was constructed from, and the trellis work of solar panels, lights and filters that ran through it. Reaching a walkway, he led Russ along it until they came to another flight of steps, that took them even higher.

"The safety roof controls should be near here."

"I see them," Russ's voice came from behind him. "To our left there's a walkway running along the side, with a line of boxes."

"That's right, they're the consoles for its power supply," Kalen said. "When the metal safety roof is activated, it extends up and over the main dome in four segments. The boxes up here govern its power supply from solar energy."

They reached the walkway and made their way to the row of consoles. Kalen studied the switches and buttons. Several green lights glowed steadily, barely visible in the strong sunlight. A buzzing sound emanated from the console, which felt warm when Kalen touched it.

"We have to re-route the circuits before we disconnect the power supply to the safety roof, so that the break doesn't register at the central hub," Kalen said.

"How long will it take?" Russ asked.

"Not long, once I get started." Kalen opened up a panel in the console.

"While you're doing that, I'll bring up the co-ordinates for the location of the transmitter." Russ took out his pad and began studying diagrams.

Kalen finished with the innards of the console and began on the switches.

"Yes!" Kalen muttered, throwing a switch. The green lights faded and red ones appeared. "That's done."

"Good." Russ glanced over the control board. The red lights shone steadily.

"I've also installed a booster for the override transmitter we're putting on the roof, to boost the signal to the servers on level twenty," Kalen said.

"By my reckoning we have to climb higher to place the override transmitter itself," Russ replied.

"That's correct," Kalen said, shouldering his pack. "The linkage system for charging the drones in-flight, is also up there. We have to duplicate what I've done here. Turn off the power to the system without alerting the central hub."

Climbing higher, the light became a glare, and Kalen lowered his helmet visor. He checked their position against the co-ordinates Russ had on his pad. They needed to get a little further up before they could install the transmitter. It would feed the override signal from the Ea-Zone's air fleet to the servers that operated the domes' entrances. Russ was not an engineer, but Kalen suspected that he had been briefed in detail about the work required. *He's only here to keep an eye on me*, he thought wryly.

Kalen paused at the sound of boots ascending the stairs below them. Glancing down, he saw a black clad soldier climbing up. Russ stiffened and drew his laser. Kalen amplified the visual of his visor and stared at the figure. The soldier saw them watching him and lifted his visor. Kalen relaxed; it was Piers. He turned back to continue upwards, until he reached a platform with a mesh floor. At one end of the platform there was another console.

"Is this it?" Russ asked, staring at the console.

"This controls the power supply for the drones' in-flight laser charging system. The laser array is housed up there, to charge the drones that fly within range of it." Kalen pointed upwards to a laser array, several meters in diameter, incorporated into the roof of the dome. A ladder led up to it. "The charging station can charge drones both inside and outside the dome. We need to turn the charging system off without alerting the central hub."

"So we can disconnect the roof lasers from this console?" Piers strode forward, staring at the console with interest.

"Yes, provided we fix the circuits so that the disconnect doesn't register in the central hub below," Kalen answered.

"I can do that," Piers said, lifting a cover off the side of the console. "If you want to go up and install the transmitter for the access override."

"Thank you," Kalen said appreciatively. He wished that Russ was an engineer as well. It would make their work a lot easier. "I'm going to use the maintenance hatch for the drones' external charging system, to get onto the dome roof and place the transmitter."

"I'll come with you," Russ said.

"There won't be much room for both of us up there," Kalen replied, feeling irritated. The close supervision annoyed him.

"I need to see that it's done. I have to come with you," Russ replied.

"If you insist." Kalen went to the ladder and began climbing up it. At the top, there was a small platform under a low hatch, adjacent to the laser chargers. Stooping under the low roof, Kalen took out a mask and oxygen canister from his bag. Russ climbed onto the platform beside him.

"We need oxygen out there." Kalen put his mask on and attached the canister. He undid the clips of the hatch. "There's an airlock between here and the outer skin of the dome."

Russ put on his mask and when he was ready, Kalen scrambled through the hatch into an enclosed space, no more than a meter and a half high. Russ came after him and Kalen shut the hatch once he was inside.

"Turn on your oxygen," Kalen told Russ, before turning off the oxygen inside the airlock, and opening another hatch above them.

Kalen stood up through the hatch, so that he was standing looking out over the roof of the dome. The surface didn't appear transparent close up but still glowed brightly in the sunshine. Over his head, the golden disc of the sun hung in a blue sky. Immediately in front of him was the external charging station, spreading over several meters. Ladder type walkways traversed the roof in several directions from the hatch, so that all of the laser array could be accessed.

Kalen ducked back inside and took the transmitter out of his bag. "Are you coming out with me? I'm going to use the ladders over the laser array, to site the relay transmitter to override the domes' entrance controls."

"You go out," Russ said. "I'll watch from the hatch."

At least he's realistic, Kalen thought, clambering out of the hatch onto one of the ladders. He checked the location he wanted and set off, crawling across the flat metal struts, wide enough to accommodate his knees comfortably. Technically, he could have walked across the roof itself, but that risked damaging delicate equipment. He found the spot he wanted, near the edge of the charging station, and set up the transmitter. It's energy cell was powerful enough to relay a signal to reach the servers, to open the port and ground entrances to the dome. Satisfied, he put away his equipment. Russ sat on the edge of the hatch, with his back to him.

Curious, Kalen looked out in the direction Russ faced. On the horizon, the air was hazy and dark. Kalen tried to estimate the distance of the dust storm. There was no wind yet at Three-Craters, and the storms could take hours to develop, if at all. It depended on the way the wind was blowing. The invasion was due to start in just over an hour. By his calculation, if the storm came, it would strike after the assault had started. He shuffled back towards Russ.

"I see it." Kalen pointed to the horizon.

"We can't worry about it now." Russ put his hands on the sides of the hatch and dropped down into the airlock.

"If the work's finished up here, we need to get down and assess the laser defenses and drone fleet."

Kalen levered himself through the hatch, shutting it behind him. He turned on the oxygen, and a quiet hiss came from the vents of the airlock.

"The others might have begun that already."

"I hope so," Russ replied as the oxygen levels increased. "We're running out of time."

Chapter Twenty-Six

Kalen stood with Russ, Halle and Jon on the roof of the central hub, behind a machinery room that regulated air flow in that section. From this position, they had used the enhanced optics of their visors, to spy on soldiers guarding a line of long range laser guns, some forty meters away. The weaponry had been placed across the roof of the central hub and along the terraces of the adjacent accommodation block. Russ had sent Piers and Rena to assess the drone fleets and laser defenses of Craters Two and Three.

"I have to find Sera." Kalen glared at Russ. "It was my condition for coming on this mission."

Halle stood to one side of Russ, staring at Kalen, white faced. He tried to ignore her, but he guessed what she was thinking. He wished that he could tell her that he'd made a mistake; that he should never have taken up with Sera, but it was too late now. Sera was his wife and he had a responsibility to her. When the fighting began, he had to make sure that she was safe.

"If you go to her now, one word from her could jeopardize our mission," Russ said.

"By the time I find her, the attack will have started. I'll only have minutes to get her somewhere safe," Kalen replied in measured tones.

"The offensive is due to start in an hour. You'll have to wait until then," Russ ordered. "We need to sabotage the main lasers first."

"They're too heavily guarded," Kalen insisted. "We can't take them out."

Russ clenched his jaw. "I don't like giving up."

Jon raised his visor and faced Russ. "There must be at least fifty soldiers up here. That's too many for us to take on. We can't do it."

"Isn't there a way to get to the lasers' power or programming?" Halle asked.

"No, the laser defenses run though separate secure systems," Jon said.

"Okay, we'll have to leave the lasers. We'll deal with the main drone fleet now," Russ announced.

"It's housed on the west side," Jon confirmed.

"You'll come with us, Trinneer." Russ fixed Kalen with an icy stare. "Once the offensive is underway, you can leave. Until then, you stay under my command."

Kalen gave a short nod of his head in acknowledgement. Russ turned away and strode towards the elevators that would take them to ground level. With a glance at Jon, Kalen followed him, cursing to himself. Russ was right, but he didn't like it. Sera could be anywhere on site and could get caught up in the fighting. If he found her, he could insist that she stay in the accommodation block. It was the safest place. The Ea-Zone wouldn't fight unarmed civilians. Or would they?

Suddenly, a mental image of the shadow wall filled his mind. The open window glowed seductively and he felt an overwhelming urge to give in to it, to let his consciousness surrender and be pulled to the other side. His surroundings faded away into a blur and instead of the half-finished city streets, he saw the glimmer of golden light that got brighter until it blotted out everything else. Somebody knocked against him and he came to with a start, the golden light and wall receding. They must be near a Uveid field, he realized. He had taken his helmet off in the elevator. He quickly put it back on again.

***

Kalen walked west with the others, towards Crater One's perimeter, south of the port control. To the north of them was the utility building, to one side of the air field. The construction to the west was only at an embryonic stage. The preparatory work had been done and foundations had been laid, but only a handful of incomplete buildings rose to any height. In places, there was charred brickwork and scorched pavements from the recent fighting. Ahead, the cliff face would eventually be terraced, but so far, only sections had been completed. There were very few people about, and Kalen guessed that work had stopped when the war began.

"We're very conspicuous here," Kalen called out to Russ. "We're probably being watched from port control."

"Keep your visors down," Russ replied, marching forward purposefully. "And keep behind me."

They carried on walking and eventually Kalen estimated that they were out of sight of the port control. Ahead, a tubular vacuum elevator ran vertically up the cliff. Russ paused to survey the cliff face.

"Where's the drone station?" Russ asked.

Jon stepped forward. "It's about halfway up the cliff, just north of the elevator. We'll see more once we're up there."

Kalen peered upwards. A dark rectangle made up of rows of polished metal boxes winked in the sunshine.

"Can we get to them from the rim?" Russ asked.

"I've serviced the drones before, but security is tight," Jon answered. "We can get up to the rim without problems, but we might not be able to get to the drones themselves."

"We should get a good view of the station though," Kalen added.

They took the elevator to the top. Kalen saw that in this section, the wide walkway running around the rim was incomplete and littered with equipment. The paving wasn't finished and construction machinery had been parked haphazardly. Two large drills stood ready to begin burrowing out a channel for the commercial lifts, that would be used to bring ground imports into the city. Girders and tracks for a transport system had been stacked near one of the dome's ground entrances, but no workmen moved about.

"They've halted work here as well," Halle remarked.

Russ bobbed down behind a stack of girders. "There'll be guards near the drone station, so be careful."

They crept forward, hugging the shadows, until they saw a small building with two soldiers guarding it. The guards wore black uniforms and berets, with their Divines fastened to the left breasts of their jackets. Both held military lasers and they were taking turns to walk up and down in front of the building.

Jon whispered at Russ's shoulder, "That's the entrance to the drone station."

Russ flattened himself against a hover truck that had been left standing empty, and stole a glance around it. "Isn't there another way down to the drones?"

"No, the only other access is from the cliffside." Jon unclipped his laser.

"We can't take the station." Kalen stared hard at the guards. "There'll be more inside and security doors."

Russ turned his head. "Are you suggesting we go down the cliff?"

"There's a ladder down," Jon said. "But we would be highly visible."

"I don't like the sound of that," Halle said unhappily.

"I'm a civilian engineer so I didn't work on the drones, but maybe we can disable them from up here if we find a good vantage point?" Kalen suggested.

"What about the power lines to the drone station?" Halle asked. "Can we get to them remotely?"

"I don't think so, Halle," Kalen said. It was the first time that he had spoken to her directly that day. She had been avoiding his gaze but now her eyes sparked with animosity. "They're under Army control and all of their systems are very secure."

Halle glared at him, anger burning in her eyes. He held her stare for a moment, so that there was a brief silence. She was very pretty even without makeup. Her fury enhanced the blue of her eyes and gave her an air of determination that Kalen had always found attractive. There was something blue around her neck. Before Halle could stop him, he snatched the pendant.

"Where did you get this?" Kalen demanded.

"Don't worry, it's a fake!" Halle yanked the pendant out of his hand.

Beside Kalen, Russ took a sharp intake of breath. "Enough. Let's find a vantage point."

They found a spot where they were well camouflaged, in the shadow of a crane, perched at the crater's rim. Lying on his stomach, Kalen had a good view of the drone station built into the cliffs below. Enclosed behind a transparent barrier, ten rows of square boxes with black metal flaps, housed a hundred drones. Next to him, Russ switched the radio on in his headset and Kalen heard him report their position to base.

Jon began to describe the military drone station, "Each box houses a drone where it undergoes diagnostic procedures and charging, ready for use. If a drone is faulty, it's removed for repair, and replaced by a spare. The power systems and repair shops are all internal, behind the outlets."

"According to my information, Unity have got at least two other drone fleets at Three-Craters," Russ said. "They also have drones in reserve to substitute for any destroyed in battle, but they can't be brought into service quickly. They take time to charge up in their boxes. That's their vulnerability."

"What about jamming the flaps? If we can stop them opening, we can ground the fleet." Kalen shifted position to get a better view. "We can't do that remotely, but we're within laser range."

"They're protected by that transparent barrier," Jon replied. "It's impenetrable to laser fire. We can't do anything until they open it."

"We're getting near time." Russ sat up and took off his Divine. "Get prepared. Take off your badges and put your stripes on. Base knows our position but we don't want to be mistaken for U-Zone."

"Are we staying here?" Halle asked.

Russ glanced at her. "We'll stay here until the offensive starts. Once I give the order, we fire on the drone station. After that, we take orders from Major Terry. Piers and Rena are already in position to attack one of the drone fleets in Crater Two."

Kalen took off his Divine and put on army stripes, the insignia of a captain in the Engineering Corps. He checked the charge on his laser and sighted the drone station. Below him, the half built city in Crater One covered the crater floor to the horizon. To the north-east, the port control jutted out from the side of the crater and further on, the buildings and terraces of the central hub and accommodation blocks were visible.

Suddenly, port control lit up in a burst of dazzling light. Almost simultaneously, white light tore through the dome in several places, creating a patchwork of light and shade. Blinding in its intensity, Kalen was thankful that he had his helmet visor. The city below gradually lit up to a burning brilliance, as sections of the dome roof let in the natural sunlight, one after the other. In the streets, tiny figures threw up their hands to shield their eyes, and ran chaotically to sparse shadows. Construction work stopped and distant shouting reached him. Beside him, Halle giggled.

"I see it was a success," Russ remarked.

"Yes, I've turned off light filters in all three domes," Halle replied smirking. "It's pretty uncomfortable down there."

"Something else is going on," Kalen said.

Below them, several teams of workers had appeared, moving with purpose in different directions. Halle let out a laugh. "I've shut down half of the mine operations as well."

Russ cast a glance over the group. "We're near the ground entrances. When they open, the Army will temporarily override the airlock controls, so the oxygen up here might get thin. Use your breathing tubes and oxygen canisters."

Kalen secured his air canister under his jacket and attached a breathing tube. Near them, sections of the walkway had begun to light up, as the roof filters shut down. Abruptly, blazing sunlight hit them and the whole walkway was bathed in white light. The soldiers guarding the station entrance flinched, throwing up their hands to protect their eyes. It won't take them long to put eye protection on, Kalen thought. They must have helmets at the station. Their advantage would only be brief, but perhaps enough.

A few minutes passed, and then, all of a sudden, the light dimmed. A black shadow fell across the half-finished city below them. Kalen looked up. Above them, a hundred or more dark craft blacked out the sky, above the dome. A thunderous roar rang in his ears and he felt the ground tremble. A loud hiss mingled with the roar resounding around the dome. Gusts of warm air swept over him and his breath came up short. Suddenly, twelve airlocks in the roof of the dome opened simultaneously and the roar became deafening as the Ea-Zone fleet streamed through them. The invasion had begun.

Chapter Twenty-Seven

Shuttle after shuttle poured into the dome of the main crater, to hover high above the city and port. Hatches on the sides of several craft opened to disgorge swarms of black shiny drones, that streaked across the sky in different directions. Other shuttles disgorged troops, who dived out, spreading the arms of their glide suits at lower levels. The deafening growl of the craft increased in volume until it became an ear-splitting cacophony.

"They've opened all the airlocks at once and aren't using the docking platforms!" Russ shouted. "The override has worked."

Kalen yelled back. "Everyone will suffocate if they don't shut the airlocks."

"They'll do it soon. It'll take time for the oxygen to escape. Get ready!" Russ ordered.

The fleet began to span out around the crater, but the bulk remained above the port and central hub. Lights at the front and rear of the shuttles twinkled and flames flared along the opposite terraces. A string of explosions tore across the roof of the central hub and adjacent blocks, and columns of smoke gushed upwards. Without warning, one of the shuttles exploded, raining pieces of twisted metal onto the buildings below.

"The lasers have started." Russ inched closer to the rim. "Fire as soon as the drone station barrier retracts."

Kalen propped himself on his elbow and trained his laser on the drone station. So far the station was inert. The barriers hadn't moved. Once they began shooting, they would only have seconds to stop the drones, before they themselves, became a target. Timing would be everything. They couldn't take out all hundred boxes. He studied the transparent barrier. It would retract into a rectangular slit around the drone hatches. He searched for its mechanism, but couldn't see anything to target.

Kalen heard a rumble behind him. The ground underneath him vibrated and all of his senses became acute. He risked glancing around. Wide doors at the base of the dome had opened. Flatbed hover trucks streamed onto the walkway, carrying soldiers bunched on top. Stopping abruptly at the cliff edge, the troops jumped out to fling themselves over the precipice. Most dived, before spreading arms and legs to activate their glide suits. Others used thrusters to shoot towards the terraces.

The action was mirrored across the length of the walkways. Hundreds of bodies shot downwards, trucks above them lining the rim. Overhead, the tail of another shuttle exploded in a lightning flash, and the craft began to topple before righting itself. Explosions ripped along the roofs and terraces where the U-Zone had positioned their laser arrays. Below, black drones darted about the front of the U-Zone drone station. The entrance doors behind Kalen, began to make an unusual buzzing sound that was amplified across the terraces.

"Unity are trying to shut the doors." Russ raised his voice above the noise. "Our primary shuttle is still in place above the dome, transmitting the override signal."

A chemical burning smell tinged the air. A black drone had fired at the drone docks, singeing the transparent barrier, leaving a glowing orange patch. The drone darted back across the front. With an almost imperceptible hiss, the drone hatches opened simultaneously. Line upon line of sharp-snouted grey drones sat ready. Suddenly, with a crack, the barrier snapped back a meter from its center line, leaving a vertical gap. Drones shot straight out in a blur before Kalen had time to fire. He aimed his laser at the vertical line of empty docks, but the Ea-Zone drones had already hit them. Flames lashed the docks' innards and then died, leaving them smoldering. Another crack and the barrier retracted a further meter. This time, several drones in the docks were hit, bursting into flames before they could move.

Kalen watched anxiously. "They're using a defense program."

Russ spoke without taking his eyes off the station. "I agree. The drones should leave simultaneously."

The successful kills attracted more of Early's drone fleet. A concentration of them hovered in front of the station, ready to strike. Kalen waited for another crack, but the noise didn't come. The barrier retracted again, but soundlessly, and he didn't have time to react. Lights blinked on sharp grey snouts and a number of the airborne black drones burst into flames. The greys streaked out through the burning debris before darting back to pick off the invaders. The drone barrier suddenly slid back entirely, and the remaining drones flew out, firing. Kalen aimed a shot at the hatches, and a fountain of sparks erupted across the boxes, before the barrier slammed back into place.

"Not much luck with that," Russ muttered beside him, watching the light show in front of them. "There are other fleets that will take on the fight in Craters Two and Three where the shuttles can't go."

Several Ea-Zone shuttles were still above the central hub and port. Lasers arrays at their front and rear winked as they fired. Full length windows had opened across the highest floor of the port control center, to expose a line of weaponry. Drones darted about in front of the shuttles, that moved intermittently. Towers of rising smoke extended towards the roof of the dome, and the air filled with the smell of burning.

Abruptly, the airlocks in the dome closed all at once, and Kalen heard the ground entrances behind him close as well. A number of large military shuttles still hovered outside, over the roof of the dome. Unity have cut off the overrides, he thought. They've found a way to interrupt the signal from our air fleet.

Below him, fighting had broken out in the city streets. U-Zone army and guards engaged the intruders. Construction workers, swinging wrenches and work tools, fell on the Ea-Zone troops that landed, and the army fired at men still in the air. Early's troops grouped at different locations, and returned fire. Explosions ripped through the streets, tearing up the buildings, sending up pillars of black smoke. Distant shouting reverberated around the crater and smoking debris fell over the city.

"Early are trying not to destroy the main buildings," Russ said. "Unity are reckless enough not to care."

"Once Unity get their troops mobilized, they'll take down the shuttles over the city," Kalen replied.

"The shuttles can land to defend key points." Russ shuffled back from the edge. "I think we're done here."

Kalen glimpsed movement near the entrance to the drone station. The two soldiers guarding the building had seen them. "Watch out!"

A burst of fire hit the end of the crane they hid behind.

"They must have seen our lasers." Russ sprang up and took aim at them. "We better move. There'll be more of them up here in a minute."

Russ crouched behind the crane, and picked up a piece of rubble. He threw it onto the walkway. Bright flashes of light burst out.

"They're watching us. We'll have to make a run for it," Russ said.

"If you go first, I can give you cover fire." Jon maneuvered into a position where he could see the guards.

"Okay, we'll go first." Russ pointed to a stack of girders a few meters away. "We'll make for that pile of girders over there."

"You go with Halle. I'll stay here with Jon." Kalen moved nearer to Jon and took a shot at the guards. Flames flickered on the roof of the building and the guards ducked inside it.

"Nobody needs to stay behind," Russ said urgently.

"Two of us can take on the guards," Kalen insisted. "We'll keep them busy while you leave."

"We'll take them out and join you on the ground," Jon added.

"Contact me when you get down," Russ ordered.

Kalen couldn't see Halle's face beneath her visor, but he detected a reluctance to leave. Russ gripped her arm and pulled her after him, stooping under the overhang of the crane and running for the girders. Kalen listened to them go, keeping up a constant stream of fire at the guards. The guards pulled back behind the doorway, but every now and again, he saw the glitter of their Divines. He wondered if they could take the drone station.

"Do you think we can get inside?" Kalen asked.

"In a word, no," Jon answered dismissively. "The guards have taken up a defensive position. The best we can do is take them out. The building is only a shell. There'll be thick security doors behind it and several barriers before we can get anywhere near the controls for the drones themselves."

"We need to find a way to destroy the station," Kalen persisted. "Only a handful of the docks were destroyed. The reserve drones will be charging now, ready to deploy."

"I've seen some of the schematics for these stations," Jon said thoughtfully. "We can't get inside."

A sharp snouted grey drone hovered near them. Jon stepped back into the shadow of the crane.

"It's seen us."

"Russ was right." Kalen jumped to his feet, pressing himself flat against the crane's side. "We'll never be able to defend ourselves against the drones."

"It's a shame to leave." Jon stared at the guards.

"I want to go to Crater Two and find Sera. She'll be working on the Uveid deposits." Kalen glanced towards the guards one last time.

"I'll come with you," Jon said.

"Okay." Kalen lowered his head and began jogging in the direction that Russ and Halle had taken. He sensed something above him and a grey drone on fire fell out of the air.

"I got it," Jon said. "But there'll be more coming soon."

"Provided we keep behind the machinery, they should leave us alone," Kalen said, cautiously making his way towards the elevator. "They won't target us if they don't have a clear line of sight."

"What about the elevator? It might have been hit."

"We'll see when we get there." Kalen kept going. Ahead, the walkway was empty of troops and the tubular structure of the vacuum elevator was in view.

"Do we risk it?" Jon asked. "Even if it's functioning, once we're inside, we can't get out until ground level."

"It drops so quickly, we'll be okay if it's working." Kalen didn't break step. There were few ways down and he didn't want to jump with a glide suit, even if they had them. He had never been trained to use one.

They reached the vacuum elevator and Kalen called the car. It appeared functional and a control panel lit up to indicate that the car was coming. While they waited, Kalen watched for the drones. The seconds seemed to draw out and he pressed the call button again. Jon moved to the side of the structure and leaned forward to see over the edge.

"The car's stopped halfway," Jon reported. "It's been shut off."

"What the planets!" Kalen cursed in disgust. He eyed the Ea-Zone hover trucks that had been parked by the rim.

Jon noticed the direction of his gaze and looked at him speculatively. "You think there may be glide suits in them? Do you know how to use one?"

"Yes and no," Kalen answered. "But we have to find a way down."

"It's the quickest way," Jon replied pragmatically.

"We'll be targets for the drones." Kalen envisaged being incinerated in mid-flight.

Across the expanse of the crater, the fighting continued, the shouting clearly audible. A smell of burning rubber stung Kalen's nose. It caught in his throat and he swiveled about to find the source. A shuttle above them was on fire. Flames licked up the sides of the craft, eating away at its casing. Its side hatches opened and men began diving out, spreading the arms of their glide suits once they were clear of the flames. The shuttle spun and tipped. It was now so near that Kalen could see the pilots fighting with the controls.

The craft veered towards them, and Kalen ducked instinctively. It's tail end swung around narrowly missing the top of the vacuum elevator. The shuttle lurched sideways, nearly hitting an abandoned drill and then swerved towards a clear space on the walkway. Suddenly, grey drones appeared, and part of the drill erupted into a ball of flame. Kalen backed up against the entrance to the elevator and fired upwards, in a wide arc. Three drones exploded and dropped out the sky.

"Set your beam to wide angle," Jon instructed, firing. Two more drones fell out of the air.

Near them, the rear of the shuttle scraped the ground, gouging the walkway in a shower of sparks. The craft swayed and then finally settled, with a deep groan. The grey drones darted forward, spewing a hailstorm of fire, at its hull. Kalen sprinted to the drill, and fired at them. Jon threw himself down beside him. Flames flared from the shuttle's rear, and the pilots began to return fire from the side hatch.

They've hit the engines, Kalen thought. The pilots have to get out before it blows.

A searing blast heated up the walkway. Above Kalen, several of the grey drones had incinerated, their burnt husks clattering onto the ground. The shadow of another craft blotted out the daylight, its front lights twinkling. Another blast hit the drones, tearing them apart, to send debris spinning downwards. A handful survived and darted towards the port. The second craft swung away after them.

Flames leapt up the sides of the shuttle and the pilots jumped out carrying bundles. They waved to Kalen and Jon and ran towards them. Behind the pilots, the shuttle became engulfed by the fire, that sent up plumes of pungent black smoke. Suddenly the craft exploded, with a cracking roar. The force of the blast spewed out pieces of burning metal and the pilots threw themselves down onto the walkway. Kalen ran over to the pilots and by the time he reached them, they had begun to get up.

"Are you all right?"

"It's only bruising," one of the pilots said cheerfully, getting to his feet and brushing flecks of burning pieces off his uniform.

His co-pilot picked up the bundles that they'd dropped. She smiled and said, "Good thing we have our helmets on."

Jon saluted the pilots. "Captain Ingeston, Engineering Corps."

"Captain Mervin, and this is Corporal Shale." The first pilot returned the salute and indicated his comrade who stood by his side, holding the bundles. "Thanks for your help."

"We're part of the advance team, under the command of Major Terry," Jon replied. "And this is Captain Trinneer."

"I have to make this quick. Here's a couple of glide suits if you need them." Captain Mervin indicated the bundles that his co-pilot held. "My orders are to take one of the hover trucks east along the walkway to join our forces. You're welcome to come with us."

"Won't that take you above the port?" Kalen asked, thinking quickly. He didn't want to use a glide suit but the port control was built into the cliff face to the east. The walkway ran behind and above it, along the rim. The entrances down from the walkway, into the port control, would be heavily guarded. The lasers had targeted that section. The pilots were going into the thick of the action.

"Yes, it will." Captain Mervin began to move off.

"We'll come with you." Jon made the decision for both of them.

***

Halle could hardly suppress her annoyance at being dragged away by Russ, leaving the others behind. "We shouldn't have left them there. You should have ordered them to come with us."

Russ answered in a firm voice, "They provided cover for us to get away. It makes sense to let them try and take out the guards."

"Where are we going?" Halle kept close to Russ as they carefully made their way along a passageway near the airfield. They had reached ground level without problem but after alighting from the elevator, had watched it take a laser hit.

"The attack on Crater One is well under control. We'll join the ground troops in Crater Two. Piers and Rena should be there."

They walked on, towards the sounds of fighting. Overhead, a number of shuttles hovered, but many had already landed. Rounding a corner, they came to a square and Halle saw one of the shuttles landing. The craft came down neatly in the square and a rear hatch opened immediately. A ramp snaked down from the hatch, and a hover truck rolled out, full of troops. Elsewhere in the square, other shuttles were landing and more trucks were rolling out.

"We're getting one of those trucks." Russ put his arm up to signal the nearest shuttle. "They're expecting us."

Chapter Twenty-Eight

Kalen and Jon sat in the rear of the truck. Corporal Shale drove and they sped along the walkway, weaving through the abandoned equipment. The truck skimmed the ground by only a few centimeters and occasionally, Corporal Shale swerved to avoid smoking debris that littered their path. She kept their speed up, handling the controls with dexterity. The drones ignored them, but the guards at the station fired as they went by, scorching the vehicle's sides. Kalen sighted them, but the truck's movement made his aim unreliable. Better to save the laser charge, he thought.

"We're joining the Second Regiment out of Base One," Captain Mervin informed them. "They're trying to take the port control. We already have the upper hand at the airfield and main terminal."

"What about the central hub?" Jon leant forward.

"Unity are still holding out, but we're gaining," Mervin replied.

Kalen gripped the side of the truck as it jolted. "What about Crater Two? We need to join the rest of our team there."

"I haven't had a report on the other craters." Mervin clutched at a hand rail to steady himself as the truck swerved again.

They made good time around the walkway and quickly passed the undeveloped area below. The buildings in this section became more crowded and terraces appeared in the cliff face. They passed above the utility center, the water tanks on its roof, still intact. Within minutes, the airfield came into view, extending from the base of the cliffs, southwards. A row of shuttles stood stationary on their docking platforms, while laser fire played out between depot buildings and the main passenger terminal. Groups of troops moved between the stationary craft, adding to the fire. Several trucks were moving northwards across the airfield, towards the cliff that overlooked it, from which the port control hung midway.

"We're nearly there," Shale announced, beginning to slow.

Up ahead, several trucks blocked the walkway. A number of soldiers milled about and beyond them, explosions and laser strikes threw up sheets of flame and burning debris. Bitter smoke trailed upwards in several places, and the babble of loud shouting competed with the sound of masonry collapsing. A shuttle had positioned itself overhead, its laser arrays winking as it fired at the port control.

"That's far enough," Mervin instructed Shale.

The truck stopped opposite the doors of an elevator and Mervin jumped out. "We leave you here. The elevator should take you to ground level. It's under our control. Good luck."

Kalen shouldered his pack and leapt down. "Thank you and good luck."

"Thank you, Sir." Jon took his leave, picking up the bundled glide suits. "We'll take these if you don't need them."

Mervin and Shale quickly disappeared into the throng near the trucks and Kalen gave Jon a questioning look. "Glide suits?"

"You never know," Jon replied.

"No, leave them," Kalen said decisively. "We don't have room in our packs."

They took the lift and reached the floor of the crater without incident. The streets at ground level were guarded by Ea-Zone troops, and they found the underpass to Crater Two without being stopped. The moving walkway had been shut off and trucks carrying Early's troops whistled past, going in the same direction as them. No one stopped to question them. Underground, the sounds of the battle were muted. The air supply units were functioning and their gentle hum leant a normalcy to the day, but every now and again the lights flickered.

Kalen wondered where Halle and Russ had gone, but discarded the idea of radioing them. "I need to find Sera Ethern. I'm going down to the Uveid deposits. If she's anywhere, that's where she'll be."

"What are you going to do when you find her?" Jon asked. "Crater One isn't safe. She can't return to her accommodation."

"If Early have control of Crater Two, I can leave her at one of the command posts until the fighting is over."

They trudged through the underpass and it finally began to slope upwards. Kalen glimpsed daylight ahead, and heard shouting. Trucks continued to stream past them carrying Ea-Zone troops. He took hold of his laser and switched it to ready. If they came out of the underpass to fighting in Crater Two, he was prepared. He fervently hoped that Early had the upper hand. Any fighting in Craters Two and Three would be at close combat.

When they emerged into the crater, Kalen saw no sign of the workforce, and no one on the half-finished buildings. The cranes stood motionless, some with scorch marks on their towers. Early's troops had control of the open area near the underpass, and lines of soldiers were moving east and north, beyond the construction site. The air was smoky and the unmistakable sounds of fighting reached him.

"I'm going to try and get below. If Sera's here, she'll be on level fifty-one," Kalen said.

"We may not be able to get down," Jon replied.

"Halle said she switched off half of the mine operations. The other half of the elevators should still be running. I have to find Sera and make sure she's safe."

"Okay," Jon replied, and began walking towards the Gate that led to the elevators to the lower levels.

They found the Gate guarded by Ea-Zone soldiers. A group of several soldiers stood near the entrance, and two more stood on each side of the Gate itself.

A young soldier with a visor covering her face, stepped forward to block their path. "Sir, I have orders to stop everyone. Where are you going?"

Kalen pushed up his visor. "We need to get down to level fifty-one."

"You can't get down, all of the elevators have been shut off," the soldier replied in an authoritative voice.

"I thought only half were out?" Kalen queried.

"The lifts got damaged in the fighting. Only some of the stairwells are open. In places they're impassable as well." The soldier was joined by two others who lingered to listen to the conversation.

"Was there much fighting down there?" Jon asked, moving forward.

"Yes, but we have it under control. Which unit are you from, Sir?"

Kalen coughed as smoke caught in his throat. "We're from the advance team with Captain Thomas under the command of Major Terry. We have orders to locate a U-Zone geologist below ground before re-joining him."

"Name? I'll check if they're being held," the soldier replied.

"Sera Ethern," Kalen said.

The soldier spoke into her radio and then returned her attention to Kalen. "There's a large number of detainees. Most of them have been rounded up and are being held on level six. There's still pockets of resistance on the levels below thirty."

"Can we go down?" Kalen persisted.

"Only as far as level six, Sir, but no further. You can check if she's there." The soldier stood aside.

"Thank you." Kalen flipped his visor down and nodded shortly to Jon.

***

The underground levels were chaotic. The stairwells were thick with cloudy grey smoke, and Kalen and Jon came across damaged sections, where the treads had broken away. The air supply units made hiccupping noises, and Kalen used his oxygen and breathing tube. Lights flickered on and off, so that everything was periodically pitched into darkness. Using flashlights, they clambered down to level six, ignoring the intervening levels and the soldiers who passed them in both directions.

Level six had been arranged as a detention center and Kalen asked a passing soldier where the prisoners were being held. They were directed to a reception area where two junior officers stood near a wide doorway, through which soldiers came and went. They were issuing orders and using their radios.

Kalen approached the nearest officer. "Lieutenant, is this where the prisoners are being held? We're trying to find a geologist called Sera Ethern."

The Lieutenant's eyes took in Kalen and Jon's rank. "Just a minute, Sir. I'll check."

"Thank you." Kalen waited with Jon, while the Lieutenant spoke into his radio.

"Not on our lists," the Lieutenant replied. "What does she look like?"

"She's about thirty with dark brown shoulder length hair." Kalen tried to think of how else he could describe her. Would her pregnancy show? "She's medium height and will be wearing one of those blue stones around her neck."

"I'll check again." The Lieutenant went inside the doorway. After two or three minutes, he returned, shaking his head. "No one of that description. We're holding mostly construction workers, a few civilians and security guards. All of them are wearing those blue stones."

"Can we see for ourselves? She may have given a different name," Kalen asked.

The Lieutenant glanced at his colleague, who shrugged. "Okay, but don't be long."

The Lieutenant gestured to the doorway and Kalen and Jon went inside. Row upon row of construction workers sat in a large hall, facing the door. Several soldiers guarded them, pacing up and down. Towards the back of the hall, Kalen saw a handful of security guards and some civilians in Colonization Division uniforms. All wore the blue Uveid pendants around their necks and appeared dazed. They sat straight legged, eyes fixed, gazing forward. There was very little noise, and the air supply units stuttered loudly against the hush of the hall. The guards watched Kalen and Jon closely.

Kalen scanned the rows of prisoners. "I can't see her."

"I can't either, but let's check at the back." Jon walked down the side of the rows.

Kalen studied each face, feeling increasingly disappointed. "She isn't here, is she?"

"No, I'm sorry." Jon skirted back towards the door.

"You didn't find her?" the Lieutenant enquired when they exited the hall.

"No, she wasn't in there," Kalen replied, pausing outside the door.

"What are you going to do with them?" Jon asked.

"My orders are to contain them on this level, while we secure the lower levels," the Lieutenant replied.

The sound of a loud siren, suddenly ricocheted loudly across the room. Kalen flinched, momentarily confusing it with the day end sirens, that had sounded twice a day before the war. Soldiers appeared from the stairwell and the Lieutenant began speaking urgently into his radio. After listening for a few seconds, he began shouting orders to the troops around him, and the other officer disappeared into the hall.

The Lieutenant turned back to Kalen and Jon. "We have to evacuate. Unity have control of the main dome's port locks. They've opened them and sent an air fleet in!"

"Go! Go!" someone shouted from the stairwell.

"We better go now," Jon urged.

"She could be below."

"That's a long shot at best," Jon replied. "Even if she was down there, we wouldn't be able to get to her."

"You're right," Kalen conceded. "Let's get up top."

More soldiers appeared on the floor and the officers began making hurried preparations to leave. Kalen heard the pounding of many boots on the stairs. He glanced towards the door of the hall and wondered what they were going to do with the prisoners. They were complacent now, but he had witnessed the madness of those affected by the Uveid.

They joined the throng of soldiers hammering up the stairs. At ground level, the fumes and noise had increased. Tiny pieces of smoldering debris floated in the air, giving off a pungent chemical smell and the atmosphere had got noticeably hotter. Just south of the Gate, Early were defending the crater. Troops positioned behind a line of trucks fought off laser fire from an army of small ground vehicles, coming through the underpass. One-seater hover guns capable of rising two meters above the ground, fired relentlessly at the Ea-Zone forces, the riders perched behind long range lasers. The hover guns swung around erratically to evade laser fire, their programming automatically detecting it.

"They've landed their shuttles," Jon yelled, as grey drones arrived to join the assault. "They've probably come from Unity's base at the fourth crater."

"Early are falling back," Jon shouted, taking aim and firing at a grey drone.

A piece of heavy masonry fell near them, hitting the ground with a thump. Another lump of stone crashed a meter away from Kalen, throwing up grit and dust. He twisted around to see where it came from. Above them, Early's troops lined the terraces in the cliffside, engaging a swarm of grey drones in heavy laser fire. Explosions rocked the terraces, ripping away chunks of the structure. The siren continued to shriek with ear piercing volume, drowning out screaming and shouting from the fighting.

"I've heard from Russ. He's in Crater Three with the others. They're trying to free the prisoners," Jon shouted.

"We should join him." Kalen lowered his head to avoid a burning section of paneling that flew by. "With the prisoners freed, we'll outnumber Unity."

***

Kalen and Jon entered Crater Three to find a raging battle. The U-Zone army had taken the terraces on the cliffside, while the Ea-Zone had taken up positions in the construction site. Early's troops lobbed laser fire from the upper floors of the half-completed buildings, which Unity were returning in equal measure. Kalen adjusted the optics on his visor and studied the construction site. Most of the buildings were shells, their interior floors remaining open. There were construction workers on the floors of several buildings. They stood or sat watching the fighting, passively, neither taking cover or flinching from the laser fire.

He sprinted towards the construction site with Jon, and found Russ on one of the high levels of a building. Halle, Rena and Piers were with him. They had joined a contingent firing lasers at the U-Zone on the terraces opposite. Several long range lasers were positioned across the length of the floor, each manned by more than one person. As Kalen came up, Halle avoided his gaze and turned her head away. At least she's okay, he thought.

"We've got our hands full here," Russ greeted them. "Unity are putting on a good show."

"Why are the prisoners just standing around?" Kalen asked. "We passed a few of them and they didn't even acknowledge us."

"We've taken their restraints off but they're apathetic," Russ replied. "We think they've been affected by the Uveid."

Kalen glanced at a worker sitting nearby, with a vacant expression on his face. He thought he saw a glitter of blue near the collar of the man's beige overalls.

"Are they wearing the pendants?" he asked.

"Probably," Rena chipped in. "There wasn't time to take them off."

"We need to take the accommodation blocks. There are more prisoners in there." Russ sited his laser and fired at the terraces.

An explosion erupted near them and part of the roof disintegrated, spewing foul smelling burning plastic, leaving a hole that glowed red hot. Another explosion on a ledge, sent chunks of masonry tumbling to the ground, far below them. Plumes of smoke drifted upwards from strikes on the lower levels and Kalen felt heat from them on his cheeks despite his visor. A blast behind them shook the floor, followed by a loud cracking sound.

Russ twisted around. "Part of the floor's giving way. They're attacking from the rear."

"We'll deal with it!" Jon shouted, swiveling to run towards the other side of the floor.

Kalen followed him, keeping his head down. There were no interior walls on this level and they covered the distance quickly. On the far side, Jon pressed himself flat against an upright girder. Kalen bowed his head and slid behind another girder nearby. Jon pointed upwards and Kalen peered out in the direction he indicated. Troops had climbed up one of the tall cranes, and were firing down at the building. The Divines on their jackets glinted in the unfiltered sunlight blazing through the dome.

Kalen shrunk back behind the girder. The angle was too difficult to get a good shot. He peeked out again. From this side he had a good view of the rest of the crater. He stared out in astonishment. The ruins on the far side had grown and now covered the bulk of the crater. A ruined city spread for kilometers from the construction site to the crater's edge in the east. In amongst the ruins, people dressed in blue roamed gracefully, appearing almost to float over the rugged stone pathways, along the alleyways and across the squares. This had once been a thriving city. *An alien thriving city.*

Jon exclaimed, "Who are they?"

"They're U-Zone. Civilians." Kalen watched the people drifting, apparently oblivious to the war raging in the rest of the crater.

"They're rebuilding the ruins," Jon said. "Look to the north. That archway wasn't there before."

"I think you're right." Kalen watched a woman of medium height, dressed in a turquoise tunic, move gracefully across one of the squares. Sera! It had to be.

A vibration passed underneath Kalen's boots and the building rocked. He staggered and grabbed hold of the metal upright to avoid falling. A thunderous growl rolled across the crater and part of the building's skeleton buckled, throwing chunks of the hard flooring down to crush a hover truck below. The tall crane swayed and Unity's troops clung on desperately.

The building shook again, and tipped as one of the corner sections crumpled, with a terrible creaking sound. A building near them began to collapse, its steel framework sagging and twisting, until it fell with a roar, sending up a cloud of dust.

Without words, Kalen and Jon scrambled towards the stairwell. The sounds of the others evacuating rang loud across the floor. Fighting to retain his balance, Kalen stumbled from girder to girder, gripping each tightly. The tremors increased and the tall crane toppled over, smashing into the street below. Part of the stairwell buckled, warping the lattice-work in the treads, and bending the handrail. Ploughing onwards, they finally reached the bottom. Outside, cracks snaked across the ground, tearing apart the fabric of the crater floor.

"The weapon! They're using the trident-weapon!" Kalen shouted, above the noise.

"How? You destroyed it." Jon glanced about them.

"They must have duplicated it. They're destroying the crater," Kalen yelled.

"Unity have taken the other two craters. They're coming in through the ground exits," Russ shouted. "We've been ordered to fall back."

"Where?" Jon asked simply.

"The airfield further north. Early will evacuate us through there. It's small but functional," Russ informed them.

"Can't we make a stand?" Jon queried.

"We're not fighting Unity. We're fighting an alien technology," Russ countered. "We can't defend ourselves against the trident-weapon."

Kalen made a decision. "You go. I'm going to get Sera."

"Don't be a fool," Russ snapped scornfully. "You'll get yourself killed."

"I'll take my chances," Kalen replied resolutely. "If I can find her, I'll join you at the airfield."

"Don't leave it too long," Russ told him.

Chapter Twenty-Nine

The ruins had grown in height since Kalen had last been in them. The ground had stopped shaking and the rumbling had died away. He tore off his stripes and replaced them with a Divine and put his laser under his jacket, where he could reach it quickly. Cautiously, he made his way amongst the stone passageways, with the strange swirling markings on the walls. He composed his face to emulate the vacant expressions of the workers he had seen, and studiously tried to avoid meeting anyone.

Occasionally, he saw people moving about in the distance, and he would take a different turning to avoid them. They hadn't sensed his presence yet, but he reckoned that it wouldn't take much for him to be exposed. The woman in the turquoise tunic had been in the north-west corner of the ruins, near the rebuilt archway. He remembered a wide passageway that ran through the center of the ruins, but decided against using it. Instead, he walked northwards keeping to the narrower alleys where there was less chance of meeting someone.

A figure at the end of a shaded passageway stood silhouetted against the harsh light. The glare behind the woman made it impossible to see her features. Kalen raised his visor.

"Sera?"

The woman entered the shaded alley. Sera's large eyes observed Kalen calmly through her black lashes. She wore her hair free, and it tumbled to her shoulders, thick and glossy. Her unlined face glowed and her full lips curved into a smile. She took a step towards Kalen.

"I knew you'd come back to me."

Kalen reached for her hands. "I've been worried about you and the baby. I'm glad you're okay."

"Of course I'm okay. Why wouldn't I be?" Sera laughed lightly.

"The fighting…"

"It can't touch us here. I've never been in any danger," she assured him.

"I've come to take you somewhere safe," he said gently.

"I am safe." A smile played across her lips.

He gazed into her eyes and then kissed her. Her lips parted under his and she folded herself into him. She felt soft and pliant in his arms and he forgot about the war and was only aware of the beautiful woman he held. The visor of his helmet was loose, and it slipped down against his forehead. He released Sera, and put a hand up to clip the visor back.

"Take your helmet off." Sera's feather-light touch stroked his forehead. "I want to see your face."

The day was hot and the shade of the walls inviting. He could afford to take a little time before they left.

"Over here." Sera clasped his hand and led him to a stone bench in the shade. "Isn't it peaceful?"

The noise had died away and they sat in the calm of a sunny afternoon. The surroundings were almost dreamlike and Kalen felt himself relaxing. He pushed his helmet up, easing it away from his sweat soaked hair. As the weight lifted, a sense of wellbeing coursed through him. He closed his eyes, savoring the moment of peacefulness after the violence of the day. The shadow wall filled his mind and the golden light through the window beckoned him.

He opened his eyes with a start and tugged his helmet into place. How could he be so stupid? A few seconds more and he would be like them. Like Sera.

She gazed at him, eyes wide. "What's the matter?"

"I'm taking you away from here." He stood up and pulled her up after him. "This way."

"Where are we going?" A confused expression crossed her face.

"To the airfield."

"In the main crater?" She pulled away from him.

"No, there's a small airfield near here."

"Why?"

He gathered her in his arms and searched her face. "Early are withdrawing. I don't want to leave you here."

"But I don't want to leave. I'm safe here. Please stay, Kalen," she pleaded.

"I can't stay. Don't you see? You've been infected by the Uveid." He lifted the chain around her neck with his index finger, dangling the Uveid stone. "This is affecting you."

A glint of something hard flickered in her eyes, but she lowered them quickly and when she raised them again, it was gone. Her gentle smile beseeched him.

"Stay here with me. We're free now."

"We're leaving and that's final. I have a responsibility to keep the baby and you safe."

He took a firm hold of her hand and led her along the alley. This time she didn't resist and he began to hope that he could get her on a shuttle. Sera picked her way over the uneven paving stones with ease, never missing her footing and put the flat of her hand out to brush the swirling patterns on the walls they passed. She began humming to herself, a quiet tuneful melody. The ruins were vast and Kalen cut across a corner until he came to the edge of them.

At the perimeter of the ruins, Sera drew back. "I don't want to leave."

Kalen reluctantly stopped walking. They were still in the shadow of the ruins and the air was a comfortable temperature. Outside, the sun bore through the dome, sending up a heat haze across the barren cracked ground. Some way from off, he could see the small military port. Shuttles were leaving, and the sound of the crafts' engines and desperate voices carried across the empty space. He couldn't drag her there, that much was certain. He had to persuade her, somehow.

He hugged her and kissed her hair, whispering, "I want to be with you."

"I want to be with you, as well." Her eyes implored him. "Why are you doing this Kalen? I thought you were happy in Unity?"

"Things change, Sera. We'll be safest with the Ea-Zone. I want our son to grow up safely. You want that too, don't you?"

"Of course." She smiled and clasped his hand again.

Kalen led Sera away from the ruins, aware that they were exposed, towards the airfield. He took off his Divine and put it in his pocket. The sky was clear of drones and he couldn't hear any fighting. With his visor raised, he squinted against the glare of the sun. Beside him, Sera seemed untroubled, moving gracefully over the uneven surface. From the folds of her tunic she produced a soft blue hat and arranged it over her hair. He peeked at her feet. She wore flat boots beneath the tunic and he caught a glimpse of her long pale legs.

"We're nearly there," he said encouragingly, as they neared the small port.

He could make out details now. Several hover trucks were parked in front of an airfield and building, near the cliff that edged the crater. Two shuttles stood on the airfield and a line of soldiers were boarding them. Overhead, the port airlocks of the dome were open, letting in Taidor's thin atmosphere.

He shrugged off his pack and found an air canister and breathing tube, and handed them to Sera. "You'll need these."

He slipped another tube into the corner of his mouth and attached it to a canister. Ready, he took Sera's hand and led her forward to the port terminal. A large group of soldiers moved around outside, their numbers swelling by others coming out of the building. Officers shouted directions, organizing the troops into groups. The first shuttle's doors closed and its ramp retracted. It rose gradually until it became a tiny spec in the mouth of the aperture, high above in the dome. No sooner had it left, then two more shuttles appeared, descending carefully to settle on the airfield.

"They're working in relays to shuttle everyone out, before Unity get here," Kalen explained.

They reached the entrance to the terminal and Kalen ushered Sera inside, past soldiers coming out. The building was cool and Kalen found an empty seat for her.

"Wait here while I ask about the shuttles."

She smiled at him affectionately and he let go of her hand and left her. Outside, he began searching for Russ and Jon. A group of troops had gathered on the concourse and they ignored him, so that he had to shoulder his way through. Satisfied that he knew no one in the group, he wormed his way out and cast about the airfield for a familiar face. He saw another group near the shuttles and walked towards them.

Without any warning, a deafening explosion erupted behind him, knocking him to the ground. He twisted around and tried to rise, to find himself blinded by dust and debris. A wall of heat beat against his visor. Screaming and shouting rang out across the airfield, and the acrid smell of burning choked the air. Through the smoke he saw that the terminal had been hit. Roaring flames shot upwards, consuming the building. He staggered up and ran towards the door, but the flames drove him back. He tried again, but two soldiers held his arms and dragged him away. The building was an inferno. Disbelief numbed him. *Sera! Sera was in there.*

Crackling flames tore through the fabric of the terminal. Stunned, Kalen watched it burn. Numbing grief coursed through him. Whatever Sera had been, she was carrying his child. Now the baby and her were gone. It seemed unreal. The shouting and people around him seemed distant, somewhere outside the bubble of his loss. Someone bumped into him, but he barely registered it. On the airfield, one of the shuttles lifted abruptly, engines shrieking, tearing free of its ramp. With doors still open, it climbed into the smoke gushing skyward.

Kalen felt a hand on his shoulder and a familiar voice asked, "Are you okay?"

He spat out his breathing tube and muttered, "Sera. She's gone."

"What do you mean?" Jon asked, now facing him.

"She was in the terminal when it was hit."

"I'm sorry," Jon said sympathetically. "But it's time to go. The shuttles are leaving."

"Where are Russ and Halle?" Kalen asked.

"The others got out except for Russ. He's this way," Jon said urgently, leading him towards the shuttles.

"Where did the strike come from?"

"The west of the crater. There's still fighting going on up there."

The soldiers had thinned out and another shuttle lifted off, quickly disappearing into the sky. Only two more craft remained, and soldiers scrambled up their ramps in equal numbers. Russ was near the shuttles, directing the boarding, moving about and keeping order. Jon and Kalen joined the end of the line to board the shuttles and soon there were only a few people left ahead of them. One of the shuttles closed its doors and took off, and the last craft began filling up quickly. Soldiers stood inside its open doors, and more troops continued to squeeze in. It's going to be tight, Kalen thought.

They finally reached Russ at the foot of the ramp. He stared at them, his eyes intense.

"Trinneer, Ingeston, you're the last. Get on board."

He still doesn't trust us, thought Kalen. He would have been relieved if we hadn't made it back.

Kalen ran up the ramp. At the top, he squeezed inside, finding a handhold. Jon and Russ came behind him. Just before the doors closed, he took a final glance outside. The terminal was still ablaze. High flames sent up bitter smoke, coloring the air grey. He pictured Sera's face and felt numb. It didn't seem possible that she could be dead. He pushed the images of Sera aside. He couldn't think about this now. They were at war and it wasn't over yet. Bodies pressed against him and he sucked hard on his breathing tube. The doors slid shut and a jolt signaled their departure. The craft rocked and he held on, cries of alarm tearing at his ears. A shower of twisted metal and burning fragments fell past the hatches.

"They've hit the other shuttle!" Russ said tersely.

"They must have been waiting for it to leave," Kalen replied.

"We're next," Jon muttered.

"The pilot's good," Russ snapped back. "We have a chance."

The shuttle abruptly tipped, and accelerated sideways. Those standing were thrown against each other. It briefly righted itself, before flying diagonally upwards. Outside, everything clouded. Smoke enveloped the craft and the interior dimmed. A hush fell over the passengers. Engines screaming, it suddenly ascended straight up. The force of the upward thrust pulled against Kalen's knees and he held on tightly to a handle.

"He's using the smoke as a shield," Russ said. "It'll disperse any laser fire."

"He's on manual, flying blind," Kalen added.

The craft lurched violently, clearing the smoke. Bright light filled the cabin. The edge of a docking platform ripped along its side with a shrill screech and the craft juddered and shook. A metal strut seemed to arrow at them, but the shuttle veered to miss it by a meter. It fell past the windows, glinting in the sunshine. They rose unsteadily, through the open airlocks, until suddenly the dome fell away. A collective exhalation of breath and gasps of relief rang around the cabin, as they flew into the open sky.

***

The post-mortem at Base Four was brutal. Kalen listened as Russ addressed a group of officers that included Commander Callard, Lieutenant Abbott, Jon, and Halle. "We've lost Three-Craters. We took many casualties including Major Terry. Our initial assault went well, but Unity got reinforcements from their base at the fourth crater. Together with the use of the trident-weapon, we were overpowered."

"How was the trident-weapon used?" Lieutenant Abbott asked.

"I think Captain Trinneer is best able to answer that," Russ said.

"They must have managed to duplicate the original weapon. It works by releasing and directing energy from the Uveid rock," Kalen explained. "It destabilizes everything around it, like an earthquake. It brought down all of the buildings in Craters Two and Three."

"The main crater largely survived, but we were overrun by Unity's reinforcements," Russ added.

"Did the workers in Crater Three escape?" Lieutenant Abbott asked.

"They didn't move until the buildings started to fall. Some got out," Russ replied.

"And we left them there?" Lieutenant Abbott sounded concerned.

"We didn't have any choice," Russ answered. "They were affected by the Uveid stones and unresponsive to instructions."

Commander Callard coughed. "We have to recognize that Unity, for the most part, are infected by an alien force. Their behavior isn't rational. We don't know if they can recover from it. The weapon they've developed comes from an alien technology. Future military action has to deal with the U-Zone on this basis."

A murmur went around the room. For a moment, their voices receded and Kalen was with Sera again, walking through the ruins. It had been so peaceful there, it was hard to accept that it involved a malevolent influence. He imagined sitting on the bench with her in the cool of the afternoon, soothing away all the hardships of the past days. A spike of loss intruded into his thoughts. Her face dissolved into the swirling patterns on the ruined walls. Someone was speaking to him.

"Trinneer, you said you'd seen the geologist?" Russ was staring at him. "I'm sorry, I mean, your wife?"

"Yes, that's right." Kalen recovered himself. "I found her in the ruins in Crater Three, but she was in the terminal when it was hit."

"Please accept our condolences, Captain Trinneer," Commander Callard said formally. "I don't want to sound callous but I have to ask you some questions. Were there other people in the ruins? What were they doing?"

"They were rebuilding them."

The room went very quiet and Commander Callard leant forward. "Did your wife say anything about that? Give any explanation?"

"No, I don't think so."

"And you didn't ask her?"

"I didn't think of it," Kalen replied, puzzled. Why hadn't he asked her?

"What did your wife say when you found her?" Commander Callard persisted.

"She said she didn't want to leave." The loss of Sera and the baby was almost too harsh for him to continue. "Something about being free."

"Hmm…do you know what she meant?"

"She also said she was safe. I think she meant in the ruins."

"Alien ruins, alien energy and an alien weapon," Commander Callard summarized and fell silent, looking thoughtful.

"Do you want me to continue with the briefing, Sir?" Russ asked.

Commander Callard switched his attention to Russ. "Yes, carry on. I haven't got any more questions."

"Although we've lost Three-Craters, we hold Morten. The U-Zone are still trying to oust us, but we've taken the city. We also hold Cherer. There's still fighting in the rest of the settlements. At the present time, the U-Zone have Central. We have our mountain bases and we're planning to launch an offensive against Central within the next few days. Once we have Central, we should have the upper hand."

Lieutenant Abbott shuffled in her seat. "What has happened to the civilians in Central and the other settlements that Unity have taken?"

"We know that the U-Zone populations are all assisting their army," Russ said, pausing briefly before carrying on. "The Ea-Zone civilians have either been executed or brainwashed, by being forced to wear those pendants."

"What about the children?"

"We think they're still holding them," Russ answered and a silence fell across the room.

The silence was broken by a corporal sitting in the corner. "Is Earth or any of the other colonies sending reinforcements?"

"No, they regard this as a civil war," Russ said. "We've reported the alien influence at play, but Earth has refused to intervene. We're on our own."

Chapter Thirty

Kalen sat with Jon in the mess hall, a plate of orange and red stew in front of him. He ate a mouthful and chewed slowly. Halle sat on the other side of the canteen with Russ. He found his eyes drawn to her, and quickly looked away. The tinkle of her laugh reached him and his gaze wandered to her again. Russ was saying something to her and she was laughing, gazing at him adoringly. Kalen's stomach churned and he put his fork down. He didn't feel like eating. As if sensing his interest, Halle turned her head and stared at him directly. He met her eyes briefly, before she quickly looked away.

Opposite him, Jon's expression was quizzical. "What's going on with her? You can hardly keep your eyes off her."

"She was my girlfriend before I defected to Unity." Before Sera; before the evil of the war. Seeing Halle made him forget Sera. Let him remember the good times and the fun they had.

"She's with him now," Jon pointed out.

"I know. I'm just trying to take my mind off Sera."

"What do you make of the alien influence on Unity?" Jon changed the subject.

Kalen considered the question. "There are shapes in the energy field, but they don't have bodies. They couldn't have built the cities or made the trident."

"Whatever built those ruins were similar in size to us." Jon finished his food. "And where are they now? Why did they leave Taidor?"

"Perhaps there were two species here?" Kalen suggested. "One had bodies and built the cities, and the others are incorporeal."

"It's possible," Jon agreed. "The incorporeal beings could still be here, taking over our people."

"If we knew what the trident was originally used for, we might have an answer," Kalen said. "Paul Neill thought it was made for communication, but I don't think so."

"Perhaps it was made as a weapon originally?" Jon suggested.

Kalen ate the last of his stew, reviewing what he knew about the trident. "I don't think the trident was designed specifically to split rock open. We couldn't direct the energy when we first used it. Who would the aliens be using it against? Their own people?"

"Or the other species that existed on Taidor?" Jon pushed his plate away.

"That doesn't make sense. They're incorporeal. A weapon like that wouldn't affect them." Even as he said it, he had a nagging doubt. There was something that he was missing in the equation. Something important. Halle's laugh distracted him and he fought the urge to stare at her again.

"What do you make of Captain Thomas's summary at the meeting?" Jon asked him in a low voice.

"I think they're overstating the Ea-Zone's chances of success," Kalen replied, trying to ignore Halle. "Cherer is too small to make a difference. Our forces are stretched already holding on to Morten."

"If the Ea-Zone can't recover Central, we'll lose."

"I admit the odds are stacked against us," Kalen replied quietly.

"What then? " Jon mused.

"There'll be an alien race in control of Taidor. Earth and the other colonies will need to be informed. I expect Earth will just quarantine Taidor."

"They've turned their backs on us," Jon said.

"They're too far away to do much anyway," Kalen reasoned. "And who would they support? They would have to come in as a peacekeeping force."

"They could have tried."

"It's too late now. The war is nearly over."

***

Halle had been enjoying her supper with Russ, until Kalen arrived in the canteen. She gazed at Russ across the table, aware of the effect that she had on him. This was a rare hour of leisure in a terrible week. The battle in Three-Craters had been a frightening experience and she was thankful that they had both got out alive. When Russ had forced her to leave without him, she had thought that she would never see him again. Or Kalen.

Now, Kalen sat by the other wall talking to Captain Ingeston, but she sensed that he was staring at her. They were deep in conversation. She wondered what they were talking about. Memories of the good times flooded back. She had spent evenings with Kalen in the bars and restaurants of Central, laughing and joking. They had often spent the night together. She had loved him passionately. It had all gone wrong when he had met that woman, Sera. Could she really be dead?

Russ sat opposite her, talking. They had finished their meal and her hand rested on the table. Russ put his hand over hers and spoke earnestly. "We have to keep fighting. We can't let them win. It will be hard, but we have a good chance of succeeding."

"I know," she tried to focus on what he was saying.

"You haven't heard anything I've said, have you?"

"You were talking about winning," Halle said.

"You seem distracted. It's Trinneer, isn't it?" Russ said astutely.

Halle smiled at him, with guileless blue eyes. "Not at all. He belongs to my past. I was thinking we could go back to my room."

"I wish I could, but Commander Callard wants me to go over the plan," Russ replied. "We'll have to make it another time."

Crushing disappointment filled Halle. "If we don't spend time together now, we may not get a chance later on."

"There'll always be another day." Russ grinned. "We'll make time, but tonight is out, I'm afraid."

"Okay," she said quietly, withdrawing her hand from under his.

"Talking about Commander Callard, he's expecting me soon. I have to go," Russ pushed back his chair. "I'll walk you to your rooms."

Halle rose to go and linked her arm in his. He made a joke and she laughed, for Kalen's benefit. Russ was too busy to be with her. She understood, but wished things were different. She wished she was back in Central and everything was normal. But it would never be normal now. She threw a glance in Kalen's direction as they left. He was still in conversation with Jon and didn't see her. I suppose he's grieving the loss of his wife, she thought.

***

A number of officers assembled for the briefing meeting, taking seats around a large table with low desk screens in front of them. Although not military, Halle had been invited to join them as a senior member of the Division. When she entered the room, she scanned the faces of those present. Kalen was there talking to an officer beside him. She took her seat and then waited for the meeting to begin.

Commander Callard opened the meeting. "Good morning. I have to inform you that the U-Zone have launched a major attack on Morten. We've had to put our plans to take Central on hold. I'll let Captain Thomas give you the details."

Russ stood up and addressed the group in grave tones. "Six hours ago the U-Zone launched an air and ground attack against Morten. They've taken the south of the city, as well as the transport terminal and shuttle port. We've been forced to take up defensive positions in the north."

A low buzz went around the room and he stopped speaking. Halle felt a sinking feeling. Everything was going the wrong way. She tried to catch Russ's eye. His gaze rested on her briefly, and she saw a reassuring warmth there. He looked away quickly and she lowered her eyes, conscious of the other people around her. She heard someone near her say "losing the war" and she suppressed a retort. They mustn't give up now. It was unthinkable that Unity might win.

Russ waited until the noise had died down and then went on, "The Ea-Zone have mobilized Base Five, Six and Seven to assist. We've been ordered to remain on standby at the present time. Unity are using the trident-weapon. They've destroyed half of the buildings in Morten. We have no way of countering it."

Russ glanced around the room. "Two other settlements have also been attacked. Trident-weapons were used at both, causing massive destruction."

Russ sat down and Commander Callard stood up. "We have a total of twelve mountain bases throughout Taidor. So long as we have the bases, we can win this war. The locations of our bases are unknown to the U-Zone. Our bases are secure provided their locations remain secret."

The room fell quiet. Halle tried to take in the enormity of what Russ and Commander Callard had said. Unity were using the trident-weapon to win, but the army bases were still safe. She looked over at Kalen who sat a few places away from her. He had listened to everything with an inscrutable expression. Next to him, Lieutenant Abbott whispered something in his ear. He inclined his head to listen and then Lieutenant Abbott sat back, her brow creased with anxiety.

Commander Callard resumed speaking, "Simply put, we must prepare for the worst eventuality - that the U-Zone take Morten. If they take Morten, they'll control our three largest settlements. We have sufficient supplies to remain at this base for the time being."

The officers began murmuring but Russ interrupted them, "We'll keep everyone informed as the reports come in. I must remind you that everything that's been said at this meeting is confidential and must not be disclosed to anyone else. For the moment, you're dismissed except for Captain Trinneer. Please stay behind."

Halle left with the others, leaving Commander Callard and Russ to speak with Kalen. She wondered what they were talking about. Something military no doubt. In time, she would find out.

***

Kalen waited while chairs scraped and the rest of the group left, except for Russ and the commander. Russ spoke first, "You have the most experience of the trident-weapon. Do you know of any way we can stop it?"

"It's powered by the Uveid rock," Kalen replied. "Get rid of the Uveid and the weapon won't work."

"I've read your report on the Uveid mine at Three-Craters. They seem to have access to a large quantity of it," the commander commented.

"They'll have to ship it around to use at different locations," Kalen said. "If they have the rock and the means to do that, they can use the weapon anywhere."

"Anything else?" Commander Callard pressed him. "You told us that you saw shapes in the Uveid energy?"

"I think the shapes that I saw are sentient," Kalen replied.

"So they built the trident?" Russ queried.

"I don't think the shapes created the trident. I also think that it was originally made for a different purpose."

"If the trident wasn't built to cause earthquakes, what was it used for? That could be the key," Commander Callard pondered.

The word "key" jangled Kalen's thoughts. A key? Could the trident have been made as a key? "What if there were two alien races on Taidor, and they fought?"

"And?" Russ asked.

"The race that built the ruined cities probably made the trident. Perhaps they weren't native to this planet and came here from somewhere else."

"Go on," Commander Callard said.

"And then there is another race. A race that are incorporeal beings – the shapes in the energy field. Let's call them simply the Uveid shapes. The two races are in conflict."

"Why would there be conflict if one race lives on the surface and the other underground in an energy field?" Russ asked.

"What if the Uveid shapes didn't live in the energy field? Suppose they were native to Taidor and the other species tried to settle here?" Kalen speculated. "Suppose there was a war? The settlors built their cities and then found themselves being inhabited by the Uveid shapes, in the same way they've infected our people."

"This is all conjecture," Russ muttered irritably.

"Maybe, but it's likely the settlors made the trident. They had bodies. They were at war with the Uveid shapes which are native to this planet. The settlors made the trident to use against the shapes. Look at what the trident does. It creates earthquakes by using the energy from the rocks. It's a key. Don't you see? It unlocks and controls the energy."

"Explain?" Commander Callard demanded.

"The settlors found a way to trap the Uveid shapes. They created the trident to imprison the Uveid shapes in the energy field. When we got near the energy field, the Uveid shapes were able to infect us. They wanted us to find the trident and use it. It is the key that unlocks their prison. Every time we use it, it releases them from the energy field," Kalen concluded.

"So we are fighting the Uveid shapes?" Russ demanded. "They're taking our people over. Influencing them to use the trident so that they are released from their prison?"

"Yes," Kalen agreed. "As farfetched as that may sound, it is a logical explanation. They want us off Taidor, in the same way as they attacked that other alien race a long time ago."

***

Later that day, Halle went to the docking bay. She glanced up from a list on her pad, and frowned. The bay extended for over a hundred meters and was filled with rows of shuttles. Originally, it had been a large natural cave and extended up to a roof twenty meters above. The cavern was well lit by strong lights around its sides and on posts along the rows where the shuttles stood. On one side, a series of huge metal doors enabled the cave to be opened up. Closed, the shuttle bay entrance was camouflaged in the mountainside, virtually undetectable.

The shuttles rested in lines according to their model. The largest were at the far end, and nearest to Halle were the smaller vehicles. Halle sighed with boredom and began walking through them, checking them off her list. Coming across a four seater, she paused to inspect it. It was a civilian craft with U-Zone markings on its hull. Captured in the war, she supposed. She prepared to walk on, but the sharp clatter of a tool hitting the hard floor, interrupted her thoughts. No one was supposed to be in the bay.

She heard another clank and she headed in the direction of the noise. Behind one of the six seater craft, someone had placed additional lighting, and moving shadows patterned the floor. The craft had been elevated off the ground and someone was working on it. She rounded its front, to find a man lying on his back underneath it. He wore beige overalls and was evidently working on its engine. Halle prepared to give the workman a dressing down. No one except her, had permission to be in the shuttle bay today. She stood over him, waiting for him register her presence, tapping the toe of one of her boots impatiently.

The clanking sound stopped and the man shuffled out from under the shuttle, using his hands to pull himself free. He wore a gold ring on his wedding finger and had a thick head of black hair. There was something familiar about him, but he had already jumped to his feet before she realized who he was.

"I'm surprised to see you here," Kalen said. His glance swept over her, taking in her blue uniform and ending with her boots.

"I didn't know anyone was down here." Halle glared at him defiantly. "You're not in the log."

"Commander Callard asked me to service a couple of the shuttles." He looked at her questioningly. "And you?"

"Checking the shuttles off a list." Halle felt her face flush.

Kalen raised an eyebrow. "That doesn't seem like a good use of your talents."

"I'm doing my bit," Halle retorted. He was scrutinizing her face now, with eyes that seemed to see right into her.

"How have you been, Halle?"

"I'm okay," she stuttered, the question catching her off balance.

"Really?" he probed. "You look tired."

Annoyance surged through Halle. "So do you!"

"I didn't mean to insult you." Kalen made an open gesture. "You always look good."

Only slightly mollified, Halle said angrily, "You forfeited any right to make comments like that when you left me."

"I didn't leave you Halle," Kalen replied, taking a step toward her. "I've already explained that."

"But you married Sera." Halle's voice wavered. She regretted the remark as soon as she had said it. He clenched his jaw, mouth compressed. "I heard what happened to her. I'm sorry."

Kalen regarded her for a moment before replying, "I have to get back to my work."

"So do I," Halle said, but didn't move. "Why aren't you in the log?"

Kalen hesitated before replying, "Not all of the craft were serviced after Three-Craters. I've been asked to look over the rest."

"Aren't they usually serviced regularly?"

"Yes they are, but Commander Callard wanted to make sure that the rest of them would be ready to fly at short notice."

"All of them?"

"Yes, all of them," Kalen replied.

"Then why are you doing it secretly?" Halle pressed.

"Do I have to spell it out to you? Why do you think you've been asked to list the shuttles? Who else knows what you're doing?"

Halle paled as she understood his meaning. Her anger left her and a deep dread took hold in the pit of her stomach, stripping away her feeling of security. The base would never send out all of its craft at once. She stared at Kalen, speechless, and then swayed as her legs went weak.

He moved quickly, putting a hand on her waist to steady her. "It's okay. It's only a precaution."

"It can't be that bad, can it?" she asked, willing him to lie. She felt the warmth of his hand through her jacket.

"You better ask Captain Thomas."

"I didn't think…" her voice trailed off.

"You're strong Halle. You'll survive," Kalen said.

She turned to him, lightly touching his arm. "I can't believe this is happening."

"Can't believe what?" a voice asked.

Halle hastily stepped away from Kalen. She hadn't heard Russ come up. He stood with folded arms and feet planted apart, digesting the scene.

"Well?" Russ enquired.

"How much danger we're in," Halle said, bracing her shoulders. "We must be prepared for the worst."

"We're in no more danger than we were yesterday. The base has been on high alert ever since we got here." Russ eyed Kalen and then spoke to Halle, "I came to find you. We made lunch arrangements, remember?"

"I hadn't forgotten. I just lost track of the time." Halle smiled at him.

Russ put the flat of his hand in the small of her back and ushered her away. Behind them, the clank of metal against metal resumed.

Chapter Thirty-One

The first reports of the outcome of the battle for Morten came through in the middle of the night. Kalen was awoken from a deep sleep by the sound of a buzzer on his desk screen. He stumbled to the desk, bleary eyed and switched the viewer on. Commander Callard's face lit up the monitor. Dark bluish circles underneath his eyes and grey stubble on his cheeks gave him an unkempt appearance. He regarded Kalen with bloodshot eyes. "Apologies for waking you, Captain Trinneer. I'm calling the senior staff to the main control room."

"Are we under attack?"

"No, there's no immediate threat, but Morten is in trouble."

"I'll be there shortly," Kalen said, and Commander Callard's face disappeared from the screen.

Kalen hastily got dressed and left his room. Walking through the corridors, everything seemed normal. Most of the personnel were still asleep and he didn't pass anyone. The air supply units hummed steadily and the strip lighting along the middle of the ceilings shone brightly. The sound of his footsteps carried down the empty passageways and he vaguely wondered how many people he was waking up.

Only a few people were in the control room when Kalen got there. Crew sat at consoles underneath viewscreens, some speaking to other bases. More screens covered an entire wall, displaying video feed from external cameras outside the base, keeping constant surveillance. Night cameras showed no movement in the immediate area. Commander Callard sat talking to Lieutenant Abbott and Russ, in a small side office. Another officer was also present, whom Kalen didn't recognize. The man was young and held the rank of captain. Kalen crossed the control room and hesitated at the open doorway.

Commander Callard paused in his discussion with the others. "Come in, Captain Trinneer. I think you know everyone apart from Captain Saul."

Kalen took a seat and waited for the commander to continue.

"Base Seven reports that the U-Zone have taken most of Morten, including the eastern accommodation blocks," Commander Callard said. "We've been ordered to reinforce Base Seven who are fighting in the north of the city. We're sending in two units at first light."

"That's about three-quarters of our active personnel?" Russ queried.

"That is correct," Commander Callard confirmed. "Captain Saul and Lieutenant Abbott will each lead a unit."

"With respect, Sir, I'm the most experienced officer. I should go in place of Lieutenant Abbott," Russ countered.

"That's why I want you here. If anything happens to me, you'll have to take command of the base," Commander Callard said resolutely.

"But I have the experience to lead a unit," Russ insisted.

"I know, that's why I need you here. The base is going to be left with very little protective resources. Most of our men and women will be in the field, together with the bulk of our armaments and shuttles."

"I understand, Sir," Russ acknowledged.

"Your experience is needed here. If we lose our military bases, we lose the war. It's vitally important that we hold Base Four. Its proximity to Three-Craters makes it strategically important."

"What are my orders?" Russ asked.

"You'll take command of the dispatch and deployment of our units. They'll join our forces at Morten secretly. The plan is to lure Unity into a trap where they'll be outnumbered. I'll give you the detailed orders after this meeting."

"Yes Sir," Russ said.

Commander Callard addressed the rest of the group. "Lieutenant Abbott, Captain Saul, you will report to Captain Thomas, who will brief you about the specifics. Captain Trinneer, you'll also report to Captain Thomas, about the shuttles. I know you've been overseeing their servicing. We have to send them out fully armed. I want you to supervise that."

"Yes Sir," Kalen replied. Reporting to Russ again, he thought wryly, remembering the way he'd ushered Halle out of the shuttle bay. So both of them would be remaining at the base. He'd listened to the exchange between the Russ and the commander, and the commander's reasoning didn't make sense. Either Captain Saul or Lieutenant Abbott could have stayed at the base.

"The destination of our forces is to remain classified until the actual attack," Commander Callard was still speaking.

Halle Rison appeared in the doorway. Kalen took in her blue Division uniform, sturdy boots and loose hair. She looked fresh and alert, and very pretty.

When Commander Callard had finished, Halle said, "You wanted to see me, Sir?"

"Ah…Miss Rison, good morning. We're sending two units out at first light to reinforce our troops at Morten. I want you to handle the communications. That is one of your areas of expertise, isn't it?"

"Yes, Sir," Halle replied. "It was part of my job at the Division."

"Good. I believe you've already been assisting in the communications room here."

"Yes, Sir," Halle said briskly. "I prefer it to administration."

Commander Callard glanced around at all of them. "Unless anyone has any questions, this meeting is over. We start preparations immediately."

***

The door to the communications room was closed. Halle pressed the entry plate but it didn't open. She wondered if security had been enhanced, and entered her high level code into the keypad on the wall. The door slid open and she paused in the doorway. Consoles and screens ringed the sides, and a center island provided seating for four more people. When fully operational, up to a dozen people worked here, but at this time in the morning, there was a row of empty seats. The only sounds came from the hum of the equipment and a whisper of voices from the radios. The lighting was low but Halle saw the top of an operator's head, behind a desk screen on the other side of the island.

"Jamie, is that you?" Halle called out. Perhaps he had dozed off in the night, she thought.

There was no reply and Halle took a couple of steps towards him, treading softly. There should have been two people on duty and her senses screamed at her that something was wrong. Stopping, she quietly backed up and peered around the other side of the island. Another operator was slumped over a console, her flaccid arm dangling down. Halle crept around the island.

A man was sitting at a work station in the corner, speaking hurriedly into the radio in low tones, "Thirty kilometers from the refueling depot, on the other side of the valley. I've sent the co-ordinates."

"What are you doing?" Halle demanded.

The man turned around and Halle recognized him immediately, but there was something different about him. His eyes were dark and unfocused. A blue pendant glinted from beneath the collar of his jacket, catching the light more than the stripes below his shoulder, the insignia of the

Engineering Corps. His initial expression was passive, but his mouth curled into a smile and his eyes became sharp. "Miss Rison, good morning."

"Why are you in here?" Halle demanded again.

"I was sending for assistance." Jon Ingeston pushed his chair back and stood up, watching her with intense eyes.

Halle prepared to run, but he was upon her in an instant. He put his hand over her mouth and wrenched her head back, pinning her arms to her sides with an almost super-human strength. He dragged her, struggling, across the room and behind the island. Forcing her to the floor, they were out of sight from the door. Putting both hands around her neck he began strangling her. She tried to shake him off and her head cracked against the edge of a console. The blow stunned her with a searing pain. She tried to scream but he gripped her neck harder and squeezed, choking off the sound. At each attempt she made to scream, he squeezed her neck tighter.

"Stop struggling," he said in a hoarse whisper.

Halle kicked out but he avoided her boots and sat on top of her, straddling her. She tried to pry his hands away from her neck but his grip was too firm. His fingers bit into her windpipe. She struggled, flailing arms and legs but she couldn't shift him. He was too strong and heavy for her, and the more she fought, the tighter he squeezed her neck. She gasped for breath, her windpipe closing off. His face was near hers now. His eyes intense black pools, exuding icy hatred. His mouth drew back into a snarl.

She kicked out, hitting the side of a chair, sending it toppling over with a crash. Jon shook her and bashed her head against the floor. The blow sent waves of pain that seemed to hit her ears. Behind Jon's head, she saw movement.

"Get off her!" Kalen shouted, swinging the butt of a laser gun at Jon's head.

The blow knocked Jon sideways, and Kalen hit him again in the face. Jon's hands fell away from Halle's neck and his body weight shifted. She gasped loudly and tried to squirm from underneath him. Kalen grasped Jon's jacket and dragged him off her. Initially stunned, Jon began to recover. He twisted around and grabbed at Kalen's legs to pull him over. Off balance, Kalen grappled with him. Halle hauled herself up, and tried to recover her breath, each inhalation painful.

Near her, Kalen struggled with Jon, sending chairs crashing over. He landed another punch in Jon's face that forced him back against a wall. Grabbing his laser, he smashed the butt into Jon's stomach, driving it in hard. Jon, doubled over, clutching at his stomach.

"He was radioing our location," Halle gasped, her voice grating painfully. "I found him in here."

Kalen didn't look at her. His attention remained fixed on Jon.

"Why?" Kalen demanded. "You know we're fighting an alien force."

"Did you really think I would abandon Unity?" Jon snarled defiantly. "For the Ea-Zone? Why do you think I left Three-Craters with you? I knew you would lead me here, eventually."

"But you helped me take the trident. You let me destroy it?"

"You're such a fool!" Jon replied, face dark with fury. "It was a duplicate. We'd already found a way to duplicate the trident."

"You set me up?" Kalen's voice was low and Halle strained to hear.

"We made sure it was easy for you to take it," Jon sneered.

"But you helped us with the attack on Three-Craters?"

"So you would trust me," Jon replied.

"Why would you do that?" Kalen demanded. A look of comprehension passed across Kalen's face. "You wanted the location of the mountain bases?"

Jon laughed, an evil, hollow sound. "Why else? Without the bases Early can't win the war. I've had to wait all of this time to get their locations."

"But the attack on Three-Craters?" Kalen asked again, puzzled.

"Didn't you ever wonder why it was so easy for you to get in?"

"You wanted us to attack?" Kalen asked coldly.

"I made sure Unity had your plans," Jon spat out. "Early was never going to win. We had the trident. We always intended to use it."

"Unity destroyed a large part of our army at Three-Craters," Kalen said, his voice inflected with restrained anger.

"Exactly!" Jon sneered triumphantly.

Halle listened feeling numb. Thoughts spun through her mind. *It had all been a trap - Unity had known they were coming. They had waited until all of the Ea-Zone's forces were engaged, and then they had struck. Now they were coming here. Jon had been a traitor all along.*

She watched Kalen slowly reverse his laser and aim it at Jon. Quietly, he said, "Traitor!"

A brilliant flare engulfed Jon, lighting up the room. For a moment, the viewscreens and consoles were bathed in harsh white light. The flames died and Jon's charred remains crumpled to the floor, the fire dying immediately. The blast at close range had incinerated nearly all of his body. A small piece of his uniform had broken free of the flames, and it smoldered on the floor. Kalen stamped it out with his boot.

"Better check that there's nothing else alight," Kalen muttered, glancing about. "The flare is usually contained."

"There shouldn't be anything here that's flammable," Halle croaked.

"Are you all right?" Kalen asked.

"I will be," Halle said painfully. "Thank you for getting him off me."

"He must have killed the other operators," Kalen said, shaking his head. "You would have been next."

"When I realized what had happened, I couldn't get out of the room in time."

"He was infected. I didn't know. I'm sorry," Kalen said, coming over to her. He put out a hand to pat her arm, and then withdrew it, as if he'd changed his mind.

Halle stared at the small heap of charred body parts by the wall. "He's told Unity the location of the base. When I came in, I heard him talking. I have to tell Commander Callard."

"If he has, it's only a matter of time before Unity get here," Kalen said, a frown crossing his face.

***

Halle waited in the communications room for Russ, after Kalen left to submit a full report. She began preparing for the day ahead, checking over the command frequencies, and tried to avoid looking at the bodies of the two operators. They sat at key stations, and she worked around them, setting up the other stations first, instead. Eventually, Russ appeared in the doorway.

"Come outside while they clear the room," Russ said, gently taking her elbow and drawing her up from her seat. "There's a lounge down the corridor where we can talk in private."

"I hit my head on the console. I'm still a bit shaky."

"Here, take my arm," Russ tucked her hand in the crook of his arm.

They walked to a small empty room, furnished with low comfortable sofas and chairs. After the door slid shut behind them, Halle sank gratefully into a sofa. Russ sat beside her and took both of her hands in his. "You've been through a terrible ordeal. I'm sorry. I should have been more vigilant. Captain Ingeston came from the U-Zone originally. I should never have trusted him."

"It wasn't your fault," Halle said. "No one could know he was infected."

"Even so, he's now put all of our lives at risk," Russ said. "We've traced his communications. In the last few hours he managed to discover the location of seven of our bases. Now that Unity have the information, they'll attack us soon."

"But we can defend the base, can't we?"

Russ said quietly, "Commander Callard has orders to send most of our forces to Morten. He can't keep them here to defend the base. Ingeston's betrayal hasn't changed that. The base is going to be very undermanned and most of our weaponry will be gone. We'll have very little left to fight with."

"Unity will be too busy fighting in Morten to come here."

"They'll come, sooner or later," Russ replied. He took a deep breath. "We've only got a few hours. I can get you out before then."

"What do you mean?"

"I can arrange for you to go to another base. One that Unity don't know the location of. You'd be safe."

"I won't go," Halle replied sharply. "My place is here. I'm not a coward."

"Once the attack starts it will be too late," Russ held her hands tighter. "You could leave now and be safe."

"I've got a job to do here," Halle said firmly. His brown eyes radiated concern and she attempted a smile. She stroked his cheek. "Thank you for offering me a way out, but I can't take it. I won't leave the base when they need me most."

"I can't say anything to convince you?"

"No, my mind is made up."

Halle leaned forward and kissed him. His lips parted under hers and he returned her kiss. Putting his arms around her, he held her close. They sat quietly for a while with Halle resting her head on his shoulder until eventually Russ stirred.

"The communications room will be clear now. We should go back. It will be dawn soon."

Chapter Thirty-Two

Kalen watched the fleet leaving, on the large viewscreens in the main control room. The larger shuttles carried drones as well as soldiers, and together with the smaller craft, constituted an imposing force. A stream of shuttles emerged from the docking bay and massed above the valley, their dark shapes silhouetted against the orange glow of the dawn sun rising behind the mountain range. The fleet would have been larger, Kalen reflected, if the Ea-Zone hadn't lost so many craft at Three-Craters. As the fleet sped away in formation, Kalen's thoughts turned to the craft they had left. There were too few to mount an effective defense.

"How long do you think we've got before Unity get here?" Kalen asked Russ who stood nearby, watching.

Commander Callard turned to them. "That depends on whether Unity split their forces, or send everything they've got at Morten."

"My guess is that they'll use the army they've stationed at Three-Craters to attack us," Russ said. "At least Jon didn't know that Base Four was reinforcing Morten."

"We've got our fleet away safely," Commander Callard remarked. "And we have plans in place if the base is attacked."

"The remainder of our fleet is ready to fight," Kalen said. "But our forces here are very depleted."

"We're nearly impregnable here," Russ answered, his gaze drifting back to the viewscreens. "It would be very difficult for them to take the base."

"If Unity took the base, they would have access to the locations of all twelve of our bases," Commander Callard added.

Kalen turned away from the viewscreens. "I'll get back to engineering now. I've got work to do."

***

Kalen returned to the shuttle bay, where he liaised with subordinate engineers and ran additional checks on equipment and machinery. Satisfied with the work, he went to check on the weapons systems. The base had ten laser and ten missile ports, carefully concealed in the mountainside. In addition, two drone stations were hidden on the south side, that normally could discharge a hundred or more drones each. With most of the drones and shuttles heading for Morten, only their lasers and missile launchers remained at full capacity, he mused.

Over the following hours, Kalen watched the reports coming in from Morten on one of the viewscreens covering a wall in his office. The control room constantly updated him and he watched with growing concern. The initial reports had been good. The fleet had arrived and the U-Zone had appeared to fall into the trap, but with the arrival of U-Zone reinforcements, the situation had reversed. The Ea-Zone were losing and soon all of Morten would be held by Unity.

Kalen had set the remaining screens to monitor the exterior of the base. Movement on one of the screens drew his attention. He scrutinized the scene. Clear blue sky and barren rock. A black spec darted across the view. Too quick to identify, but it had to be a drone. He stared hard at the image and then stared at each of the monitors in turn. There it was again. *They know where our cameras are*, he thought, with a shock. *The drones are avoiding them!*

The deafening wail of a siren rang out, in three sharp bursts. There was a pause and then it rang out again in another three short bursts. After another pause, the siren emitted its screeching signal in one long final burst before falling silent.

Commander Callard's face came on a viewscreen. "We've picked up a fleet coming this way."

"I saw the drones on the external monitors," Kalen said.

"We saw them too," the commander replied.

"They knew where the cameras were."

"Your point?"

"If Captain Ingeston told them, they may know where the lasers are," Kalen replied.

"Let's hope not."

Kalen pressed buttons on his console. "The lasers are ready for use."

"Our drones?"

"Ready, Sir, but only fifty remaining."

"Good, we're deploying our lasers first," the commander said.

"Aren't you going to use the drones or shuttles, Sir?" Kalen asked.

"Not immediately."

"But Sir, our lasers and the missile launchers alone aren't sufficient to fend off an attack," Kalen pointed out. They were keeping him in the dark about something.

"The drones will provide cover for the shuttles when we use them. Just make sure they're ready."

The screen resumed showing the external video feed. A fleet of shuttles darkened the sky. They hovered ominously above the valley as if waiting for something. Kalen guessed that there were fifty or more of them. Within seconds, a massive burst of light flared on the mountainside. Almost immediately, the base retaliated, launching a missile that streaked across the blue sky. One of the shuttles exploded, throwing out a hail of twisted metal into the valley below. Kalen cursed - Unity were deliberately provoking attack to get a fix on the base's laser and missile positions.

Another explosion erupted in the sky; a craft became a spinning fireball that spiraled down to shatter on the ground, leaving debris strewn over the sandy surface. This won't last for long, Kalen thought. Unity won't take too many hits before they come at us with everything they've got. He checked the shuttle bay viewscreen. The shuttles stood ready, but no pilots were boarding. He wondered where the crews were. Why was the commander waiting so long to deploy the shuttles?

There was another blast on the cliffside. This time Unity had taken out one of Early's missile launchers. A couple of Kalen's viewscreens went blank. He realized that they were trying to take out the video feed. Several of Unity's shuttles came into view, and then dispersed to ring the mountain. They hovered, waiting.

He watched the last of Unity's shuttles take up position. There was a brief pause and then the assault began. As one, Unity's shuttles began firing, and the mountainside erupted in a hellish maelstrom of explosions. The base retaliated with sweeping laser fire, and launched missile after missile at the fleet, red fire streaking across the sky. Despite one or two hits, the majority of Unity's shuttles remained unscathed, swinging about so that Early's weapons had difficulty getting a lock on their target.

Kalen wondered where Unity's drones had gone. He scrutinized the screens, looking for them. The drones were near the missile and laser ports, firing straight into them. Jon must have told Unity their location, he thought. The extent of Jon's treachery shocked him. He tried to block Jon out of his mind. Jon had been infected. For how long, he would never know.

Kalen called the commander. "The drones are targeting the missile and laser ports, Sir."

Russ's face came on screen. "We know. We're fighting them off."

"You've got to send our drones out," Kalen shouted.

"Those aren't the commander's orders," Russ replied sharply.

"If the drones get into the base through the ports, we won't be able to hold it. They're small enough to dodge our fire and get into the ports around the sides of our weapons."

"I'll be issuing further orders soon," the commander said, and ended the call.

Kalen returned to watching the viewscreens. He lost another screen when its feed was interrupted, but the remaining screens gave him a good view of the battle. One by one, Early's missile launchers and lasers were being destroyed. Soon, we'll have no static defenses left, Kalen thought. We have to use the shuttles and drones now, or the base will be taken.

One of Unity's shuttles inched closer to the mountainside and opened a side hatch to disgorge a swarm of grey, sharp nosed drones. These were different from the ones already engaged in the attack, Kalen observed. Not as big as the others, they had thin, elongated bodies. They'll be able to get through smaller gaps, Kalen thought with a feeling of despair. He forced himself to concentrate. He must detach himself from any emotion and focus on the job in hand. He watched, almost transfixed, as the new drones headed for the weapon ports, and disappeared inside.

Within two or three seconds, all of the viewscreens went blank, before flickering back to life with Russ's face displayed multiple times across them.

"Attention all personnel. U-Zone drones have penetrated the missile and laser ports. We are trying to contain them, but if they breach the weapons bays, they will be able to invade all areas. Ensure that you are armed and keep a watch for any incursions in your sections. If you sight a drone or are subject to attack, report it at once to central command in the control room and deal with the drones locally, if you can. We are assembling teams to cut off these attacks but inevitably some may get through. We'll update you further once we have more information."

All but one of the screens switched back to their previous views. Now Russ was looking directly at Kalen.

"Trinneer, you heard that?"

"Yes I did. How far have they penetrated?"

"They've got into every single one of the missile ports and five of the laser ports. We've shut off the weapons bays but the drones are burning their way through the interior barriers, and they've entered the subsidiary weapons control room in section three. We're still operating the weapons remotely, but the drones are destroying the feeds to the weapons systems to disable them."

"They haven't got into our own drone ports?" Kalen asked.

"Not yet, we've kept them shut," Russ replied. "We believe that once Unity's drones get into the base proper, they'll target the main control room and shuttle bay."

"So we still have our drones?"

"Yes, we've got fifty standing ready. Our priority is to deal with Unity's drones inside the base, they pose the greatest threat."

"We could use our own drones to stop them."

"We'd lose too many. We're going to use them with the shuttles." Russ twisted away from him and nodded to someone outside Kalen's field of vision. "We're expecting the drones to break through into section three, imminently. It's near the shuttle bay and once they're in, they'll go for it. I've already got a unit over there, but I need to redeploy them. I want you to go to section three and take over. I'm sending Piers and Rena to meet you and they'll be under your command."

"Yes, Sir," Kalen acknowledged formally. "I'll go immediately."

"Good luck." Russ's face flickered out.

Kalen spun around and opened the weapons cabinet next to the door of his office. Opening it, he selected three long military lasers, two more handheld lasers to add to the one he already carried, and picked up the equipment pack that he kept there. Reaching for a helmet and gloves, he slung the lasers over his shoulders and hoisted the pack onto his back. He was already dressed for combat and he pulled his helmet on to complete the suit.

Outside his office, he heard running footsteps. He sprinted along the passageway towards section three, passing five or six soldiers running in the opposite direction. One of the soldiers had his visor open and Kalen thought that he recognized the man. Momentarily unable to place him, Kalen searched his memory and an image of the man by the serving bar in the canteen came into his mind. *He's one of the canteen staff. The non-combatant personnel are defending the base!*

Kalen carried on running and within minutes neared section three and the subsidiary weapons control room. The sound of shouting, heavy scuffling steps of several people moving about, and the whoosh of weapons fire reached him, before he could see anything. He smelled burning and slowed, approaching the corner of the corridor cautiously. He mustn't run straight into the laser fire. He must assess the fight first; there might be an advantage in surprise.

He flattened himself against the wall and took the peep stick he carried, from a pocket in the front of his jacket. The bendy metal stalk tipped by a tiny camera at one end and a small screen at the other, had been designed for engineering use but was the perfect tool for this, he decided. He bent the stalk quickly and held it out, so that he could see the scene around the corner, on the small screen. The wall bordering the weapons control room had a hole in it, charred and still smoking around the edges. Two small grey drones darted about the corridor, firing towards a group of four soldiers who had taken cover behind the opposite corner. Several smoldering drone husks lay on the floor of the corridor, discharging coils of smoke.

Kalen heard heavy footsteps pounding along the corridor behind his back. He glanced around and saw Piers and Rena jogging towards him. He pushed his visor up and beckoned to them to join him, putting a finger to his mouth to indicate silence. He nodded as each came up and showed them the view on his peep stick.

"I'm going to take out those two drones," he whispered. "Be ready to back me up."

Pulling his visor down, he readied his military laser. "Here goes."

Kalen sprang forward, and fired his laser on wide beam at the two drones. One of them exploded instantly into a small fireball and dropped to the ground, but the other darted away before coming straight at him, lights twinkling at the front. Abruptly, it exploded in a bright flash and fell to the floor in a smoking mess. Rena's arm brushed Kalen as she lowered the laser she held.

"Good shot," Kalen said, stepping out from behind the corner.

"Thank you," Rena replied, following him.

"We're here to relieve you," Kalen shouted at the soldiers already there.

"Thank you, Sir," one of the soldiers replied, before turning away to leave hastily down the other corridor.

"There's another drone coming through," Piers yelled urgently, raising his weapon.

"Take cover at this corner and I'll go to the opposite side," Kalen ordered, sprinting to the position that the other unit had vacated. "We can't stop them getting in, but we must stop them from going any further. Hitting them from two sides will be more effective than one."

A drone sped towards Kalen and he fired, but it swerved upwards as if anticipating his shot, and came on again at a greater height. *It's trying to get past me,* Kalen thought, bringing it down. Three more drones entered the corridor to take its place, the first two splitting so that each streaked off in a different direction, whilst the third fired alternately at the corners where Kalen, and Piers and Rena stood, as if giving covering fire to the other two.

The hole in the wall continued to smoke and got larger. The drones are still burning it out, making it easier for them to get in, Kalen thought. Soon, we won't be able to contain them. Was there a way to seal the hole? He didn't have anything to use and even if they could seal it, that would only be a temporary solution - the drones would soon burn another one. No, all they could do, was stand and fight, but it would be a losing battle.

Kalen watched a drone fly over Piers and Rena. They hadn't stopped firing, but the drone had escaped. In that moment he realized that they had lost the battle and used his helmet radio to contact Russ. "A drone's escaped into the second corridor. We can't contain them."

"Acknowledged," Russ replied tersely. "Send Rena after it, but remain at your position with Piers. Out."

"Rena, trace that stray drone and destroy it," Kalen instructed. "Then ask Captain Thomas for further orders."

"Yes Sir." Rena took off.

Kalen nodded at Piers, who continued to direct laser fire at the drones, incinerating the small machines, one after the other. Twitching metal carcasses littered the floor, exuding pungent smoke that rose in thin wisps. A small grey shape hurtled towards Kalen and he ducked swiftly. He got the impression that it had flown over his head, but before he could see where it had gone, another came at him. He swung his gun up and hit it squarely and it fell to the floor with a plop. Before he had time to think, another drone flew at his face, dropping within centimeters of his visor when he hit it, but others passed over his head, continuing at speed along the corridor, to penetrate deeper into the base.

Kalen heard Russ's voice through his radio. "Trinneer and Piers, drop back to section one. We're going to close off parts of the base."

"Will do," Kalen said, waving at Piers. "Did you hear that Piers?"

"Yes," Piers replied.

"Give me covering fire while I come across to you," Kalen said. "Now!"

Kalen ran across the corridor to Piers, keeping his head low and jumping over the burning metal debris on the ground. Reaching him, he slowed only slightly and Piers turned and sprinted after him along the corridor. Kalen headed for section one, in the core of the base. The main control and communications rooms were located there, and he wondered what the commander had planned. It was vital to save the shuttles. The shuttle bay was accessed by thick metal doors that were usually kept shut, and an interior airlock for use when the external doors were open, but these would not withstand an assault indefinitely.

Several running soldiers came into view, ahead of Kalen. He continued running with Piers behind him, until they reached an intersection in the passageway, where people had grouped. Kalen glanced around for a senior officer and spotted a corporal giving orders to a small contingent of men and women. He appeared to be placing them in defensive positions along the mouths of adjoining passageways.

Kalen called Russ. "We're at the perimeter of section one. Have you further orders?"

"Just a minute," Russ replied.

After a short pause, Commander Callard spoke, "Trinneer, come to the main control room."

"Yes, Sir," Kalen responded, walking quickly through the throng of uniforms and taking a corridor that led to central command. *The base can't survive unless Commander Callard has a good plan,* he thought. The drones were inside and difficult to stop. After taking out the weapons systems, they would systematically kill all of the base personnel. Assuming defensive positions alone, wouldn't be enough to save the base; the commander had to do something more, something that would clear the corridors of those deadly machines. Kalen turned the problem over in his mind until the germ of an idea began to grow.

Chapter Thirty-Three

Kalen paused at the door of the control room and punched the entry panel. Inside, an air of brisk efficiency pervaded the room; personnel wearing headsets sat before desk screens, that showed interior and exterior views of the battle raging around them. In the center of the room, Commander Callard and Russ stood before a bank of large viewscreens. Russ also wore a headset, taking verbal reports from operators situated around the room and conferring with the commander. Both were focused on the screens but the commander turned as Kalen came up.

"We're pulling back," Commander Callard said to Kalen. "We're sealing off sections two, three and five of the base which have suffered the worst incursions. We're still fighting the drones in sections four and six where our own drone stations are. The shuttle bay is in section four so it's imperative that we keep that open."

"Understood." Kalen waited for the commander to go on.

"We have metal doors between each section that can be used to seal them off individually. The drones won't be able to penetrate the barriers." Commander Callard's eyes returned to the screens. "We're nearly ready to go."

"The last of the personnel have left the affected sections," Russ confirmed.

"Good, proceed," the commander ordered.

Kalen watched heavy doors sliding across several corridors. The video feeds showed numerous small grey drones still within, firing in groups of two or three, at various electrical installations. Some had burned through to the interior of junction boxes, and worked destroying cabling and switches.

"They'll destroy all of the feeds to the lasers and missile launchers, if they're not stopped," Kalen remarked. "There's also quite a few in the corridors of the other sections."

"They came in through the weapon ports in sections three and five, so now that we've sealed those sections off, no more should get into the rest of the base," the commander said. "We need to do something quickly before they disable all of our weapons systems."

"Even if there's a way to destroy the drones inside, more will come in through the weapon ports unless those are sealed," Kalen said.

"We can't seal the ports without shutting off our guns," Russ replied.

"You're an engineer, Trinneer. From all accounts, one of the best. Is there a way to flood the area with an electrical charge to fry the drones programming?" the commander asked.

"In theory it would be possible to use radio frequency pulses to confuse the drones' electronics and disable them, but the pulses have to be targeted. If you flood the whole area, all of the electronics in those sections will be disabled, including our own weapons systems," Kalen explained.

"So we need a method of delivery?" Russ pressed.

"If necessary we could sacrifice ten of our own drones," the commander conceded.

"They're not really equipped for the job. We would also need to open the section doors to get them inside. I've got a better idea," Kalen said. "We can use the ant and spider bots that are used to repair the air supply and other internal systems. They're small and designed to go through the air ducts. We can adapt them and adjust their programming to emit directed radio frequency pulses at the drones to disable them."

Russ stared at Kalen without saying anything for a moment and then his face broke into a smile. "Good idea.

Those bots are standing idle in engineering and we've got a lot of them."

"It'll only delay the inevitable," Kalen cautioned. "If Unity continue to send drones through the laser and missile ports, eventually they'll succeed in destroying all of our weapons systems."

"But we can send enough bots to disable the drones as they come in. It'll buy us more time," the commander said. "Go to engineering and put it in hand."

"I'll instruct the team what to do and keep you informed," Kalen confirmed.

***

The first spider bots ran through the air supply ducts of section three, transmitting images back to the viewscreens in the base's engineering depot. Kalen watched their progress on the screens, while five other engineers worked behind him on the rest of the bots, Rena and Piers amongst them. He had decided to send the spider bots in first – their bodies incorporated the tools necessary to cut through the filters and grills of the air ducts, to reach the corridors where Unity's drones continued to burn away vital equipment.

Each spider had been adapted to send out a radio frequency pulse that would disable Unity's drones. They had been programmed to go to the corridors in all three sections and once within range of the drones, target them individually with the pulse. The spiders themselves would be unaffected by the pulse – Kalen and his team had fitted them with a device that bounced emissions from their fellows, to avoid confusing their own electrical systems. After the spiders came the ants, similarly equipped.

Kalen watched the metal slats of a grill glow orange and begin to warp with heat. A spider's pincer grasped and twisted it until the slat broke away. Using a second pincer, the spider seized the broken end and bent it back, repeating the process with both appendages until it had created a large enough hole to climb through. A sharp grey snout, lights twinkling, abruptly filled the hole. The drone juddered and spun around, falling away from the hole to drop to the floor, innate. Good work, thought Kalen.

The spider ran through the hole, providing Kalen with a glimpse of the corridor, before running up the wall to perch just under the ceiling. More spiders streamed out of the air duct after it, taking up similar positions along the corridor. Kalen checked their functions on his handheld pad. All now transmitted the radio frequency pulses and the effect on the drones was evident. Drones jerked and spasmed before falling to the ground or simply dropped mid-flight out of the air.

Kalen surveyed the progress of the spiders and ants in the other sections. Equally good, he decided, but still only a short term solution. More drones were coming through the weapon ports and would soon outnumber the bots which had begun to lose power. There was no way to recharge the bots except to recall them. He couldn't do that effectively - the charging systems had already been damaged by Unity's drones. *We can't hold them*, he thought.

"We're being overrun, Commander," Kalen reported. "The drones will soon take down all of our electrics in the sealed sections."

"We've already lost sixty percent of our lasers and missile launchers," Commander Callard replied. "We calculate that we have thirty minutes left at the most before we lose the rest of them. Is there anything you can do to slow it down?"

"I'm sorry, Sir, but there's nothing more I can do. You must consider alternative options. According to the diagrams I've seen of the base, some of the primary cables run through those sections, which control lighting, heating and life support for the rest of the base. I believe that's why Unity attacked those areas first."

"You're saying that they'll shut us down completely?" Russ interjected. "They can shut off our air supply?"

"That's correct; even to section one. If that happens the base won't be able to function at all. The only way to defend the base is to send out the shuttles and drones to stop the attack."

"We're aware of that, Trinneer," the commander said drily. "But we haven't got enough shuttles or drones to ensure a victory by ourselves. Unity's forces far outnumber ours. We've requested assistance from the other bases and we're waiting for reinforcements before we send them out."

So they're not planning to use the shuttles yet, Kalen thought with alarm. *How long are they going to wait?* "The position is getting critical, Sir."

"We've managed to clear out most of the drones from the corridors in sections four and six but there are still a few stray ones out there. Section one is still clear of them," Russ added.

"Wait for further orders, Trinneer," the commander said sharply and broke the connection.

The other engineers had been listening to Kalen's voice and they had stopped what they were doing. In front of them, the last of the bots still awaited adaption, but there was only a handful left. Kalen returned their silent stares and shrugged without comment.

"Might as well finish the job," Piers muttered and bent to pick up a bot and work on its underside.

While half of the viewscreens showed images of the corridors with the bots and drones, the other half transmitted views of the exterior of the base and the battle that still raged. More of Unity's shuttles had arrived to disgorge drones, or fire at the base's missile placements and lasers. The base continued to defend itself, but its missile and laser fire had become spasmodic. Intervals of two or three minutes now stretched between missile fire, and the laser fire had become infrequent, with very few successful strikes.

Behind Kalen, the last of the bots had been sent off and the other engineers joined him, to stand watching the viewscreens.

"Where are our reinforcements?" Rena asked.

"If they don't come soon, we've lost the base," Piers remarked gloomily. "I don't understand why we're not using our own drones or shuttles."

"They're ready to go," Kalen confirmed. "I'm simply waiting for the word."

A thunderous rumble penetrated the depot and the ground tremored. It seemed to Kalen as if the whole base had moved. The sensation reminded him of the ground shaking in Crater Three when Paul Neill had used the trident-weapon. He scanned the viewscreens and saw the cause. A direct hit on one of the missile ports. A rugged depression several meters wide, dripping flaming rubble, scarred the side of the mountain. The rock face above it had crumbled, threatening a landslide. *We can't hold out much longer,* Kalen thought.

Another strike hit one of the laser ports, causing a searing fireball to erupt, blazing against the blue sky. It sent up plumes of black smoke, and showered the scarp with red hot pieces of rock and twisted metal. The fire began to die quickly in the thin atmosphere, leaving a deep depression where the laser port had been and exposing part of the structure of the base. A screaming missile streaked across the sky and one of Unity's shuttles exploded with a roar. The craft burned brightly, spinning out of control towards the ground. The engineers behind Kalen cheered and waited for the base to fire again, but nothing happened. They watched tensely as Unity's shuttles pulled back and reformed, so that they hovered in a line around the base. Without warning, they fired simultaneously, blanketing the mountainside with laser fire. *Our weapons ports can't survive that,* Kalen thought. *We must get orders soon to use the shuttles.*

Russ came on Kalen's radio. "Trinneer, we're going to evacuate the base."

"What about the reinforcements?" Kalen asked.

"We've had word that they're not coming and Morten has fallen. Laser ports have been destroyed in section six and the drones have got into the rest of the base," Russ said urgently. "I want you to take Rena and Piers with you and escort the personnel in the communications room to the shuttle bay. Send the rest of your team straight there." Russ dropped his voice. "The commander is going to sound the alarm in a moment. There's something else that I need you to do."

Kalen listened as Russ briefed him further on the evacuation plan. When he heard the details, Kalen realized that evacuation had always been a contingency the base had prepared for. Now, his life and the lives of everyone on the base, depended on how well those plans were implemented.

Chapter Thirty-Four

Halle had stayed at her post in the communications room watching the battle on viewscreens mounted on the wall. Six other operators were with her, and each time one of their long range lasers was destroyed, a hush had fallen over the room. She had heard the reports that Morten had fallen and now the base was in danger. She had monitored the transmissions between the crews manning the lasers and missile launchers, and heard their desperate screams as each position had been destroyed. Reports that more drones had got into the base came in and she wondered if they would get into section one. She fingered the small laser she'd attached to her belt and switched off the safety catch. Glancing towards the door, she satisfied herself that it was closed, and out of her peripheral vision saw her desk screen flicker.

Russ came on screen, looking tired and drawn. "Halle, we're sounding the alarm for general evacuation."

"What?" she stammered. "We're giving up?"

"We haven't got any choice. Once the alarm sounds you must leave and go straight to the shuttle bay. Make sure that you're armed and keep an eye out for Unity's drones."

"Is everyone leaving?" Halle asked.

"Yes, tell your people in communications to leave immediately and get to the shuttle bay. I've sent Captain Trinneer and a couple of others to give you a hand in case you run into any drones, but don't wait for them. They'll meet you on the way," Russ said urgently.

"What about you? You'll be in the bay?" Halle searched his face. She had the feeling that he was hiding something from her.

"I'll follow you down there. Someone has to make sure everyone gets out. I'll be on the last shuttle."

"I won't see you?" Halle felt her eyes moisten and she blinked quickly to dispel any tears. This isn't the time to cry, she thought.

"We don't have much time, Halle. Good luck." He gave her a weak smile.

Halle stared him. She saw something in his eyes that she couldn't read – was it sadness? "But…"

Halle's words were drowned out by the deafening sound of the siren that let out a continuous blast, chilling in its purity.

Russ mouthed the words, "Goodbye. I love you."

Her desk screen went blank. She turned and shouted at the others, "We have to evacuate. Everyone must go to the shuttle bay."

She heard the sound of running footsteps in the corridor. The footsteps multiplied until there was a storm of noise coming from the passageway. Her colleagues began to gather their things together, scraping back chairs and standing up. Halle reached for her jacket and slipped it on and stood up. All of the screens had died and it seemed strange to her, that they should be abandoning their posts like this. For an instant, she imagined Unity's soldiers entering this room, gold Divines shining on their jackets and seeing it deserted, the screens dark.

The others reached the door before her, and it slid open onto the bright corridor beyond. A man ran past, his boots thudding across the floor, and her colleagues ran after him. Halle took a last look around the room and prepared to leave. A feeling of profound disquiet pervaded her and she felt an overwhelming desire to see Russ. She hesitated at the door, and on impulse turned towards the central control room, instead of the shuttle bay. If he was to be on the last shuttle out, she would be there with him, she decided.

Halle hurried along the corridor and where it branched, she took the left fork that led to the command center. The corridor was quiet. No soldiers ran down this passageway; no sounds of running footsteps or voices. Ahead, something grey and shiny moved through the air towards her at speed. She gripped her laser, bringing her arm up quickly as she fired. The drone burst into flames in a shower of sparks and dropped to the floor. *That was close,* she told herself silently. *I must be more careful in future.*

Another branch in the corridor puzzled her. Had she come the wrong way? Where was Russ and the rest of the crew from the command center? She should have passed them by now. Halle stopped running and fought to catch her breath. Turning around, she swiftly trotted back the way she thought she had come. She heard a soft whirring noise behind her. Too late, a voice in her head screamed. Throwing herself to the floor, she twisted around to fire at the drone. It hovered about a meter off the ground, tilted at a funny angle and it's snout lights twinkled. In that second, Halle felt the heavy knowledge of certain death and everything seemed to slow. As she stared at the drone, it exploded with a crack and dropped. The whiff of burning tickled her nose.

"If it hadn't already been damaged you would be dead," Kalen said, coming to stand over her, laser still in his hand. He reached to take hold of her arm and pulled her up. "What are you doing here? You're supposed to be on the way to the shuttle bay. You're running in the wrong direction."

"I was going to the command center," Halle replied, stumbling to her feet.

"This isn't the way to the command center." Kalen looked puzzled. "You're going towards the drone station. When I saw you weren't with the others I came to find you."

"I was trying to find Russ," Halle stated baldly.

"You might see him in the shuttle bay," Kalen said. "We have to go there now. No more detours."

Kalen led Halle at a trot, through empty passageways. At each corner, Halle prepared to see drones and her heart thumped with exertion and anxiety. The corridor lights flickered and some went out while others dimmed. The gentle hiss of the air supply units suddenly stopped and the bitter smell of burning filled the air. Their boots clattered across the floors and their shadows danced beside them on the walls.

"Everyone's already at the shuttle bay," Kalen explained. "We must hurry."

Halle willed herself to carry on running, despite the cramping pains building in her legs. They turned a corner and then she heard movement and voices ahead of them; officers shouting instructions and the harsh sound of many shuttle engines. The wide interior doors of the bay were open and inside the bay, she saw that the exterior doors were still closed and the shuttles were parked in rows ready to leave. Soldiers were directing the boarding, and orderly lines had formed. She scanned the bay looking for Russ.

"Where's Russ?" she asked Kalen. "I can't see him."

"I can't see him either," Kalen said. "He must be directing operations from somewhere else."

"I must find him," Halle insisted.

"There isn't time, Halle," Kalen said sharply.

"I want to wait for him. I can go on the last shuttle with him," Halle replied stubbornly.

"You can't do that. We have to go now," Kalen said, putting a hand on her shoulder.

"But I haven't said goodbye to him properly," Halle said.

"Don't be silly, Halle. Captain Thomas asked me to make sure that you got away safely. So that's what I'm going to do. The shuttles are about to leave."

She looked desperately about them. The floor was emptying of people fast and there was no sign of Russ. The pilots were running through last minute checks and the shuttles' engines roared.

Kalen reached out and gripped her arm. "Please don't argue with me. Our shuttle's over there. You must come now."

She let Kalen propel her behind the rows of shuttles, to an empty one standing near the end. It was a four seater and for a brief moment she hoped that Commander Callard and Russ would arrive to join them. Miserably, she climbed into the front seat, hesitating briefly to scan the bay again for Russ. She couldn't see either the commander or him on the deck. She waited while Kalen waved towards one of the officers in charge.

"I've room for two more in here," Kalen shouted.

"You're okay to go," the officer yelled back. "We've got enough shuttles."

Kalen went around to the other side of the shuttle and climbed into the pilot's seat, fastened his seatbelt and turned the engine on. He pressed a button on the shuttle's console and the doors slid shut with a hiss.

"Halle, buckle up and put on a helmet – there's one in the locker in front of you. This is going to get rough."

Halle fastened her seatbelt and checked to make sure it was secure. That simple act had a finality about it that she found hard to put into words. It symbolized a leaving, not just of the base, but of Russ and this part of her life. Somewhere deep inside her psyche, was the knowledge that things would never be the same; that this heralded a new chapter in her life or even her death. She raised her eyes and from the limited viewpoint of the shuttle, she surveyed the bay again, abortively, for Russ.

"Unity's army is waiting for us outside," Halle said. "How are we going to get out?"

"The drones will cover us," Kalen assured her.

Halle turned her head away from Kalen and watched the leaving preparations in the bay. Nearly everyone had boarded and two officers were doing final checks. They walked down the lines of shuttles, counting off the occupants and using their radios. Finally, the officers nodded to each other and made their way to a shuttle that already had a pilot, and boarded it. Halle twisted her head around to get a better look and realized that she could see no more people on the ground – everyone had boarded.

"Where's Russ?"

"You asked that before," Kalen replied, flicking switches on the console. He dipped his head to listen to his helmet radio and then said something into his headset in a low voice that she couldn't hear.

"There's no one left on the floor?"

"There'll be a shuttle waiting for him," Kalen answered, concentrating on the craft's instrument panel.

"You haven't even told me where we're going?"

"We're going to Base Nine."

"Unity's drones will come in when the bay doors are opened," she pointed out. "How will Russ get out then?"

"Just a moment. I have to use the radio." Kalen turned his head slightly, away from her, and whispered into his headset, paused and then she heard him say, "Acknowledged."

Halle waited for him to finish.

He glanced across at her. "We're just about to go. I need to concentrate on getting us out of here. No more talking for now."

Halle fell silent and suddenly the bay doors slid up and daylight streamed in, lighting up the massive bay. Two other rows of shuttles stood between their shuttle and the doors, and Halle vaguely wondered if that put them at a disadvantage; if they were one of the last to leave, they could be more vulnerable to attack. The growl of the shuttles' engines around them, increased in volume. Beside her, Kalen had tensed.

"We move as soon as we can, so brace yourself," Kalen told her.

The first line of shuttles suddenly flew forward, shooting out of the bay in a storm of roaring engines. Thundering out, the second line followed them. With a force that threw Halle back into her seat, their shuttle hurtled out into the sky. Kalen swung it around violently, so that it passed within meters of the mountainside. All about them, explosions ripped through the air, as shuttle after shuttle was destroyed. Pieces of twisted burning metal bounced off their hull, and Kalen swung their craft about so that it pitched and rolled to avoid the onslaught. Finally, he soared upwards towards the sun. Below, Early's meagre fleet of drones darted in and out of the melee, lasers blazing.

Kalen steered the shuttle on a course that took them above the mountain. Below them, the battle still raged. How many had they lost? Halle wondered. Where was Russ? Had he got out? She glanced at Kalen, but he was busy with the shuttle's controls. He'd cut her off when she'd asked about Russ, but she had to know where he was. Halle opened her mouth to ask the question, but before she could utter a word, a blinding flash lit up the sky with a white light that seared her eyes, despite the craft's tinted windows.

Dazzled, she blinked her eyes and peered out. For a moment she couldn't comprehend the enormity of what she saw.

She let out a short scream, "No, no – it can't be."

An explosion had destroyed one side of the mountain below them. Smoke and flames surged out of the mountainside in volcanic intensity and an avalanche of rocks tumbling down, leaving massive jagged hollows in its wake. The mouth of the shuttle dock filled with rubble and fires raged from several points across the mountain's steep slopes. A black scar appeared in the sheer cliffs, and rocks rained over it in a grey storm, throwing up dust when they smattered against the lower slopes. A sheet of smoke hit them and Kalen veered away to avoid it.

"It's the base!" Halle cried. How had it happened so quickly?

She glanced towards Kalen but he remained focused on flying the shuttle, his eyes flickering between the console and the windows, constantly checking their position and scanning the sky. He said nothing, his mouth molded into a thin line of concentration and a frown furrowing his forehead.

"It's the base. It's been destroyed. Did you see?" Halle demanded.

"Yes, I saw. The whole base has gone," Kalen said unemotionally, without shifting his gaze away from the craft's console. "I'm turning northwards."

"How? Unity can't have destroyed all of it?"

The sky around them had now cleared and they left the mountains behind. They flew parallel to another mountain range, far to their left, over a dry plain. A handful of other shuttles appeared as black specs on the horizon, far away. Kalen pressed a switch on the console and the nose of the shuttle gently rose up increasing their height. She heard the tinny sound of a voice coming from his helmet radio and heard him say "Confirmed."

"I don't understand," Halle insisted. "How could Unity have destroyed the whole base so quickly?"

"It was rigged to blow, to stop Unity getting it," Kalen said, not looking at her.

"What do you mean?"

"Commander Callard's orders were to destroy the base rather than surrender it."

"You knew this?" How was it that she hadn't known? Why hadn't she been told?

"I didn't know until we were in the shuttle," Kalen said, sounding sincere. "I'm not army, so I wasn't privy to everything."

"So they set the charges remotely?" Halle asked. She stared at him. "Answer me."

"No, someone had to be there, to make sure." Kalen refused to meet her eyes.

"Commander Callard?"

There was another pause, and then Kalen said quietly, "No, as I understand it, two officers were required."

Halle stared at him aghast. "Russ?"

Kalen didn't reply.

"You're telling me Commander Callard and Russ were both there?"

"Yes, I'm sorry. They wouldn't have survived."

"No!" she screamed. "You lied to me! You told me that Russ would be in the shuttle bay!"

Kalen finally turned his head and looked at her. "No, I didn't lie to you. I thought he would be in the bay. When you kept asking where he was, I radioed from the shuttle to find out. I didn't know he wasn't coming until then."

Halle saw sympathy in Kalen's face and for a moment she detested him for being there, with her, instead of Russ. How could Russ have kept this from her? She felt her eyes well up and dabbed at them with the back of her hand.

"Russ is dead?" Halle asked again in horror. "He lied to me. He said he was coming as well."

"He had his orders. There's nothing you could have done."

Halle tried to swallow the tears that coursed down her cheeks. It was hard to believe that Russ was gone. She had been talking to him only half an hour before. Perhaps it was all a mistake.

"Didn't they have a safe room or somewhere they could go, when they blew up the base?"

"So far as I know, there was nothing like that," Kalen replied.

"Or another way out, so they could escape?" Halle pressed. She wanted Kalen to lie to her, tell her that Russ was still alive. She needed him to give her hope.

"Stop it, Halle. They had to be in the control room to make sure that the whole of the base was destroyed. He's gone. I'm sorry, but there's no chance that he's still alive."

Halle sniffed back her tears. She felt her anger rising. Unity had done this. She hated them. She looked out of the window. The air was clear and the only mountains she could see were so far away, they looked tiny.

"I can't see any of the other shuttles," Halle said.

Kalen glanced out of his side window. "The shuttles were ordered to go to different bases; the ones that Unity don't know about. We were to take different routes if necessary. We're not far from Base Nine now. I'll call them. I'll put it on speaker so you can hear as well."

Kalen flipped a switch on the console and said, "This is Captain Trinneer, out of Base Four requesting permission to land at Base Nine. Please acknowledge."

"This is Base Nine," a voice responded. "We are under attack. Do not come here. I repeat. We are under attack. Do not come here. Please acknowledge."

"I acknowledge. Out," Kalen replied and the radio went silent.

"What are we going to do now?" Halle asked.

"We'll try for another base," Kalen said. "But if Base Nine is under fire it means that Unity have coordinated their attack on a number of targets simultaneously. It also means that they've had intelligence about the location of our bases from more than one source. Ingeston didn't know the location of Base Nine."

"The other shuttles are going to get the same response."

"I'll try Base One. Ingeston had no knowledge of its location." Kalen flicked the radio to another frequency and Halle heard him say, "This is shuttle two nine eight. Base One, please respond."

There was silence and Kalen said again, "Base One, please respond."

Kalen waited and when there was still no response, he repeated, "This is shuttle two nine eight. Base One, please respond."

Kalen sat back and let out a deep sigh. "It looks as if Unity got to Base One as well. I'll try Base Two."

Halle listened as Kalen tried to contact Base Two but there was no reply.

"What does that mean? They can't have attacked all of the bases, can they?" Halle asked.

"It's possible," Kalen said. "They had the resources. They only needed the locations. There's two more I can try."

Kalen leaned forward and pressed buttons on the craft's console. "I'm amplifying the radio signal and trying different frequencies," he explained. "If I can't get a response from the last two bases, we'll have to reassess our position."

Halle sat almost rigid, still numb from the knowledge that Russ was dead. She pictured his face, at the end, tired and drawn. She tried to push the image aside, and remember the way he had looked, the first time she had seen him, eyes sparkling, lips twitching into a smile, confident and powerful. He had mouthed the words, "I love you." Why hadn't she ever told him that she loved him? Had she loved him? If she had asked herself the question that morning, she would have been unsure of her answer. But if the definition of love was measured by the amount of grief she felt at losing him, then by that definition, she had loved him. Ironic, she thought, that she could only recognize her love for Russ by losing him.

A voice from the radio interrupted Halle's thoughts. "This is Base Eight."

"This is Captain Trinneer, out of Base Four. Seeking permission to land at Base Eight. Please confirm," Kalen replied.

"This is Base Eight."

The signal cut out and a crackling sound came from the speaker. Kalen adjusted the radio. A digital display flickered brightly, the figures changing rapidly until settling at a different frequency. Kalen sat back.

"Base Eight, please confirm permission to land," Kalen said.

A voice came from the speaker. It was so faint that Halle could hardly make out the words. "This is Base Eight. We are under attack. Permission denied. Inadvisable to come here. Please acknowledge."

"Acknowledge that Base Eight. Suggest alternative base?"

Kalen's voice betrayed no emotion. He's so matter of fact, Halle thought, he could almost be ordering food.

There was a brief silence before the reply. "This is Base Eight. We have received intelligence that all of the bases are under attack. We suggest that you seek an alternative destination. Good luck Captain Trinneer. Out."

The radio went dead and Kalen switched it off. "That's the last of the bases. I couldn't get a reply from the other one either. We'll have to find somewhere else to go."

Chapter Thirty-Five

Halle's thoughts were reeling. It seemed impossible that all twelve mountain bases were under attack. Unity had taken Central, Morten and Three-Craters, the three largest cities on Taidor. Had they taken all of the settlements? She hadn't heard – such sensitive information was classified.

"Do you know if the Ea-Zone still hold any of the smaller settlements?" she asked.

"I don't have that information. But even if they did, it's probably only a matter of time before Unity takes them as well." Kalen kept his eyes forward, adjusting the controls to slow the craft. "We need to save fuel."

"What about one of the construction sites?" Halle suggested. "I know that there is a large site in the north at Area Sixteen."

"I don't think it would be advisable to go there without certain knowledge that the Ea-Zone hold it. The construction sites weren't protected when Unity originally struck. I remember hearing talk that the U-Zone had taken most of them by surprise."

"Where then? Surely there must be pockets of resistance?"

"I don't know of any. They've taken Cherer," Kalen said grimly. "Let's face it, the Ea-Zone have lost the war."

"Do we surrender?" Halle asked. "I saw what they did to the civilians in Central. They were using the Gates to kill them. They might kill us, too."

"You're right. If we surrendered, they'd probably kill us or make us wear those mind numbing Uveid stones." Kalen took his hands off the console and gave her a long look.

"I can't believe that everyone from the Ea-Zone is dead or imprisoned," Halle reasoned. "There must be a resistance force somewhere."

"You're probably right," Kalen agreed. "But we don't know how to find them or contact them. We need to run through our options."

"We could land the shuttle somewhere near a settlement and take our chances," Halle suggested.

"That's very risky. If the U-Zone are in the vicinity they'd pick up the shuttle even before we land. We could get shot down." Kalen creased his brow, frowning. "The shuttle doesn't carry enough supplies to sustain us for days if we were to land further out."

"There's an observatory at the pole," Halle said.

"We've got the same problems as heading for the construction sites or smaller settlements."

Halle felt a sinking feeling in the pit of her stomach. She studied Kalen's face. He wasn't looking at her, but sat staring into the middle distance, as if he were thinking. He hadn't displayed any of the anxiety she felt.

"How can you be so detached about this?" Halle asked him.

Kalen's eyes focused and met hers. "Getting emotional won't solve anything. I've got an idea, but it's a bit extreme. I think it's our only way out."

His hands worked over the console and the shuttle began to climb. Bending forward, he opened one of the front lockers underneath the instrument panel.

"Why are we climbing? Where are we going?" Halle asked perplexed.

"We're leaving Taidor." Kalen handed her a breathing mask and an oxygen canister. "Put these on and switch on your helmet radio. We shouldn't need the oxygen masks but the ascent could interrupt the air supply so better to be prepared."

She looked at him in surprise. "We can't leave Taidor. The shuttle won't get us to another planet."

"This shuttle is designed with a dual system for short space flight. It's got a strengthened body and is pressurized." Kalen took out a mask, and clipped it to his helmet, positioning it over his mouth. "Have you got your radio on? You should be able to hear me through your headset?"

Halle fiddled with her mask and helmet until she had it in place. "We need an awful lot of thrust to leave the atmosphere."

"I think we've got enough fuel to do it, and reach one of Taidor's moons," Kalen replied.

"But there's no one there," Halle objected.

"Two of the moons originally had research stations on them. The third had a settlement on it."

"Aisus?" Halle queried, trying to remember what she knew about the moon.

"Correct," Kalen said. "People settled on Aisus fifty years ago, long before we began colonizing Taidor."

"But there's been no contact with Aisus for over forty years." Halle searched her memory. "The Division prohibited any contact with the settlement."

"The settlement should still be there," Kalen replied, staring at a digital display on the console. "I'll check the coordinates and calculate the fuel we'll need to be sure we have enough."

"The Division only issues no contact orders in serious cases." Halle thought hard. "The settlement might not exist anymore."

"There's no reason to think that it doesn't exist," Kalen replied confidently.

"We don't know why the Division cut them off," Halle objected.

"We'll have to take a chance."

"We know nothing about them. They might not welcome us," Halle said.

"Would you rather stay on Taidor?"

"No, but what if you're wrong? What if there's no settlement?" Halle asked. She imagined arriving at the moon and finding it deserted; an arid dead place. They would be stranded, without the means to survive. She glanced around the shuttle, trying to work out what supplies they had. Whether there was enough food or oxygen for a day or a week would make no difference. Ultimately, if Aisus were uninhabited or they failed to find its inhabitants, their air would run out and they would die horribly, slowly, in an alien environment.

"The atmosphere is the same as Taidor, but there's less gravity. There must be something there," Kalen replied, programming their new course into the shuttle's onboard computer. "I've set the co-ordinates. We have enough fuel to reach Aisus but not enough to come back again."

Halle could think of nothing more to say about Aisus. They were taking a chance, but what was the alternative? A terrible death in the jaws of a Gate, or being made to perform slave labor, mind numbed by an alien force. Whichever way she looked at it, there were no palatable choices. She imagined Russ talking to her; telling her, "Take a chance." Russ would do it, if he were here. In that way, he had been like Kalen.

"In a minute I'll switch over to the secondary system and start our ascent," Kalen informed her.

"What should I do?" Halle asked. "I've only been off world in the larger commercial shuttles."

"Check that you're securely fastened in your seat. When we go into full thrust, the shuttle will vibrate but don't worry, the hull is designed for this and will hold. The engine will get noisy and you'll find that the G-force will increase as we accelerate. It will only take us a few minutes to leave the atmosphere and once we're through, the pressure will ease immediately."

"Okay." Halle tightened her seat belt and sat back.

Most of Kalen's face was covered with the oxygen mask but he still had his visor up. His helmet covered his black hair and ears, but the way he moved was so familiar to her, that she still felt the old attraction that had originally drawn her to him. But he'd left her for Sera, she reminded herself. His words came back unbidden into her head, "Captain Thomas asked me to make sure that you got away safely." Russ had sent him. Russ had known that he was going to die, yet he had sent her to his rival. She would never forget Russ, but it wouldn't be a betrayal to love Kalen – if Kalen wanted her. For the moment, the events of the day had drained her of nearly every emotion except grief and fear, and she struggled to have even hope.

The small shuttle continued to climb until they were high above Taidor. Halle could see the peaks of mountains, spread out far below them. *This could be the last time I see Taidor*, she thought.

"I'm switching over to the secondary system now and bringing the thrusters online," Kalen said, his hands poised over the controls. "Are you ready? This shuttle's so small that you'll feel the pressure more than in a commercial shuttle. You'll feel a lot of pressure on your chest but it won't last long."

"I'm ready," Halle confirmed.

Kalen pressed a panel on the console and the engines roared, the nose of the shuttle veering upwards, so that they ascended vertically. An enormous pressure forced Halle into the back of her seat and her lungs felt as if they were being squashed by a huge weight. The shuttle vibrated violently, shaking everything inside, and as their velocity increased, the pressure and shaking got worse. The light changed and the shuttle's engine screamed as it fought to leave Taidor's atmosphere. Halle clenched her hands together and gritted her teeth, determined not to appear nervous.

Within minutes, the shuttle abruptly broke free of the atmosphere, and Kalen cut the thrusters. The engine stopped howling and the pressure eased off Halle's chest. She relaxed and looked out of the side window. Below them, the curve of the planet Taidor, was visible.

"Are you okay?" Kalen asked. "Landing won't be so uncomfortable."

"I'm fine," Halle said. "How long will it take us to get to Aisus?"

"It's going to take about eight or nine hours in this."

"Do you think we'll ever come back to Taidor?" she asked.

"Probably, when Unity's defeated. Then we can go back."

"Do you really believe that?" Halle questioned. "Unity have taken the planet. The Ea-Zone have no weapons or troops left. The U-Zone have killed or enslaved nearly everyone."

"We have to hope, Halle," Kalen said in a low voice. "We don't know what's going to happen. I expect that eventually Earth will send a force to gain control again."

"We've lost everything," Halle said.

"We've got our lives. We can start again," Kalen said briskly.

"Start again?"

"There's something I want to say while I have the chance. I'm sorry that I hurt you. Try not to hate me."

"I don't hate you," Halle replied, surprised. She'd been angry and hurt when he'd defected to Unity with Sera, but she'd never hated him.

"Good, because we've only got each other now. We're going to have to work together to get through this." Kalen's eyes met hers, seeking her agreement.

She dropped her gaze. *He still doesn't want me*, she thought. *He's just being practical. I'll never be Sera. I'll never be the woman he wants to marry. I was just a fling to him, someone to laugh with, but not to fall in love with.* Somehow having him sitting so close, made it all worse. She thought about Russ again. Had she used him as a substitute for Kalen? He was like Kalen in so many ways. If she had, did it matter now?

"That's Aisus, isn't it?" Halle pointed to a small pale disc in front of them.

"Yes, we've got a long way to go," Kalen said. "I suggest you get some sleep."

"What about you?" Halle remembered what Kalen had said about working together. He was right; their lives depended upon partnership. She couldn't sleep through the entire journey and leave him piloting the shuttle alone.

"I can manage."

"Why don't we take turns," Halle suggested. "If you can put the shuttle on automatic, I can keep watch while you sleep."

"Okay, but I'll take the first watch. You get some sleep." Kalen smiled at her.

"If you say so." Halle closed her eyes and tried to relax but the events of the day flooded her mind. She tried to make sense of it all. Everything that had happened had brought her to this moment, to this shuttle, to be with Kalen. Perhaps it was meant to be? Did she believe in destiny? That was a question for another day, another place, but perhaps she was fulfilling her destiny. The thought gave her comfort and she curled up in her seat and fell into the heavy sleep of exhaustion.

***

Kalen had slept deeply while Halle kept watch. He stirred when she shook his arm and opened his eyes to find that Aisus loomed large before them, filling the shuttle's windows. Pockmarked by craters, it hung in space, a giant pale orb. He felt his heart rate quicken. Their lives depended on what they found there – they didn't have enough fuel to go back. Would they find people, or something else? No one had had contact with Aisus in over forty years. He glanced at Halle.

"We're nearly there," she said, eyes bright.

He yawned and stretched before checking instrument readings on the console. "Everything is okay. We shouldn't have any trouble getting down."

"What's that?" Halle sat up straight in her seat.

Kalen looked up. "What the…"

Ahead of them, hundreds of black spots were silhouetted against the moon. Over the next few minutes, more dark shapes came into view. The spots flew in formation, like a giant flock of birds. Kalen switched the console viewscreen to full magnification and studied them carefully. He saw large shuttles with missile and laser ports and a blue and white square design on their sides. He wondered where they had come from. He'd never heard of craft from Aisus being seen - commercial shuttles that used this sector would have reported them.

"They can't be from Aisus," Kalen said. "Space going craft on this scale would be known on Taidor."

"It's a fleet, heading towards Taidor," Halle exclaimed.

"It's certainly a fleet and heavily armed," Kalen stared at the console screen. "Those are military craft but I don't recognize the markings on their hulls."

"Let me look," Halle bent towards him and stared at the screen. "That's the planet of Borle's insignia."

"Are you sure?" Kalen stared at the screen again. "I thought they had yellow in their design."

"They changed it very recently – after you went to Unity."

So Unity had deliberately kept him ignorant of the change, Kalen thought. Why did that surprise him? What else had they kept from him? "I knew Earth had refused to come, but I didn't hear anything about Borle."

"Russ told me that the Ea-Zone had appealed to Borle for help," Halle said excitedly.

"That would make sense. Borle's in this solar system. With those numbers the Ea-Zone has a chance now."

"Unless they've come to help Unity," Halle murmured.

"I hope not," Kalen said grimly.

"Is there any way we can contact them?" Halle asked.

"They know we're here. The specifications of those military shuttles enable them to detect craft as small as this one from hundreds of kilometers away. If they'd wanted to contact us we would have heard from them. I expect we're so small that they know we're not a threat."

"Can't you try?" Halle persisted.

"I will but don't get your hopes up. They'll have their orders, so it's unlikely they'll stop or make a detour to pick us up. And do you really want to be plunged into another battle?"

Kalen switched the radio to transmit. "This is shuttle two nine eight out of Taidor calling the Borle fleet. Please respond."

Kalen waited for a minute and when there was no response, he repeated, "This is shuttle two nine eight out of Taidor for the Borle fleet. Please respond."

"Acknowledged shuttle two nine eight. This is Commander Herring. Please explain your status."

"This is Captain Trinneer, of the Early Colonial Time System, lately under the command of Commander Callard, on course for Aisus, with one other. Permission requested to join your fleet."

"You are a long way out, Captain Trinneer. We are aware of the situation on Taidor. I regret that I cannot spare any of our craft to pick you up. We have orders to proceed directly to Taidor."

"Understood. Will you report our position and relay a request for rescue from Aisus? The conditions there are unknown and we won't have enough fuel to leave."

"I'll pass on your request but as you know, Captain Trinneer, all contact with Aisus is prohibited. I cannot confirm that anyone will attempt a rescue mission."

"Extreme circumstances are driving us there. I wish the fleet good luck," Kalen said.

"Good luck to you as well. Out." The commander disconnected the call.

Halle looked disappointed.

"You didn't think that they would pick us up, did you?" he said softly. She had pushed her oxygen mask down and her large blue eyes held Kalen's gaze. He wished that he could put his arms about her, but she had loved Russ, not him.

"No, but at least they know where we are. Perhaps they'll come and rescue us," she replied.

"You heard the commander - it's unlikely," Kalen said. "Don't have any unrealistic expectations. We're on our own, but we're nearly at Aisus. We'll soon reach the settlement there."

The last of the fleet passed in front of the moon and disappeared from view. Kalen concentrated on the task ahead. Despite the assurances that he'd given Halle, there was no guarantee that a settlement existed on Aisus, and if it did, that they'd allow them to land. As they approached, the details of craters and mountain ranges on the moon's surface, became visible. Kalen looked desperately for signs of a settlement. He had to start their descent soon – they had to land, settlement or not.

"I can't see any lights or cities," Halle said.

"We'll see them when we get a bit nearer," Kalen assured her.

"Do you think so?"

"Of course, we'll see the settlement soon."

"We'll be able to go back to Taidor if Borle defeats Unity," Halle said. "The people on Aisus must have some form of interplanetary transport."

"I expect so." Kalen smiled and took hold of her hand. "The war will soon be over and then we'll go back."

He squeezed Halle's hand. She didn't pull away and he felt encouraged. She'd told him that she didn't hate him. That was enough for now. Perhaps in time she would forgive him for leaving the Ea-Zone. How he had missed her. He glanced over to her and she met his eyes. Anxious, but at the same time bright with hope. She clasped his hand, twining her fingers around his. He felt her tremble and took a deep breath. The shadow wall had gone. This was it. There was no turning back. They had the whole of their future before them.

About Lucy Andrews

Lucy Andrews grew up in the north of England, near the Scottish borders and qualified as a lawyer. After working for most of her professional life in London, she decided to pursue her interest in artificial intelligence, which led to a research degree in cognition and neuroscience. Lucy now lives by the sea in Sussex where she spends much of her time writing fiction and walking in the beautiful English countryside.

Social Media

Facebook: https://facebook.com/LucyAndrewsAuthor

Twitter: https://twitter.com/LAndrewsWrites

If you enjoyed this story, check out this other Treeberry Press book by Lucy Andrews:

Crater's Edge

The year is 2235 and Earth is colonising the planets. Work on the new city at Three-Craters has nearly stopped. Deep underground, strange accidents and power failures plague the site and the miners believe that the place is cursed. Kalen Trinneer is sent to investigate but finds that Three-Craters will not give up its secrets easily. Is the site really cursed? Do the answers lie in the other time zone whose population share the planet? Kalen's search for answers takes him on a dangerous journey where he finds love and betrayal, a journey that doesn't end until he eventually discovers the truth about himself and the society in which he lives.